BLIND DATE

A HUNTER AND TATE MYSTERY

BRENDA CHAPMAN

Title: Blind Date / Brenda Chapman

Names: Chapman, Brenda, 1955 – author

Description: Series statement: A Hunter and Tate mystery - #1 Edited by Allister Thompson. Cover Design by Laura Boyle Published by Ivy Bay Press, First Edition March 2022

ISBN Trade Paperback: 978-0-9784284-0-2; ISBN ePub: 978-0-9784284-1-9; ISBN audiobook: 978-9784284-2-6

For Ted, now and always

Vengeance is in my heart, death in my hand, blood and revenge are hammering in my head.

— William Shakespeare, *Titus Andronicus*

PROLOGUE

Clare Daniels looked over her shoulder a third time before breaking into a run. The normally busy street was deserted. An autumn fog had settled across the city while she was inside the hospital, and porch and streetlights glowed a pale yellow through the gauzy haze. She shivered inside her wool coat, chilled through by the dampness. The page of a newspaper brushed against her legs, tumbling past in a fresh gust, making her jump like a startled rabbit. She stopped running and breathed deeply to still her racing heart.

Paramedics had brought in a kid with a gunshot wound to his stomach at shift change. The flashes of fear in the boy's tough face had gotten to her more than usual, so she'd stayed to help prep him for surgery. It was a busy night in the Ottawa Civic Hospital ER, and the skeleton crew of nurses was glad of the help. Changing out of her uniform an hour and a half later, she'd almost called for an Uber, but the twenty-minute walk would help her to decompress, or so she'd thought before setting out — before the exhaustion, the darkness, and the fog had her mind playing tricks, imagining that she heard footsteps following a distance behind her.

At the corner, she slowed to a walk and pulled out her cell phone. A car's headlights cut through the mist and caught her in their beam. She squinted into the glare. The car slowed as it drew alongside her, sidling like a john looking for a pickup. The passenger window started to slide down. "Yeah, that's right, I'm a scaredy-cat bitch," she said into the dial tone, averting her face and picking up her pace. The car eased past, and the taillights disappeared around the corner. She let out her breath in a frosty white stream and checked again over her shoulder as she tucked the phone into her pocket.

She started jogging. The cloud cover was low and blocked out the moon and stars. Leaves swirled across her path with every gust and crunched under her feet. At the next corner, she crossed the street and slowed to a walk, catching her breath and exhaling in short, white puffs. The sidewalk fed past some sketchier townhouses, and she moved into the centre of the road, out of the shadows.

Two blocks farther on, she could see with some relief the two-storey, square brick house where she had an apartment, a holdout to the new builds that crowded in on either side. There were five units, one basement and two on each floor above. She had one of the smaller apartments on the second floor across from Josie Wheatly, a teacher at Broadview School. Josie had only moved in three months before, but they were bonded by a hometown farther north in the Ottawa Valley. They weren't best friends by any means but shared the odd glass of wine when they were both free.

She stopped outside the building and looked up. The lights were on in Josie's apartment, even though it was nearing 2:00 a.m. *You go, girl!* she thought. Josie had talked about her boyfriend Rory a couple of times. He was a soldier on assignment in the Middle East somewhere and supposed to be home at the end of the month, but Clare was almost certain he'd gotten early leave, likely to prepare for their Christmas wedding.

She strode up the walkway to the front door and used her key to enter, then climbed the stairs as quietly as she could so as not to awaken any of the other tenants. She paused with her apartment key in the lock and looked over at Josie's closed door. She could hear some noise coming from inside and smiled at the thought of Josie and her fiancé. They had a lot of catching up to do. She took a step closer, but it felt wrong to eavesdrop and jeopardize their fledgling friendship, so she spun back around and pushed her own door open.

Inside, she stood silently, listening for any noises within her apartment before locking the door, slipping out of her coat, and kicking off her shoes. She was paranoid, no question, but living alone in a big city made her cautious. Hard to believe her parents hadn't locked their doors when she was growing up. Sometimes progress was a step backward.

Sleep. I need to sleep.

She padded into the kitchen for a glass of water on her way to the bedroom. As usual, she checked to make sure none of her possessions had been moved since she left that morning. If she hadn't been so exhausted, she'd do a thorough search of every room, even looking in the closets and under the bed. Her obsessive compulsion would have to slide for one night. If someone wanted to molest her, they'd have to find a way to keep her awake. She managed a quick trip to the washroom before stripping and climbing between the cold sheets. A minute later, she was sound asleep.

In what felt like no time at all, she opened her eyes.

Bright morning sunshine was pouring through the window. "Nooo," she wailed and flung an arm over her eyes. She groaned and rolled onto her back. Why hadn't she thought to close the curtains? She turned her head and looked at the clock. Less than five hours of sleep. A headache swelled behind her eyes. She tried to return to oblivion, but after half an hour of drifting in and out, she threw back the covers. May as well not waste a day off. Four seven-to-three shifts followed by yesterday's four to midnight had her internal clock all messed up, and it would take the full round of nights to switch that around. She sometimes wondered the long-term consequences of shift work but always shoved the thought aside. No point worrying about something she had no control over.

On her way to the kitchen, she stopped in the bathroom and swallowed a couple of painkillers. Her cell phone rang in her purse on the hallway table as she was pouring water into the coffee maker. She raced down the hall, fumbled through her purse, and pressed the right buttons before the phone went to voicemail.

"Mom, no, I was up." *And why would you call me this early if you thought I wasn't?*

She listened to her mother's ramblings and tried to be kind. Her mother lived alone in Almonte, a thirty-minute drive away. Clare visited her too seldom these days. "Mom? Mom, hang on a sec. I hear a noise outside in the hallway. Yeah, not sure…" She unlocked the door and pulled it open. A white cat darted past her into the kitchen.

"That's strange. Josie's cat was scratching at my door and now…" She stuck her head into the hallway. Josie's door appeared to be shut, but she must be awake if the cat had gotten out. Snow Boy was Josie's baby, and she'd be worried if she couldn't find him. "Just a sec, Mom, I'm going to knock on my neighbour's door and return her cat." If Josie and Rory were awake, perhaps they'd be open to sharing a cup of coffee. It would be nice to meet the guy who'd won Josie's heart.

She kept the phone away from her ear because she could hear her mother's voice clearly with the receiver in her hand and crossed the hall, knocking softly at first with progressively harder raps. The door seemed to give under the pressure and swung open of its own accord. She held the phone to her stomach and called Josie's name.

Silence.

That's odd. Maybe she's in the shower.

Clare stepped into Josie's hallway and listened. A hair-raising, keening sound was coming from the back of the apartment. Clare raised the phone to her ear. "Mom," she said quietly, "can I call you back? No … no, nothing's wrong. I'll call you back. Ten minutes, yeah."

The carpet muffled her footsteps as she walked slowly toward the back rooms. She checked inside the living room and kitchen on her way past but saw nothing out of place. With every step, the unsettling noise was getting progressively louder, and her heart pounded harder in response.

"Josie?" she called as she reached the doorway to the bedroom. "Snow Boy was in the hall, and he ran into my apartment." She swallowed and thought about turning around instead of making a fool of herself. The bedroom door was ajar, but she had to push it open to see inside. *Please forgive me for this intrusion.* "Josie, is everything okay?"

She gave the door a gentle shove and froze.

Josie lay on the bed in the fetal position, her naked legs tucked in tightly under her arms. Her whole body was rocking back and forth, back and forth, strands of long blonde hair hiding her face. The keening stopped for a moment but started up again with the same haunting intensity. Crimson blood stained the top sheet scrunched below her legs.

"Oh my God, Josie." Clare's legs functioned while her mind struggled to take in what she was seeing. She crossed the space and knelt beside the bed, reaching out a tentative hand to touch Josie's wrist. The shriek that erupted from Josie's gaping mouth wasn't human. Her eyes snapped open, but whatever she was seeing was not in the room. She resembled a cornered wild animal as she scrambled to the far side of the bed, as far from Clare as she could get. Fresh splotches of blood marked the pillow where she'd been lying. The smell of blood and acrid body odour intensified with her movement.

"I'm going to get help. You're okay now. I won't let anyone hurt you anymore." Her words were too loud, swelled by hysteria, and it took all her nurse's training to calm herself down. She fumbled with the phone and punched in 911. The dispatcher made her repeat the address.

She found a blanket in the closet and tucked it over Josie's shivering, nude body, careful not to touch anything on the bed. The police would need to collect samples to begin mapping the trauma that had been inflicted in order to make a case against Josie's attacker. She searched for sources of bleeding but didn't see any deep wounds. A slash on her forehead and another on her neck had bled a lot but were only seeping now. Clare guessed they'd been made by a knife, but luckily, they were superficial cuts. She crouched next to the bed and spoke soothingly, repeating over and over that Josie was safe, that help was on the way. Gradually, she touched Josie without her pulling away and smoothed back her hair, wet with sweat and matted in tangles. After several seconds, Josie went still, her breathing shallow. Her pulse was weak under Clare's fingertips.

"Where are you, damn it?" Clare asked, picking up the phone again. Josie was crashing. She was about to hit redial when the buzzer sounded from the downstairs foyer. "Oh, thank God, thank God."

She backed out of the room and ran down the hall to let them in, relieved to have someone else take charge of the horror.

CHAPTER 1

The room was shadowed in stripes of predawn darkness when Ella slipped out of bed and trod across the cold floor, down the short hallway into the living room to stand in front of the window. She craned her neck to see the small front yard and street below. Weak rays lightened the night's darkness, and the conifers in the yard across the street swayed in a wind that had kicked up while she was asleep. A strong gust rattled the windowpane, and a moment later the first raindrops pelted against the glass.

Her top-floor apartment was chilly, and she returned to pull the comforter from the bed and wrap it around her naked body. "Coffee," she muttered, taking the few steps into the galley kitchen. If Felix's money transfer didn't show up in her account today, she'd be forced to go to the food bank, much as the idea hurt. She'd picked rent over a full belly this week and would need to get food where she could.

The kettle whistled, and she poured boiling water into a mug with a teaspoon of coffee granules. She stirred in two spoonfuls of sugar to quell the rumblings of hunger before settling at her desk in the alcove next to the living-room window. As the heat warmed up the space, she shrugged off the blanket. Tony and Sander, the guys in the second-floor apartment below, controlled the thermostat in her apartment as well as theirs. They had it set to rise by a few degrees at 6:00 a.m. in time to heat the house before they got out of bed to get ready for work. The pipes shuddered and clanked as one of them ran a shower. It would take a few hours for the tank to reheat so that Ella could take hers.

Aside from the desk and chair, a ratty two-seat couch was the only furniture. Greg took the nicer pieces when he moved out a month before, six weeks after he'd moved in. Instead of replacing the pieces with new stuff, she'd visited the Sally Ann and selected whatever would get her by on the cheap. Perhaps foolishly, she'd spent part of her severance on a state-of-the-art computer system: an analog microphone, audio interface, headphones, and editing software. *Plan ahead*, her then-editor liked to say, and for once she'd taken his advice. He probably hadn't meant for her to drain the last of her bank account a week after being terminated from the paper, but at least she'd been smart enough to move to this apartment when the whispers of downsizing had begun circulating around the office in April.

As per her routine, she checked email first after logging on. Nothing from Felix, but she figured that her secret benefactor was likely still in bed. She opened the podcast that she'd uploaded the day before and checked comments. Ten new ones and only one negative. Followers had jumped by two hundred and sixteen. She'd have to remember to send the stats to Felix. It'd be something uplifting to keep his interest in her stories from waning. *Screw that noise*, she thought. The last story was a good piece, and it shouldn't matter how many people clicked on *follow*.

She'd found the story riveting, a teenager selling drugs at his school who was responsible for his own brother OD'ing. He'd spoken with more honesty than she believed possible once he realized he'd be completely anonymous. Heartbreaking story. Bad home. Sucked into the criminal life like a piece of dirt into a vacuum cleaner. There but for the grace of God…

She got up and checked the cupboards. The fridge. A stale box of crackers and the stub of a block of cheddar cheese that had lost its neon orange hue were all that remained. The breakfast of champions. A message pinged as she settled back in front of the computer, munching on a cracker. Felix.

U there?

In the flesh. What's up?

Idea for show. Rape vic.

A break in text. Three dots jumped while he typed at the other end. She waited, anxious to know if the victim was still alive.

Name Josie Wheatly. Teacher. Assaulted 3 days ago. Civic Hospital hood. In hospital.

She thought for a moment before typing.

Angle?

Human interest. How respectable girl got into that position.

Maybe. I'll look in2

Good. Thx. later

He signed off Messenger, and she lifted her hands from the keyboard and leaned back with the plate of crackers and cheese resting on her lap. She stared at the picture of Bart Simpson taped to the wall as she ate. *Eat my shorts.* Her stomach gurgled.

She'd never met Felix, not that this was — his or her —

real name, although she thought of the person as a man because of the name's gender. He'd contacted her online when she was covering a story the year before about gang shootings in the east end. She had still been working at the paper, and he'd reached her through her work email. From the get-go he was vague about his affiliations. His email address was untraceable — she knew because she'd tried to track it down. Her best guess was that he was embedded in the police service or an organization closely affiliated. He might even be a reporter or the partner of a reporter. She chose to believe he was on the up-and-up. In any event, he had inside knowledge about ongoing cases that he was willing to share with her. Well, not exactly share. More like guide her toward a story with hints on where to find the evidence. The motivation appeared to be making the public aware of certain injustices and victims who were falling through the cracks. He even paid a minimal amount after she followed up on his suggestions. She considered herself an undercover investigative podcaster for hire. A rogue Charlie's Angel.

Her email notified that a new message had arrived, and she opened it to find a transfer of four hundred dollars. She accepted the money and toasted the screen with a cracker. She'd be able to stretch the funds to last the month but needed to come up with another story if she was going to eat in November. That or find a real job.

But what was the fun in that?

Ella carried out a Google search going back a week for local news stories about the rape and found nothing. She typed in the name "Josie Wheatly". There was only one person by that name in Ottawa with a Facebook page that foolishly wasn't private. She opened Josie's homepage and started gleaning information. Birthplace: Toronto (but grew up in Almonte). Twenty-nine years old. Education: B.A. majoring in English from U of Toronto. B.Ed. from Queen's. Relationship status: not specified. Occupation: teacher. She had 819 friends and posted almost daily. Ella scrolled through her photos.

The woman was pretty, with wide brown eyes, curly blond hair that she kept shoulder-length, average height (when compared to those standing next to her), and slender. Favoured workout clothes, jeans, and frilly blouses. Cowboy boots of soft brown leather with two-inch heels. She didn't appear to have a significant other but posed with various friends and people Ella assumed were her family, often with a drink in her hand. Some months back, she had posed with a man in uniform in a couple of pics. Brother? Boyfriend? It was hard to tell, but Ella couldn't find him in any of the more recent photos.

She went back to Josie's main feed and started trolling through her posts, working backward in time. Her last entry was a week ago on the fifth of October, two days before the attack. She liked to repost jokes and recipes. Was especially fond of kitten and puppy videos. Owned a Persian cat named Snow Boy that was featured in an annoying number of pics. In August, she'd posted a chain of photos from a trip to Chicago with her mother. June and July had been spent partying with a revolving cast of friends. *School's out for the summer.*

At the end of July Josie had moved into a different apartment building, the same month Ella had moved to this apartment in the Glebe. The street was familiar, the house at the corner more so. She enlarged the photo and read the house number. Her heart started pounding double-time at the coincidence. She scolded Josie under her breath. *Silly, silly girl. Broadcast your life to the world and make yourself an easy target. What in the hell were you thinking?*

SHE WAS PUTTING on her leather jacket when the sound of excited barking came through her front door. She yanked it open, and her downstairs neighbour Tony's miniature dachshund, Luvy, jumped up on her legs before scooting past her and racing around what little space there was in the apartment. The dog ended by stretching out on the area rug under Ella's desk, staring up at her with sorrowful brown eyes, head resting on her front paws.

"Nice try, dog," Ella said, but Tony leapt up the stairs from the second floor before she had a chance to crawl under the desk to scoop her up. He carried a plate of grapes and sliced melon that he handed to her, saying, "You're welcome," as he slid past her into the apartment.

"You and Luvy moving in?" she asked, selecting a piece of cantaloupe. A moan rolled up her throat. The fruit tasted like a sun-kissed July day, juicy and sweet.

"Thought you could use some male company now that Greg's vacated. Where did you say the fucker went anyway?" He picked up a pencil from her desktop and twirled it from one hand to the other.

She shut the door and crossed the living room to sit in her desk chair. "Off to find himself, so that could be anywhere with a barstool."

"He did like the drink. You know you're probably better off, right, Ella?"

"I miss his half of the rent money."

"You can do better."

She wasn't sure he believed that but thought, *Okay*. She

asked, "Where was this honesty when I'd come home to the three of you deep into a bottle of Glenfiddich?"

"We thought you liked him, so Sander and I were being supportive. Bonding with your chosen one."

More like in lust with her chosen one. Greg had told her a couple of times that they'd suggested he try swinging the other way. He believed they'd have followed through if he'd shown any interest. Tony pointed at her jacket. "Were you heading out?"

"I'm working on a podcast and doing some research. Shouldn't you be getting ready for work, or do you lot wear kimonos to cut hair these days?"

He wriggled his chest like a stripper inside the silk fabric. "First client is this afternoon." He bent over and picked up Luvy. "Don't stay stuck up here all the time, girl. Not good for your mental health."

"I like my own company."

"Well, come downstairs and see us any time you feel lonely."

His eyes had that sympathetic look that she hated when it was directed at her. She waved her hand in the air as if to say she had no need of companionship. "Sure. Say hi to Sander for me."

"He already left for the office. We'll throw a dinner party on the weekend if you're free."

They both knew that she would be. Her social life had been Greg. She also knew that the dinner party would just be her and the two of them. A pity meal. She shrugged. A girl had to eat. "What can I bring?"

"Just your sunny self."

After he'd gone, she tucked the fruit plate into the fridge and grabbed her knapsack. The sound of running water filled the stairwell as she passed Sander and Tony's apartment. It was comforting to know they lived below her, even if she made little effort to keep the friendship going. Greg had been the one they liked being around. The bon vivant. She reminded herself to come up with an excuse to take a rain check on the meal. She didn't like being a charity case, even if she could do with some decent food.

The ground floor had been vacant all month, but paint cans were lined up in the hallway. Her Polish landlord, Alex, was having the apartment primped for new tenants. This house was old and showing its age in a posh, trendy part of town. The well-to-do neighbours on the street had asked Alex on numerous occasions to stop taking in boarders, but he was a stubborn old coot and continued to insert poorer tenants into their pristine world. It was his way of giving them the finger. She had to like him for it.

Her bike was under the stairwell near the back door. She hauled it out and down the front steps onto the sidewalk. She kept side bags hooked onto the back rack for groceries, and she'd install winter tires in a few more weeks. She'd lucked out when she found this baby for sale on Kijiji from a woman moving out of the country. The bike was old but a lovely cobalt blue with a black leather seat and gold bell.

The sky hadn't managed to rid itself of the low, grey clouds, but the early morning rain had ended and the wind had eased to a soft breeze. She cut east down Third Avenue, past Corpus Christi Elementary School, and crossed Bank Street at the lights. Bank was the main artery running through the Glebe neighbourhood and lined with an eclectic array of shops, bars, and restaurants that drew people from all over the city. The street cut the residential section in two. The east side of the neighbourhood ended at the Queen Elizabeth Driveway, which ran the length of the Rideau Canal.

She crossed the Driveway onto the bike path. She

could turn left and ride north all the way into the downtown, but instead she pointed her bike in the opposite direction and headed into the west end of the city. She biked past garden beds, now cleared and put to sleep for winter, and swathes of lawn graced by old growth oak and weeping willows. The path wound past wealthy homes with large, widely spaced yards that sat atop a hill on the other side of the Driveway.

She continued past Dow's Lake, manmade and small as lakes went, and up a steep hill into the Experimental Farm, enjoying the assortment of trees and bushes that led to a large red barn and outbuildings where government scientists and agriculturalists carried out their research. A working farm in the middle of a city of a million people was a rarity and one she hoped would never be gobbled up by greedy interests. The earthy smell of cow dung and tilled soil mingled with the odour of the decomposing leaves.

All too soon, she biked past the last stretch of trees and gardens and found herself at Carling Avenue and six lanes of traffic. She crossed at the lights and wound her way through residential side streets in the neighbourhood behind the Civic Hospital, where Josie Wheatly was being treated. The street where Josie Wheatly lived wasn't listed on her Facebook page, but Ella knew exactly where to find the house. She biked there first to see if any other tenants were home. Maybe she'd luck out and Josie would be back in her apartment. The wail of a siren was fast approaching, and Ella swerved to the side of the road and craned her neck to look behind her as an ambulance raced past on the cross street.

She watched until it rounded the corner and then followed in its wake. The ambulance hadn't gone far. It was stopped halfway down the street, the siren turned off abruptly while the pulsing red light continued to strobe from the roof. She got off her bike and rolled it closer. Two paramedics scrambled out of the cab and raced up the sidewalk into the wide-open door of a house. A second siren grew louder from behind her, and moments later a police car swerved around the same corner and pulled up behind the ambulance. A female cop leapt out and strode toward the front door while her partner remained in the car, talking into his headset.

Normally Ella wasn't that person who watched someone else's medical crisis unfold. They deserved their privacy at such a vulnerable time, but today she remained rooted in place, eyes fixed on the entrance. The house was the same one showcased on Josie Wheatly's Facebook page, the house number prominently displayed above the door. Eighty-eight Kinnear. The same house that Ella had lived in before she moved this past summer to Percy Street. Josie had taken up residence in the apartment she'd vacated on the second floor. The one with the creaky floorboards in the hallway and the drafty window in the kitchen that had to be forced open when humidity swelled the frame in the sweltering heat of midsummer.

The coincidence was jarring. It was unsettling enough for Ella to wheel her bike toward the crowd of onlookers drawn out of their homes by the sirens and commotion. She left her bike helmet on, and those neighbours who knew her from when she lived on the street glanced past her without a second look. She stopped behind two young mothers holding babies and waited.

Twenty minutes later, a white Volvo pulled up, and a woman with a medical bag got out. Ella recognized her stooped posture and frizzy brown hair from her days on the crime beat. Brigette Green, Coroner. The sight of

Green made her realize that there'd been a death, and she instinctively clasped a hand over her heart.

The two women in front of Ella exchanged shocked looks, and one of them said, "Leona got a text from one of the tenants. First the poor girl was raped and now…" She looked down at her baby as if to make sure he wasn't listening. Her voice dropped. "She hanged herself."

Ella rolled her bike away from the gossiping women onto the street, her mind buzzing, scrambling to make sense of what she'd overheard. The assault was now a death. Why had the hospital let Josie Wheatly go home if she was so traumatized? Why hadn't somebody stayed with her? None of this made sense.

Ella pedalled as fast as she could away from Kinnear Street in a vain attempt to put distance between herself and the pain of what had transpired — the violence that had desecrated her old apartment. Yet as fast as she could go, she couldn't outride the thought that kept echoing around in her head.

Josie Wheatly could have been me if I hadn't lost my job and needed a cheaper place to live. Whatever evil gained access to that apartment missed me by mere weeks.

CHAPTER 2

By the time Ella rode the bike path into her neighbourhood, she'd come up with a plan. When she got home, she'd undertake a more thorough background check on Josie Wheatly, including a call to Paul O'Brien, her one remaining police contact. They hadn't spoken since she left the paper, but he'd never refused to help her. Then tomorrow she'd bike back to Kinnear Street to talk with Clare Daniels, the woman who'd lived across the hall from her. She and Clare were friends on Facebook, a social media site she rarely used, but Clare's posts should give a clue to her nursing schedule at the hospital. She was a frequent poster who gave away more than she should, in Ella's opinion. Clare was the best person to fill in the blanks about what had happened to Josie Wheatly. The plan calmed her, and instead of cutting off the canal bike path at Third Avenue, she kept going toward the downtown. Staying in motion kept the unease in her belly from spreading.

The day had warmed, and while not sunny, the threat of rain was remote. The low clouds acted as a cozy blanket that kept the warmer air swaddling the earth.

The canal passed by the Conference Centre and the Westin Hotel and ended at the Rideau Centre, a sprawling two-storey mall with a glassed-in walkway over Rideau Street. Exiting the mall through the back entrance, one was smack in the middle of the ByWard Market with flower vendors and rows of outdoor stalls selling autumn vegetables, baskets of bright red apples, a jumble of pumpkins laid out on the ground, maple syrup, and souvenirs for the tourists who thronged the streets and cafés. On a normal day, the noise and busyness appealed to her. Wandering through the crowds made her feel a part of the community without the need to interact. Today, however, she wasn't in the mood to mingle.

At the Rideau Street intersection, she turned left instead of continuing straight ahead into the Market. The sidewalk sloped below a concrete underpass where street merchants sold homemade jewellery and art and where buskers played for money. If Danny stuck to his routine, she'd find him there.

She scanned the vendors and smiled when she saw him leaning against the concrete wall near the far steps, strumming his beat-up guitar and singing a Dylan standard, "Knockin' on Heaven's Door." She swore he'd been wearing the same rainbow-striped poncho and blue jeans for the past ten years. He had on his battered leather sandals, and she thought that his feet must surely be cold. He smiled when he saw her but kept singing, head thrown back, long brown hair swaying in time. When the song ended, he lowered his guitar and jumped across the space to hug her. While still in his embrace, she dropped a twenty into his empty guitar case and watched it settle amongst the quarters and loonies.

"Hey. Elle. Good to see you, sis."

She released his boney shoulders and drew back. "Are you keeping well, Dan?"

"Yeah, can't complain. Had a cold last week, but it's better."

"Where're you staying?"

He shrugged. "You know. Here and there, but mostly the Mission. I'm covered."

"You know that I have room for you. The weather's getting colder. Why don't you come stay for a while? I'd love to have you."

He smiled, and for a moment they were fifteen years younger, when life was simpler and he was her happy little brother. "I'm fine, Ellie, but thanks."

"You always were too proud."

"I've got you on my emergency list."

"I hope you take me up on my offer before it gets to that point."

He studied her. "What's going on? You seem upset about something."

She thought of telling him about the unsettling morning and the woman who hanged herself in her old apartment. She decided unburdening herself wouldn't help. "Everything's good. I just needed to see you." His stare made her bottom lip tremble, and she forced a smile. "Say, can you play 'Time in a Bottle' for me?"

"Croce? You got it."

He returned to his spot, picked up his guitar, and started strumming. His voice was untrained and raw, his face angelic. Every note he sang made her want to wrap herself around him and shield him from the world's nastiness and pain with her body — to make him stop taking heroin or whatever street drug busking allowed him to buy. But she'd tried to save him more than once, and this was where he'd ended up. She had to let him be … for now.

He looked up between lines, and when the song ended, she blew him a kiss and mimed writing with a pen. She held a hand to her ear. *Call me.* He smiled and nodded, but she knew full well he wouldn't contact her. He never did. She gave a final wave and started back the way she'd come, gutted to be leaving him again but knowing the choice wasn't in her hands. On her way home, she'd detour into a grocery store and buy some food to last her a few days. Keeping busy meant she didn't have time to stop and think.

BACK AT HER APARTMENT BUILDING, she hauled her bike inside and tucked it under the stairs. She pulled the tote with her purchases out of the saddlebags and climbed the two storeys to her apartment. It was too early for wine, so she made a pot of tea and positioned herself in front of the computer.

The news outlets were restrained in their reporting on Josie Wheatly's death, but a few local sites mentioned her tragic passing. The cause of death wasn't yet being given, but one could surmise from the facts. Josie had only just arrived home from the hospital after being assaulted. She was depressed. Her family asked for privacy in this difficult time. It didn't take a genius to figure out she'd killed herself.

Paul O'Brien picked up on the first ring. "Yeah, Detective O'Brien here. How can I help you?"

"Paul, it's Ella Tate."

His pause was brief, likely not expecting to hear from her ever again. She hadn't returned his call after the paper laid her off. "Ella, how the hell are you? Haven't heard from you in a dog's age."

"Good, I'm good, Paul. I'm freelancing and have an investigative podcast where I go into depth on local cold cases or whatever's in the news."

"What's the name of it?"

"*Crime in the Rear View.*"

"*Crime in the Rear View*. Good name for a series. I'll have to give it a listen." He was typing something, the keystrokes clicking in her ear. His voice sounded distracted. "So why'd you call me today?"

"I'm doing a show about rape victims and was on my way to interview Josie Wheatly."

"I don't think she's available."

His droll sense of humour was the top reason she liked him. "I hear it was suicide."

The typing stopped at his end. "Listen, Ella, I'd like to help you out, but not over the phone. Why don't we meet for a drink at the watering hole after my shift? I'm done at eight."

The idea of staying in for the night was enticing, but this might be her only chance to get the background information. It meant making her way back downtown. It also meant staying busy.

"I'll be there."

He grunted his assent and ended the call.

She checked her phone. Nearly five o'clock. If she ate supper now, she'd have lots of time to walk to their rendezvous. Her mouth salivated at the thought of the pork chop chilling in the fridge after a long stretch of Kraft Dinner and hot dogs. She'd splurged on a couple of bottles of wine but wouldn't open one until she got back. Funny how things she'd taken for granted became special treats on the downslide.

O'BRIEN WAS SITTING at the bar with both hands wrapped around a tall glass of beer when Ella slid onto the stool next to him. His eyes shifted from the television behind the bar to her and back to the baseball game.

"You cut your hair," he said before raising the glass to his lips. "Suits you."

"Thanks. You're looking good too."

"It's my junk food diet. Doing wonders for my figure." He patted his belly before raising two fingers to the bartender. "The usual?"

"Sure."

The bartender approached. "The lady will have a vodka tonic, two ice cubes and a lime twist. And could you bring us a bowl of nuts?" He looked sideways at her and grinned.

"I'm impressed."

"Memory like a steel trap. I also remember that you pick the olives off pizza and have an aversion to standing in line."

"Keep talking, and I'm going to think you have my picture taped to your bulletin board at work."

"No need for a photo. You're unforgettable." He reached over and patted the back of her hand resting on the bar. His voice became gentle. "You doing okay, Ella?"

"Can't complain."

He gave her face a searching look, and she didn't shrink under the scrutiny. He broke eye contact and drained his glass as the bartender set down their drinks and slid a bowl of nuts between them. "So, you want to know more about Josie Wheatly?" O'Brien asked.

"Well, I was toying with the idea that her assault — rape — would make a good in-depth podcast, but now it might be even more important to tell her story."

O'Brien hunkered lower over his drink, head bowed.

"You could link the rape directly to her suicide. In my book that makes it murder."

"Morally, anyway. Do you have any suspects for the rape?"

"No. Likely won't find any, if you want my opinion. I've had a look at the file, and whoever did it was a pro. No forensic evidence."

"What did Josie say when she was interviewed afterward?"

"She wasn't."

"What do you mean?"

"She was brought to the hospital unconscious, and when she woke up early afternoon, she was hysterical. The doctor had to sedate her, so we couldn't interview her then. We focused on doing forensics on her body and her clothes and apartment. So that was the first two days gone without speaking to her. The third day, she was recovering physically but said she was groggy and was having trouble remembering what happened. The decision was made to hold off one more day before taking her statement. Her mother was with her constantly from the morning she was brought in but was satisfied enough with her progress by the end of that last day to go home to Almonte, a half hour away, to get some sleep. She was exhausted, as you can imagine. She planned to return first thing in the morning and spend the day with Josie, possibly taking her home to Almonte if the doctor said she was well enough to leave. A victim support worker had visited twice without being able to interact with Josie and was also scheduled to return that morning. Unfortunately, Josie left the hospital without checking out at the nurses' station in the early morning hours when staff was at a minimum. The hospital staff had tried calling her mother as soon as they found Josie gone from her bed, but she was in the car driving and didn't pick up. As soon as she realized her daughter was gone, she rushed over to the apartment and found her hanging from a door frame in her bedroom. She called 911, but there was no chance of saving her."

"That's just … bloody, bloody tragic." Ella tried to focus. "Didn't someone go to check her apartment when they knew she was missing from the hospital?"

"Change of shifts and other priorities. Short answer no, but we were definitely going to track her down."

"Did Josie tell anybody what happened in the assault? Her parents? Hospital staff?"

"Apparently she didn't. It's hard to know what to make of her silence."

"You haven't mentioned a boyfriend."

"He's been out of the country on military duty but on his way back. Name's Rory Leavitt, and he was her fiancé."

"Shit. What a terrible homecoming."

"The good news for him, though, is that he's not a suspect for the rape."

"I don't think that will be his top concern when he hears she's dead."

"No, I suppose not." Paul watched the ballgame for a bit and pumped his fist at a home run.

She squinted at the TV. "I thought you were a diehard Jays fan."

"I am, but the Jays missed the World Series again this year, so the Red Sox are the next best thing." He drained his beer and pushed the glass away from him. "Well, it's been a long day, so unless you have another burning question?"

"Did anybody living in the building see anything?"

"The woman on the same floor found her after the assault. Clare Daniels. You could start there." He pushed off from the stool. "You take care, Ella. Don't be a stranger."

Now would be a good time to tell him that she'd lived in Josie's apartment up until three months ago, but he was in a hurry to leave, and the information seemed irrelevant. They'd never met up at her apartment, and he had no reason to make the connection. She raised a hand in a half-wave. "You too, Paul. How many more years before you hang up the shield?"

"I'm hoping to be on my boat somewhere in the Caribbean next winter. I'm pushing sixty, and enough is enough."

"Yeah, you've done your time."

She watched him leave but stayed to finish her drink and the bowl of nuts. Sad to think a free bar snack was the healthiest food she'd had all week aside from the plate of fruit Tony'd given her.

The rain was over for the evening when she stepped outside, and she decided to walk home. An hour of exercise and fresh air might help her fall asleep. She'd been getting by on four hours since Greg left. This new podcast story was going to be a challenge and might be just the thing she needed to get her life back on track and into a routine.

CHAPTER 3

O'Brien hesitated and looked back at Ella before he pushed open the front door. He waited for a young couple to enter and exited the bar. He'd expected her to call him long before now. The fact that she hadn't could be taken as a good sign. The things he'd set in motion were working. He hoped so, anyway. He'd parked a few streets over and retraced his steps, thinking about Ella. She was waif-thin and with her short hair looked elfin in her oversized sweater and leggings. Her skin had always been pale but now verged on translucent. He knew she'd hate his concern, so he kept his distance, but that didn't stop him from worrying. He'd been sending people to drop money into Danny's guitar case and monitored his movements from afar when he had time. Whatever he offered never seemed to be enough.

He glanced across the street. Young people had congregated outside the door of a pub, and their voices rose every time the door opened to let out loud pockets of rock music. A couple of them were openly passing a joint back and forth. One of them raised his eyes to look at O'Brien, but he didn't react and the moment passed. Walking a few steps behind on the opposite sidewalk was a man with his hood up, hands in his pockets and chin tucked inside his black jacket. O'Brien wouldn't have noticed him except that they were walking at the same pace. O'Brien picked up speed to see if the hooded man did as well. At the corner, he looked over but the man had disappeared.

A stab of pain shot up from his stomach. He should have skipped the second beer. Whatever was going on in his digestive system could handle one drink but not two. He'd cut out spicy foods and ate small meals, and that seemed to help. His doctor had told him it was likely stress causing this upset to his system but had asked him to come in anyway to run some tests. O'Brien had agreed to the appointment in the morning but now thought about skipping. He'd see how he felt when he woke up. His cell phone vibrated in his pocket. He pulled it out and checked caller ID. Brigette Green working another late night. He accepted the call. "Good evening, Dr. Green. What keeps you at the lab this late?"

"The Wheatly suicide. I'm scheduling the autopsy for tomorrow afternoon at two. I know it's not usual for a suicide, but I convinced her mother."

"Why?"

"The previous assault and the method of death. I've noted some ... anomalies. See you at two." She clicked off.

O'Brien gasped as another sharp pain shot up from his ribcage. He put both hands on the trunk of the nearest parked car and pressed while he waited for the spasm to pass. "Goddamn it," he said. The pain eased, and he crossed the street to get to his car. His mind was already mulling over Green's call. If her suspicious meter was engaged, the Wheatly suicide could get upgraded. Suicide was bad, but murder was a hundred times worse.

CHAPTER 4

Two a.m. Ella was wide awake, hunched over her computer, reading articles about the psychology of a rapist. The mug of tea next to her on the desk was cold and long forgotten. She'd absorbed the information from the scientific journals with mounting anger and disgust.

She learned that men who raped might admit to having initiated nonconsensual sex even as they denied that they'd committed rape. They often started on their trail of abuse young, as early as high school or college. Many stopped after one or two times crossing the line, but a percentage continued — united by their lack of empathy and remorse. The fact that stood out for her was one that she'd long known: men who raped and were never caught seemed ordinary, the boy next door. The guy you'd pick to walk you home after a school dance. *The friend who had a beer with your dad after raping your little brother.*

She stretched and rubbed her eyes. Counted to ten. *Don't go there*, she thought. *Stick to the present, to Josie Wheatly.* Was this how the assailant wormed his way into Josie's world? Was he someone she knew and trusted? The second, equally chilling scenario, was that he was a stranger who somehow forced his way into her apartment. Ella didn't know which was worse. The rapist would be equally as hard to uncover, no matter his relationship with her, but her death had made finding him considerably more difficult.

"Motive," she said into the empty room. "Why choose Josie Wheatly? *Why choose the woman who moved into my apartment?*"

The moon was out. A nearly full orb cast a silver stream of light into the room. "This is the fairy hour," Danny used to say when they first moved to Ottawa and they took late-night walks around the city streets. His anxiety had prevented him from sleeping, and she'd kept him company even when she'd longed for her bed.

The weight of the day washed over her in a whoosh, and her head began to throb behind her eyes. She reached over and turned off the computer and the desk lamp. She was wearing a long t-shirt over black leggings but had wrapped herself in a blanket at ten o'clock when the thermostat kicked into its night-time mode. The sheets were cold when she slipped between them, and she curled into herself like a cat. She closed her eyes and worked to slow her breathing. She shivered and thought, *If Greg were here he'd wrap himself around the length of me and snuggle his face into my neck. We'd heat up the bed like a couple of furnaces, and the covers would end up a twisted jumble on the floor halfway through the night.*

She'd slept better then, when Greg was in her bed, even when she felt smothered by his body touching hers, his breath warm on her cheek. Now she had the entire mattress to herself, but she kept to one side of the bed. The fairy hour was the time of night when she missed being with him the most.

THE NEXT MORNING, Ella leaned against her bike across from her previous home on Kinnear. It was a crisp fall day, but the sun was shining like a bright penny, and the hopeless feeling she'd been carrying around was sinking lower in her belly. It was hard to stay in the pit of black despair with sunshine caressing the top of her head like a heat lamp. The frantic activity of a day ago was gone. A woman walking her corgi stopped in front of the house and stared up the walkway, but she'd moved on by the time Ella crossed the street. Ella tucked her bike out of sight around the corner of the house and pressed the intercom for Clare's apartment. Clare should be home, if her Facebook postings were anything to go by. A few moments later, the intercom crackled and Clare's voice echoed through the cramped space. "Yes? Who is this?"

"Clare, it's me. Ella Tate. Do you have a minute to talk?"

Silence. "Ella? Of course. I'll buzz you in."

Clare greeted her at the top of the stairs and hugged her, even though they'd never hugged when they'd lived across the hall from one another. "I'm so glad to see you," she said, and Ella could tell that she'd been crying. Fresh tears glistened in her eyes before she turned to start down the hallway. "Come in. Come in. Do you have time for coffee?"

"I do. Thanks."

Clare led Ella into her living room and had her sit while she poured them each a cup in the kitchen. An oversized white cat was sleeping on the floor in the sun. It stretched out to full length, watching Ella for a moment before curling up and closing its eyes again. When Clare reappeared with the tray bearing two mugs, cream, and sugar, she'd recovered her composure. "You're looking well, Ella. I like your hair shorter."

"It's made my head lighter." Ella touched the nape of her neck. It was a foolish move to go so short, since it cost money to keep up. She'd already decided to grow the length out again. "When did you get a cat?"

"It's … it was Josie's cat. I'm allergic but can't bring myself to give him to the humane society. She called him Snow Boy."

"He's well fed." Ella had never owned a pet. She'd thought about it but wasn't sure she'd make a good owner. She took a sip of coffee. There was nothing to be gained by spinning a tale about why she'd shown up after three months with no contact, so she got right to the point. "That's really why I'm here. Josie Wheatly."

Clare's face crumpled. "Oh, Ella, I'm sick over what happened to her." She bowed her head and inhaled deeply, then raised her eyes and stared at Ella as if assessing how much she knew. "You're aware she died yesterday, right?"

Ella nodded. "Yes. I came by to speak with her late morning, and I saw the police and the ambulance. Word spread about her … suicide."

"Her poor mom found her. She'd come to take her home. Josie was assaulted last week in her apartment. Did you know that too?"

"Yes. The entire chain of events is tragic. After I was let go from the newspaper and moved into my new place, I started up a true crime podcast show." Ella set a business card on the table between them with the podcast site. Clare picked up the card and studied it. Ella added, "When I came by yesterday, I wanted to talk to Josie about the assault and shine a light on the issue. Now she's dead, and I believe it's even more important to get her story out."

Clare put the card back on the table. "Josie was a

guarded person, no matter the image people had of her. I'm not sure she would have wanted to become the subject of your podcast."

"Maybe not, but she'd have wanted justice. I'm sure you agree we owe her that." Ella sounded pompous to her own ears. Yet she honestly believed in seeking the truth. Truth was her lodestar. Not working for the paper gave her the freedom to do whatever it took to peel away the layers of lies and corruption to get the real story. It wasn't as if she had much more to lose job-wise if the case went sideways.

Clare leaned back in her chair so that a brilliant shaft of sunlight streaming through the window illuminated her face. The harsh light wasn't flattering. It washed her out and accentuated the tired lines around her eyes and mouth, even though she was in her late twenties. She took her time answering.

"If it was anyone else … but I trust you to do the right thing, Ella. You always avoided the sensational when you were a reporter." Decision made, she slapped her thighs in a startling show of enthusiasm and leaned forward. "What do you need me to do?"

Ella was flattered to learn that Clare had followed her work on the paper but was surprised at the same time. They'd never discussed her articles when she lived across the hall. She took a small tape recorder and microphone out of her backpack. "I'll ask you questions about Josie and will sprinkle bits throughout my podcast. Don't worry, I'll be selective about what I use, so no need to edit yourself when you speak."

Clare looked wary but nodded.

"Just let me get this set up and pretend we're having a chat over cups of coffee."

"I think I can do that."

Once Clare started talking, the floodgates opened. Ella felt like her therapist, gently encouraging and prodding for more detail, trying to get some decent soundbites. Clare's reliving of the morning she found Josie's body was podcast gold, but it was her recollections of their high school years in Almonte that interested Ella the most.

Clare: *We grew up in the small town of Almonte where everyone knows everyone. Josie was a few years older than me, and I used to be jealous of how popular she was, you know, with the boys and teachers. I was a social misfit back then and shy as all get out. (small laugh) Josie had this natural outgoing personality. She was pretty and liked to party. When she moved in here three months ago, all those teenage insecurities of mine came flooding back, but she'd changed from what I remembered. She wasn't so … I don't know, careless about other people's feelings.*

Ella: Can you remember an example of when she was insensitive to somebody?

Clare: *Sure. We were in the school gym decorating for the autumn dance. Sort of a big deal in a small town. The grade nines were asked to take care of the decorations, a scary task since we were the newbies. Anyway, another not very popular girl named Christine led up the decorating committee, which included me and another girl. We worked for a few days making decorations with corn husks and dried leaves and other stuff from around the area. We worked all morning setting up and thought we'd done a good job, that is until Josie and a couple of her entourage came into the gym. Josie said it looked like a kindergarten class had vomited up some art projects. They all had a good laugh, even though we were right there. They just didn't care. (She put a hand over the microphone.) You won't use this, will you? It's got nothing to do with what happened to her.*

Ella: No, but it gives me a picture. What was your relationship like after she moved in here?

Clare: *We used to share a glass of wine now and then, usually on a Friday evening if I wasn't working at the hospital. We weren't* *bosom buddies, but she kind of grew on me. She wasn't that party girl any longer, and she seemed more thoughtful. She taught grade four and said it was an okay profession for now, but not where she saw herself down the road.*

Ella: Did she say what else she wanted to do?

Clare: *Well, she was engaged to a guy in the armed forces named Rory Leavitt. He was due back in the country soon, and they planned to get married around Christmas. That might have meant some travel. Other than that, she never said much about her plans.*

Ella: Was Rory from Almonte as well?

Clare: *No, his mom, Maureen, moved to Almonte recently. She's on the same street as Josie's mom, Cheryl, which is how Josie and Rory connected, you know, through their mothers. Josie said that since both their moms are widows, they've become good company for each other. She met Rory in Ottawa, but I never had a chance to be introduced because he's been stationed overseas since before she moved into your old apartment.*

Ella: How did she hear about this place anyway?

Clare: *I told my mom the apartment was empty, and she must have told Josie's mother. They're good friends too, although my mom lives a few streets over. With the way things turned out, I'm sorry now that I said anything.*

Ella: Where did Josie live before moving here?

Clare: *She had a basement apartment in the East End, but she wanted to be closer to Broadview School, where she was working.*

Ella: Did the super ever fix the tricky front door?

Clare: *No, but we all knew to shut it hard. Even Josie was aware because I told her.*

Ella: But it might have been mistakenly left open?

Clare: *(looking uncomfortable) It's possible.*

Ella wrapped up the interview without learning much else of use. She was putting the tape recorder into her knapsack when she stopped to ask Clare a question that had been nagging at her. "Would you say that Josie was happy, you know, with her life?"

Clare thought for a moment. "I was surprised to find out she was a teacher. Didn't match with what I remembered about her. I thought she was destined for a more glamorous life. Maybe an actress or interior designer or real estate agent to the wealthy. There wasn't the excitement I would have expected when she spoke about her future, especially when she talked about getting married and having kids. Strange how people can change."

"Only those who decide to grow up." Ella followed her toward the door. "Thanks, Clare, and take care of yourself. I'll let you know when the podcast goes live."

They hugged again, a little less awkwardly this time, and Ella stepped into the hall. She waited for Clare to close her door before crossing the hall to her old apartment. The door was locked when she tried the handle. It would have been good to get inside to get a feel for Josie. She could take some photos for the podcast web page, but she didn't dare break in. Instead, she settled for some snapshots of the building from across the street before she got on her bike and started winding her way down side streets on her way to Broadview School.

CHAPTER 5

Ella arrived as the school lunch break was about to begin. She loitered near the front door and approached the first person who looked like a teacher. Turned out Ms. Tiffany St. George worked in the classroom next to Josie's and agreed to chat during the ten-minute walk on the way home to eat. As luck would have it, St. George was a bit of a talker, and she invited Ella inside while she heated up some soup.

Her house, five blocks from the school, was a bungalow built in the eighties and in need of some serious maintenance. The concrete front steps were crumbling, and the siding had slipped sideways in several places. Inside wasn't much better. In the entranceway, the wallpaper had yellowed and peeled in long strips near the ceiling. The wood floors needed a sanding and a coat of varnish. On the way through to the kitchen, Ella noticed that Tiffany had a thing for roosters. The picture above the fireplace and the art in her kitchen were on theme. Rooster ornaments lay scattered on every available surface.

"Sure, go ahead and tape, but don't use my name. The

school frowns on us being in the news. There's nothing negative that I could say about Miss Wheatly, so I don't mind speaking about her teaching skills."

She appeared so earnest that Ella had to chew back a laugh. Tiffany reminded her of one of those doorbell-ringing, religious zealot, married-to-the-job types — believers in all that was correct and righteous to the exclusion of logic. She turned on the tape recorder and set it slightly out of the teacher's sightline. Tiffany quickly forgot that she was being taped, and Ella encouraged her with nods and smiles.

The most telling bits:

Ella: How well did you know Josie Wheatly?

Tiffany: *Josie taught at the school for three years. Grade four the entire time. The kids adored — absolutely adored — her. I mean, she had this way of relating to them, and she was so darn much fun. Some of the parents were worried about how much time the class spent on art projects and singing and such, but they had no idea how much preparation went into these activities. Sure, her classroom got boisterous sometimes, but those were happy kids. Happy, happy kids. They're going to be devastated when Miss Wheatly doesn't show up to teach them because of the terrible decision she made. She must have been in so much pain to take that desperate way out. (deep sigh) The assault precipitated that, of course. I might have thought her stronger … you know, emotionally, but trauma affects people differently, and who are we to judge? Well, she's at peace now, and I'm sure going to miss seeing her smiling face every weekday morning.*

Ella: What was Josie like as a colleague?

Tiffany: *(slight grimace) Friendly, but she didn't spend much time in the staffroom. We sometimes asked her where's the fire, she'd leave that quickly. She liked to get to the school early and do her prep* *before the kids showed up, and she usually left soon after the bell rang at the end of the day. She seemed efficient. Certainly confident and knew her own mind.*

Ella: Did you know anything about her personal life?

Tiffany: *Well, she wore a honking big engagement ring. (loud laugh) The diamond must have cost her young man a few months pay. I know she came from up the Valley somewhere. Arnprior or Almonte or Cobden? Not sure.*

Ella: Was she friendlier with any of the staff that you noticed?

Tiffany: *Well, she sometimes shared a joke with Mr. Rivington. He teaches grade six. He's our school catch. (tittering laugh) Oh, soup's ready. Would you like a bowl?*

Ella: No, but thank you. I'll be going and let you eat your meal in peace. Thanks so much for this. I can see myself out.

AS SHE LEFT THE HOUSE, Ella couldn't help but think, *Talk about damning with faint praise. Ms. St. George could give lessons.* She inhaled gulps of fresh air on the front step and thought over her options. School would be back in session soon, and she wouldn't have a chance to speak with the hot Mr. Rivington. She'd have to make another trip.

She mulled over the two interviews as she biked home in the autumn sunshine. She pedalled through the Experimental Farm, following the bike path down the hill to Dow's Lake and along the canal that wound past autumn flowerbeds of purple aster and scarlet chrysanthemum. The bushes and trees were seminude, their leaves spiralling in singles or clusters to the ground like so much confetti. The water in the canal was dark and muddy and smelled of dead fish.

Josie Wheatly was still a half-formed person, but the picture was getting less blurry. She was a woman settling for a life that she hadn't planned on and didn't appear totally suited for. Had her restlessness made her reckless? Was the assault random or personal? Ella had no answers, but she'd only just started digging. The next step would be to borrow a car and make the trip to Almonte, but first she'd do some research to find the address where Josie's mother Cheryl lived and figure out who else might have known Josie —whether someone from her past hated her enough to rape her and drive her to suicide.

But first, a visit to her happy place.

IF ELLA HAD one true friend in this world besides Danny, it was Finn Nyberg. They'd met in seventh grade when his family emigrated from Sweden and settled in Edmonton, Alberta. Back then, Finn was a scrawny kid with blonde hair to his shoulders and an almost nonexistent English vocabulary. He had eyes like shiny blue marbles that watched and assessed but gave nothing away. He wasn't any match for Jason Bryson, the biggest boy in their class, a man-boy with both parents over six foot and an extra birthday on the rest of them, having failed grade two. Jason was a dumb, oversized bully who got a hate on for Finn from the moment Mrs. Holland sat the two of them next to each other. Finn took the jabs, taunts, and ridicule without once reacting, even as his English steadily improved. Ella knew for a fact that he understood the names Jason was calling him a few months into term. Unbeknownst to anyone, Finn's father owned a boxing gym downtown, and Finn was spending time after school and on weekends learning how to defend himself … and he kept this a secret until the day Jason Bryson decided to turn his attentions on Ella.

School was almost done for the summer, and all the kids were squirmy, wanting to be outside and not putting in time working at their desks. Jason was being more obnoxious than usual, making farting noises whenever Mrs. Holland's back was turned and misbehaving whenever she was busy elsewhere. She must have reached her breaking point that particular day, because she held up his science project in front of the class and went on for ten minutes about what a piece of crap it was before deciding to hold up Ella's as an example of what he should aim for next time. She concluded by cracking a joke at Jason's expense. Ella made the mistake of laughing along with the rest of the class. Sometimes teachers get even without thinking through the consequences.

Jason was waiting for her after school, and he followed a few paces behind as she pretended to ignore him, yelling out obscenities and calling her names when nobody else was close enough to hear him. She arrived at the entrance to the park that she had to walk through to reach the bus stop. She could hear Jason breathing hard close behind her and turned to face him. He lurched forward and shoved her off the path toward some trees. She could still remember the terror that made her freeze up so that she couldn't fight back. It was at that moment that Finn arrived on the scene out of nowhere. He told her afterward that he'd been following them for a while. He pulled her away from Jason and got himself between them. He'd grown over the year without her even noticing and was now only a head shorter than Jason. All that training in the gym paid off, and that was the last time Jason ever bullied either one of them. Jason was damn lucky Finn hadn't put him in the hospital. From that day on, she and Finn were inseparable. He even followed her and Danny to Ottawa and opened his own Nyberg Gym. Their friendship had altered once he started dating Adele, but the connection was still there.

Ella wheeled her bike into the hallway of Nyberg's Gym on Catherine Street, where it wouldn't be stolen, and made for the lockers. The change room was empty. She quickly put on the workout clothes she kept in a locker reserved for her. Finn was working with one of his protégés, but he gave a wave as she crossed to the stationary bikes. After a brief warm-up on the mats, she biked for half an hour, varying the tension to give her legs a good workout. She moved from there to the weights. Finn finished with his client and came over to spot her.

"Hey, Ella. Been a few weeks. Where've you been?"

"I had some things going on." She was lying on her back and grunted with the effort of pushing up fifty-pound barbells.

"You and Greg break up?"

"Yeah." She lowered the weights, took a deep breath, and pushed them up again. "He decided I was too much work."

If Finn was surprised, he hid it well. He waited a beat. "His loss."

"One would like to think."

When she was done with the weights, Finn left to work with a new patron, and she picked up a skipping rope. After minutes of vigorous jumping she put on the boxing gloves to take a round out of the punching bag. Finn returned as she was tiring.

"Want to take me on?"

She looked over at the empty boxing ring roped off near the back of the gym. The idea of going a round with Finn was appealing, but she'd already been working out for an hour and a half, and fatigue was making her limbs heavy. The two-week hiatus hadn't done anything for her stamina. "Rain check?" she asked, giving one last jab at the bag.

"You getting soft on me, Ella?"

"I'm not as young as I used to be. How about a coffee instead?"

He nodded, and she followed him to his office at the front of the gym, where he could see who came and went. He poured them each a mug from the pot on top of the filing cabinet before taking his seat behind the desk. Ella flopped down in the visitor chair.

"Good God, Finn. How long has this coffee been sitting there? It tastes like it could remove stomach lining." She lowered the mug and wiped her mouth with the back of her hand.

"Puts hair on your chest." He smiled and sipped. "So how're you really doing with Greg's departure?"

She thought over her answer, trying to be honest with herself. "Nostalgic. I liked him and thought we'd last … well, last for a bit longer anyhow."

"He came by last week."

She straightened. "Now why would he do that?"

"He mentioned that he'd moved into a new place, but we didn't have time to get into it. He worked out for an hour and then left."

"Did he seem okay?"

"I guess."

She relaxed back into the chair. "Well, it's a free world, but I wish he'd find another gym. It's not like there aren't lots in the city."

"Did he really break up with you, or was it the other way around?"

"I might have suggested we spend some time apart, but

he was the one who moved out. He said that I was, and I quote, emotionally closed off. He couldn't see putting up the white picket fence or having kids with me until I got my shit sorted."

Finn didn't agree or disagree. "How's the podcast coming?" he asked instead.

"I'm following a story. Do you know that teacher who got raped last week and died yesterday?"

"Vaguely. Is that what you're working on?"

"Yup, and the odd thing is that she was the one who moved into my old apartment." She waited to see if Finn also found this a strange coincidence, but he was watching someone through the glass and his attention was divided. He looked from the window back to her and seemed to be trying to refocus. "Should make a sad but important story. What's your next move?"

"I'd like to borrow your truck tomorrow, if I may. I want to visit Almonte, where the victim's mother lives, and talk to a few people."

"Yeah, no problem. I'm in at nine tomorrow, so you can come by and get it. I won't need it until five or so. I told Adele I'd pick her up after work since our car's getting serviced. She's got some parent-teacher meetings and has to stay late."

"Perfect." She set the nearly full mug of coffee on the desk and stood. "Well, I have places to be, things to do, and I can see that you're ready to get back on the floor. How is Adele, by the way?"

He picked up his cell phone and stared at it, his thoughts miles away.

"Finn?"

"Sorry, yeah, well, she's grumpy and hungry all the time. She keeps telling me that she looks like hell, even though she's glowing and gorgeous. She's into her eighth month and slowing down."

"This too shall pass." She paused, "No pun intended. Say hi for me."

"I'll do that. See you tomorrow, Ella."

"Tomorrow."

CHAPTER 6

Ella got a late start the next morning. Almonte was in Lanark County, a half-hour drive southwest of Ottawa and famous as the birthplace of James Naismith, inventor of basketball. More recently, the town was known as the filming location for several Hallmark Christmas movies. She imagined the fairy-tale village charm would induce many city dwellers to want to move there, but the reality was that most would be bat-shit bored after a week.

She arrived at lunchtime and decided to treat herself to a table on the Heritage Café Bistro's patio next to the Mississippi River. It was a brilliant fall day, and the sun had heated the air so that she didn't need a jacket. There wouldn't be many more such days before the winter chill forced everyone inside. The server sat her at a table overlooking the falls, and she read the menu while waiting for him to return with a glass of red wine. Hungry after a week of barely eating, she ordered the butternut squash and bacon mac and cheese, then settled back and watched the cascading water while letting her mind wander.

Before long, her thoughts returned, as they always did,

to the puzzle of Josie's rape and suicide. It was astonishing to think that only a week ago Josie was leading a normal life, teaching grade four and waiting for her fiancé to return home. She'd have been planning her wedding, with all the excitement and parties that entailed. Could the rape have derailed her so completely and so quickly? Ella knew the trauma would have been intense, but from what she'd learned so far, Josie was not a weak or unstable woman. Her mom was there for her. Her fiancé was on his way. She had support. Why did she choose such a desperate way out without giving herself any time at all to heal?

An hour later, Ella drove across town to pay her respects to Josie's mom — or that was what she'd told Cheryl Wheatly when she called to set up an appointment the day before. Ella was frankly surprised when Josie's mom agreed to see her, not certain she would have in the same position. The Wheatly house was a bungalow on a quiet dead-end street lined in oaks and elms, a cozy-looking home in a bucolic setting. Ella stopped and took a few photos before hurrying up the walkway.

Cheryl Wheatly greeted her at the door and brought her into the living room. Ella turned down the offer of tea. Unease made her speak too quickly. She apologized for her intrusion before explaining her real reason for being there — the true crime podcast and her goal to shine a light on the terrible rape and death of her daughter. Cheryl sat silently throughout her spiel, back ramrod-straight while Ella fumbled through her explanation. When she stopped talking and took a breath, she knew that she shouldn't have come. Not enough time had passed since Josie's death, and Mrs. Wheatly's silence was indictment enough. She gathered up her bag and prepared to apologize a second time before making an awkward exit.

Cheryl looked at her then. "I used to read your articles

in the paper. You always wrote with such compassion. You were careful with the truth. If you honestly believe this will help others who've experienced a similar tragedy, I'm willing to tell you about my girl."

Ella sank back into the couch cushion. "I know this isn't easy."

"Talking about Josie helps me."

"I'd like to tape our conversation, but I'll edit the interview and will be respectful in what I select."

"Fine."

Cheryl was a smaller, older version of the pictures she'd seen of Josie, with short blonde hair and the same pale eyes behind blue-rimmed glasses. She stared vacantly off in the distance while Ella set up the recorder and placed the microphone between them. Cheryl glanced at the tape recorder and nodded for Ella to get started.

Ella: Did Josie tell you anything about her assault last week?

Cheryl: *No. She was unconscious when she was brought to the hospital, and the doctor sedated her after she came around because she was so upset. She was also confused and said she didn't remember what happened. This is normal, I understand. The police planned to interview her the day she checked herself out.*

Ella: Can you describe her injuries?

Cheryl: *(after a long pause) Well, she was viciously violated and had cuts on her face and hands. She'd been struck in the head and bled quite a bit. The doctor told me all the wounds were superficial. I know that she would have recovered from all her physical injuries given time. The rest…" Her voice trailed away.*

Ella: Do the police have any idea who did it?

Cheryl: *No leads. They're going through her phone and laptop. So far, they haven't told me anything.*

Ella: I understand she was engaged to be married.

Cheryl: *Yes, Rory Leavitt, her fiancé, was due home from active service in the Middle East at the end of the month. He's on his way back to Canada now.*

Ella: Please tell me about Josie.

Cheryl: *You mean what she was like as a person?*

Ella: Yes, it would be good to get a picture of your daughter.

Cheryl: *Josie was an only child and grew up to be a beautiful, caring woman who loved kids. She had a great sense of fun and liked nothing better than getting together with friends and family. Parties and family suppers were top of her list. This is a small town, and people are close. She also loved to travel and liked adventure. She and Rory had a trip planned to Machu Picchu next month and had lined up a guide for the trek. I understand it's quite arduous. Josie loved to challenge herself.*

Ella: Had she always wanted to be a teacher?

Cheryl: *Oh my, yes! She had a way with the kids. They trusted her, and she always knew how to speak to them on their level, even the troubled ones. She cared. I guess that's the secret.*

Ella: Was Josie worried about her safety in Ottawa at all?

Cheryl: *No. She'd just moved into her new apartment close to the school where she taught, and it's in a quiet, middle-class neighbourhood not known to have any serious crime. She was at a very good place in her life. I never in a million years would have thought that she'd take her own life even after... after the horrific attack in her apartment. She was always so strong. When her dad died two years ago, Josie was the one who got me through it. She wouldn't let me wallow and ... well, I know she wouldn't want me to do that now either.*

. . .

Ella didn't have the stomach to probe any deeper and wrapped up the interview without gaining much else that she could use in the podcast. What she did have was heart-breaking enough. Mrs. Wheatly agreed to send some photos of Josie for her to use on the podcast page.

Before setting out from Ottawa that morning, Ella had made an appointment with one of Josie's high-school girl-friends in Almonte, but the woman had left a message cancelling while Ella was on her way to the town. No explanation, but Ella figured she needed time to grieve. Interviewing Cheryl has been emotionally draining, and Ella wasn't sorry to take a break from another encounter. She had enough information from the three interviews anyhow to do the first instalment of Josie's life story. She was eager to get back to Ottawa to begin editing the piece. She'd check in with O'Brien for an update on the case in the morning before posting her first broadcast later that day.

Felix emailed as she was finishing her supper of sausages, French fries, and a store-bought salad. She'd been skipping vegetables lately because she couldn't afford them and never knew a forkful of lettuce could taste so good. She clicked on the message. Good news. Felix had secured a sponsor for the show and would be topping up her pay. All she had to do was incorporate the attached audio file into her shows at two different spots: directly after the intro and halfway through the podcast.

She closed her eyes before clicking on the link and prayed to God that Felix hadn't sold their souls for a few bucks. She'd draw the line at hemorrhoid cream, hair removal products that promised to change one's life for

$19.99, or, worse yet, pharmaceuticals. No way she'd be in big pharma's pocket. She needn't have worried. Once again, Felix was on the same wavelength. She'd be plugging a pub on Bank Street not far from her apartment. No conflict of interest or cringe-worthy ad. Did this mean Felix had a place in the 'hood? They'd never exchanged addresses, but it was possible they lived near each other. Or maybe he knew where she lived. She wasn't sure how she felt about that.

She closed her email and opened the podcast file. She thought that the best part of making these podcasts was splicing them together. She loved recording her commentary and inserting clips from the interviews. She even had an appropriately haunting opening musical score she had recorded one summer evening in her apartment. Danny and another buddy had come by to play an acoustic arrangement that Danny had created for her show. The quality of the sound was surprisingly good. Ella smiled at the memory of that evening before she got down to work. When she checked the clock at 1:00 a.m., she had the better part of the podcast put together.

Normally, she started reading the online news around this time, but tonight she put the computer on sleep mode and prepared for bed. She was meeting with Paul O'Brien first thing in the morning to catch up before he started shift, and she couldn't be late. It took her a while to nod off. Her mind was full of questions about Josie and what led somebody to the attack in her apartment. How had she left herself so vulnerable? Was it as simple as the front door not locking when somebody went out that evening?

As Ella began to drift, Danny's theme music replayed in her head. She wondered where he was holed up for the night. The anxious feeling that filled her every time she thought of him out there alone kept her from falling asleep. She started going over the Wheatly case so it would be fresh in her mind when she met up with O'Brien in the morning. It wasn't long before she was jolting in and out of consciousness … and not much longer before she was down for the count. For the first time since Greg left, she slept five straight hours without waking.

THE DAWN RUMBLED IN. Lightning jagged intermittently across the sky. Rain gusts pummelled the roof and lashed against the windowpane. Ella put on her raincoat and left her bike at home. Walking quickly, she took Third Avenue to Bronson, where she headed north six blocks until she reached a favourite greasy spoon café. She could see O'Brien waiting for her through the plate glass window. He looked tired, grey stubble on his cheeks, eyes bloodshot. It crossed her mind that he'd been on a bender. She didn't remember him as being a serious drinker.

"Hey, buddy," she said as she slid into the booth across from him. She shrugged out of her dripping raincoat and spread it across the seat next to her. "Thanks for seeing me again so soon and letting me pick your brain about the Josie Wheatly case."

Daisy was already on her way over, waving the coffeepot. She'd piled her grey hair into an odd topknot that looked like a bird's nest about to fall out of a tree. "The usual?" she asked, and O'Brien and Ella nodded in unison. They hadn't eaten here in months, but Daisy hadn't forgotten them.

"How's your research coming?" O'Brien asked before taking a sip from his refilled mug.

"I managed to get some good background from Josie's mom and another teacher. I also got a few clips from Clare

Daniels who lived across the hall from Josie. Thanks for the tip, by the way." She considered not revealing that she'd lived in the same apartment as Josie but decided that might seem odd if it came to light later. "Josie moved into that apartment after I moved out three months ago."

O'Brien stared at her. Blinked once. "Exact same apartment?"

"Exact."

"That's an odd coincidence." He fiddled with the handle of his coffee mug. "If I tell you something, it has to be off the record for now."

"Okay."

He leaned across the table and lowered his voice. "I don't have a lot to share, but evidence is pointing toward murder, not suicide."

"You're kidding."

"We have video of her leaving the hospital with a man, but he was careful to keep his face hidden. He was wearing dark, baggy clothes, so it's hard to make out his size. He was definitely taller than Josie by maybe a foot."

"Was he forcing her?"

"Looked like he had a grip on her, kind of propping her up. He took her down the stairwell, as far as we can ascertain, and out the fire exit. There's the briefest shot of them going out the door."

"It was probably whoever assaulted her. Came back to finish the job."

"That's the working theory."

"She could identify him."

"Or at least give us more information to help us find him." O'Brien toyed with the teaspoon. "If you hadn't moved when you did…"

"Don't think that hasn't crossed my mind."

"Well, lucky timing for you, but not for Josie Wheatly.

Life can be odd that way. Not worth losing sleep over."

They both straightened back in their seats as Daisy arrived with the food: scrambled, sausage, and brown toast for Ella, two over easy, bacon, and white toast for O'Brien. She'd even remembered that Ella took peanut butter and O'Brien preferred strawberry jam. They thanked her and dug in. Ella used the time to mull over the implications of Josie's death being a murder.

O'Brien finished eating first and pushed back his plate. "Was a time I'd light up a smoke to cap this off. Still miss the ritual of it. You ever smoke, Ella?"

"Nuh-uh. The science was out by the time I was old enough. I figured the cons outweighed the temptation."

"Smart." He paused. "Ever see your folks?"

"No." She tried to meet his eye and find out what he was getting at after all this time.

He shrugged. "Their loss. Look, I have to get moving. You'll keep what I told you under your hat?"

"That's a given, but I'd sure appreciate updates when you can. Breakfast is on me."

"I'll be in touch. Take care of yourself." He seemed to want to say more but stopped, busying himself by standing and putting on his raincoat. She watched him saunter over to Daisy at the cash and drop some money on the counter. Ella shook her head and mouthed *thanks* when he turned at the door. He waved and stepped outside.

Daisy came over to remove his plate. She stood next to Ella with one hand on her ample hip. "You two haven't been in for a while," she said. "Nice to have you back."

"Good to see you too, Daisy."

Daisy moved away to serve two construction workers who'd taken seats at the counter, and Ella finished the last bites of her meal before following O'Brien outside into the rainy morning.

CHAPTER 7

Danny huddled deeper into the thicket of bushes and wiped drops of rain from his forehead. The pine and balsam branches overhead offered some protection, but the rain was heavy and dripped through the boughs. He'd left his gear at the shelter, sweet-talking the care worker into watching it for him, only taking along his guitar. If someone stole any of his other stuff, he could deal with it. Just not his twelve-string.

He was winded from running and tried to slow his breathing so that he couldn't be heard, squatting on his haunches and peeking out from amongst the foliage. The panic in his chest eased. He appeared to have given whoever was following him the slip.

A few hours earlier, during a break in the rain, he'd walked up Rideau Street to visit his buddies in front of the Rideau Shopping Centre. The rain had driven Cal and Bernie away from their usual panhandling corners, and he met them in front of the main entrance of the mall. Bernie and Cal lit up cigarettes from a crumpled pack that Cal pulled from his jacket pocket. Then they crossed at the lights to make their way to the protection of the underpass, where they could smoke out of the drizzle and away from the angry looks of passersby.

"Hate this bloody fuckin' weather," Bernie said, shivering inside his thin jacket. Danny studied him to see if he was on something. It looked like he was needing a fix, but it was always hard to tell with Bern. He'd be cold and shivering even on a hot day.

"A guy was asking about you a day ago," Cal said, tapping Danny on the arm with two fingers. "Wanted to know where you busked on Tuesdays."

"Maybe some music producer from Nashville hoping to discover the next big star," Bernie joked.

Cal grinned. "Don't forget us little people when you're being driven around in your limo with more blow than you can put up your nose in one lifetime."

"You'll be the first two I dump when I'm rich and famous, you can count on that." Danny gave Cal a gentle shove on the chest, and Cal wrapped an arm around his shoulders and squeezed.

"Won't get rid of us that easy."

"Don't I know it." Danny smiled at Cal. "Say, what did this guy asking for me look like?"

"Motherfuckers!" Bernie yelled. His eyes flashed with wild excitement, spittle gathering at the sides of his mouth.

Cal's and Danny's smiles flipped over. Cal turned his head to look at Bernie and rolled his eyes.

"Goddamn federal government. Always got their hand out. Screwing the little guy. Why, if I had the power, I'd round up every last one of their sorry motherfucking asses and I'd..."

And … he's off, thought Danny. Bernie building up a head of steam was like a jet plane taking off. There'd be no reasoning with him for love nor money. He'd once owned a small business selling electronics, the failure of which he blamed on government red tape, even though he'd run the store and his marriage into the ground all on his own. Danny knew exactly the trajectory this particular rant would take and started backing away a small step at a time. Sure enough, Bernie's arms started waving and his hands formed into fists. He began jabbing at the air in front of him like Muhammad Ali while his voice rose to a shout laden with curses. He'd forgotten the two of them were there, now totally consumed by his self-righteous anger. Danny could see Cal also putting space between himself and Bernie. They exchanged furtive, feeble waves before turning and hurrying toward the opposite exits. Bernie'd be spending the night in jail if past episodes were anything to go by.

Danny usually busked in the ByWard Market for the afternoon, but the lousy weather meant he wouldn't get enough coin to make up for getting soaked. He thought about taking on a rescue dog to keep him company. A black Lab maybe, or something smaller that he could tuck inside his jacket. He'd heard a dog brought in more money, but one might also keep him from being allowed into the shelters. Just didn't know if it was worth the trouble. Besides, what would he do with a dog when he flipped his life around and got a real job?

The drizzle had turned into a light rain when he was nearly at the spot where he usually played his guitar. A guy wearing a black jacket with the hood up was leaning nearby against the brick wall a few feet from his corner. The uneasy feeling that started when Cal said a man was asking about him returned. Danny walked past him to the end of the block before turning to look behind him. The guy in the black jacket was no longer leaning against the wall. Danny scanned both sides of the sidewalk and located him facing into a store window with his head lowered. Danny watched him for a second until the light turned green, then crossed the street and hung right, walking briskly south toward Rideau Street, his guitar case slung over his shoulder and banging against his back. Another block on and he turned to have another look. A couple of people were walking arm in arm toward him. He caught a glimpse of the black jacket behind them.

That was when he started running.

He raced through the tunnel where he'd left Bernie yelling into the wind twenty minutes earlier, but there was no sign of him now. Danny made it to the other side of the underpass and up the concrete stairs. He ran across the cobblestones, past the Convention Centre, and down the incline to the bike path that ran alongside the canal. On a better day, the path would be crowded with people strolling, jogging, biking, but the cold rain was keeping them indoors. Limping past the National Arts Centre outdoor café as exhaustion set in, he kept going until he reached the stretch of bushes and trees where he'd spent many a night during the summer heat waves. He left the path and pushed past branches until he found a nice flat spot under the trees. The spot he was crouched in now, waiting for darkness to fall, waiting out the threat with no idea who the man was or why he was after him.

The rain stopped shortly after evening shadows stretched across the path. Danny had nodded off in his hideout and slept a while longer, dreaming that he and Ella were kids again, safe inside the fort they built in the woods at their cottage. Ella was reading to him from a book, and her voice was lulling him like a soft breeze into a contented doze. He jolted awake, sad to realize that he was alone, that he was no longer that boy. His dreams were becoming so vivid. It must be a side effect of detox. He liked going to sleep now. Not like before, when he'd wake up with his skin crawling with bugs that only he could see. By the time he was fully awake and ready for the walk back to the shelter, the cloud cover had blown up the waterway to let the nearly full moon cast silver shards of light across the canal. Danny stood and stretched his cramped legs. He stepped tentatively from his hiding place and looked up and down the bike path. No signs of movement. He reached back for his guitar case and started walking.

He was shaking after a few minutes, needing a fix of methadone to take the edge off. He wouldn't tell Ella about his latest attempt to quit until he was clean for longer than two weeks. Disappointing her again was not an option. He'd lasted all day without needing anything, and that had to be progress, but he'd stop at the free clinic for a shot on his way to the shelter. They'd told him to check in anyway. The nurse he liked would be working. Maybe she'd have time to chat for a bit. He'd have asked her on a date if this was a different life. Maybe he could still get to a place where a woman like her would look at him twice.

He could see the glow of the Arts Centre not far off in the distance, the pockets of light glittering across the water. The smell of damp, rotting leaves reminded him again of the dream and the woods. He wondered if Ella ever thought about those years, if she remembered that time with the same fondness. Those long summer days when they hung out with Finn and their cousins, Lance, Marianne, and Sally. That part of his childhood had been good, at least.

A shadow emerged from the fringes of the path a few feet in front of him. He jumped sideways, startled at the sudden rush of movement. The shadow lurched until it was almost on top of him, and a hand shoved him hard against the fence railing. Danny raised an arm to push his attacker away but wasn't fast enough to stop the flash of metal that ripped into his stomach. A searing pain made him gasp in cold air as he doubled over, still skewered on the blade. The person grabbed Danny's shoulder and wrenched, withdrawing the knife and pushing Danny backward. Danny grabbed his belly and felt the warm gush of blood on his hands. He dropped to his knees. Footsteps pounded away from him, receding down the pathway in the direction he'd come. The guitar case thumped against the pavement as Danny slid sideways and rolled on top of it. He tried to scream. He wasn't sure if he had before things went black and the pain ebbed away.

CHAPTER 8

Ella spent the entire afternoon recording and rerecording her Josie Wheatly podcast. She incorporated bits of the taped interviews with Josie's mom and Tiffany St. George, careful to keep the teacher's name out of it. Still, anyone who knew Tiffany's voice would know it was her. Ella stuck to her more positive comments, as she'd promised. Her wrap-up commentary cast doubt on the suicide theory without letting on that she knew Josie had been murdered. Risking her source would be reporter suicide. She and Paul O'Brien had been through too much for her to break his trust now.

The podcast went live at four o'clock. Ella copied the link to a few well-connected social media sites, Twitter being the main vehicle to get some clicks. Her name was still well known around Ottawa, and soon the post was retweeted by some news outlets and reporters. Sherry Carpenter, an ex-colleague from the paper, sent a private message congratulating her on a terrific piece. She asked to meet for a drink the next day. Ella thought over the wisdom of seeing her again before deciding it might be good to reconnect and smooth over the awkwardness. Ella had heard through the grapevine that Sherry took a pay cut to keep her job at *The Capitol.* She covered the political beat at City Hall and was a good writer.

The rain was still pelting against the window, but the wind had died down when Ella checked the time. Four thirty, and a few hours of daylight left. She'd been sitting at her desk all afternoon, and her muscles had stiffened. The large bag of chips she'd munched on all day had left her over-salted and bloated. It was time to go see Finn and work on some cardio.

She packed a gym bag and called for an Uber. Perhaps not the best use of her meagre funds, but the cold, wet weather dictated. Finn was teaching a boxing lesson to a couple of teenagers when she entered the gym, so she changed and warmed up on the mats before getting on the treadmill. After half an hour, she moved to the elliptical. Finn tossed her a towel when she stepped off a half hour later.

"Two days in a row, Ella. You're going to get fit if you're not careful."

She wiped the sweat from her face while she caught her breath. "Not if my aching legs are the measuring stick. I feel like I've been run over. I'm going to cool down and have a shower." She looked around. They were the only two left in the gym. "Unless you want to close up now. I can shower at home."

"Take your time. I have some paperwork to get through." He hesitated. "We could go for a beer if you like after you clean up. I can drop you off at home."

She couldn't remember the last time they'd had a drink together. He was always in a hurry to get home after work. "I'd like that. Adele won't mind if you're late?"

"No worries on that score."

The rain had finally stopped, and darkness had settled

in when they stepped outside. The air was perfumed with the after-rain smell of wet leaves and earthworms. There was a pub around the corner, so they decided to go on foot and come back for Finn's truck after their drink. Finn was preoccupied, and they walked along the wet street without saying much. It was a slow night in the pub, and they took a table between the gas fireplace and the window. Ella could do without the Irish jigs playing through the sound system, but at least the music wasn't loud enough to give her a headache. After the server brought them a couple of craft beers, Finn leaned forward and put both hands around his glass. "Do you ever miss those times when we were kids, hanging out with Danny and your cousins?"

"Not really. Marianne and Sally were never all that friendly, always competing with me … or maybe I was the one competing with them. They were better in school than I'd ever be, and Lance was a natural athlete, expected to make the NHL. Aunt Ruth always had the newest everything in her house and dressed like a fashion plate. They made me feel inferior. I preferred hanging out with you and Danny when they weren't around."

"Which wasn't that often. I didn't know you felt that way." Finn swirled his glass in the moisture on the table. "Adele's starting to question whether she wants to stay married to me. I'm not certain if it's the hormones from being pregnant or what, but she's depressed and thinks she's going to be shit as a mother. Says she's going to give up the baby if I don't want it, because she can't do this any longer. I'm not sure what to do."

This was the last thing Ella had expected to hear. "Finn … that's awful. You have to know that this is coming from the pregnancy. The hormone changes can wreak havoc on a woman. Has she talked to her doctor about how she's feeling?"

"She said she doesn't need to speak with anyone. I put in a call anyway and am waiting for her doctor to contact me, but I'm not holding out much hope that he'll be able to get through to her."

"Was Adele … unhappy before she got pregnant?"

Finn lowered his head and spun the beer glass around in a wet patch on the table. "We were in a rocky place about a year ago. She was involved with someone at work."

"Oh, Finn, I'm so sorry. I had no idea."

"Yeah. The guy's also married. When he broke it off with Adele, he told her that he and his wife were going to work on their marriage and he'd taken a job at another school. She said that she was ready to recommit to our marriage too. She got pregnant a few months later, and everything seemed solid. Then this guy got back in contact with her. Messed up her head."

"He sounds like a first-class jerk."

"You'll get no argument from me."

They hadn't shared personal problems since Finn married Adele, so Ella knew things were bad. He'd only ever spoken well of Adele, and Ella had envied their devotion to each other. The truth was unsettling. She dropped her voice and said out of the side of her mouth, à la James Cagney, "You want me to take him out for ya? Break his kneecaps maybe?"

Finn grinned. "Not going to solve anything in my marriage, but thanks for suggesting a satisfying movie solution."

"Things will be okay, Finn. Adele will figure out what's important once she holds the baby."

"I hope you're right."

She hoped she was too. They both knew there were no guarantees. Finn raised his head, and Ella felt the silent connection pass between them. There was a time he'd been the only one keeping her from taking a bottle of sleeping pills, when everyone in her life had turned their backs. She'd be there for him now no matter what.

"So how 'bout them BoSox?" he asked, lifting his glass and draining the last of his beer. "Looks like it might be their year to go all the way."

FINN DROPPED her off in front of her apartment. She watched until the red glow of his taillights disappeared around the corner before starting up the walkway. She didn't know Adele that well. Finn had met her through one of his friends, and she'd always been aloof toward Ella. For her part, Ella thought Adele was flighty at their first encounter and had been surprised by Finn's early infatuation. Even more surprised when they eloped. She'd deliberately stayed out of their married life and only saw Finn when she dropped by the gym. It would take a while to digest the reality of his marriage.

Tony must have heard the front door opening, or he was looking out the window and saw her get out of Finn's truck. In any case, he was waiting outside his apartment door on the second floor when she walked up the staircase. He waved a bottle of red wine in the air. "Up for a nightcap?"

She was tired and grumpy but couldn't think of an excuse to pass by him without looking rude. Not to mention she could do with another drink. "Lovely," she said and followed him inside his apartment and down the hallway to the living room, the sight of which made her breath catch every time. He was the one with the decorative flair, or so he'd told her more than once. To her eye, the room was outlandish and garish, but everything somehow worked. The art on the walls was modern and vibrant, oil paint laid on thickly in wide brush strokes. There were high ceilings and floor-length drapes of crimson velvet, matched by jewel-toned furniture: a couch in emerald green and Queen Anne chairs in peacock blue. Plush, white, shag rugs lay scattered across the dark hardwood floor. Tony said Alex agreed to let them have the floors redone but refused to pay for the work, so he and Sander went ahead anyhow. Unlike her cramped, dark garret, this unit was blessed with floor-to-ceiling French doors that led onto a small balcony where Tony grew herbs and cherry tomatoes.

Some classical music was playing in the background as she sank into one of the chairs and accepted a full glass of wine. The wine tasted like a summer day in Paris — or how she envisioned a summer day in Paris — and she savoured the bouquet on her tongue. Tony never did or consumed anything on the cheap. "Where's Luvy?" she asked, scanning the corners of the room.

"Sander took her for the nightly constitutional. He usually visits with a friend around the corner but shouldn't be too long." Tony stretched out on the couch. Tonight he was wearing a gold brocade lounging jacket and silk pajama bottoms the colour of overripe plums. Since she'd last seen him, he'd dyed his shoulder-length hair forest green. The scent of jasmine wafted up from the diffuser on the glass coffee table.

"I listened to your podcast. It was insightful but left many questions unanswered. Do you believe Josie Wheatly was a victim of foul play, or did she die by her own hand?" His eyes fixed on hers with laser focus.

"You'll have to wait for the next instalment." She smiled and sipped her drink, pleased that he'd deduced as much as he had from her vague inferences at the end of the podcast. "I had no idea you followed my podcast."

"Religiously, girl. Do the police have any idea who assaulted her in the first place?"

"Not that they've told me."

"But you do have an inside source? It seems obvious that you do."

She nodded, slightly disconcerted that he'd figured that out too. "But they can only tell me so much."

"It's so macabre but exciting at the same time. I love murder mysteries, guessing whodunnit. I must have been a private detective in my previous life. Sander says I've got the most analytical brain he's ever encountered."

"That's quite a compliment."

"Of course, he said it when we were first dating. That *is* the time when one will say anything to get into the other person's pants."

She took a larger gulp of wine and remained silent, not sure of the correct response. Tony was given to self-aggrandizement, but he often seemed to be camping it up rather than serious. She didn't know him well enough to tell if he was poking fun at himself or not.

They both turned at the sound of the apartment door opening. A second later, Luvy's toenails clicked toward them down the hallway. "Hey, Tony," Sander called. "You'll never guess who I ran into. Your crush Greg was..." Sander skidded into view on his stocking feet. He was wearing his usual plaid shirt, baggy jeans, and ball cap. Sander was a jock, loved football, was into weightlifting and drinking beer. Ella had no idea how he and Tony got together, but she did know that he'd dated women before Tony came along. He blushed at the sight of her. "Oh, hey, Ella. Didn't know we had company."

Tony laughed at Sander's *faux pas*. "And where did you

see the delicious Greg? Ella doesn't mind if we talk about him, do you, Elle?" He held up the wine bottle in Sander's direction.

"He was walking a block from here, heading toward Bank Street." Sander's embarrassed eyes flicked from her to the wine bottle, and he nodded for Tony to pour.

"Did you talk to him?" Tony asked as he got up and walked over to the drink caddy to get a glass.

"He wasn't too pleased to see me at first, but yeah, we chatted for a minute. He's staying with a friend across the bridge in Ottawa South."

A twenty-minute walk from their place. Ella was hoping he'd moved farther away but wasn't surprised that he hadn't. Both guys were staring at her, waiting for a reaction. She shrugged. "Probably a drinking buddy. Lots of bars over there."

"So you had no idea who he was moving in with?" Tony laughed. "I don't know if I could let Sander go that easily." He exchanged a look with Sander that said, *I told you so. Ella isn't capable of deep feeling.*

"Greg is free to live with whoever the hell he wants. We. Broke. Up." She pounded each word separately in place of Tony's head.

"And you don't care a whit, is that what you're telling us, girl?" Tony snapped his fingers. "Gone and good rid … dance to bad rub … bish."

"That's about the size of it."

"Tony's just bummed that Greg moved out. He doesn't have many friends." Sander dropped onto the couch next to him and mussed his hair. "Love you."

Tony feigned a pout. "I have friends. Lots of friends. Carloads of friends, in fact."

"Little clown carloads maybe."

They started pushing each other, and Sander wrapped

an arm around Tony's neck and pretended to punch the side of his head. They'd been together three years and were still openly affectionate. Ella couldn't imagine. She'd never lasted more than a year with anyone. Scratch that. Four months with anyone.

She drained her glass and stood up. "It's been a long day, and I should push off. Thanks for the wine, Tony."

"Don't be a stranger," he said, extracting himself from under Sander's arm. "Supper is still on the back burner for the weekend."

"Keep me posted."

She climbed the stairs and entered her apartment, turning on the lamps, and checked that everything was as she left it. Josie's murder had her spooked. She could very well be the one assaulted if she hadn't lost her job and needed to move to a cheaper place to live. She unscrewed her precious bottle of wine and poured another glass that she sipped while waiting for the computer monitor to warm up.

What was Greg doing back in the neighbourhood? He'd made it quite clear that he wanted nothing to do with her until her attitude about their relationship changed — which it had not. He hadn't lived in this apartment long enough to make any friends aside from Sander and Tony. So what was the draw that brought him back? She knew exactly who he was living with. She'd known from the minute he told her that he was moving out, because where else would he go but back to Lucy, his old girlfriend across the bridge on Grove Avenue? She had never stopped calling when Greg had lived with Ella. Greg said Lucy used to cry on the phone when she'd had too much to drink.

She couldn't lie to herself. Knowing he'd actually moved in with Lucy stung for a bit, but she shut that regret down damn fast. Greg was handsome and funny and sweet most of the time. They got along really well, but she'd known it wouldn't last. Letting him go before he got too attached was the kindest gift she could have given him … given herself. But what was he doing back here? Why did her heart beat faster knowing he was nearby?

She flipped open the podcast analytics. Over six hundred views already and twenty-two shares. This was the best first-day release yet. Felix and the new sponsor should be pleased. Eight people left comments, all positive. Two of them raised the possibility that Josie Wheatly had been murdered. No message yet from Felix about the podcast, but this was to be expected. He only reached out sporadically, usually with an idea for a show or an angle to investigate.

She spent an hour reading the news online, had a second glass of wine, and flopped into bed soon after one o'clock. Whether she passed out or fell asleep from exhaustion, she was soon oblivious to the world and managed to stay unconscious until her cell phone rang at 6:00 a.m.

CHAPTER 9

"Is this Ella Tate?" A woman's voice, one she didn't recognize.

"It is."

"Please hold."

Ella was standing naked on the cold floor and leapt back to the warmth of her bed. Normally she'd hang up on someone who called this early and put her on hold, but the urgency in the woman's voice kept her waiting. She heard the sound of the receiver being fumbled at the other end. An intake of breath. A man's voice this time.

"Ella Tate?"

"That's me."

"Do you have a brother named Danny Tate?"

Her heartbeat quickened. "Is something wrong? Where is he?" She took a breath, calmed herself down, and tried again. "Yes, I have a brother named Danny Tate."

"This is Dr. Fournier. I'm sorry to tell you that Danny was stabbed last night and is in critical condition at the Ottawa Civic Hospital. We stabilized him and operated to stop the internal bleeding, but he'd lost a great deal of blood before he was found."

"Is he conscious?"

"He slips in and out. He managed to give us his name, and we tracked down his doctor at the free clinic. Your name and phone number are on file there as his next of kin. I'm sorry it took so long to sort out who to call."

"I'm on my way. Please let him know I'll be there soon if he comes around again."

"He's in ICU. I'll leave a note with the nurses that you're allowed in to see him. The police are also here, so I imagine they'll be checking your credentials."

"I'll be sure to bring ID."

She raced around the apartment, throwing on clothes, going to the bathroom, and trying not to panic. She took her second Uber ride in two days, even though the hospital was a few kilometres away and she normally would have biked. Her foot drummed on the floor of the car the entire way. They stopped at so many red lights that she wanted to hit something with her fist, but she stopped herself by focusing on looking out the side window. Danny had never been in a street fight that she knew of. He avoided confrontation. *The doctor said he was stable.* Who would attack her gentle-spirited brother who never said boo to a soul?

She was out of the car before it stopped completely, and the driver yelled at her as she slammed the door. She didn't stop to apologize and raced through the main entrance. She got directions from reception and rode the elevator to Intensive Care. A female police officer checked her identification before a nurse brought her to see Danny. He was in a space screened off with dividers and lay pale and still, hooked up to a heart monitor with an IV dripping clear liquid into his arm. An oxygen mask covered his face, and the sound of his laboured breathing almost made her fall to her knees. She moved beside him and gently took his hand. The nurse waited next to her.

"Who brought him in?" Ella asked, her eyes not leaving Danny's face.

"A couple of teenagers found him lying on the bike path that runs along the canal near the Arts Centre. Luckily, they were smart enough to call 911, or Danny likely wouldn't have survived the night. We operated on him to stop the bleeding in his stomach. He hasn't woken up yet, but he's stable. We'll need to monitor him for the next twenty-four hours. Are your parents still alive?"

"They are, but neither of them is in contact with Danny or me."

"Would you like us to notify them about Danny's condition?"

She took a moment to think. "I'm not sure they'll care, but if you think this is necessary…"

"It's whatever you believe Danny would like. His condition is stable for the moment but still precarious."

"They live in Edmonton." She tried to weigh the options. Would Danny want them to know, or would it upset him even more when he woke up? "It's complicated," she said, glancing at the nurse.

"Well, as his contact of record, I'll leave this up to you." The nurse's eyes were curious, but she didn't probe.

"My brother's an addict. I suppose you realized that when you spoke with his doctor at the clinic."

The nurse picked up Danny's chart. "He's been taking methadone for the past two, almost three weeks. He was past due for a shot, so this was administered to keep him comfortable."

"He was detoxing?"

"Yes."

Ella turned and stared down at her brother's face. She

stifled the sob that filled her throat. “Can I sit with him for a while?”

“Certainly. I won’t be far if you need me.” The nurse pulled a chair to the head of the bed and showed Ella the button to press in case of emergency.

“Thank you.”

She sank onto the chair, all the while holding Danny’s hand. “Why didn’t you tell me you were getting clean?” she whispered into his ear. “I’m so proud of you. When you’re ready to leave here, you can come stay with me. I won’t hear no this time. I’ll make that chicken dish you like so much and the chocolate cake.” She rested her cheek against his arm. “You can’t leave me, Danny. You can’t. You’re all I’ve got.”

He didn’t become conscious while she sat with him. The nurse returned after twenty minutes, took her to a small waiting room, and told her that someone would be back to speak with her soon. Soon stretched into two hours. Other people came and went, visiting their own family members in the ICU. The nurses smiled encouragingly at her whenever they passed by. Occasionally one stopped and asked if she needed anything, but she always shook her head. The thought of food made her want to throw up.

She was alone in the waiting room when the cop finally came to speak with her. Officer Grant didn't have any more information than she already knew, and Ella had nothing to give in return. He handed her a business card before leaving and asked her to call if she thought of anything that could help track down the person who hurt Danny. Dr. Fournier entered a few minutes later and took the seat next to her. The doctor was young, with a wide smile and soft black eyes. Ella liked him immediately, and this feeling grew once she realized that he came directly from another surgery to speak with her about Danny.

"Your brother's a fighter," he said. "The knife went into his stomach and pierced part of his liver. We operated to stop the bleeding and repair the damage shortly after he arrived by ambulance. We're replenishing the lost blood and giving him a saline drip along with painkillers. I know that he's trying to kick a heroin addiction, so we're being careful about the amount. I'm concerned about infection, so I've also started antibiotics. I have to add that Danny's physical condition has been weakened by his time living on the street. He's anemic and undernourished."

"When will we know…?"

"If he's going to make it? Forty-eight hours should give us a better picture of his recovery time. He's in good hands here. You should go home and rest. The nurses have your number and will call you if there's any change."

"Should he still be unconscious? Is this a bad sign?"

"He was thrashing about, so we gave him a sedative. He needs this time so his body can heal. He won't wake up for any intelligible conversations today." Dr. Fournier patted her arm. "Go home and try not to worry. We'll take good care of him."

SHE DECIDED TO WALK. The day had turned mild, and the autumn colours were just past their peak. Enough leaves had fallen to brighten the sidewalk and gutters where they'd gathered, but those left on the boughs made a brilliant display against the backdrop of satin-blue sky. Half an hour later, when she reached her street corner, her stress had lessened, although her worry for Danny hadn't gone away. She needed to stay busy. The police would do a cursory look into the crime, but they'd be unlikely to go above and beyond for a homeless heroin addict. It would be up to her to bring the bastard to justice.

She climbed the stairs to her apartment, tiptoeing past Tony and Sander's door, hoping that Tony hadn't heard her enter the house. Luckily, "My Heart Will Go On" was blasting from their stereo, drowning out the click of the front door and her footsteps in the stairwell. He only played Céline when Sander was at work. It was well past lunchtime. She wasn't hungry but made a peanut butter sandwich and ate it at her computer while she looked up the addresses for the Ottawa Mission and the free clinic nearby. Before putting on her jacket, she called the hospital and asked about Danny's status. The nurse told her there was no change but that this was to be expected for at least another day with the sedatives they were giving him.

It seemed like a good idea to leave her bike at home, since it could get stolen. Most homeless people weren't crooks, but it only took one junkie to steal the bike to sell for a hit or a bottle. She walked to Bank Street and caught a bus that took her downtown to Parliament Hill. She walked east from there, past the Château Laurier onto Rideau Street. She continued on past the Rideau Shopping Centre until she reached Waller, where she veered right. The Ottawa Mission was a solid red-brick building on a busy corner across from some high rises and next to a city parking lot. Men stood smoking in groups on the sidewalk or sat on the grass median as well as in the parking lot. One guy drank from a twenty-sixer of rye and passed it to his buddy. She'd judged these men for their addictions and lifestyle before Danny joined them.

A man wearing a black suit jacket and stained brown dress pants stepped forward from the shadows as she passed by on her way to the Mission entrance. "Looking for someone, pretty lady?"

She inwardly cringed but pasted a smile on her face. "My brother Danny was staying here. He's about six foot, long brown hair, always carting around his guitar. Do you know him?"

"Everybody knows Danny."

"Did you hear that he was stabbed?"

"Everybody heard that he was stabbed."

"Does everybody know who stabbed him?"

"No."

"Any rumours?"

"Wasn't none of us."

She reached into her pocket and handed him five dollars. "Thanks, buddy. Say, do you know who Danny hung around with yesterday?" She'd pulled out a second five-dollar bill, and his eyes went from it to her face.

"You can ask for Cal. He's inside getting some grub."

She handed over the second five. She wished it could be more, but she had to eat this month too. She entered through the cheery blue main doors, and a volunteer greeted her. Ella said she was Danny's sister, and he escorted her into the dining room, where he pointed Cal out to her. Cal nodded to the volunteer before he turned to leave and pointed at the chair across from him. She sat. Nobody else was within earshot.

"You look like him," Cal said, leaning back in his chair and picking up the coffee mug. He shoved his tray of dirty dishes to one side. "Same big sea-green eyes with ungodly long lashes. Yours fake or what?"

She smiled. "Not fake."

"We always kid Danny about his girly eyelashes." Cal's mouth turned sideways. The wry grin made his face elfin. She guessed him to be in his fifties, but he could be younger. His hair and beard were completely grey, and the lines in his forehead and around his eyes were etched deep. "Have you seen Danny in the hospital?" he asked.

"This morning. He's hanging in but still critical. You were with him yesterday?"

"For a bit. He showed up late afternoon with his guitar. Bernie, Danny, and me walked to the underpass across from the Rideau Centre, and Bernie started into one of his rants, so Dan and I headed for opposite exits to put distance between us and Bern. It was the last time I saw your brother. Usually he busked in the Market on Tuesdays, but it was raining and cold, so he said he was taking the day off, like I was from panhandling."

She knew exactly where Danny would have set up if it hadn't been raining. He was a creature of habit. "Did Danny say anybody was threatening or bothering him?"

"Nope. He never gave anybody any trouble neither. Danny was liked by everybody."

"Did he owe anyone money?"

"Not that I know of. He didn't need to borrow 'cause he made money busking."

She wasn't sure if she was asking the right questions and took a second to think. "How did Danny seem when you met him yesterday?"

Cal frowned as he appeared to be reaching back in his memory. "I dunno. He was getting off the drugs and seemed clearer, if you know what I mean. The jitters were disappearing. He looked over his shoulder a few times when we met up. I dunno if he was watching for somebody. Oh yeah, that reminds me. I told him that this guy was asking the day before where he busked on Tuesdays. We joked about it."

"What guy?"

"Never saw him before. He was hanging around out front of the Mission."

"Young, old?"

"Hard to say. I wasn't exactly in my right mind when I met the guy, and it was dark out. He was wearing a hoodie." Cal shrugged.

"If you see him again, try to get a name and description. Give me a call if he comes around."

"I could use the phone here."

"Good. This card has my number."

"Danny left his stuff with one of the volunteers. All except his guitar. You can ask to keep his gear while he's in the hospital. It'll be safer with you."

"I'll do that. The police have his guitar, apparently. Thanks for talking to me."

"We're all pulling for Danny. Tell him that Cal says to get out of that hospital bed and haul his sorry ass back down here. Tell him we miss him."

"I'll be sure to pass that along as soon as he wakes up."

CHAPTER 10

The clinic that Danny frequented wasn't far from the Mission, so Ella dropped by on the off chance somebody would be free to speak with her. The waiting room was full, not an empty seat in sight, and a line-up at reception trailed across the room to the entrance. When she finally reached the front of the line, she gave her name and phone number with a request for Danny's doctor to call when he was free. She knew the impromptu visit was a long shot, so she thanked the woman at reception and left half an hour after arriving, none the wiser about her brother's attempt to detox or the support he'd been receiving.

When she left the clinic, she stopped on the sidewalk and checked her phone for messages from the hospital. She hadn't missed any while inside. Waiting for news about Danny was like a throbbing toothache that was always present, even when she tried to block it from her mind.

It was nearing two thirty. She needed to keep moving, or the worry would take over. She started toward Rideau Street. Danny would be busking on his corner in the Market if this was a regular Wednesday. Not the same corner as on Tuesdays, but only two blocks over, nearer to the fruit and vegetable stalls. All of the vendors knew him and gave him fruit after he performed. Danny was particularly fond of cherries in the summer and McIntosh apples in the fall. Small treats in a life dependent on the kindness of strangers.

She walked past Danny's corner, imagining him there. She pictured his sweet smile, the one that lit up his face whenever he'd see her approach. He'd always finish his song before giving her a hug. Lost in thought, she almost didn't hear her name being called. She stopped walking and waited as Paul O'Brien waved and crossed the street on his way toward her with a younger man, taller and leaner than O'Brien, following behind. If this new person was a detective, he'd joined the force after she had stopped working the crime beat.

"Ella," O'Brien said when he reached her.

The one word held enough sympathy to sink her. "You're assigned to Danny's stabbing." Her voice was harsh and stopped O'Brien from expressing his condolences aloud. She looked from one man to the other. "Have you found anything?"

"Not yet." He studied her face before half-turning. "Ella Tate, meet Detective Liam Hunter. Hunter's the lead on this case, but I asked to tag along since his partner's on training. Ella is Danny's sister." O'Brien's sad eyes met hers. She could be all of seventeen again, the first time they met on the afternoon when he'd taken her statement.

"Sorry about what happened to Danny," Hunter said, breaking the moment. She turned her head and stared at him before nodding. She supposed it was a good sign that he used Danny's name. It meant that he saw her brother as a person and not just a homeless drug addict. His expression was intense, his eyes sky-blue and hard to escape. Her shoulders relaxed, and she realized how tightly wound she'd become since spotting O'Brien walking toward her.

"Thanks. Have you got any theories as to what happened to him?"

"We're still retracing Danny's movements from yesterday. He left the Mission midafternoon and met a couple of buddies in front of the Rideau Centre. He left on his own shortly afterward, heading in the direction of the Market. His friends don't remember seeing him after that. It was raining heavily off and on, and Danny wasn't in his normal routine. One of the vendors saw Danny around four o'clock walking past the corner where he played when the weather was better. She thought he left in a hurry and found this odd because he normally would have come over to say hello and get an apple from her." Hunter's voice had an Irish accent that was soothing to her ear. He had the same ruddy complexion and black hair as many of his countrymen. She could picture him herding sheep in the rolling green hills and drinking beer in a pub with his mates. She'd been to Ireland with Danny when he turned eighteen, her birthday gift to him after he got out of rehab the first time.

"Did the vendor see anybody following him?" she asked.

"She didn't notice, but that doesn't mean there wasn't."

"He was detoxing with clinic support. I'm not sure for how long, but that would mean this wasn't over drugs."

"It could have been random," O'Brien said. "Wrong place at the wrong time."

"I'm not convinced." Ella glanced at him and back at Hunter. "Somebody was asking about him the day before this happened. He wanted to know where Danny busked on Tuesdays."

Hunter pulled a notebook and pen out of his pocket. "Description?"

"Cal didn't have one. He's another guy who lives at the Mission."

"Cal's last name?"

"I don't know it, but if you ask for Cal… He was one of Danny's friends that met up with him yesterday afternoon."

"I spoke to a guy named Bernie, but he didn't give me any other names. I'll track down Cal."

"Thanks. Maybe he'll remember something since we spoke."

Hunter put the notebook away and signalled to O'Brien that they should get moving. O'Brien touched her forearm. "I'll give Hunter your phone number, and he'll contact you if he has more questions or something to tell you about the case. You take care of yourself, Ella."

"And you, Paul. Nice meeting you, Liam."

"Sorry it wasn't under other circumstances," Hunter said. "I'll be in touch soon. I have Danny's guitar to return to you."

"Yes, I want to keep that safe for Danny."

Ella took out her phone as she started walking and checked messages again. Nothing. She shoved the phone back into her pocket and quickened her pace as she headed west toward Parliament Hill. A notification pinged on her phone as she drew even with the Château Laurier. She looked at the sender's name and cursed. She'd forgotten all about the drink with her ex-colleague Sherry Carpenter at six o'clock. They'd agreed to meet at a pub in the Glebe. If she hurried, she might make it with a few minutes to spare.

CHAPTER 11

Liam shot O'Brien a glance as they stopped to survey the ground where Danny Tate spent his Tuesdays busking. He didn't think it was his imagination that O'Brien and Ella Tate had a relationship extending beyond cop and victim. Something in the way they looked at each other spoke of a deeper familiarity.

Danny's busking spot was across the road from a fruit vendor next to a brick building on the corner. It was a prime location to busk with lots of foot traffic from two directions. The woman who ran the fruit stall said Danny was a creature of habit. Only the nasty weather that Tuesday had kept him from playing.

"Place has been cleaned by street sweepers since Danny last played here," O'Brien observed, coming up beside him. "We aren't going to find anything, especially since he didn't play on Tuesday."

"Danny walked past her stall that day if the fruit vendor wasn't mistaken. It's possible he crossed paths with his assailant in this location." Liam pointed farther up the street. "Still want to come with me to the Mission?"

"In for a penny."

They fell into step.

"Ella's not the most open of people," Liam said. "You two known each other long?" He glanced sideways at O'Brien. He kept his face neutral, but Liam saw evasion in O'Brien's eyes before he looked away.

"I was working out of Alberta, and her family was living in Edmonton, oh, about ten years ago now. There were charges against a neighbour for corruption of a minor. Danny was the minor. The neighbour got four years and made the child sex registry."

"Jesus. Could that have anything to do with his attack?"

"Bit of a stretch, given the passage of time. The family's still out west far as I know." O'Brien's voice tightened. "It has a lot to do with Danny being hooked on drugs and living on the street, though."

They passed a woman obviously turning tricks on the corner, but she saw them and slipped into the shadow of a doorway. Liam watched an oncoming man in a business suit who'd started walking toward her veer off at the last second. He had no doubt that he and O'Brien had *cop* written all over them.

"Lunch break for our civil servants," O'Brien said dryly. "Sitting at a desk all day is a tough job and requires some relief."

Liam had no comeback. His mind was still on Danny. "What part did Ella have in the trial?"

O'Brien took a while before answering. "She brought the charges. She was only seventeen, and most kids that age would have backed down, given the pressure from her family. If you want to know more than that, you'll have to ask her, or you can look it up in the news archives. It was a big story for a while."

They reached the cross street before Rideau. O'Brien

stopped walking. "Ella and I have stayed in touch off and on over the years. I try to make sure she and Danny are doing okay. I never liked how the case shook down, even though there was a conviction. They lost their family over it. I tell you, though, Ella has more guts than anyone I know, even if she comes across as the prickliest pear in the bowl."

Liam turned to face him. "I'm sure she values your friendship."

"I believe she does. Listen, I'm thinking about retiring one of these days and was hoping you'd be able to keep an eye on Ella and Danny when I'm gone."

"What would you want me to do, exactly?"

"Make sure they're not in any trouble. Maybe confirm some facts about cases when Ella needs help with her true crime podcasts. She used to be the crime reporter for *The Capitol* until cutbacks three months ago. She's a good writer. Fair and objective. Does her research."

Liam hesitated. What exactly was O'Brien asking of him? Feed Ella information about ongoing cases? He opened his mouth to give a noncommittal answer, but O'Brien had started walking again. "I'm only asking you to think about it," he said over his shoulder. Liam followed a few paces behind. He thought that O'Brien must have seen something in his expression that made him shut down the conversation … and that was just fine by him.

CHAPTER 12

Sherry was seated at the bar, talking to the bartender, when Ella arrived. A nearly full glass of red wine sat in front of her, so Ella knew that she hadn't kept her waiting long. Sherry broke off her conversation when she saw her and jumped up for a hug.

"It's so great to see you," she said before they separated.

Ella tried to place her perfume's scent. Fresh rain and lemon balm. A hint of brown sugar. "It's been a while."

She ordered a beer, and they took their drinks to a table next to the window that looked out at the people walking past on Bank Street. Ella thought about how much she enjoyed living in this quartier of Ottawa. She liked the eclectic vibe — bohemian, student, and wealthy all rolled into one. A balance of old and new. The Glebe butted onto the Rideau Canal, and the stately three-storey brick houses were interspersed with new condos. Thankfully, apartment buildings were low-rise and blended in with the houses. Mature oaks and elms shaded the streets. Shops and restaurants lined this stretch of Bank, and people from the surrounding neighbourhood walked here to buy groceries and to drink expensive cappuccinos in one of the numerous coffee shops.

"So, how've you been keeping?"

Ella pulled her eyes away from the street view. "Well, I started a podcast…"

"Which is really terrific. You have me hooked one hundred percent."

"Thank you. It's an interesting venture for sure. I live a few minutes' walk from here, so my apartment's in a decent location. Being let go from the paper might have been a blessing." She held back on the subject of Danny. An hour catching up with Sherry and putting him out of her mind seemed like a good idea. Plus she hated being the recipient of anybody's sympathy. "And how about you? Are you still enjoying working at the paper?"

Sherry made a pouty face. "It's different with so many of the old guard gone. I know I should be grateful to still have a job but … well, can I say that I envy you?"

"You can say it, but you have no reason to." She studied Sherry's face. She was late-twenties, pretty in a bubbly cheerleader kind of way. When they first met at Sherry's job interview for the paper, she'd had mousy brown hair. It was now dyed a flaxen blond in keeping with the editor's preference for fair-haired reporters. She was petite but curvy and manipulated men with her looks, but this assessment did her a disservice because she was also smart. A survivor in an industry that ate up young women and spat out their aging bodies like chewed wads of gum. "Are you working on anything interesting?" she asked.

"I'm on the City Hall beat, so a lot of drudgery with the odd titillating bit. I'm not writing op-eds, just covering the facts. The opinion pieces are left to a more seasoned reporter, and by this I mean Derek Milestone." Sherry grimaced before taking a sip of wine.

Ella thought, *so the rumour mill got it wrong when they said you landed my crime beat.* She asked, "Is that old windbag still there? I wonder how he managed to evade the chopping block." She held up a hand. "No, don't tell me. He kept a file of blackmail-worthy information on everybody at the paper and in the political arena. Nobody would dare cross him."

"He's always dropping hints at meetings about all the secrets he's gathered on people of influence over the years. I thought it was so much bullshit."

"How else do you explain that he's such an odious man and still has one of the plum jobs?"

"You may have a point. He's a good writer, though." Sherry rested her elbows on the table and leaned forward. "François Canard is in a tough spot. He's walking a high wire between hard news and creditors."

"I don't envy him. He wasn't happy to have to let so many of us go." She'd like Canard as a boss. He'd always treated her like one of the guys, a rarity in her experience, up until he took over the paper.

"I have a proposition for you."

"I'm listening."

"I checked some sources after I listened to your last podcast. Word is that the Josie Wheatly suicide is going to be changed to murder. You must have kept an inside source, if I heard your podcast correctly."

Ella tilted her head from side to side as if playing coy and smiled.

"I want off the municipal beat but need a scoop so Canard starts seeing me as more than a reporter of transit cock-ups and city tax hikes. I'd like to cover crime like you did."

"And you think I can help you get the gig?"

"I believe we can help each other."

Their gazes locked in a moment of mutual assessment. Ella had spent her career working alone, building contacts and not sharing. She'd deliberately avoided climbing up the corporate ladder and had to admit that this inability to suck up might have led to her getting the shaft. However, the idea of teaming up with someone who had inside access that she didn't anymore was a carrot. The question was how far could she trust Sherry? "I could keep you in mind," she said finally and broke eye contact, "or you could let me know when you have something and we can see from there."

Sherry laughed. "You're as tough to pin down as they say."

"Oh yeah? What else do they say?"

"That you're crusty as hell and hard to get to know. Milestone called you a ball-breaker. I actually think these are compliments, especially coming from that dick."

"Well … maybe. Listen, I won't promise anything, but I'll keep you in mind if I have something worth sharing."

"And I'll start asking around about the Wheatly case." Sherry raised her wine glass in Ella's direction and grinned. "Here's looking at you, kid. This could be the start of a beautiful friendship."

Or not, Ella thought as she drank.

CHAPTER 13

Ella didn't think she'd be able to sleep. Her brain was working overtime, but her exhausted body won the battle sometime between 2 and 3:00 a.m. It was a pleasant surprise to roll over and see morning sun streaming through the open window. The clock read ten to eight, so later than her normal wake-up time. Must be her lucky day.

The air in the room was chilly, and she had no interest in getting out from under the covers. She lay a while longer in her snug bed, watching the play of light and shadows on the far wall, trying to centre herself for the day ahead. The hospital hadn't called with bad news in the middle of the night, and she took this as a good sign. Danny had made it through to the morning.

Regardless of what was happening in her personal life, she needed to get enough material to come up with the second episode of the podcast. Hopefully, Paul O'Brien had an update about the investigation. He should be able to confirm if Josie's suicide had been upgraded to murder. It'd be good to get the green light to dig deeper into the case. A gym workout later in the day would be her fallback if she got nowhere with her research. Keeping busy was the only way she knew how to cope. The only way she could control her fear about Danny.

Music thumped up through the floor below. She recognized Tina Turner's "Private Dancer," another Tony go-to comfort choice. Sander must have left for work early because Tony would never play his music this loud otherwise. She sighed and pushed back the covers. It was time to get the day under way anyhow.

The water in the shower was lukewarm, the tank nearly drained by Tony or Sander, likely both. The pair was getting on her nerves this morning, more so than other days. A cup of instant coffee helped to warm her, and she took a second cup to her desk. While the computer booted up, she checked messages. Felix had sent one of his rare missives, and she opened it first. *See attached. Password: xTy451* was all it said. She clicked on the file and pasted in the password. It took her a second of astonished reading to realize what this was. A full police report on Josie Wheatly's death, including a forensics report. "Who the hell are you, Felix?" she said under her breath. "And how did you manage to get your hands on this classified information?"

She skimmed the report before settling in for a more careful reading. When she finished, she sat back in her chair to ponder what the new information revealed. Josie died by hanging, but she'd consumed an almost lethal dose of sleeping pills and alcohol about twenty minutes beforehand. Coroner Brigette Green concluded that based on the amount ingested, the accelerating effect of the undiluted alcohol, and Josie's recent injuries, it was highly unlikely that she could have strung the rope, gotten herself on the chair, and hanged herself. Moreover, evidence indicated that Josie had ingested the pills and liquor in the kitchen where the bottles were found and died in the bedroom, opposite ends of the apartment, as Ella well knew.

The light from the window bathed Ella in warmth as she raised her head and stared outside. The obvious conclusion was that whoever assaulted Josie had come back to the hospital to take her home so that she could be killed without interruption or witness — so they could make it look like a suicide. Ella believed that whoever this person was, they had meant to kill her on the night of the rape but miscalculated. This indicated a novice or someone just getting their violent career underway. Perhaps he'd raped before, and his behaviour had now escalated into murder. Maybe he believed that Josie could identify him, and he couldn't let her live.

Felix had included a second file that consisted of two photos: a close-up head shot and a full body shot of Josie posing with her fiancé. Josie had wheat-blonde hair like hers, but Josie's was shoulder-length and wavy, whereas Ella had cut hers into a pixie style after the breakup with Greg. It had been a need to change things up. Ella held the head shot closer. Josie's eyes were darker than Ella's green, and her jaw was squarer, but they both had the same high cheekbones. They were close to the same build and height, however, and this gave Ella pause. Could somebody have mistaken them? At a distance, they'd be difficult to tell apart if someone didn't know she'd cut her hair. The similarity was unsettling but not conclusive. She reminded herself that sometimes a coincidence was simply a coincidence.

She sent Felix a return email. *Safe to make conclusions public?*

The answer arrived seconds later. *Family has report. Use anonymous source.*

Of course.

His final message came a few seconds after that. *Sorry about your brother.*

Ella sat with her hand resting on the mouse and stared at the screen. How did this person know about Danny? Her unease with Felix was growing, but she had no idea what she should do about it.

After a quick breakfast of an apple and slice of cheese, she crept downstairs past Tony's door, not having the energy to deal with his endless questions and *joie de vivre.* She retrieved her bike from under the stairs and made it outside without any sign of him. It was another cool day but not raining, even though the cloud cover made the morning feel like evening. She put on her helmet and took the direct route down Third Avenue to the canal. Her legs ached from the two workouts, and it was a battle pedalling against the wind and biking up the hill into the Experimental Farm. An ambulance raced past as she reached the hospital property twenty-five minutes later, the siren shattering the silence and putting her on edge. She locked up her bike near the main entrance and went inside, taking the elevator to ICU. She entered Danny's room and put a hand over her mouth. Someone else was lying in Danny's bed, and for one awful moment she couldn't catch her breath.

A nurse hurried into the room behind her, and Ella spun around to face her. The nurse spoke before she had a chance to ask. "Your brother stabilized and was moved early this morning to a ward on the floor below. We needed the space." She didn't look Ella in the eye when she spoke. Ella didn't need it spelled out. Danny had no money, no extra insurance. He was moved to make way for someone with the means to pay for a private room. Ella didn't blame her. It was the system that treated people according to their means. At least Danny hadn't been turned away.

"Did he wake up?"

"No, but his vitals were strong."

"Do you know the room number?"

"I can check."

She led Ella to the desk and completed a computer search. "Three twelve." A red light was flashing, and she glanced up and smiled. "One of the impatient patients paging for service."

"Then don't let me keep you. Thanks ... for everything."

The nurse rounded the desk and stopped next to Ella. "Danny's a fighter. You hang in there too."

Ella nodded and watched the nurse stride down the hall and enter a room. Then she took the stairs to the floor below and started down the hallway, counting off room numbers. Danny's room was midway down the corridor. She scanned the space. Three beds and Danny's next to the door. He was hooked up to machines. A heart monitor, oxygen mask, a drip that injected a steady supply of medicine into his body. He was flat on his back, his long hair spread out around him on the pillow, eyes closed. A nurse was standing next to the head of his bed, fiddling with the drip. Ella's eyes dropped to a man sitting on the other side of the bed.

"I figured you'd show up sooner rather than later." Detective Liam Hunter stood and set a newspaper on his seat. "If you have time, we can talk over coffee once you've had a few minutes with Danny."

"Yeah, I have time." She looked at Danny and back at him. "We can go have coffee now so I don't hold you up. Danny isn't going anywhere." She stepped closer to the bed and rubbed her fingertips along the back of Danny's hand. Then she checked that he was still breathing. She looked at Hunter. "Let's go."

They took the elevator to the cafeteria on the main floor. Ella grabbed a table while Hunter lined up for their coffee. She studied his back while he fished in his pocket for money. He was an unassuming man. He held himself loosely, like he was at ease in his body. She imagined he frequented the gym regularly and played a team sport of some sort. He stepped aside and smiled at an older man waiting behind him. They exchanged words and both laughed.

Hunter took quick glances at her as he approached the table, holding a tray with both hands. He set a mug in front of her and dropped a small handful of creamers and packets of sugar between them as he sat down. "Forgot to ask how you like your coffee."

"I guess you're hoping I don't say black." She picked up a couple of creamers and slid some packs of sugar into her pocket for coffee at home. "Have you made any progress on who knifed my brother?"

He was watching her, his eyes dropping to her hands as she ripped open a creamer and poured the milk into her cup. "Danny's well-liked in the homeless community," he said. "Nobody has any idea why somebody would try to kill him."

"I knew that already. Have you found out anything else?"

His eyes rose to her face. "Could what happened when you both lived in Edmonton have anything to do with why your brother chose to live on the street? Could it have anything to do with why he was stabbed?"

She inwardly cursed Paul O'Brien. "What've you been told?"

"Nothing helpful. O'Brien said you'd both had a rough time, but that's it. He also said you'd tell me whatever was necessary to advance the case, and it wasn't up to him."

She took back her curse. *Forgive me, Paul.* She slumped back in the seat and slurped from her mug, looked around the room, and bought some time. “Whatever happened ten years ago has nothing to do with this,” she said at last. “Danny’s an addict. He must have crossed somebody in his world.”

“Yeah, maybe, but never hurts to look at the whole picture and rule stuff out.” Hunter tore open a creamer and a couple of sugars and poured the lot into his coffee. He stirred the cup by sloshing the contents back and forth. He fixed his gaze off into space, and she kept quiet while he thought. “We suspect it was the man asking about Danny the day before. The fact he kept his face hidden is suspicious. He was young, white, and medium height, but that’s all we know.”

“Well, that’s more than I managed to get out of Cal.”

“I caught him on a good day.”

“While I agree this guy is the main suspect, I still think you need to keep an open mind. There’s no proof he did it.”

“Agreed.”

“So where do you go next with this investigation?”

Hunter took a deep breath and let it out slowly. “I’m not going to bullshit you, Ella. We both know that the chances of solving his assault are slim.”

“You’re giving up.”

“No, I’m not giving up, but unless someone comes forward, I haven’t got much to go on, to be perfectly blunt. I’m researching past knifings in the downtown and looking at ex-cons living in the area. I’d like to tell you we’ll get the guy, but that would be hopeful at best.”

“Don’t sugar-coat things on my account.”

“You don’t strike me as someone who needs a sweet fix.”

She took one last slurp of coffee and pushed her chair back from the table. "I'm going back upstairs to spend time with Danny, since we seem to be finished here. Thanks for the coffee." She stood and took two steps then stopped and spun back around. "Say, is Hunter your real last name, or did you change it for, you know … symbolism? Detective hunting his prey. Tracking down the bad guys."

His lips twitched, but he held back the smile. "I come from a long line of Irish Hunters. I'm the first bona fide detective, though."

"Well, don't let me keep you from your dogged search for the truth."

He touched two fingers to his temple in a mock salute. "I'll contact you when I've got something to report."

She scowled. "You do that."

Her anger was directed at him, but her ire included the entire justice system and the stigmatization of marginalized people. She'd had limited hopes for Hunter finding Danny's assailant, but those were already dashed.

She spent half an hour sitting by Danny's bedside, speaking words of encouragement into his ear and watching his chest rise and fall. He reminded her of a frail bird, hurt and trapped. The need to get moving and to make somebody pay for him being in this bed ate away at her. When the nurse returned to check his vitals, Ella slipped out and was on her bike a few minutes later, pedalling like a motocross racer back the way she'd come. Liam Hunter's question may have been a shot in the dark, but it had gotten her worried. She needed to contact some people — to make sure her past and Danny's hadn't come back to destroy them.

Her first call was to her parole contact, Kiki Hicks. She caught Kiki parking her car in the lot outside her office in downtown Edmonton. They hadn't spoken in five years, and she took a few seconds to place Ella's voice. When she did, it was as if time had peeled back.

"Ella, of course. How the hell are you?"

"Sorry I'm calling out of the blue, Kiki, but I need to check up on him."

"No worries. He's still living at the same address. No change. Why, has something happened?"

"Danny was assaulted a couple of days ago and is in the hospital. I wanted to be certain Jamieson wasn't involved."

"I'll check my sources but don't believe he could be. Last time I saw him, he seemed … diminished. I suspected he was ill, but he didn't mention anything in particular, and I didn't probe."

"I'd appreciate if you could have a closer look at his movements. Thanks, Kiki."

"How's Danny?"

"Not good, but he's hanging in."

"Well, give him my best, and you take care too. I'll be saying prayers for you both."

Ella never knew how to respond to the prayer offer, so she didn't. "You have this number?" she asked instead.

"I'm writing it down now. Talk soon."

After the call ended, Ella looked up the number for Collins Bay Penitentiary. It took a few tries, but the third woman she spoke with finally rerouted her to someone willing to answer her questions. Ella had decided on a shortened version of the facts.

"I was a reporter on the crime beat and covered a couple of your more violent inmates. They weren't too pleased with my articles. One of my family members was assaulted last week, and I'm checking to make certain it wasn't related to my past work. I need to confirm that neither prisoner got early parole."

"What you're asking is public information, Ms. Tate, so I can share the facts. Names?"

"Gino Robertson. Doing twenty-five years to life for killing his wife. The next is Eddy Calhoon. Twenty-five years for multiple rapes."

A pause. She heard keys clicking on the other end. "Ms. Tate? Both are still under lock and key."

"Well, that's good to know. Thanks for checking." She was about to hang up.

"We keep a good eye on their mail and listen in on their phone calls. The files don't show anything worrisome."

"I appreciate you telling me."

"I'd want to know too if I were you."

She sat for a while after they disconnected and thought about where to search next. The frustrating fact was that Liam Hunter was probably right. Whoever knifed Danny had been careful. He or she had left no clues and kept their face hidden. Unless they did something stupid or knifed more victims, she might never uncover their identity.

She opened her computer and began a search for stories within the last two years in Ottawa where knifings were involved. The list was surprisingly short. Turned out guns were the new weapons of choice in the downtown core. She checked out all the stories and discounted most, since the assailant was known or the attack was gang-related. This left a couple of names that she crossed off the list after further research. The number of random, unprovoked stabbings was rare and unusual in a city of a million people. She couldn't find any attacks similar to Danny's. Either he was extremely unlucky — wrong place, wrong time — or somebody had targeted him. If the latter, one glaring question remained: why?

The inaction frustrated her. She started pacing around her small living room as she tried to come up with a plan. Her cell phone rang on her desk as she was walking past. She glanced at the number before picking up.

"Hey, Sherry. Got something?"

"I think so. Josie Wheatley's army boyfriend Rory Leavitt was in the country the day she was killed."

"You're kidding. How come the police don't know that?"

"He took early leave and was intending to surprise her."

"How'd you find out?"

"I have a source." Sherry paused. "Do you want to take a drive? I'm leaving in twenty minutes but can pick you up if you give me your address. He's in Almonte staying with his mother."

"I'll be downstairs waiting." She texted Sherry her address and grabbed her jacket and keys on the way outside.

She pondered the significance of Rory's early return as she stood on the sidewalk watching for Sherry's car. Josie's mother Cheryl had believed that Rory was still overseas when she'd spoken with her. He must have stayed silent about the timing of his return to Canada, even after Josie's body was found. Not exactly the actions of a devoted fiancé with nothing to hide. Ella thought about calling O'Brien to tell him the news but quickly shelved the idea. It was prudent to see what she and Sherry uncovered before the police took over. No point in giving away a perfectly good lead before it had a chance to bear fruit.

CHAPTER 14

Sherry drove a battered Ford Focus. Ella guessed the original colour to have been green, but rust had taken over, making this assumption iffy. The front bumper hung at an angle, and she carefully skirted around it to the front passenger side. Sherry had already cleared a space on the seat, although coffee cups and candy wrappers took up most of the floor area. The smell of stale coffee and days spent chasing stories reminded Ella of her years on the paper.

"Welcome aboard." Sherry grinned at her from behind oversized sunglasses. She stepped on the gas before Ella'd gotten the door shut.

"What's the rush?" Ella grabbed on to the dashboard to stop herself from sliding into it.

"I like to drive fast."

"No kidding." Ella tugged at the seatbelt and took a few attempts to straighten the strap before she could buckle up. "Are you living in this heap or what?"

"Almost. But this heap beats taking the bus."

"Not by a hell of a lot."

They rehashed the case on the thirty-minute drive to

Almonte and reached the outskirts of the town shortly after two o'clock. Sherry asked, "How do you want to play this? I can imagine Rory isn't going to be too forthcoming if he had anything to do with her death."

"I'd say be sympathetic and slide in your questions when it feels right. You don't want him to know you have suspicions about his involvement."

"Yeah, keep him off balance. Chime in whenever. We can be a tag-team."

"Sure, thanks." Ella was willing to let Sherry run the interview, since this lead came from her research. Staying silent would give her room to watch Leavitt's reactions more closely.

Sherry parked across the street from the two-storey house nearly hidden by oaks. She craned her neck to see up the pathway to the front door. "Let's hope he's home."

"Wait, you didn't set up an appointment?"

"He wouldn't return my calls."

"Might have been a signal that he doesn't want to be interviewed."

"Then we'll use your charm to get in the door." Sherry grinned and pointed in the direction of Ella's heart. "You have some charm twinkling in there somewhere, don't you?"

"What do you think?"

"I think you'd do anything for a story. Your fearless exploits are legend around the water cooler."

"Maybe once."

"Where does that reckless courage come from, Tate? I sure wish I had some of what you've got."

Ella scrunched up her face. "It comes from hating to let bad guys get away with their crimes."

"Well, you're my hero."

"You should get out more."

They exited the car. Sherry was wearing faded jeans and a red silk blouse under a jean jacket. The blouse was unbuttoned to show off her cleavage. She saw Ella staring. "What, too much?"

"He's just lost his fiancée. I doubt he's looking for a date." She wanted to say more, like how Sherry didn't need to use her body to get a story, but she shut up. Not her business.

Sherry didn't say anything but casually did up a couple of buttons as they walked to the front door. Ella rang the bell and stepped down next to her. "Over to you," she said.

"I think you should take it."

Ella looked at Sherry's profile as they waited. Her chin was up and her shoulders were set rigid as a board. She wanted to tell Sherry to get over herself but figured this wouldn't help matters any. She turned to face the lady standing in front of them. Shoulder-length grey hair on the unruly side. Eyes the colour of melted milk chocolate. Tentative smile. First impression was that this was a kind woman, not overly confident meeting strangers. "Yes, can I help you?"

Ella waited a beat to see if Sherry would jump in. She didn't. "Mrs. Leavitt? I'm Ella Tate and this is Sherry Carpenter. We were hoping to speak with your son, Rory."

Her smile widened. "Why, I'm so glad you're here. Please, call me Maureen. Rory needs some friends to talk to because he's keeping things bottled up just like his father used to, God rest his soul. Rory's out back. Follow me."

"No, we're from…" She started to correct her, but Maureen was walking into the house, and Sherry had stepped in after her, effectively blocking Ella's path.

Mrs. Leavitt led them down the hallway and through the kitchen onto a back deck. "I'll pour some coffee. You girls get comfortable," she said, leaving them to watch

Rory below them on the lawn, practising his kick-boxing moves.

He was dressed in black biking shorts and a tight, long-sleeved t-shirt. His feet were bare, his hair shorn into a buzz cut. *He's one beast of a man,* thought Ella. *Muscles up the ying-yang, as Finn would say*. "I'm not sure this is a good idea, Sherry. We should have identified ourselves as reporters to his mother."

Sherry was already moving toward the steps and ignored her. Rory stopped mid kick and looked up at them. Ella got a better sightline on his face. He had a classic square jaw and the same oversized lips as Mick Jagger. The identical brown eyes as his mother, but his were shrewder and not nearly as kind. He strode over to Sherry before she could set foot on the grass.

"I'm so sorry to disturb you," Sherry said, her voice hushed and sombre. "We wanted to offer condolences for your loss."

"And you are?"

"I'm Sherry and this is Ella. She lived in the apartment building that Josie moved into a few months ago. Ella has a podcast that talks about difficult crime cases. We were both devastated about Josie's assault and now her tragic death."

Ella had to hand it to her. Sherry had skipped around the fact they were both reporters, but she'd given him enough about her podcast to plead innocence if he later challenged their integrity. Rory's antagonistic stance relaxed. The sliding glass door creaked open behind Ella.

"Here we are," Mrs. Leavitt said, setting a tray on the patio table. "Why don't you sit and chat? I'm off to the grocery store." She gave them an encouraging smile before disappearing inside. Ella tamped down her unease at being left alone with Rory, who may or may not have killed his girlfriend.

Rory shook his head but climbed the stairs behind Sherry and took a seat at the table. He slid a cup of coffee toward Ella and another in Sherry's direction so they also lowered themselves on to the chairs. He stared at Ella. "You knew Josie?"

"We know a lot about her. I was on my way to see her when I found out she'd died."

"Yeah, it was a shock. I'm still trying to work through what happened." His mouth was hidden behind the coffee mug. He watched her while he drank.

The guy's hiding something, she thought. "When did you find out?"

"When I first got to Almonte."

"Clare Daniels told me that you were due in Canada at the end of the month."

"Clare … oh yeah, the woman across the hall. Well, that was the plan, but I decided to take early leave. I was in Montreal for a few days and then was going to surprise Josie on the weekend. I stopped off in Almonte on Thursday afternoon, and that's when I found out she'd died. My mother was distraught because she hadn't been able to reach me."

"So you didn't know for a few days about her death or even that she'd been raped? You didn't have a cell phone?"

"Nobody shared the rape news with me after it happened. Josie didn't want me to know, apparently. It was one of the few legible things she was able to communicate. I had to buy a new phone when I got back in the country and hadn't gotten around to it. I tuned out for a few days to destress and adjust to being away from the war zone."

"She was a brave woman."

His expression tightened, as if somebody had wound a winch connected to all the muscles in his face. His voice dropped and hardened. "Whoever did this to her needs to pay."

She took a large gulp of coffee and set the mug down, hoping Sherry picked up on the danger. They needed to get out of here before this army-trained killing machine figured out why they were really there. Sherry seemed oblivious, and Ella starting to wonder about her people skills.

"I understood that you met in Ottawa. I thought you lived there," Sherry said. She started to twirl a strand of hair around and around in her fingers but stopped when she saw Ella staring at her. Rory's eyes ping-ponged over to Sherry.

"I did. I do, but my mother moved to Almonte, oddly enough before I met Josie. Our mothers live on the same street, and that's how we linked up. Her mother had passed along a package for me to deliver to Josie in Ottawa, and we started dating soon afterward. Best day of my life when I met her." He paused and swiped at an eye. "I'm staying here until after the funeral."

"Which is when, exactly?" Ella asked.

"It'll be at the Brock Funeral Home two or three days from now. There'll be a notice in the paper." He ran a hand over his jaw. "Say, how did you know Josie again?"

"I lived in the same apartment building. Sherry, I think we should be going." Ella stood. "Again, we're very sorry for your loss, Rory. Everyone who knew Josie speaks highly of her. She'll be very sorely missed."

His eyes darkened, and anger and grief rippled across his face. He slumped back in the chair, lowered his head to his chest, and put a hand over his eyes.

"We can see ourselves out," she added.

Sherry followed her outside, but she wasn't happy. "I

was only getting started. We didn't even get into his overseas work or their relationship."

"You didn't feel the threat in there?"

"No. What I felt was a scoop in the making, and now all I'm feeling is disappointment."

Ella couldn't let this go. "Not identifying yourself as being from the media when we first gained entry put us both in a precarious situation, something I'm certain you know full well. The longer we talked to Rory, the more uncomfortable I was getting. He doesn't strike me as a man who likes being fooled. I don't mind taking risks, but only ones that are calculated. I'm also not a fan of using the sex card to get information. I think that working alone is the better way to go from here on out."

"Don't hold back."

"I'm doing you a favour."

Sherry maintained a sullen silence all the way back to Ottawa, and Ella was happy to see her taillights speed away when she climbed the steps to her front door. "Buck up, buttercup," she mumbled, unlocking the door. "Sulking's not a becoming look."

She checked that the lock clicked shut and started up the stairs. Seemed like their beautiful friendship had ended before it even got started.

CHAPTER 15

The noise level in the office dropped off as admin assistants and officers started to shut it down for the day. O'Brien had been put on hold. He leaned way back in his desk chair and rested his foot on a bottom drawer that he'd pulled out for this express purpose. As he waited for someone to come on the line, he watched Hunter leave the Sarge's office. He was carrying a file and turned around at the door to say something to her.

He'd often wondered what Staff Sergeant Greta Warner did on her days off. She was notoriously private, but there were the rumours. He wasn't sure how many of them he believed. The one about her being separated from her husband of five years seemed valid. He knew a lot of officers whose marriages didn't last, his own included. In any case, she'd been taken to task a few times in the past for poor judgment and was known for her abrasive personality. He was among those surprised when she got promoted to staff sergeant. He put a hand over the phone's mouthpiece as Hunter approached.

"Anything important?" he asked.

"Not really. Sarge okay'd my overtime and assigned a

couple of officers to do one last blitz of the Market to see if anyone saw something the day Danny Tate was stabbed. She's not convinced it will do any good but relented after I kept pleading my case."

"Good luck."

"Yeah, I know. I'm gonna need it."

A woman's voice started talking in O'Brien's ear, and he held up a finger for Hunter to wait for a minute. He listened and said thanks before hanging up. He looked at Hunter. "That was a contact in Edmonton running a check for me on Gordon Jamieson."

Hunter's expression was quizzical at first. He nodded as he placed the name. "The guy who did time for abusing Danny when he was a kid."

"That's right, his uncle through marriage. Danny was only fourteen when Gordon was caught. The abuse had been going on for a year. That was ten years ago, but the man could have bided his time to get even. As it turns out, nature is getting even in her own way. Jamieson is bedridden and not expected to live much longer. The big C."

"So he's a dead end." Pause. "Seems like your sense of humour is rubbing off, and I'm not sure if that's a good thing."

O'Brien shook his head but didn't allow the snort to escape. "I sent Ella a text to meet up tomorrow. I want her to know."

"You and Ella seem to have a unique relationship."

"We go back a long way, and I think a lot of her. She's smart as a whip. Doesn't care jack for the trappings of life, and she's loyal to a fault. But I've told you this already."

"A prickly pear, I believe you said."

He grinned. "Her most endearing quality. You have to get to know her, Hunter, which, as we discussed, I'm hoping you will. Start by reading some of her old news articles. She's incisive and cuts to the heart of issues, sticking to the facts. She's not into giving her own opinion, like a lot of journalists today, although she can be blistering when it comes to corruption or cruelty. She's made a few enemies in the prison population over the years."

"I already know that I wouldn't want to be on the receiving end of her scorn."

O'Brien studied him. "She's a voice that we can use. Never forget that."

"I understand, but I'm still not certain about … well, what we discussed the other day."

"And that's wise, but keep an open mind. We steer the narrative, and remember, she's on the same side."

Hunter nodded but didn't say anything. Not for the first time, O'Brien wondered if he'd made the right call asking Hunter to become Ella's person on the force when he retired. Hunter was a good detective, but he wasn't easily readable. An unobtrusive man. He sat quietly in the room but gave valid insights when he decided to speak up. O'Brien stood and put on his jacket. "Well, I'll see you tomorrow. I'm quitting on time tonight for a change."

"Hot date?"

"Could say."

Hunter grinned and saluted before leaving him alone with his thoughts. O'Brien sighed and looked down at the message scribbled on a pad next to his phone. *Call Dr. Sharma.* The blood test and X-ray results were back. He knew a doctor's office only called if there was bad news. The tiredness and pain in his gut he'd been feeling over the past year must mean something, but the prognosis could wait until tomorrow. Another day of ignorant bliss wouldn't matter in the big scheme of things. He'd use the bit of time to get his head around the idea that he was likely going to have to retire sooner than he'd planned.

The ByWard Market was hopping, and he was late, so instead of making a tour of the side streets to find an empty spot, he snapped off a ticket and drove into the parking garage. The garage was nearly full, but he found an empty place on the fourth level near the stairwell to the street. He walked down the steps and onto George Street, pausing at the entrance to scan the stream of passersby.

It was a short walk to the Laff on York Street, oldest pub in Ottawa, fully named the Château Lafayette House, where his two retired police buddies were waiting for him, a pitcher of cold beer and three glasses on the table. They'd snared a spot with an unobstructed view of the World Series game on the big screen, and poutine and corndogs were on the way. O'Brien took the vacant seat and gratefully drank from his glass before they began dissecting the pros and cons of the two baseball teams. They'd spend the next three hours watching the game and catching up on their lives, although he wouldn't mention his medical problems or anything that came close to personal. These were his oldest friends, but he wasn't the kind of man to burden anyone with his problems.

He shut off his internal voice and let himself relax. Normally he'd be watchful, ever the cop checking out the other patrons, sizing up threats. But tonight he was tired and decided to let go of the stress. The game was a close one, and he had money on the Red Sox. The bar crowd cheered and groaned with every play. O'Brien's eyes passed easily over the man in the baseball cap and hoodie sitting in the corner, drinking pints. He didn't notice hoodie guy pay up his tab and slip out the door in the dying minutes of the game.

CHAPTER 16

This time, Ella didn't make it past the second floor when she returned home. Tony opened his door and poked his head out when she reached the landing and invited her in. She declined, and he trailed behind her up the stairs to her apartment.

"Sander not home yet?" She took a couple of tries with her key before unlocking the door.

"He's working late. Where've you been all day?"

"Hospital this morning. Almonte this afternoon."

"Sounds like the makings of a story. Who's in the hospital?"

"My brother Danny." She paused. "He was stabbed on the bike path next to the canal."

Tony clutched his t-shirt in the approximate location of his heart. "My God. How is he?"

"Not great. I'm about to call for an update."

"Well, get to it, girl." He was inside her apartment before she could close the door and flopped down on the couch, watching her. "I'll wait here to be sure Danny's okay."

"Make yourself comfortable."

"Thanks, I am."

She phoned the hospital and paced around the small space while she waited to be transferred to Danny's floor. A nurse finally came online and told her Danny was still unconscious but hadn't worsened. They'd stopped giving him sedatives, so he should wake up soon. She'd call if Danny's condition changed. Ella lowered her phone. Danny continued to linger in limbo, and she was helpless to do anything.

"Well?" Tony sat on the edge of the couch, staring at her. "How's Danny?"

"No change." She sat down in her desk chair. "Do you need something, Tony?" After her outing with Sherry, she'd used up her store of patience.

"Actually, I want to do something for you. Sander's going to a work conference in Phoenix tomorrow, and I have some free time. I could help with the research for your podcast. I'd be Watson to your Holmes. Havers to your Lynley. Sonny to your Cher."

His eyes could have taught puppies to beg for scraps. She almost laughed at the ludicrousness of his idea. She stalled, hoping he'd retract his offer. "I thought Sander was home for the weekend."

"The colleague who was supposed to go to Phoenix fell ill yesterday. Everything was paid for, so Sander was chosen as the replacement. That's why he's working late. He's got to give a workshop and is scrambling to get materials together. Anyhooo, I'm all yours if you want me."

She asked jokingly, "Do you happen to know anybody in the Armed Forces who can get their hands on a soldier's itinerary?"

"As it so happens, I do. One of my regulars is an admin assistant at headquarters."

She blinked. This could be a stroke of good fortune,

but she was weary after her ugly afternoon with Sherry and not convinced that taking on a helper was a good idea. "I don't have any money to pay."

"Being in on the chase is payment enough. Should I give my client a call? I can dangle a discount on his next haircut as an enticement to look up the information."

"All right. Consider this your trial run." She shook her head. "Sonny Bono? Really?"

Tony clapped his hands. "Sonny may not have been a sleuth, but he and Cher were a dynamite team. You won't regret this. Now, all I need are the details for the quest and I'll be off."

"I do recall their marriage didn't end well." She wrote down Rory's name but had little else to add. "He's army and lives in Ottawa when off duty. His mother lives in Almonte at this address. That's all I know. He arrived back in Canada about a week ago and says he spent the first few days in Montreal before going to Almonte on Thursday. His fiancée was Josie Wheatley, the woman who was raped and subsequently died."

"I know all about *that* horror. I've listened to your podcast three times. Made notes. Would you like me to text you what I find on this covert assignment?"

"Perfect."

Tony hopped up and pumped his fist over his head all the way to the door while singing "We Are the Champions." He turned with his hand on the knob. "Alex has some tradesmen working downstairs starting tomorrow. He asked me to let you know." Winked. Swayed his hips. "Could be some bumping and grinding going on."

She groaned. "Too easy, Tony. Let me know when you find out something."

"You got it. Your bloodhound partner's on the scent."

He slammed the door, and the sound of his footsteps

retreated down the stairwell. She had little reason to hope he'd find anything, but the assignment had gotten him out of her apartment and made him incredibly happy. *Nothing wrong with both outcomes,* she thought. She turned on her computer as her phone pinged a message. Paul O'Brien wanted to meet over breakfast. He had something to tell her. She sent a confirmation that she'd be at their greasy spoon by seven thirty, and he replied seconds later with a thumbs up.

She scrolled back through the messages and froze like a hare in the headlights. A text from Greg. Her finger pressed *open* before she had a chance to reconsider and hit delete. *I heard about Danny. Let me know if I can help in any way.* How did he hear about her brother? Only a few people knew. She thought for a second before typing. *No need but Thx.*

Best to end contact quickly before regret made her do something foolish. He was back with his old girlfriend who wanted the same things he did. She wouldn't be drawn into a conversation that would likely end with him asking to come over.

She tossed the phone onto a pile of papers and forced herself up from the desk. In the galley kitchen, she poured a glass of wine from the open bottle in the fridge before starting on a meal. Supper tonight was a grilled cheese sandwich with a side of dill pickles, the perfect bitter accompaniment to the cheap plonk that Tony would surely have poured down the toilet if he were here.

She caught up on the day's news on her computer before calling the hospital one more time. Danny still hadn't woken up, but his heartbeat was holding steady. No infection from the wound, so this was one hurdle crossed. Her worry settled for now, but it was still a low-grade buzz, constantly with her, threatening to flare into full-blown panic if Danny's condition worsened.

She shut things down and crawled into bed around nine o'clock, worn out from the day. Sleep came quickly. She awakened just as suddenly out of a deep sleep, her heart thudding, fear paralyzing her in place. She stared into the darkness of her room, lying on her side, scrambling to gather her thoughts, listening for sounds. What woke her, and why was her heart beating like a metronome? She'd been dreaming of Danny but couldn't grasp on to his fading image now that her eyes were open. A premonition that something had happened and he was sending a sign through the ether prompted her to slip out of bed and go down the short, darkened hallway to the living room to find her phone.

She connected to the switchboard. The woman who answered put her through to the nursing station on Danny's floor. She waited in a brilliant shaft of moonlight pouring through the window, tree limbs swaying black shadows across her face as she stood anxious and shivering in the cold apartment. There was a clink outside on the landing, and she pivoted. She'd left the lights off but could see well enough in the murky light to the door. Her heartbeat picked up speed and she stepped closer, aware suddenly of her nakedness. Carefully, silently, she lifted the dangling chain and eased it into the slot. A woman's voice began speaking into her ear, asking which patient she was enquiring about. She moved back into the shadows, grabbing her raincoat from the wall hook as she passed by. "Danny Tate," she whispered and watched in horror as the door handle slowly turned.

It wasn't Danny's spirit leaving this world that had woken her. Whoever intruded into her dreams was very much alive and standing outside her door.

CHAPTER 17

She frantically searched the apartment for a weapon. The only object halfway suitable was a bike helmet, which wouldn't do much damage unless she managed to get a few solid hits in. Even then, she wasn't sure she'd have much of an advantage unless she managed to knock the person out.

She raced on silent feet across the room in the darkness into the kitchen. Her hand wrapped around the handle of the carving knife and yanked it from the wood block. All the while she was on the move, the night nurse was speaking into her ear, updating her on Danny's condition. No change, she said. She instructed Ella to go back to bed and check again in the morning. "Thanks," Ella whispered and ended the call before her brain thought to ask the nurse to send the police to her apartment. She'd have had to tell her where and why, so perhaps it wasn't the best use of her time anyway. She stood in the kitchen doorway with the phone in one hand and the knife in the other, shaking.

Should she call 911 or wait to see if whoever was outside tried to force their way inside? What if it was a drunken Greg? Or obnoxious Tony back with a plate of fruit? Neither seemed likely, but not outside the realm. Should she call out? Confront them head-on and ask what the hell they were doing? *And what if it's the same man who raped and killed Josie Wheatly?* The logical part of her brain knew this was an insane idea, but the knowledge didn't stop her from tiptoeing into the living room and picking up the raincoat from the chair where she'd dropped it. She was braver once the coat was on and zipped but still uncertain of her next move.

The door handle was turning again. A clicking noise sounded, as if the person was fidgeting with the lock. Ella tightened her grip on the knife and moved silently into position next to the door. The lock was cheap, and it would only take seconds for them to pick it open. Sure enough, she watched as the door swung inward until the chain caught and held with a sharp bang. The sensation of being a few feet away from someone who was breaking into her home was almost an out-of-body experience. At the same time, it was hard to control the adrenalin pulsing through her in rising waves. She was torn between wanting to call 911 and staying as silent as she could to give herself the element of surprise when they got inside and she attacked. The element of surprise would be gone if the person heard her speaking on the phone, but perhaps that would make them flee? But what if the opposite happened? What if they became violent instead? The chain wouldn't hold for long if they were determined. She might not have time to tell the dispatcher where she lived, let alone how long it would take the police to get here. She opted for silence and raised the knife to shoulder level. Hopefully the sight of the knife would be enough to scare them off.

The intruder dropped something onto the tile floor outside her door, and the clang was loud enough to make her jump. Almost immediately, Luvy started a frenzied barking in Tony and Sander's apartment from the floor below. She heard a rush of movement outside the door, followed by footsteps pounding down the stairwell. She ran over to the living room window and craned her neck to see the sidewalk in front of the house. She couldn't make out the figure in the darkness. It turned in the opposite direction to her window and was quickly out of sight. A few seconds later, a frantic knocking shook her apartment door.

"Ella? Ella? Are you okay?" Tony's voice bellowed through the crack in the door. He pulled on the handle. The chain rattled, and there was a loud thunk as the door held in place.

"Tony, hang on."

She left her lookout and ran through the living room and down the short hallway to let him in. He was as dishevelled as she felt, his green hair tangled and sleep creases in his left cheek. He'd thrown on a gold robe over red silk pajama bottoms, and his feet were bare. Luvy stood behind him on the landing, looking down the staircase and growling as if she was ready to take on anyone and everyone. Who knew such a big bark could come out of such a little dog? Ella almost laughed at the image of her ten-pound saviour.

"What happened?" Tony asked. He was panting from his run up the stairs. "Why's your door ajar?"

"Someone was trying to break in. Luvy's barking scared them off." She slowed her breathing and downplayed her fear with a shrug, trying to slow her pounding heart before she suffered a stroke.

"My God." He ran his fingers down the door frame. "Look at these marks. They were made by a crowbar. The wooden door jamb is solid oak, though. Your intruder must have gotten frustrated and decided to try the lock pick instead." His eyes were now clear of sleep. "Have you called the cops?"

"To what end? The person is gone now and not likely to return tonight."

"Do you think this has anything to do with your podcast?"

"God knows."

"I'm checking downstairs. How did they get through the locked front door?"

"They seem adept at breaking in."

They took the stairs in single file with Luvy leading the way. The front door lock had also been forced, and the door refused to shut properly. "We have to call Alex in the morning first thing," Tony said, straightening from his inspection of the door jamb. "He won't put this through insurance and have his rates hiked, knowing him, but he'll need to get the locks fixed."

Tony followed her back upstairs and into her apartment. They assumed their usual positions, Tony rocking forward on the couch so that his elbows were resting on his legs and Ella in her desk chair facing him.

"You should at least file a report. What if this person decides to come back?"

"Then Luvy will have a go."

"I'm serious, Ella. What if Luvy hadn't woken up, and this person got inside your apartment?" He seemed to focus in on her for the first time. "Do you always sleep in a raincoat? Whatever possessed you to buy a coat that gawdawful colour?"

"It was the only piece of clothing handy. And I happen to like lime green. Brings out the jade tone in my skin." She waved a hand in the air as if her attire was of no consequence. "Anyway, I doubt very much whoever tried to get in will be back. I'm going to get a better lock tomorrow. One with a deadbolt. I'll even pay for it if Alex won't."

"Good idea. I will too, but I'm quite sure I can talk Alex into paying. He needs to update his security and enter the twenty-first century. Never heard of video cameras? Hello." He paused. "You and I are going shopping one day soon, girl. It's past time your wardrobe entered the twenty-first century too."

"Good luck with that. Where's Sander? Surely he's not still sleeping?"

"He caught a late flight tonight to Phoenix. He's worried about the presentation and wanted to see the setup. He has things to work out." An unhappy look crossed Tony's face, and she didn't probe. She wasn't the person to question someone else's relationship. Tony stared into her eyes. "I'd like to call the police."

"If you do, we'll be up all night. I'm meeting a cop friend for breakfast tomorrow. How about if I fill him in and see what he advises? Those crowbar marks in the wooden door frames aren't going anywhere."

"Okay, but only on the condition you come sleep in my apartment. I'll take care of calling Alex about security while you meet your cop friend."

This was not where she saw the conversation heading. "I'm fine here."

"No arguing. We have a spare room already made up with fresh sheets. Otherwise, Luvy and I will be sleeping on your couch. I'll brook no argument."

His face was set. If she was honest with herself, she wasn't keen to sleep in this apartment alone until there was a better lock on the door. She stood. "Then let me get something to wear, and I'll come with you."

"Anything is better than that gaudy green raincoat." He shivered. "Has nightmare written all over it."

Her eyes welled up as she rummaged through her messy drawer to find a t-shirt, using the time to pull herself together. Now that the threat was over, she allowed herself a moment's weakness before she picked out a favourite long white tee and slammed the drawer shut. She leaned on the dresser and swiped at her eyes with the back of her hand. She told herself that accepting Tony's generosity should not make her weep. Her body was simply reacting to the fear and what could have happened. When she finally joined him in the living room, her eyes were dry and she'd regained her equilibrium. She bent down and rubbed the dog's head. "Lead on, Luvy," she said.

Tony held the door open for her and followed her downstairs to his apartment. He poured them each a healthy slug of Scotch, and she took hers to bed in the spare room. She didn't think she'd be able to relax, but having Tony and Luvy in the next room made her feel safe. She was soon sound asleep and stayed that way until the sun shone through the window. She had just enough time to return to her apartment, shower, dress, and get on her bike to meet O'Brien for their seven thirty breakfast date.

CHAPTER 18

Daisy motioned for Ella to sit at any table and followed her with a full pot of coffee. "Expecting your gentleman friend?"

"Yes, and I'm surprised he didn't beat me here. I'll wait to order until he arrives."

"No rush." Daisy reached across another table and grabbed a newspaper left by a previous customer. "Catch up on the day's news while you wait."

"Thanks, Daisy."

Ella scanned through headlines, looking for an update on Josie Wheatly's case. The article was buried on the last page of the news section. The police were calling her death suspicious, so they were easing into the murder call as they assembled the evidence. Likely O'Brien invited her to breakfast to give her the inside scoop.

She set the paper aside and checked her watch. It wasn't like him to be late for anything, and he usually sent word if he was delayed. Several customers had found seats, eaten, and been on their way since she arrived. She checked her phone, but there was no message that he was waylaid.

Daisy returned with the coffeepot. "Ready to order?"

"I guess. The usual, please. Looks like my date got called in to work."

"Happens. I get stood up regularly myself." She winked and sashayed back to the counter while Ella tried to imagine her as a femme fatale. Daisy looked like somebody's plump grandmother, but looks could be deceiving. She had to remember to tell O'Brien. He'd be amused.

She sent him a text before her food arrived, and he still hadn't responded by the time she finished eating and went outside to unlock her bike. She was disappointed, but there was always breakfast tomorrow to catch up on his news. It was sunny but not particularly warm, and she was happy that she'd pulled on a thick fleece before leaving her apartment. She pedalled the direct route up Carling Avenue to the hospital and arrived before nine o'clock.

A new nurse was looking after Danny this morning. She was younger and not as outgoing as the last one, carrying out her duties with quiet efficiency. She told Ella that Danny spent a restless but stable night.

"What does that mean — restless?" Ella asked.

"He was thrashing around more than usual and seemed closer to gaining consciousness. You may find he wakens today."

"That's good then?"

"The doctor will be in this morning, and he'll explain everything and can update you on Danny's condition." The nurse turned away, fiddling with the IV tube.

She didn't respond to the hope in Ella's voice, and this worried Ella. Danny's skin was pale and dry like an old man's. "Do you have some lotion that you use for backrubs?" she asked.

"Of course." The nurse left and returned with a bottle. After she moved away to check on the other patients in the room. Ella started massaging lotion into Danny's arms, avoiding needles and tubes. All the while, she spoke softly to him about the weather, his music, how much she missed hearing his voice. She shifted her ministrations to his feet and calves and massaged the muscles with lotion that smelled of lavender and vanilla. If he'd been restless in the night, he was calm now, his limbs dead weights. She couldn't see any signs of awakening in his face.

She stayed all morning and through the lunch hour. She'd brought a book of poetry and read aloud to Danny, attempting to drown out the moans of a man in the next bed. If she had the money, she'd move Danny to a private room, but that was not going to happen. She heard the doctor speaking to his interns in the hall. She tracked the squeak of their footsteps on the polished floor in and out of rooms until they finally appeared inside the doorway.

Dr. Fournier nodded at her before checking Danny's chart and shining a penlight into each eye. The interns gathered at the foot of the bed while he made a more thorough examination of her brother.

"Is he doing better?" Ella asked when she couldn't bear waiting any longer.

"He's stable, but his pulse could be stronger." Dr. Fournier nodded to the interns, and they moved over to the next bed while he remained. "I think Danny's through the worst, but the knife wound caused a great deal of internal bleeding and damage to key organs. The years of drug use weakened his immune system, a factor we can't overlook. He was also malnourished. We're giving doses of methadone through the tube to keep his body from detoxing. I'm concerned that he hasn't gained consciousness yet, but this could be his body's way of healing."

"The nurse said he was restless during the night."

"I won't lie to you. His condition is grave, and this

could still go either way, but I'm hopeful. The signs are encouraging. I'll be back this afternoon to check him again and will let you know if there are any changes."

"Thank you, Doctor."

He patted her shoulder. "Keep the faith. He's in good hands."

She stayed with Danny until one o'clock and used the time to call Tony. He was happy to report that Alex had lined up a locksmith for two o'clock, and she promised to be back by then. Tony wasn't pleased to hear that she hadn't told O'Brien about the break-in, but she assured him that she would handle things once she left the hospital.

The nurse who'd been in ICU the day Danny was brought in stopped by to see him on her way to lunch. "How's he doing?" she asked, coming close to the bed and looking down at him.

"He's still unconscious but stable, or so I'm told."

"He's had a tough time." She put a hand on his forehead. "No fever." She glanced at Ella. "He has a sweet face. He looks a lot like you."

"The same parents will do that to a person, although I never thought of us as sweet-looking."

The nurse laughed, and then her expression turned serious. "I finally contacted your mother."

"And how did that go?"

"She was polite. Thanked me for the information before she hung up."

"My parents aren't coming."

"I won't hold out false hope." The nurse studied her for a moment but didn't ask the obvious.

"Thanks for checking on him."

"I'll come back at the end of my shift and sit with him for a bit. Try not to worry."

Too soon, it was time to leave. Ella would have liked to

crawl up onto the bed and wrap herself around Danny's body. Transfer some of her energy into his, warm him back to life. Instead, she kissed his forehead and whispered into his ear. "Don't leave me, Danny Tate, you hear? I'll be back tomorrow. You keep fighting and think about waking up soon."

CHAPTER 19

Tony and Alex were standing on the sidewalk when Ella arrived on her bike. They were talking and watching a guy installing a new lock on the front door, but they turned as she glided up behind them.

"I hear you had quite the night," Alex said. He was a balding Polish man, five foot four with black glasses and a round belly, a study in contrasts standing next to the tall, lean Tony, although they had an identical concerned look on their faces.

She straddled her bike with both feet on the pavement and leaned on the handlebars. "I'm just sorry whoever got in damaged the locks and door frames, Alex."

"We can always fix those." He glanced at Tony. "I'm getting cameras installed on the front and back doors. The security guy should be here next week to set them up."

"It'll be like trying to get into Fort Knox." She pulled her bike onto the sidewalk.

"The painters are working in the first-floor apartment. They'll be here through the weekend."

"Have you got a new tenant moving in?"

"I'm advertising after the painting's done. I'll see you

both later."

Knowing Alex, he wanted to increase the rent and figured the paint job would help get maximum dollar — well, maximum on his scale. Even at that, he kept rents lower than expected in this neighbourhood. He was a gruff man but liked to help people out. She was a case in point.

Tony followed her into the building and waited while she tucked her bike behind the stairs. He handed her three new keys, one each for the front and back doors and another for her apartment. "Courtesy of Alex. New deadbolts all around," he said. "Ones not easily picked."

"I assume Alex is paying?"

"He had no choice after the guilt trip I laid on him. He'd have agreed to have a twenty-four-hour, armed, security guard on duty if I'd pushed much further."

"Ever thought of going into sales?"

"Actually, I've always wanted to be a cop. Or was that I always wanted to *do* a cop?" He tapped his chin and pretended to think.

"Yeeeeah, right." She gave him a look and walked past the open door to the ground-floor apartment. Two men in coveralls were moving around inside. One was painting baseboards a glossy white while the other was using a long-handled roller on the ceiling.

"Ever think about moving downstairs to the bigger apartment?" Tony asked as she started up the stairs.

"I'm happy where I am."

"Not sure how."

"What do you mean by that?" She stopped and glared at him, but he didn't appear to notice.

"You're living in cramped quarters with nondescript second-hand furniture — well, what there is of it — consuming a diet seriously lacking in nutrients. Your clothes are functional at best. Your boyfriend moved out, and you're riding around the city on a bike that looks as if it's been through the Blitz. Might be time to up your game."

"Are you done?"

"For now."

She turned back around and continued climbing. *Welcome to the world of poverty,* she thought. Muttering loudly enough for him to hear, she said, "At least my hair isn't forest green."

Tony passed his own landing and continued climbing to her apartment door. "Why are you still here?" she asked.

"To fill you in on my assignment."

What had she been thinking when she recruited Tony to help with research? He'd already annoyed the hell out of her, and she'd been home less than ten minutes. "Aren't you cutting hair today?"

"I cancelled this morning to look after the security problem. I'm going to the shop in half an hour and will put in a late evening as a result. I can only stay a minute because I have to take Luvy for a walk before I leave."

Hearing that he'd be gone the rest of the day lightened her mood. She pushed the door open and motioned for him to enter. Tony flopped down on the couch. His hair fell across his face, and he brushed it to one side. He was wearing a silky purple shirt, open to show off his chest, tight black pants, and chocolate-coloured desert boots. His green hair contrasted with the black stubble on his cheeks. Ella was still smarting from his criticism about her lack of style. Her grey fleece, blue jeans, and black running shoes might not stand out, but at least she was comfortable. She plopped down in her desk chair and slung one leg over the arm. "So what did you find out?"

"I've touched base with my soldier boy, and he's calling me later today with the information about Rory Leavitt and his trip home from overseas. I'll be texting you with the findings when I get them."

"So you haven't actually got anything to tell me?"

"Only the update. I also wanted to ask if you've reported the attempted break-in yet, or would you like me to handle it?"

"I'm having trouble reaching O'Brien, but I've left messages. I've asked him to meet up for breakfast tomorrow but have yet to confirm."

"Could our intruder have anything to do with your podcast and the Wheatly case?"

"Possibly."

"I worry for your safety, Tate." He extended a hand and wriggled his fingers. "Let me see your cell."

"I'm not sure how this is going to solve anything." She dug in her pocket and passed him the phone while telling him her password.

Tony typed with his thumbs for several seconds and passed it back. "I put my phone number into your contact list under Tony. You can call me anytime. I think we should have a word or phrase that you use if you're being threatened."

"Such as?"

He thought for a bit. "It has to be a word that could come up in a conversation but not one that's so common you'd likely use it anyway. How about: another late night?"

"So if someone's pointing a gun at my head and they let me call you, I slip 'another late night' into the conversation?"

"Exactly."

"Consider it done." As if this would ever happen.

Tony seemed satisfied and got off the couch. "You don't know how great this is to be part of your team. I'll check in later. I also put you on my speed dial."

She tucked her chin into her sweatshirt and didn't comment, much as she wanted to tell him that he was mistaken. She wasn't a team player. She wasn't the person he wanted on his speed dial.

He stopped at the door. "What are you doing with your money, if I may be so bold as to ask? Surely you got a severance package and must be collecting unemployment?"

"None of your business, is it?"

"No, I guess not. Just curious more than anything. Pretend I never asked."

After he was gone, she flipped through the day's news stories on her computer while thinking about the Josie Wheatly case and her brother's attack. It seemed as if she was treading water, barely keeping her head above the waves. If there were leads for her to follow up on from either attack, she wasn't seeing them.

She pushed back her chair and started pacing around the small space. If she sat for much longer, depression and obsessive thoughts would slither their ugly way into her and twist her guts into a knot. Before she'd let that happen, she put on her duffle coat and a black skullcap and went downstairs to haul out her bike one more time. She needed a workout that would exhaust her body and soul. An hour in the gym would keep her mind occupied and give her a fighting chance at a decent night's sleep.

FINN WASN'T in his office. The university student, Maisie, was on duty and spotting a guy lifting weights. She gave Ella a wave on her way to the change room. The stationary bikes were all in use when Ella emerged from the locker room, so she started with stretches on the mats before moving on to the punching bags and elliptical. Maisie wandered over to chat as she reached down to pick up a skipping rope.

"Hey, Ella. Finn should be back anytime now. He told me you might be in." She flexed her biceps as she talked. She was the strongest five-foot-two woman Ella knew, with several weight-lifting trophies on her mantel to prove it. Her long auburn hair was braided in a ponytail. She'd told Ella that she was studying to be a doctor and planned to work overseas in one of the poorer countries before starting up a practice in Canada. Ella had no doubt Maisie would accomplish everything she set her mind to.

"I thought he worked Fridays."

"Usually, but he wanted to go with his wife to her doctor's appointment." Maisie picked up a skipping rope. "I've been worried about him lately."

"He's got a lot on his mind with the baby coming."

"Yeah, maybe that's all it is."

"You don't sound convinced."

"I don't know. He's preoccupied and taking more nights off than usual. I worked last night too, and he didn't come lock up like he usually does. He didn't say anything to you about being upset … or something?"

"I don't know what to tell you."

"I guess like you say, having your first baby can be stressful." She shrugged before moving away to work with another client. Ella watched her for a minute and wondered what it was that Maisie had left unsaid.

There was no sign of Finn when she finished with the punching bag, so she took her time cooling down and stretching. She'd planned to delay showering until she got home but took one now to kill time before getting dressed. It was nearly five o'clock when she left the change room. Her dawdling had paid off. Finn was standing near the main entrance, talking to Maisie. He was still wearing his jacket and ball cap and unlocked his office door while Maisie waited and followed him inside. She pushed the door shut before Ella could make it across the gym to reach them.

Surely you're not having a fling with Maisie, she thought and immediately chastised herself. Finn wasn't that kind of guy. Still, the uneasy feeling lingered. He had changed since he'd married Adele. Knowing now about the trouble in his marriage had led her deeper into unknown territory, and she didn't know how to read him anymore. She waited a minute before crossing to the office and rapping on the door. There was movement on the other side before Finn yanked the door open, scowling, until he saw that it was her.

"Hey, Ella." He grabbed her in a quick hug. "We're going over this week's schedule, but I think we're okay for the next few days." He came out of the office, and Maisie had no choice but to step out as well.

"I'll see you in two days then," she said and smiled. "Don't be a stranger, Ella."

"I don't plan to be."

After she'd gone, Finn and Ella stood staring at each other. "Everything okay?" she asked.

"Never better." The sarcasm in his voice was unusual.

"Anything you want to talk about?"

"Not really. So, how's Danny?"

"The same. Holding on but not waking up. It's as if his body doesn't want him facing the pain."

"Perhaps nature is giving him some time to heal. Who knows what damage the drugs he was taking all those years have done to him?"

"He was clean for the past while. He never told me."

"He probably didn't want to disappoint you again if he slipped."

"I'd have liked to know that he was trying to get clean so I could have helped him. Anyhow, moot point now. How was Adele's medical appointment?"

He shrugged. "Everything's right on schedule, but don't change the subject. You did try helping him, Ella. Two extended stays at the rehab place. You're still paying off the loans. You've been the best sister a guy could ever ask for."

"And I'd do it all again in a heartbeat. I'd do the same for you. Listen, Finn, if you ever need—"

He cut her off. "I never should have burdened you with my marriage woes. I feel bad about that, so let's pretend I never said anything."

"If that's what you want."

"It is."

She'd planned to tell him about the attempted break-in the night before, but not when he was in this odd mood. She shifted her bag from one shoulder to the other. "Guess I'll get moving then. I'll be back in a few days, hopefully."

"Okay. Take care, Ella. I've got a client waiting for a lesson, so sorry we can't talk longer." He gave her a peck on the cheek and left before she had a chance to ask more questions.

She watched him with his client for a minute before pushing the heavy front door open and stepping outside. Finn's friendship had been one of the few constants in her life, but nothing ever stayed the same forever. He had a wife and child on the way, and she had to accept that they were his priorities. The guiding principle of her life since she was old enough to form one was that the only person she could truly count on was herself. Grief only came when she forgot.

CHAPTER 20

Ella stopped at the grocery store and picked up a few dairy staples, cramming a carton of milk, small tub of yoghurt, pound of butter, and package of cheese into her knapsack. Tonight's dinner would be scrambled eggs with a strawberry yoghurt chaser. No vegetables, but at least some fruit. Well, a trace of fruit.

A wind had come up, making the last few streets of her bike ride more challenging. She slowed even more as she rounded the corner and saw a black sedan parked in front of the house. It wasn't a car she recognized, and after the incident of the night before, she approached cautiously. Tony was likely at work, and Sander was away. The guys painting the downstairs apartment would have quit for the day. Should she turn around and wait for the car to leave? She pondered this idea for all of ten seconds before going around the block and approaching the car from the rear. Better to face them head-on, out in the open.

A man was sitting alone in the driver's seat with his head bent, reading from a paper resting on the steering wheel. Every so often, he lifted his head and looked up the street, then lowered his head and resumed reading. He was wearing a black wool cap and black jacket, and it wasn't until she eased up next to the window that she saw his face. She rapped on the glass and got a certain satisfaction when he jumped. Hunter turned the key in the ignition and rolled down the window.

"Is this a social call?"

His expression stayed grim. "Don't you answer your phone?"

"I was at the gym. My phone was in my locker. Is there anything I can help you with?"

"I have something to tell you. Can I come inside?"

She didn't know him well enough to read his expression, but he looked upset, and she thought he'd gotten news about Danny's case that she wasn't going to like. "Sure." She walked her bike onto the sidewalk and waited for him.

He set aside the papers he was reading and got out of the car. He held the apartment door open while she rolled her bike inside, and once she had it tucked away, he followed her upstairs. The door to Tony and Sander's apartment opened as they passed by, and Sander started to step into the hallway. He ducked his head when he saw them and moved back inside, shutting the door firmly behind him.

"That's strange," Ella said.

"What's strange?"

She glanced at him over her shoulder. "Nothing. It's just I thought that person who went into the apartment was out of town."

It took some jiggling of the key to get it to work in the new lock, but she managed and they entered her less than spacious digs. She tried to see the apartment through fresh eyes and had to admit that while it suited her, not everyone would be impressed. A desk and chair filled the space under the small window, which was closer to the ceiling than the floor. Her computer equipment took up all the room on the desk. A couch and a floor lamp were the only other furniture. The bathroom at the end of the hallway next to the bedroom was large enough for a shower but not a tub. Hunter stopped and looked around.

"You haven't got any pictures on the wall, well, except for that Bart Simpson over there, which is hardly artwork. Not an art lover?"

"I like art. Just don't want to have to look at the same paintings day in and day out."

"Could be why you're not married."

"What do you mean?"

"Looking at the same man ... or woman ... day in and day out. Takes a certain mindset."

"Are you married, Detective?"

"Haven't had the pleasure."

"This place was furnished better until my boyfriend moved out a few weeks ago, and turns out most of the stuff was his. I haven't gotten around to redecorating."

"Sorry to hear that."

She wasn't sure if he meant that he was sorry Greg moved out or that he'd owned the bulk of the furniture, but it didn't matter. "Would you like to sit down?" She pointed at the couch.

He shook his head. The grim look returned. "There's no easy way to say this. I know you're friends with Paul O'Brien, so I'm really sorry to have to tell you that he died sometime last night. Looks like a heart attack."

She couldn't have heard correctly. "No. That can't be true."

"I'm really sorry. Please sit. Can I get you some water or a drink of something stronger?" His eyes were concerned, and he made a move to hold onto her arm.

She shook him off and turned away. "I can't believe he's gone."

"For what it's worth, I only worked with him this last bit and thought he was a stand-up guy. He spoke highly of you."

"I've known him since I was seventeen." She was feeling off balance and lowered herself awkwardly onto the couch. "We were supposed to meet for breakfast this morning."

"He was found in a parking garage at close to midnight." Hunter stood for a few seconds, looking down at her. "Where do you keep your alcohol?"

"There's wine in the fridge."

"Nothing stronger?"

"No."

He went down the hallway and into the kitchen, and she heard him opening cupboards and the fridge while she sat and stared at nothing. He returned with a half-filled glass of white wine and handed it to her. He sat next to her and urged, "Have a sip. It'll help with the shock."

She drained the glass and closed her eyes as the warmth filled her chest. She rested her head against the couch back. "Does his ex-wife know?"

"Somebody's contacting her. She lives in California, and it's taking a while to track her down. Tell me," he hesitated, "how did you and O'Brien meet?"

She opened her eyes and watched him for a few seconds. Was he fishing or only making conversation? She decided to find out how much he knew. "Paul was a cop in Edmonton. We met there."

Hunter's expression gave nothing away. "Just how close were the two of you?"

"We weren't sleeping together, if that's what you're asking."

"No, that wasn't where I was going with that question. I'm simply wondering how good a friend he was to you."

"We met up now and then over the years. He was always supportive." The words downplayed one of the most enduring relationships of her life. What she didn't say was that O'Brien had been her rock throughout Gordon Jamieson's trial. He'd helped her and Danny relocate to Ottawa and had gotten the grants that allowed her to take journalism at Carleton University. He'd followed her and Danny east several months after they arrived.

Hunter's voice softened. "I know about the trial. I know that O'Brien was the arresting officer."

She was still for a moment, gathering her thoughts. Of course Hunter knew about the trial. He'd have researched Danny's life history for the case. She shrugged. "Paul looked into what happened and laid the charges. He's been a part of my life ever since."

"That must have been a tough time for you and Danny and your family."

"Tough. Good word." She stood. "I'm feeling better, so don't let me keep you any longer, Detective. I imagine you have somewhere to be."

He followed her lead and got to his feet. "The coroner is having a look to determine the exact cause of death. Paul had diabetes, so it might not have been a heart attack that killed him. I'll let you know about any arrangements for a funeral once we contact his ex. Did you know her?"

"We met a few times, but she left O'Brien not long after the trial. She'd been having an affair with the next-door neighbour. He didn't like to talk about her."

"I guess not." Hunter frowned before starting toward the door. "I'll be in touch. You take care of yourself."

"Thanks for coming by to tell me in person."

"I'm sorry for your loss."

She listened to his footsteps clomp down the stairs before going into her bedroom and curling up under a blanket. She was cold and shivered uncontrollably. She closed her eyes and tried to squeeze back the tears but couldn't stop them from sliding down her cheeks and soaking the pillow. This had to be the worst week of her life, and it was far from over. The dread and sadness inside her were growing, and she was helpless to do anything about it.

CHAPTER 21

Ella woke at 2:00 a.m., hunger propelling her out of bed. Her head ached from weeping and a lack of food, and her legs wobbled as she lurched toward the kitchen. She poured the last of the wine into a glass before making two peanut butter sandwiches and taking the meal to her computer. Two bites and a sip of wine and she began to feel human. She took a deep breath and centred herself. She tried not to think about Paul O'Brien. Danny. The attempted break-in. Focused on how this had always been her favourite time of day.

The night's silence settled around her, and the darkness soothed like a warm bath. The feeling of aloneness was familiar, and she was at ease in her solitary state. Her time with Greg had been an anomaly. She'd be lying to say that she hadn't liked being part of a couple, but she'd returned to her comfortable place … on her own. Nobody else to dance around, placate, or consider.

Her computer screen flashed into life, sending a bright bluish glow into the room that made her squint until her eyes adjusted. She took the last bite of sandwich number one and wiped her fingers on the blanket wrapped around her shoulders before clicking on the email icon. Three new messages. She opened the one from Felix first. *Breakfast tomorrow at your usual place. 8 o'clock.*

She raised her eyes from the screen. Chewed on a fingernail. Why meet her now? And how did Felix know about her breakfast place? Hers and O'Brien's. What kind of insanity had she let herself get drawn into by accepting this anonymous person's help? Her instinct was to shut this connection down immediately yet the need to find out who killed Josie Wheatly and curiosity about Felix overrode her unease. She sent her reply, accepting the date, and clicked on the second email, this one from Sherry Carpenter, whom she hadn't heard from since their ill-fated trip to Almonte.

Sorry how things ended. I'm still willing to share intel if you are. Meet up soon? Something had prompted this half-assed apology, but she wasn't interested. Sherry was more work than Ella was prepared to expend. She hit delete and opened the third email. The last message was from Tony Venditto. She hadn't known his last name. Nor could she figure out how he got her email address until she remembered that the podcast contact page linked to this address.

Hey Girl. Got that info you asked for from my hunky army bud. Soooo hard to believe. I'll be up tomorrow to fill you in. T.

"Couldn't just put what you found in an email?" she muttered under her breath. She didn't type a response to him either. Hopefully he had something worthwhile to report, because it was time she taped another podcast about the case.

She opened a news app and read an article about melting ice floes that didn't improve her mood but took her mind out of its loop. A new email message popped up on the screen as she was about to shut down and go to bed.

Her hand hesitated. What was Greg doing sending her a message this time of night? She clicked on his name.

Can't sleep. Out walking. Do you want to meet up for coffee sometime soon? I miss you. She pushed back from the computer and stood to scan the sidewalk in front of the house. The closest streetlight pooled a wide arc of yellowish light one house down, far enough away that her yard was in near darkness. The message had come from Greg's phone. She searched the shadows, trying to see him, not sure if she wanted to or not. It was unsettling to think that he could be nearby, watching her apartment. Sander had met him a street over only a few days ago, so he'd been roaming this neighbourhood for no good reason that she could think of. She stepped back into the room and moved closer to her apartment door. She leaned her ear against the wood and listened for sounds of someone outside. If it was Greg who'd tried to break in the other night, he wouldn't be able to pick the new locks as easily. The idea that he would do such a thing was crazy, but how well could one ever really know somebody? They were together less than a year. He was angry when he moved out and said that she'd regret her decision. In the middle of the night, the words seemed more threatening than they did at the time.

Satisfied that nobody was creeping up the stairs, she padded across the floor to her bedroom and tried to clear her mind of stressful thoughts. She reminded herself to invest in a bottle of something stronger than wine as she began to drift away.

WHEN ELLA PHONED the hospital in the morning, a new nurse told her that there was no change in Danny's condition. He'd spent a restful night but hadn't regained consciousness. Ella thanked her and tucked her phone into her knapsack before dragging her bike out of its storage place under the stairs. The rain had started before she woke up, and a strong wind was thrashing the boughs around like waves in a gale. She secured her bike helmet over the hood of her raincoat before stepping outside. Her coat flapped open in a gust of wind, and she stopped to zip it up. The greyish light had a dismal feel, the cloud cover low and ominous. A rumble of thunder sounded off in the distance to the northwest in the vicinity of the Ottawa River. Storms often tracked along the river's path from farther north in the valley, blowing through the downtown and eastward. One part of the city could have a torrential downpour while another section remained as dry as toast. She thought that this morning no part of the city would escape the steady, cold rain.

She arrived at the diner tired, hungry, and wet after battling to keep her bike upright. A crack of thunder directly above her head had her hastening indoors after securing the bike to a metal post. She shook the raindrops off her jacket at the door and took a look around. Daisy was pouring coffee for a table of two construction workers seated next to the window. A couple of men were at the counter, eating. Neither looked at her as she found a seat at the far end of the restaurant where she could watch the door. Daisy sauntered over, waving the coffeepot and pouring a cup without asking.

"Your gentleman friend joining you this morning?" she asked.

"No." Her fallback was to say nothing and to find a new place to eat breakfast, but O'Brien had liked Daisy. She had a right to know why he would never be returning.

"Paul O'Brien, the man I always sat with, suffered a heart attack and died a few evenings ago."

"Good Lord." Daisy's eyes filled with tears. "You must be devastated. He seemed like such a good friend to you."

"He was. Thanks."

Daisy stood in place for a few moments, holding on to the coffeepot, biting her bottom lip and shaking her head slowly from side to side. Before walking away, she asked, "Can I get you the usual then, sweetie?"

"Perfect." Ella nodded and looked down at the table, focusing on the salt shaker.

She ate her eggs and toast slowly while reading the newspaper that Daisy had dropped on the table along with her meal. Daisy refilled her coffee mug before taking Ella's empty plate back into the kitchen. Three more construction workers entered with a gust of wind and rain. They sat near the window and immediately checked their phones. Ella lingered over her coffee while Daisy took their order. The front door opened again, and a fourth guy with a hardhat and yellow vest joined their table.

This is ridiculous, Ella thought. *Felix isn't coming.* She started putting on her raincoat, cursing Felix under her breath as she did. Daisy saw her getting ready to leave and raised a hand for her to wait while she poured a fresh round of coffee for the men. She walked over to Ella's table, waving the coffeepot and reaching into her pocket with her other hand. She pulled out a scrap of paper. "Almost forgot when I got busy. I was told to deliver this message after you finished eating. Said they were a friend and wanted to surprise you but had something to do first so they couldn't join you for the meal."

Ella took the paper. It was from Felix, instructing her to go out the back way and look for a blue SUV. Daisy waited until Ella raised her eyes. "Back door's unlocked. You can enter again without a problem. Do up your raincoat, dear. It's still raining cats and dogs."

"Thanks, Daisy."

At least if something bad happened to her in the parking lot, Daisy would be able to fill in the police. She put on her coat and walked down the hallway, past the washrooms and the kitchen, and stepped outside into the downpour. The parking lot was small. Two cars were wedged in next to each other, and a navy SUV idled alongside the back fence facing the road. She dodged puddles and rounded the front of the SUV to climb in through the unlocked front passenger door. A woman was sitting behind the wheel, watching as she shook the rain out of her hair. Ella returned her stare.

"Are you Felix?"

She smiled. "I'm one half. There are … were two of us."

This isn't what she was expecting to hear. "How does that work, and why are you being so secretive?"

"Let's say our jobs would be in jeopardy if anyone found out. I'm working in Victims' Services. Paul O'Brien asked me to help him out with the Felix project. He didn't want you to know he was behind the emails."

"No way."

"Yes, it's true.

Ella swallowed hard. It took a moment before she could speak without her voice cracking. "I can guess why O'Brien helped me out, but why did you get involved?"

"I'm sick of watching people get away with murder and other egregious crimes. I often have information that I can't ethically share. Paul came up with the idea to prompt you to investigate in the hopes you'd dig out the facts … as you've done so admirably many times. He liked the idea of staying at arm's length. He said that it was safer for everyone." She grinned. It was hard to tell how old she was, but Ella guessed early fifties. A hoodie was pulled up over her hair, but a light brown and grey strand had escaped. She was wearing gigantic sunglasses, even though it was raining. This woman didn't trust her as much as she professed. She seemed to read Ella's mind. "I can't be seen with you," she added.

"Then why take this risk?"

"I think Paul would want you to know. I sent the emails to you from an untraceable account my son created. He's a genius that way. He and Paul were close."

Ella watched the woman's hands squeezing the wheel. "You and Paul were close too."

"We were together six years. I still haven't taken in that he isn't coming back. I don't know what I'm going to do."

"I'll find another source."

"That's not what I meant." She paused and checked in her rear-view mirror. The rain was pattering on the roof. The windshield was blurry with streaks and steam from their breath. "We didn't broadcast our relationship around the station. Nobody in our offices knew we were an item."

The fact that O'Brien had been in a good relationship eased something in Ella's chest. It was a comfort to know that he hadn't been lonely in the last years of his life. She thought for a moment. "Do you know what he was going to tell me?"

She nodded. "He was worried about you after Danny's stabbing. He checked into Gordon Jamieson and found out he's dying of cancer and not capable of making a trip to Ottawa. He wanted you to know."

"Thanks." His final act was to look out for her. She forced her voice to remain steady. "Tell me, are they certain he died of a heart attack?"

"That's what I'm hearing. Why?"

"Just making sure. Is there anything else?"

"Only that I'd like to continue making contact when I have something for you to follow up on. I'll understand if you want to break the connection."

"Let's keep going as we are for now. O'Brien found a sponsor for the podcast, and I can look for others. To be honest, I never liked the idea of being paid by a secret source, but I needed the money."

The woman swivelled her head around to face her. "Paul was paying you?"

O'Brien. They stared at each other, silent for a moment. "It wasn't necessary," Ella said. "I'd have searched out the stories without payment. You don't need to keep sending it."

"I'd like to, but my son is going to university next year, and I'm the only provider. I'm already paying for my daughter's four years." She smiled. "Take care of yourself, Ella. I know that Paul was extremely proud of you. He said you were like a daughter."

Her cue to leave. Their entire exchange had taken less than two minutes. Ella put her palm on the handle and turned to look at the woman. "Paul was a good man. The best." She pushed the door open and hesitated. "I worked the crime beat for several years and know how frustrating it is to see someone guilty get away with it. What was your breaking point?"

"We prosecuted a young man who raped a university student. In this case, he got off and went on to rape two more women before he was caught and sentenced. Evidence was disallowed that could have stopped him after the first victim. Her life was put under a microscope, and her character went through a meat grinder."

Ella nodded. "I'll be getting the next podcast out this

week." She added, "And just so you know, I never reveal a source."

"I'm counting on that." The woman looked straight ahead at the street. "I was on my way to visit Josie Wheatly that day in the hospital. I wish I'd been able to help."

Ella pondered her situation as she biked slowly home through the falling rain. As a reporter, she'd come close on a couple of occasions to entering that grey world of getting a story by any means possible. Every time she'd pulled herself up short, not liking where the investigation had taken her. Integrity wasn't something you could barter away and then get back. O'Brien and this woman had steered her investigations without giving her complete access to all the facts, but she could imagine the repercussions if this collaboration ever came to light. The woman had a lot to lose, more so than her. The question was whether helping victims outweighed the risks. She was more convinced now that it was.

She thought about how the woman had been careful not to reveal her identity. She'd worn loose clothing, a head covering, and glasses so that Ella would have difficulty picking her out of a police line-up. On the plus side, Ella knew where she worked, and she'd memorized the license plate. With a bit of legwork O'Brien's partner wouldn't be anonymous to her much longer, if she chose to carry out a search.

O'Brien's silent involvement was like a blessing, a belief in her and what she was doing. She only wished he'd trusted her enough to talk about the secret alliance before he died. She'd have given him an earful for putting his job on the line for her. Then she'd have hugged him and thanked him from the bottom of her heart.

CHAPTER 22

The painters were back in the ground floor unit as Ella started up the stairwell to her apartment. They had the door propped open, and one of them waved his paintbrush in her direction while the other was crouched with his back to her, working on the baseboards. Her shoes squelched on the floor tile, and she dripped like a faucet all the way to the third floor. She was no sooner through her door than Tony came bounding up the steps with Luvy in his arms. He was wearing a baggy orange tracksuit straight out of the eighties and bright yellow sneakers. He'd dyed his hair a pewter grey. *There's no way in hell this man is taking me shopping for a new wardrobe*, she thought.

"You're back. I came up earlier, but you'd already gone out. Hot breakfast date?" He was panting, and Luvy licked his neck as he stood waiting for her to step aside so he could enter.

"I was hungry."

"You must have been to go out in this weather." He settled Luvy on the couch while she kicked off her shoes and socks and went in search of a towel to dry her hair.

She put on leggings and socks and a warm fleece while she was at it. The kettle was whistling at full boil when she entered the kitchen.

"Thought you could do with a hot beverage," he said, pouring water into the mugs. "Nothing like a cuppa after a carefree romp through Ottawa on one's clunky bike in a thunderstorm whilst in search of bacon and eggs."

"You know the way to a girl's heart." She gratefully accepted the tea, and they went into the living room and assumed their usual positions. Her voice was grumpy. "I wouldn't call my bike clunky."

"Let's say nobody would be foolish enough to steal it." He took a sip of tea. His eyes were excited, bright buttons above the rim of the cup. "Soooo, my army boy came through. He confirmed that Leavitt left his post in the Middle East early."

"That's right. Leavitt said that he was spending a few days in Montreal before surprising Josie on the weekend. We already knew that."

"But what we didn't know is that he was in Canada five days before Josie died. He also didn't reveal to you that he came home early on compassionate family leave. He told his sergeant that his fiancée was bedridden with a serious illness."

"So he lied to his sergeant in order to return to Canada early. Five days. That's three more than a couple."

Tony leaned forward. "He did indeed lie to his sergeant and to you, but we will track him down and find out why. Josie's service is this afternoon, and I'm going to be your date. I have the car since Sander's away. We should be on the road by eleven."

She held up a hand to stop him. "Whoa there, cowboy. I wasn't planning to go to the service." Funerals were her least favourite pastime. She studied his face to see any sign of distress, since she knew Sander had been in their apartment the day before. Should she say something or play along? Did she even want to know?

"If you're worried about having absolutely nothing suitable to wear, don't be. I picked you up a little something and will bring it up before I put on my suit."

"I'm not..."

"This will be a good opportunity to stake out Leavitt. Maybe we can even get him alone so you can ask pointed questions about his lying ways. I'll be right behind you, making sure he doesn't pull anything nasty."

She was intrigued by Tony's delusional belief that he could save her from an attack by a man trained to kill. She cocked her head to one side and asked, "And how do you propose to do that? He's a solid mass of muscle with experience taking down his enemies."

"The point is I'm a witness."

"Small comfort after I've had my head bashed in."

"I'll keep my video camera running. He won't get away with it. Not with me as your backup." Tony set his mug on the floor, picked up Luvy, and headed for the door. She'd grown used to his toss-off lines meant to be over the top. She still wasn't entirely sure when he was kidding but was beginning to think it was ninety-nine percent of the time.

He called from the hallway. "Have your shower, and I'll pop up with your outfit. I'll put it on your bed. Leave the door unlocked, and I'll make sure nobody enters. Luvy is the perfect guard dog. She barks at her own shadow."

"Is being left alone too much to wish for?" she asked as she stripped for the shower. She still couldn't figure out how Tony had become her sidekick when all she'd ever wanted was to get rid of him. She suspected he and Sander were having major problems, despite their overt affection of the other night. Helping her was giving him something else to focus on. His need to be busy shouldn't matter, but somehow it did. She was curious to know more about him. To scratch beneath the persona that he so carefully cultivated.

The black dress that Tony left for her was surprising in its simplicity. The cut was elegant, scooped neck and long sleeves, cinched at the waist and draping silkily to right above her knees. It was a perfect fit. He'd also left a pair of low-heeled black shoes and a silver necklace with a dove pendant and pearl drop earrings. She put everything on to show him with no intention of wearing the outfit to the service. Even without knowing the cost, she knew the ensemble was way outside her budget.

Tony was waiting in her living room. They both whistled at the sight of each other. He was wearing a black suit with a lavender shirt open at the neck and his hair pulled back into a ponytail. She'd forgotten how handsome he was under his crazy dyed hair and outlandish clothes — well, outlandish by her standards but probably on trend with everyone else. He had the young Brad Pitt vibe going on today.

"You look … astounding," he said. He made a motion with his finger, and she spun around. "Good lord, girl. You've been hiding your light under a bushel of ill-fitting clothes."

"The dress is lovely, Tony, but too rich for my blood. I can't possibly wear this."

"You can and you shall. Everything is from a second-hand store and my treat. I'll be offended if you turn down my gift horse."

"Tony, I can't possibly—"

"Let's get going, or we'll miss the show." He tossed her a grey wool coat that he'd been holding behind his back and turned to leave. He stopped after a few steps and spun around to look her up and down one last time. "I have exquisite taste, if I say so myself."

She stared at his retreating back for a moment before putting on the coat, which also fit perfectly, and followed him down the stairs. If dressing her gave the man so much pleasure, who was she to steal his joy? The free drive to Almonte was also difficult to pass up. Sometimes the best line of resistance was to hold your tongue and swallow what was given to you. It wouldn't kill her this once.

THEY WERE the last ones to enter the chapel at the funeral home. All the pews were filled, and they were forced to stand, squeezed in with thirty other mourners at the back. It appeared that half the town was here, both elderly folks and those Josie's age. They got a few curious looks, likely because everyone in town knew each other and they were strangers, but the service began and all eyes became fixed on the front of the chapel.

Ella preferred to do her grieving alone. She wasn't a fan of organized religion or the dogma meant to keep people bound in senseless rituals. Tony, on the other hand, seemed energized by the crowd and listened raptly to the service, bowing his head and closing his eyes to pray, swaying and singing along to the hymns, even if he was a word behind. Ella would have liked to distance herself from him, but they were packed in too tightly.

She searched the backs of seated people's heads and glimpsed Rory Leavitt's buzz cut whenever those behind him shifted position. He was sitting with his mother Maureen in the front pews reserved for family. Josie's mom Cheryl was in the pew across the aisle. Ella would have thought that all of them would be seated together.

She tuned out most of what was said except when a girlfriend of Josie's got up to speak about her life. The girlfriend who'd cancelled her interview. The takeaway was that Josie had liked to party and have fun, but she had settled down after university. She'd loved teaching and had been looking forward to building a family with Rory. They were soul mates, and Josie had considered herself the luckiest woman in the world. She had been the truest, sweetest friend anybody could ever have. Ella wondered how much of this sugary outpouring was true. Would this girl have given a more honest portrait of Josie in the cancelled interview?

One last hymn and prayer and the minister invited everyone for tea and sandwiches in the Serenity Lounge before raising his hands for the final blessing. Tony whispered into her ear, "I hope they have those yummy cream cheese pinwheels with a cherry in the centre."

"You're a man of refined pleasures, Tony."

"I know what I like."

They waited for the family to pass by and joined the throng walking to the reception. Once they entered the lounge, the sombre quiet of the chapel disappeared as people greeted each other and the murmur of voices rose and fell. Tony headed directly for the tea urn and poured them each a cup. He left her a second time to fill a plate with sandwiches and squares and motioned Ella over to a table so he could set his teacup down while he ate.

"Sadly, no pinwheels if you're searching for one, but help yourself," he said, biting into an egg salad sandwich triangle. "So what's the plan?"

"What, you don't have one ready to go?"

"I'm the helper and you're the main event. The Sonny to your Cher, remember?"

She was about to respond when Clare Daniels

appeared next to Tony. "That was a lovely service, wasn't it?" she asked.

"So lovely," agreed Tony.

"Josie had a lot of friends," Ella said to stop him talking. She gave him a look, and he picked up his tea, excused himself, and wandered away. He was more perceptive than she'd imagined. She looked at Clare. "Have you heard anything more about her assault and death?"

"The police have been all through her apartment and our building and interviewed each of us a couple of times. They don't seem to understand how none of us saw or heard anything."

"You didn't hear anything?"

"Well, nothing that helped. I came home late from working a shift the night she was assaulted. I heard noise from her apartment and thought she had company. To be honest, I believed her fiancé was home early and they were making up for lost time. If I'd known … well, the guilt is going to be with me for a long time. I was also working the morning she died."

"And the others in your building didn't hear anything?"

"Not that I'm aware."

"Did you see Rory Leavitt before the murder?"

Clare met her eyes. Looked away. "Maybe. I thought so at the time."

"But you aren't so sure now?"

"Two nights before Josie's assault, I saw her get out of a car with a man in the driver's seat. She was laughing when she stepped out, and I heard her say, 'Thanks for the date, darling.' Of course, I thought it was Rory, but when I spoke with him he said that he hadn't seen her since he returned from his tour of duty. He was going to surprise her on the weekend."

"The guy in car, you didn't see his face … or perhaps a buzz cut?"

"No. I was walking on the sidewalk on the passenger side. Josie stopped laughing when she saw me, but she turned right back to talk to whoever was in the car, and I kept going into our building." Clare was quiet for a moment. "I listened to your podcast with my interview, by the way. It was good."

"Thanks." Ella leaned closer. "Off the record, Clare. Did Josie ever say anything negative about Rory? Even as a joke?"

The evasive look was back on her face. "I'm not a gossip, Ella. I hope you know that."

"I do, but this isn't gossiping. It's trying to figure out what happened to her."

"I know, but still anything I tell you wouldn't feel right."

Ella followed the track of Clare's eyes, searching the room until they focused on Rory. He was standing near the door with his mother, and they appeared to be quietly arguing. Tony hovered nearby. It was time to wrap up her chat with Clare and get over there. "It was nice to see you again, Clare. I hope next time it's under better circumstances."

"You can get your old apartment back if you're interested. It'd be good to have you living in the building again."

Good and creepy. "I'm settled in where I am, but thanks for thinking of me." Ella backed away, but Clare stepped forward and reached out an arm to hug her. After a long moment, they broke apart.

"Don't be a stranger," Clare said.

"I'll be in touch." Ella smiled and turned to walk over to Tony only to find him, Rory and Maureen gone. She searched the crowd near the door and couldn't see any sign of them. She wove her way through the small groups of people standing about chatting and entered the foyer. Tony and company were nowhere to be seen. She hurried toward the main entrance and stepped outside into the bracing air. She scanned the lawn and started walking toward the parking lot. When she rounded the corner of the building, Tony was sauntering toward her, a cat who swallowed the canary grin on his face. He reached her and took hold of her arm.

"Ready to leave?" he asked.

She pulled back and surveyed the parked cars, looking for Rory. "Where are Rory and his mother? Did you dispose of them behind the garbage bin?"

"So the lady has a sense of humour. Who knew?"

"Tell me what happened."

He let go of her arm. "Rory and Maureen were arguing because she wanted him to stay and circulate, and he wanted to get the hell out of here. He said that everyone talked about Josie as if she was a saint, and it was all bullshit. I followed them outside, where Rory got into his truck and squealed out of the parking lot, leaving his mother standing by her lonesome. I asked if everything was okay, catching her at a weak moment. She said that Rory was upset because Josie had broken up with him in a letter while he was overseas, and that was the reason he came back early."

"So Josie got cold feet. I'm not surprised based on what others said about her being an outgoing, party kind of girl."

"Do you want to go corner him and get a confession?"

"Tempting as that might be, I think we'd best leave the police to handle his interrogation. Let's go home, and I'll record my podcast. You didn't manage to get any of that on tape?" She was half-joking and surprised when he patted the phone in his pocket.

"Every juicy word."

They started walking. "You're good at this, you know that, Tony?"

"I've been reading people my entire life. It's the only way a gay boy like me makes it through alive." It was a sobering statement even though delivered lightly.

She linked her arm through his. "Well, however we both got here, I'm glad that we did." And oddly enough, she found herself meaning it. He looked at the ground and nodded. She cleared her throat. "Let's go home, partner, and figure out our next move."

CHAPTER 23

Her podcast went live at seven o'clock. She was taking a chance putting out information that the police may or may not have ferreted out about Rory Leavitt and the reason for his early return to Canada. She rationalized that the cops could have uncovered the information as easily as she had. Bottom line, she was a reporter, and reporters wrote scoops, consequences be damned. The public's right to know the truth trumped all else.

She sat back in her chair and waited. It wasn't long before likes and comments started pinging. Twenty-four positive and one negative that gave her pause.

You always twist the truth. Someday you'll pay, bitch.

More than negative. Threatening. Repulsed, she deleted the message, not wanting its nastiness to be viewed by others on the podcast page. Trolls were the cockroaches of the Internet, hiding behind anonymous accounts and filling social media with their venom. They weren't worth her time.

Supper. She was running short of food again, but hunger had her searching the fridge until she pulled out a small slab of cheese and a yoghurt. The bag of bread on the counter had begun to grow mould, so she tossed it into the garbage bin before gobbling down the cheese and yoghurt. She forced herself to ignore her body's need for more sustenance. She reminded herself that she'd survived on less for longer periods of time.

It was too late to go to the hospital, so she called instead. The nurse on Danny's floor reported that he was still unconscious. Resting comfortably. She'd only begun her night shift and promised to call if there was any change. Ella thanked her and stood holding the phone with the dial tone buzzing in her ear, reluctant to let go of the line to Danny. They hadn't uttered the word coma, but she'd done some research and knew he was likely in one. He shouldn't be unconscious this long after surgery unless something had gone wrong. She had to trust that Dr. Fournier and his team were doing all they could to bring him out of it and not think the worst. There was nothing she could do except keep busy.

She spotted her handbag on the couch and set the phone down. It took a moment for her to find the scrap of paper with Felix's licence plate number. Holding it in her hand, she hesitated. Should she pursue this woman's identity or let her keep her anonymity as she so obviously wanted? She mulled over the options for all of fifteen seconds before reaching the only decision ever really on the table. She couldn't stray from her life's creed: always learn as much as she could about everyone affecting her life, whether friend or foe. Do not leave anything to chance.

She completed a basic Google search but as expected found nothing. This was the point when she'd ask O'Brien to track down the plate. She sat motionless for a few minutes, running the last conversations with him through her head. He'd seemed off his game, his skin paler than normal. She began scrolling through her phone contacts until she found the name of the woman in the licence bureau. Brooke Wong used to track down the odd plate for her when she wrote for the paper. Rather than call, she sent a text with her phone number, asking Brooke to contact her when she had a chance. She was careful not to write anything that could come back to bite either of them.

It was going on eight o'clock and too early to go to bed. Muffled music filtered through the floor from Tony's apartment. She thought about going down to see him but couldn't muster the effort. She wasn't up to talking to anybody anyway. She opened her last bottle of cheap plonk and poured a glass that she set on her desk while she clicked a song on YouTube from Joni Mitchell's *Blue* album. *I wish I had a river.* She raised her glass toward the shaft of moonlight coming through the window. "Here's to you, my old friend," she said. "May you travel safely to your final home." She drank and thought about Paul O'Brien, who'd been one of the few constants in her life. Only he, Danny, and Finn had remained close from her early days. If Danny didn't make it … she couldn't finish the thought. The pressure on her chest made breathing hurt and tears gather in her eyes. She finished her wine in a couple of gulps and poured another full glass. She took the drink to bed and drank in the darkness until the glass was empty and the day floated away.

THE RINGING of the phone wakened her. It took a few seconds to orient herself in the darkened room. When she finally realized where the sound was coming from, she leapt out of bed and ran into the living room, where she'd left her cell on the desk. Why couldn't she remember to bring the phone into the bedroom when she went to bed? By the time she clicked on the receive button, the caller had hung up without leaving a message. She checked call display but didn't recognize the number and decided to disregard the call. Most were from telemarketers anyway, since she rarely gave out her number.

The sun was barely over the trees, long, shadowy fingers of light giving a dappled, whitish glow to the room, but she was now wide awake and sleep was over. The hunger was back, however, but it was too early to get groceries. She put the kettle on before heading to the shower and drank a cup of instant without milk after getting dressed in yesterday's jeans and a fresh black turtleneck under a white hoodie. She pulled on her boots and a windbreaker and left the apartment by eight o'clock.

She stepped as silently as possible down the stairs, past Tony and Sander's apartment, relieved when their door stayed closed. On the ground floor, she hauled out her bike and was opening the front door when she looked toward the street. "Not again," she muttered under her breath. She rolled the bike back under the stairs and went outside, walking directly to Hunter's car parked next to the curb. She bent down to see inside the passenger window. He was speaking on his cell phone, staring at something across the street, and jumped when she rapped on the window. He said something into the phone before putting it into his pocket and getting out of the car.

"I was just calling you."

She felt in her pockets. Checked her knapsack. "Damn, I left my phone upstairs. Why were you trying to reach me?"

"I listened to your podcast. Do you have time for breakfast?"

"I was on my way to see Danny."

"I can drop you off afterwards."

Her stomach growled. "I'll eat with you, but I want to come back here so I can get my bike."

"No problem."

She got into his car. It smelled of pine air freshener and strong coffee and was spotlessly clean. Hunter drove with relaxed ease, the fingertips of his right hand on the steering wheel, his eyes scanning the road and the side streets as they passed. "Any preference?" he asked.

She looked at his profile. "Go to Bronson and turn right. There's a greasy spoon at the corner of Gladstone that I like to frequent."

He nodded. A smile curved up the right side of his mouth. "I know of it." He glanced at her. "I hear your brother's holding his own."

"So I'm told."

They drove the rest of the way in silence. The rain from the day before had ended, but the cloud cover still hovered low and thick. The trade-off for the gloom was a warmer day, so she guessed that was something. Still, she was having difficulty fighting the black mood that threatened to drag her under. This wasn't her favourite time of year by any stretch, but this year the season was taking despair to a whole new level.

Daisy was serving another table when they entered, but she reached them with a pot of coffee as soon as they were seated. She looked from Hunter to Ella and gave her a wink as she filled her mug. *Does she think I'm here on a date?* Ella shook her head to signal that Daisy had misinterpreted the situation.

"Usual?" Daisy asked without missing a beat.

"Usual for me."

Hunter ordered pancakes and bacon and waited for

Daisy to move out of earshot. "What proof do you have that Josie broke up with Rory Leavitt before he left the Middle East?" he asked. He was staring at her, and she forced herself to concentrate.

"His mother told my assistant at Josie's funeral service yesterday. I have it on tape if you need to hear the words with your own ears."

"Thanks, I'd appreciate that."

"I'll send a copy to your email address."

"I need to ask: do you have any proof that he killed her?"

"I'm not ruling out the possibility, but no, I don't have any proof. I'm surprised you and your colleagues weren't at the service."

"Sergeant said it wasn't necessary." He let the statement hang in the air for a moment like the glaring oversight it was. He rested against the back of the booth and seemed to be thinking something over. "Sometimes I forget you were a crime reporter." He rephrased when he looked at her face. "*Are* a crime reporter. I'm guessing you still abide by the protection of your sources."

She nodded.

He studied her as he drank his coffee. He set down the mug and rubbed a hand across his chin before resting his elbows on the table and leaning in. "I know O'Brien was feeding you information."

"How—"

"He told me. He also filled me in on Danny's … about the trial."

"I didn't realize you two were that close."

"He was getting ready to retire. He wanted someone he could trust on the force looking out for you and your brother."

"Do you know about Felix too?"

"Who?"

"I guess that's my answer." She slumped back in her seat. She'd have liked to punch O'Brien and hug him at the same time. God, she missed him. "O'Brien was a good man," she said.

"That's why I'm going to try to fill his shoes, starting with a nudge today in a new direction. Plus I'm beginning to see that you're as resourceful as O'Brien said you were."

"I'm listening."

"Like you, we'd uncovered that Leavitt was back in Canada a few days longer than he first indicated. The news that Josie broke it off with him is new, however. We found some of her emails arranging dates with other men, which appears to support her change of heart about tying the knot."

"That could be a motive for Leavitt to kill her if he knew," Ella said. "There was a level of torture to her assault." She was happy when he seemed not to realize she knew more about the autopsy than she should have.

"I can't give details, but it's an angle we're pursuing. The thing is…" His voice trailed away. They were silent as Daisy set their plates on the table. She returned to refill their coffee before leaving to serve a couple of new customers sitting at the counter.

"I love their pancakes," Hunter said, pouring maple syrup over the stack.

Ella picked up her fork. "Do you eat here often?"

"A couple of times with O'Brien. We worked together for just a few months, but it was enough time to know we liked and trusted one another."

"This is where we always met up."

They exchanged glances before lowering their heads and busying themselves eating. She was startled by the stark grief on his face and wondered if hers was a mirror of his.

"I'm sorry I haven't more to report on Danny's attacker," Hunter said. "Random assaults are difficult when there are no witnesses."

"I keep hoping he'll be awake when I go to visit or phone to check on him."

Hunter waited until she met his eyes. "I think what you did … standing up in court for your brother … took a lot of courage."

"Maybe. My parents haven't spoken to me or Danny since."

"See, that's what I don't understand. How could your parents take the side of your pedophile neighbour over the two of you?"

"It should have been simple, but there were a lot of dynamics in play. My father knew Gordon Jamieson since they were kids. They were in the same unit in the navy and did tours of duty together. Hell, they even married sisters and bought houses next to each other in Edmonton. We're all related. I spent my childhood hanging out with his three kids — my cousins."

"Making what happened even more heinous."

"If you choose to believe it happened. Dad and Mom said Gordon would never harm a child, let alone his nephew. He's a God-fearing Baptist, and pedophiles would never belong to their congregation. My father's words, I kid you not."

"The court documents said you walked in on Gordon with Danny."

This wasn't a memory she dredged up if she could help it, but for some reason it felt important for Hunter to believe her. "Gordon was the assistant coach for Danny and his own son Lance on the local hockey team. He'd drive them to practice and games, including tournaments in other towns. Dad worked shift in the oil patch and was often away. Dad believed Gordon was stepping in when he couldn't, but that's when Gordon started grooming Danny. With Dad away, it was open season. When I walked in on the two of them, the abuse had been going on for over a year … and yes, I know what I saw. Danny was bent over their dining room table with his pants around his ankles and Gordon behind him with his pants down." The memory made her shudder even after all these years. She set down her fork and clasped her hands together under the table.

"It's still hard to fathom why your parents took Gordon's side."

She worked to keep her voice steady. "The judge believed us and found Gordon guilty. He got four years, was out in two, followed by parole. His name's on the sex registry. My parents and Aunt Ruth — she's Gordon's wife and Mom's sister — were convinced by Gordon that Danny and I made it all up to get attention. They said Danny wasn't much of a hockey player and was jealous of Lance and all the praise showered on him because he was a natural athlete. They believed I wanted to spite my two cousins, Marianne and Sally, because they were much prettier and more accomplished than I was." She gave a sideways smile. "They both went to university and married into money, so maybe my parents were right about them going places while I proved to be a failure in just about everything."

"I wouldn't say that. Did Lance go on to become a professional hockey player?"

"No, he dropped out after juniors, although I heard he's coaching now. He has a wife, two kids, and a good teaching job. He still lives in Edmonton, last time anyone updated me."

"Did Gordon molest any other boys?"

"None that came forward, which didn't help our case. My brother Danny was always a kid who wanted to please people. He was sweet and polite. It took a lot for him to testify at the trial. All of my cousins stood up for their dad. They haven't spoken to me or Danny since we brought charges. It was sad how they turned on us, since our two families and my friend Finn were always hanging out. Finn's the only one who believed us. You can't pick your family, I guess."

"I'm sorry to make you bring this up. Can't be a memory you like thinking about."

"Don't apologize. Danny and I live with the effects of what happened every day. The only good news this week is that Gordon's in the final stages of cancer. I'll break open the champagne when that monster's gone from this earth for good."

CHAPTER 24

Ella only remembered that she should have told Hunter about the attempted break-in at her apartment after he'd dropped her off and driven away. Reporting it seemed pointless anyway, since two days had passed, and the trail, if there even was one, had gone ice-cold. Still, she didn't look forward to telling Tony that she'd again neglected to raise the attempted break-in with the police.

By the time she biked through the Experimental Farm to the Civic Hospital, she was in a better headspace, ready to sit with Danny for a few hours and read to him from the poetry book she'd tucked into her knapsack. He loved poetry as much as he loved singing and playing his guitar. She'd found a dog-eared book in his belongings and hoped that reading some of his favourite poems aloud might be a way to bring him back to her.

The nurse was making adjustments to Danny's IV when Ella stepped into the room. She was the one named Sophia who'd worked the previous day shift. Ella placed her in her fifties, plump, with crinkly eyes and a shy smile. The bed next to Danny's was empty, giving them a bit of privacy. Sophia glanced at Ella and then looked meaningfully toward the corner space at the foot of the bed. Ella turned her head and stared as Sophia slipped past her and out the door. Ella blinked.

"Mom?"

"I meant to be gone when you got here. I'm sorry if I upset you."

"Don't be sorry. I didn't think you'd come."

Her mother was smaller than she remembered, her face more deeply lined and looser at the jaw line. Her hair used to be blonde like Ella's but was now a soft grey. Her eyes, however, were still the same sharp dark blue. "You've cut your hair," she said.

Ella self-consciously touched the nape of her neck. "I wanted a change. Does Dad know you're here, Mom?"

"As far as he's concerned, I'm visiting your cousin Marianne in Peterborough. She moved there with her husband and three kids when he got a job in a law firm. She's about to give birth to her fourth, and I've come to help out. I'll be spending tonight and the next week at least at their place, so I'm not exactly lying to your father. I needed to see Danny."

"He's been unconscious since he came out of surgery."

"I know. I've called a few times and spoke to the nurse just now. She's very nice. And how are you, Ella?" Her voice was mildly defiant, as if she was preparing for an attack, but her eyes were uncertain.

A glimpse at the insecure side of her mother left Ella off-kilter. Her mother was a devoutly religious woman who always saw the world in black and white. Right and wrong. No room for grey. She could only imagine the soul-searching it took for her to come here against her husband's knowledge. Yet how could Ella forgive her mother for shunning them, along with their father and the rest of the family, these past ten years? For believing she and Danny were capable of making up their uncle's abuse? "I'm getting by," she said.

A smile flitted across her mother's face. "I followed your column. You're a fine writer. Gifted. I'm not sure what side of the family you got that from."

There was so much she wanted to say. Questions she needed to ask, but all she could do was look down at Danny and bite her bottom lip. Maybe the fact her mother was here said all she needed to know for now. She heard the rustle of clothing and sensed her mother standing next to her. She smelled of rosewater, and Ella squeezed her eyes shut, trying to stop the flood of memories.

"I've forgiven you — both you and Danny for bringing charges against your uncle and … leaving like you did."

Ella took a moment to absorb what she'd said before an anger pulsated through her that was truly frightening. She clasped onto her elbows and forced herself to count to ten, then opened her eyes and said, "*We* did nothing to be forgiven for. *We* told the truth."

Her mother was silent for a moment. She spoke quietly. "I understand if you're angry, but remember, there are always two sides."

"There aren't two sides to abuse, Mom. We didn't make anything up. I can't understand how you could take his word over ours."

"Well." She moved away from Ella, back toward the foot of the bed. Ella kept her eyes on Danny's still face and breathed deeply in and out. In and out.

"I wanted to see you so many times, but your father … he's stubborn."

It was the closest her mother had ever come to criticizing him, to admitting they weren't in sync. "It's okay, Mom. I know."

"I don't want you thinking that I agreed with everything that went on." She picked up her purse from the floor. "I have to go. When Danny wakes up, tell him I'm praying for him, will you do that, Ella?"

"Of course."

"You take care of yourself. I pray for you too."

Ella hesitated. She should say something, but by the time the words formed in her head, her mother was gone. She lowered herself onto the chair next to Danny and tried to still the shaking in her hands. For so many years, she'd dreamed about a reunion, and now that her mother had come, her anger had ruined everything. She reached over, took Danny's limp hand, and rested her forehead on his arm. She could run after her mother and say she was sorry, but she stayed seated. The years that her mother had refused to acknowledge her and Danny kept her rooted in place. Her mother could have believed Danny back when the abuse happened. She could have taken his side. A mother should always protect her children.

"I'm sorry, Danny," she whispered. "At least she came. Maybe when you wake up, we can visit her and go from there."

Please wake up, Danny. Please come back and we can go on together like we always have.

Please don't leave me here all alone.

SHE STAYED through lunch hour and read the entire book of poems aloud without any sign of movement from Danny. A different doctor checked him on her rounds but had nothing encouraging to tell her.

"Sometimes they wake up from comas on their own and other times they slip away," she said.

Ella appreciated her honesty, even though it wasn't what she wanted to hear. It was unsettling for the doctor to say the word *coma* for the first time. When Ella was in this room with Danny, finding out who killed Josie Wheatly or who put him in the hospital became unimportant. She was thankful she'd eaten breakfast so she didn't have to leave to buy food. Sophia brought her a cup of tea and biscuits at two o'clock. She sipped the tea and talked to Danny about the things they'd do when he got out of there. Then she dozed in the chair for a bit and woke when the nurse returned to check on him.

"He knows you're here," she said. "I firmly believe that."

"I'll stay a little longer."

She held Danny's hand and sat in the chair with her head resting on the bed. She was so tired that she couldn't keep her eyes open. The exhaustion after too many nights without a decent sleep had caught up to her. She wasn't sure how long she slept, but she awoke to Sophia rubbing her back. Dr. Fournier and another nurse were in the room, and her eyes darted from them to Danny.

"I'm so sorry," Dr. Fournier said. "Danny's heart stopped at 4:12. He's slipped away."

"No." She shook her head, not able to let this truth sink in. How had she slept through all the noise and commotion? Sophia was murmuring comforting words as she staggered to her feet. The tubes had been removed from Danny's arm, the heart machine turned off. His face was waxen and so still. He looked like he was that young boy again, without a care in the world. Peaceful. She raised a fist to her mouth.

"Would you like some time alone?" Sophia asked.

Ella nodded.

"Is there anyone we can call to come be with you?"

She thought of Finn but dismissed the idea. He had enough on his plate without her troubles. Her mother would be in Peterborough, awaiting Marianne's baby. "No, I'll be okay. Could I … sit with him for a while?"

"Of course. Take as long as you need."

They fussed for a bit before leaving her alone with Danny. The curtain surrounded his bed, giving a semblance of privacy, although she could hear a patient cough and wheeze in his bed at the other end of the room.

She felt Danny's presence. It was as if he were sitting next to her, trying to comfort her before he left for good. She closed her eyes and gave in to the warmth of his presence. She put off believing that he was gone and never coming back.

She stayed with Danny for an hour, enough time to tell him how much she loved him and to say goodbye. Sophia was waiting when she finally stepped into the hallway and told her where they'd be taking his body after Ella said that she didn't have a preference. A funeral director would be in contact to discuss arrangements. "Should I call your mother?" she asked.

"I'd appreciate if you would. Thank you for all you've done." She stumbled onto the elevator. The weight of Danny's death was disorienting. She got off on the wrong floor and wandered to the end of the hall before realizing. Back in the elevator, she made it to the ground floor and half-sprinted toward the main entrance, needing to feel fresh air on her face. She stopped and turned when somebody called her name.

She'd rushed right past Finn, who was standing alone off to the side, next to a pillar. Before she could say anything, he'd crossed the space between them and pulled her against his chest. "I'm so sorry," he said into her ear. "I'm so, so sorry."

She bobbed her head up and down, and he released her but kept an arm firmly around her waist. They walked without speaking toward the main doors. When she trusted herself to talk without breaking down, she asked, "How did you know?"

"The guy who lives below you."

"Tony?"

"Yeah, he called the hospital to check on Danny, and the nurse told him. I've come to take you home."

"My bike—"

"We'll put it in the back of my truck."

It was strange to think of someone she barely knew looking out for her. This hadn't been the norm in her life, and she wasn't certain how to process Tony. "Can we go to the gym?" she asked. "I need to take a round out of a punching bag, or I'm going to go crazy."

"Whatever you need, Ella."

They arrived at the gym soon after seven o'clock. The inside lights were off, and the parking lot was deserted. "You're closed already?" she asked.

"Yeah. Maisie decided to take a break, so it's only me for now."

"I thought she liked working here."

Finn's jaw tightened. "She did. The thing is she thinks we..."

"I don't need to hear it, Finn. Honestly."

"Yeah, you're right. Maisie's embarrassed enough."

They entered by the side door, and Finn punched in the alarm code. They both went to change and met up in the gym.

"Warm ups first," he said and led her to the mats. They stretched and jumped rope for five minutes before going over to the punching bag. Finn held on while she pummelled it.

The need to scream and rage lessened with each blow. After she was all but spent, they put on protective gear, laced up gloves, and went into the boxing ring for a couple of rounds.

Finn was an efficient, methodical boxer with a deadly right hook. He'd taught her all the tricks of the trade, and while she'd never bested him, she usually held her own. Grief and weariness had slowed her reflexes, but Finn didn't make her pay as he usually would have. By the middle of the second round, she should have been flat-out on the mat, but he continued to dance around her and backed off instead of landing a solid punch when she left an opening. She wanted to chastise him for going easy, but that would have taken energy, and it was all she could do to stay on her feet, fending off his reach and trying to get in punches of her own.

After she landed a half-hearted jab, Finn stepped away and dropped his gloves. "Enough. How about we go clean up and get a beer around the corner?"

"I'm not sure I'd be good company tonight. I'm sorry, Finn."

"Then I'll drive you back to your place. I won't take no."

She usually showered at home but was so sweaty and exhausted that she stripped and stepped into one of the shower stalls. She stood under the stream of hot water, eyes closed and face upturned. The water washed away the tears that slid down her face. She remained this way for five minutes until her grief eased. Then she washed her hair and soaped away the layer of sweat.

Finn was in his office, poring over a ledger, when she finally joined him. He looked up and studied her for a moment. His eyes were sad, but he smiled when her eyes met his. "All set?"

"I am." She attempted a grin. "Thanks for being here, Finn. It means a lot."

Instead of saying anything, he rounded the desk to wrap her in a hug. "Anytime, my friend. Anytime. Danny was a light who's left us much too soon. Know that I'll always be here for you."

CHAPTER 25

Finn asked if she'd like him to come upstairs for a while, but she told him to go home to Adele, that she'd be fine. The truth was she needed to be alone. She watched his taillights disappear around the corner before unlocking the front door and climbing the stairs. Tony's door remained closed as she trudged past.

Inside her apartment, she stood in the centre of the living room, torn between wanting to rip the place apart and collapsing onto the floor. A third choice won out, one that would keep her from thinking about Danny. She sat at her desk and turned on the computer. Her last podcast was doing well, with over three thousand views. Five hundred and ten new subscribers. The new comments suggested Rory Leavitt should be investigated and complimented her reporting. Whoever left the threatening comment earlier hadn't weighed in again.

She opened her phone and clicked on her texts. Three from Sherry Carpenter asking her to call. She wanted to make a return trip with Ella to Almonte to question Leavitt. Ella hit delete three times. Liam Hunter had left two messages, one in the morning and the second an hour ago. The first said he needed to speak with her. The second said he'd heard about Danny and hoped she was doing okay. He'd try to connect soon.

I'm not doing okay. As long as whoever did this to Danny is out there, I'll never be doing okay.

She heard a soft knock at the door to her apartment. She didn't want to see Tony but couldn't ignore him either. She put the chain on before opening to look into the hallway. Nobody was standing on the landing, so she unchained the door and opened it wider. At her feet was a twenty-sixer of Scotch, no note. She bent, picked up the bottle, went back inside her apartment, and locked the door. Half a bottle later, she passed out fully dressed on the bed.

SHE WOKE LATE. The sun was beaming bright and cheery through her bedroom window, as if the horrible day before had never happened. She groaned and flung an arm over her eyes. An elf with a jackhammer was drilling inside her brain. It took a moment to fully wake up and to realize that somebody was actually pounding on her apartment door.

"Hold on!" she yelled and rolled off the side of the bed on to her feet. She grabbed the dresser to steady herself. The room righted itself after a few deep breaths. "This is going to be bad," she predicted as she wobbled on shaky legs down the hallway. She threw caution to the wind and flung the door open without checking. Tony was standing a few feet away, holding a tray covered by a cloth in one hand and a carafe of coffee in the other. Luvy scampered past into her apartment as she stood staring. Tony motioned her to step aside and followed the dog into her living room, the smell of bacon and coffee lingering behind him.

Her stomach roiled. "I'm not sure this is a good food day," she said.

"It'll help with what ails you." He moved the Scotch bottle and set the plate on her desk before disappearing into the kitchen. He rummaged around in the cupboards and returned with two mugs. He'd brought a small pitcher of cream and a sugar bowl from his apartment and added generous amounts to both their coffees. He handed over a mug and took his seat on the couch.

"Have a piece of bacon," he said. "The grease will soak up some of the alcohol from last night."

"Worth a try." She selected a crispy one and chewed while watching him. "Why are you being so good to me?"

He tossed back his hair. "Because."

"That's it? Because?"

"Sure. Because covers it." He sighed. "I'm sorry about Danny. I never met him, but I liked his vibe."

"He was a drug addict playing his guitar for spare change and living on the street."

"Exactly. What's not to admire? He was doing his own thing."

"Well, doing his own thing got him murdered."

"Sadly, life has no guarantees."

She sipped from the mug and finished eating the strip of bacon. "Thanks for the bottle you left outside my door last evening, even if I don't look thankful this morning. My stomach isn't used to single malt, I guess."

"Think how much worse you'd feel if you'd consumed your usual gut-rot." He grinned and paused. "So, I have a couple of clients at noon in the salon and then am all yours for the rest of the day. What are our plans?"

Now was the time for her to cut off this odd relationship, even if he'd grown on her. "I like to work alone."

"And you are. But you need a wingman. Someone to take care of those pesky details while you're out getting stories."

"What's in it for you, Tony? Seriously. I can't pay."

"I don't expect money." He shrugged. "I'm bored, and helping you makes me feel good. It's as simple as that."

Time passed while they stared at each other. A wave of nausea torqued upward from her stomach. "All right," she said, breaking eye contact. God, she felt rough. Part of her welcomed the pain that kept her from thinking. "I might need to lie down for a bit. Check in with me after you get home from work."

He beamed and stood up, holding Luvy under his arm. "Grand. I left some painkillers in the kitchen. We'll see you anon."

She raised a hand and waved weakly. "Anon."

SHE AWOKE from her nap to the sound of a phone ringing. The caller hung up before she got out of bed, but they tried again a few seconds later. This time when she stood, her head wasn't spinning and her stomach had settled into a low-grade queasy. She dashed across the floor and picked up her phone, but again, she was too late. Liam Hunter's name and number came up on the call list, and she tapped on his number. He answered on the first ring.

"Where are you?" he asked.

"In my apartment. Where are you?"

"Parked on a side street around the corner from your place. Do you have time to meet?"

"I'll come downstairs to let you in."

"Be there in a few secs."

She raced into the bathroom, splashed water on her face, and brushed her teeth. Her skin was pale in the mirror, and her hair was spiked up like a porcupine getting set to shoot off its quills. No question she was feeling better than she looked. A hangover would do that to a girl.

Hunter stood with his back to the door when she pushed it open. He was wearing a black leather jacket and jeans over black boots. He spun around and looked at her through dark sunglasses. "Sorry about your brother. His death is a tragedy that never should have happened."

"Thanks." She turned and crossed the foyer to the stairs. He shut the door and followed several steps behind. She left her apartment door open for him and went into the living room. The plate of food Tony had brought still sat on the desk, the eggs rubbery and the toast stone-cold. She picked up a piece of bacon as Hunter stepped into the room. He looked around before taking Tony's usual place on the couch. He sat forward with his elbows resting on his knees. "I've been trying to reach you all day."

"What time is it?"

"Ten after one."

"I slept in."

Hunter nodded but didn't comment. He glanced at the plate of congealing eggs and the half-empty bottle of Scotch before looking down at his hands. "I wouldn't bother you if this wasn't urgent. Some disturbing information has come to light that affects you."

"I'm listening."

"As you know, I requested an autopsy on Paul O'Brien's body."

"So, was it a heart attack or diabetes?"

"Neither, as it turns out. Forensics came back late last evening. He was struck from behind. The bruising on the back of his head wasn't consistent with a simple fall. There's also slight bruising from a needle mark in the back of his neck. We believe he was injected with a drug that stopped his heart. The tox screen isn't completed yet and will take a few more days. In any event, he was found in a parking garage next to his car, so there was certainly opportunity for someone to waylay him."

"Good God." She bent at the waist and inhaled deeply, trying to stop herself from passing out. It took a few moments for the black dots to clear from her eyes. She raised her head. "Could this have to do with of one of his cases?"

"We don't know. The coroner also found liver cancer. O'Brien likely didn't have a great deal of time left." Hunter stared at her, looking as if he was having trouble saying what was on his mind.

Knowing he was so sick should have made O'Brien's death easier, and maybe it would, given more time. Yet this didn't take away from the fact that someone had taken his last days and months in an act of immense cruelty. Realization dawned. "You think this has something to do with me. With Danny."

"Two people close to you were murdered. A woman who moved into your apartment was raped and then murdered a few days later. You're the common link."

"This seems—"

"Unbelievable. I know. We need to take the possibility seriously and figure out who could be behind this and why."

"Let me get this straight. You believe the same person who killed Josie Wheatly killed Danny and Paul O'Brien?"

"I admit it's a long shot, but I can't rule out that it's also a possibility."

"Does your boss believe this as well?"

"Not exactly." He shifted, and the expression on his face was pained. "Staff Sergeant Warner thinks I haven't nailed down enough evidence to support the theory."

"So you could be wrong?"

"I could be. The question is, are you willing to take the chance if I'm right?"

CHAPTER 26

Ella chewed her bottom lip while thinking things over. She couldn't deny that two people in her life had been murdered within a week. Combining their deaths with Josie Wheatly's attack in her recently vacated apartment and the pattern was alarming. She looked at Hunter. "Somebody tried to break into my apartment a few nights ago. They got into the house and were working on my door when Luvy — the dog that lives in the apartment below — sounded the alarm."

Hunter rubbed a hand through his hair and scowled. "Good God, Ella. Why didn't you say something before this?"

"I meant to tell O'Brien, but he never met me for breakfast, and then I found out he died and the attempted break-in slipped my mind." She glared at him when she was done. He'd put her on the defensive when she'd done nothing wrong.

"Still."

"Yeah, no need to tell me. Tony's already been on my tail about it."

"Tony?"

"One of the guys who lives in the apartment below me. He's somehow become my assistant." She added, "Our landlord Alex installed better locks and ordered cameras because of the incident. We're like a high security bunker even without Luvy, the guard dog."

"Well, that's a relief." In case she didn't get the sarcasm, he frowned again before adding, "I'm not convinced this new information will change my staff sergeant's mind about all the murders being connected." He took out a notepad and pen from his jacket pocket. "We need to make a list of anyone who might hold a serious grudge against you. We can probably narrow the names to men, since Josie Wheatly was raped, but if you're at odds with either gender, don't hesitate to name them."

"You're assuming the rapist and the killer of three people is the same person."

"I don't believe in coincidence."

"So why doesn't your boss feel the same way?"

"She's a stickler for proof."

"I'm going to have to go through my files to come up with people I ticked off during my reporter years on the crime beat. Some of them are still in prison. More than a couple are dead."

"Include those too. We can always rule them out later."

"I think the dead ones might already be ruled out."

"They could have a loved one seeking revenge."

"Well, that's the definition of a long shot."

"Or the definition of thorough."

She held up a hand to end the pissing match. "Did you find out why Leavitt lied about when he returned to Canada?"

"I gave him a call. He said that he wanted to surprise Josie and got the dates mixed up when he first spoke to us because he was so shocked by her death. It happens more often than you'd think."

"Okay, but what about her breaking up with him before he flew home? Perhaps the surprise fell flat and she rebuffed him in person. We all know that women are most at risk when they leave their partner. He's top of my list for her murder, and news flash: I never met him or anyone in his family before she died. No connection. No reason for him to kill my brother or O'Brien."

Hunter took his time answering. He seemed to be trying to see behind her eyes into the workings of her brain. "Leavitt told me that he didn't believe her letter. He figured once she saw him again, they'd be back on track. He seemed credible. Surely you don't put these three murders down to coincidence? We need to look for someone who knew you and all the victims. I believe there's a connection."

"Danny led a dangerous lifestyle that caught up with him. O'Brien likely had more enemies than I do. Josie had an upset fiancé trained to kill. Three different killers are a distinct possibility."

Hunter stood and looked down at her. "You sound like my staff sarge. I don't rule out three killers, but I'm not ruling out one either. My advice is to be careful until we know exactly what's going on. Stay away from isolated places. Keep your doors locked and don't go out at night alone."

"I'm not a fool."

His face said, *I'm not so sure*, but he nodded and waited a few beats like a comedian holding off the punch line for maximum laughs. "But your life choices have led you here." He waved a hand around her small and poorly furnished living room and gave a half-smile. "I'd say your judgment hasn't always been the soundest."

She sat staring out the window long after he'd clomped down the stairs, and the front door of the house had opened and slammed shut. She swallowed hard to keep the caustic bile from welling up from her chest into her throat. Liam Hunter was a sanctimonious, judgmental, male know-it-all, and she'd met many of his kind throughout her life. She wouldn't give him the satisfaction of finding out that she was also worried that the cases were linked. All she needed was for him to start babysitting her.

She punched her fist onto the desk before picking up the last piece of cold bacon and chewing on the tough meat as she booted up her computer. She'd search through old news articles she'd written before going through her paper files. Not the way she'd planned to spend the rest of the day, but at least she'd be busy. Hunter could waste his time looking at cold cases if he wanted. Who knew? He might even find someone from her past with a huge axe to grind. And while he was busy digging up her past, she'd have space to continue with her own searches without tripping all over him.

FELIX HAD SENT a text before lunch. Paul O'Brien's autopsy report was in an attachment with a password sent in a separate email. The email account where this originated was new and anonymous. The message was carefully worded. *I know this will be difficult to accept. Will continue digging at my end. Delete after reading.*

Ella took her time going through the report. It confirmed everything Hunter had told her earlier about O'Brien's death. The coroner, Brigette Green, had also noted the cancer throughout his liver and pancreas.

Ella deleted the report and looked out the window.

Felix didn't appear to know that Hunter had taken on O'Brien's role as her police source, and she wondered about getting them to connect. Would Hunter think this collaboration a step too far? She couldn't risk alienating him completely. Not yet. Not until she found Danny's killer, because she needed Hunter's eyes and ears, annoying as they might be.

She liked to keep track of a story by making notes. It was easier to see connections when everything was laid out on a page or two. She hadn't accumulated the facts on paper yet for any of the murders and spent the next hour typing the names of people and timelines for all of the cases. All three of the murders. Each got its own content page, but she merged them into one timeline. Her memory was good, and everything that happened over the past week was still fresh.

She was jotting the salient points from her interviews when a forgotten lead popped into her head. Tiffany St. George had said that Mr. Rivington, the staff heartthrob, spent more time with Josie than anyone else on staff. She'd meant to go back and interview him, but he'd slipped off her radar with everything else going on. It was nearly two thirty. There was time to eat something and bike over to the school before classes ended for the day. The big question was: eat what? If she allowed for November rent and payment on her loans, she had exactly one hundred and eighty dollars to get through the next couple of weeks. She needed to tighten her belt an extra notch, both metaphorically and physically. A threadbare existence was doable but exhausting. Still, she had to eat something.

Done with her filing for the day, she got on her bike and went to the closest store on Bank Street. She stuffed a loaf of bread, jar of peanut butter, cheese, eggs, pasta and sauce, toilet paper, and toothpaste into her saddlebags.

After a quick pedal home, she wolfed down a sandwich before getting back on her bike and taking her beaten path through the Experimental Farm and side streets to Broadview School.

The students were streaming out the doors onto buses or into the waiting arms of their parents as she arrived. Several swarmed around the bike rack, so she stood to one side while they unlocked their bikes and put on their helmets. Her clothes were damp with sweat, and she shivered as she waited. Within minutes, they were all gone and she locked up her bike and entered the school carrying her helmet. She signed in at the office. The receptionist directed her to Mr. Rivington's classroom at the end of a long hallway lined in kids' artwork and smelling of day-old tuna sandwiches, rotting apples, and an industry-grade cleaning product. Her footsteps echoed in the nearly empty hallway. Only a couple of kids lingered outside one of the classrooms, but a teacher stepped into the hall and shooed them home. She smiled at Ella before going back inside her room and closing the door.

Mr. Rivington looked up from his desk and saw her standing in the doorway. His eyes flicked up and down her body in the briefest of movements that she wouldn't have noticed if she hadn't been watching him so intently. *The man's a player,* she thought. She moved deeper into the room. "Mr. Rivington? Sorry to bother you, but would you have a moment to speak about Josie Wheatly?"

"May I ask who you are?"

"Ella Tate. I host a true crime podcast and have been looking into Josie's assault and death. Ms. St. George suggested I speak with you."

"She did? Well, I guess I can spare a few minutes. Grab a chair." He pointed to the desk directly in front of him, but she chose to sit on the desktop rather than wedge herself onto the seat. This way he didn't have the height advantage, although he certainly had the size competition won. Even sitting, he looked tall and fit with the physique of a boxer. His sleeves were rolled up to the elbows, showing off muscular arms and arty tattoos. Finishing off his he-man look were a square cut jaw and carefully tousled hair with golden streaks that had to come from a salon. She wondered who'd win in a battle between Mr. Rivington and Rory Leavitt. Either man could have done damage to Josie Wheatly if so inclined.

"Ms. St. George said that you were friendly with Josie."

"I'll bet she did." He picked up a pencil and began tapping it on the desk.

She was curious about his reaction and would have liked to probe the sarcasm but held off. "Can you tell me about her?" she asked instead.

"Josie was a wonderful teacher and just a … a special woman. Zany sense of humour, great with the kids, and a supportive colleague."

"You knew she was engaged to Rory Leavitt?"

"I knew."

"Did you talk about him at all?"

"He wasn't the focus of our conversations."

"Were you interested in taking her out?"

His pupils darkened. "It didn't matter if I was. She made it clear early on that she wasn't interested in dating anyone from work."

What wasn't he telling her? "Was she interested in dating men outside of work?"

"She was engaged."

"But she broke it off before Rory came home. He got the dreaded Dear John letter while he was on tour."

Rivington ran a hand through his hair. "I didn't know she followed through." He was quiet for a bit. The pencil-tapping picked up speed. "I ran into her one Sunday afternoon by chance at the Parkdale Market, and we went for coffee across the street. Not a date, and I doubt she would have even gone for coffee with me except that there we were. She was unusually talkative about her situation. She told me that she didn't see herself married. Fidelity wasn't in her DNA. She confided that she'd dated a few men through a singles site. Said there was something exciting about going on blind dates."

"From what I've heard, it's mainly losers on those sites. People posting pictures of themselves from twenty years ago, making up shit."

He smiled. "She said she was good at weeding out the undesirables. Guys in the grocery store or at the gym hit on her all the time as well."

"Did she date them too?"

"She had standards, but I think the odd time. She never named names, if that's your next question. We only talked about it that one time."

She was getting a bad feeling looking at this hulk of a teacher who was attracted to a woman who serial-dated everyone but him. Jealousy and anger might be natural reactions. She feigned a sympathy she didn't have. "Must have been difficult being so close to her and not being included on her dateable list. Many men would be upset."

He dropped the pencil and leaned back in his chair. "I'm not most men. Getting women to go out with me has never been an issue, and honestly? It was her loss. I'm also far from stupid. Somebody else killed Josie, and I hope the cops catch him and put him away for good. The only anger I feel is for the scumbag psycho who raped and killed her — and maybe some for you for thinking I'd do something that heinous to a colleague and a friend."

CHAPTER 27

The office was in mourning. Liam nodded at the other detectives in Major Crimes as he made his way to his desk. Somebody had placed a vase of red roses on O'Brien's desk. The flowers looked out of place and only made Liam sadder than he already was. He slung his jacket over the back of his chair and opened his email. The first message he read was from Greta, asking him to stop by her office when he arrived. He left the rest unopened and looked across the room. Her door was partly open, so she was likely waiting for him. He took a last look at O'Brien's empty chair and got to his feet.

"You wanted to see me, Sarge?" he asked after knocking and taking a step inside.

"Shut the door and take a seat."

She finished typing whatever it was she'd been working on while he waited. He studied her profile. Brown hair cut in a bob that fell to her jawline. Half-moon glasses perched on the end of her nose that she wore for reading. A strong jaw and long neck, partially hidden by the starched collar of her navy shirt. She bit her bottom lip while she worked. She must have felt his gaze on her because she took her time typing, stopping once to drink from her coffee mug. He was about to say something about coming back later when she lifted her hands from the keyboard and swung her chair around to face him. She dropped her glasses onto the desk.

"I've assigned Boots and Jingles to the O'Brien murder, and you'll be answering to them as well on the Wheatly and Tate cases. Be sure to keep them in the loop about what you've been up to."

Eric Bottes and Wayne Jorgenson. Boots had been O'Brien's partner at one time and must have asked to be on O'Brien's case. Hunter didn't question his demotion to second fiddle on Danny's file because she expected him to put up resistance. He'd have to work it out with Boots and figure a way around her.

"O'Brien's death intersects with Danny Tate's attack," he said.

"They knew each other, but the attacks were completely different. One of them was a knife in the stomach and the other was a blow to the head and drugging. I'm not seeing a strong connection between the two."

"I know we've been over this, but I believe someone is targeting people close to Danny's sister, Ella Tate. Up until three months ago, Ella lived in the apartment where Josie Wheatly was attacked and killed."

"So how is that a factor?"

"I haven't nailed it down yet, but I'm working on it. Ella tells me someone tried to break into her apartment a few nights ago."

"Did she report it?"

"No."

Greta took her time answering. "There's something about this Ella Tate woman that makes my Spidey sense tingle. Could she be looking for publicity for her podcast?"

"That thought never crossed my mind."

"She supported her brother's sojourns in residential rehab. He was costing her."

"She appears to have genuinely cared for him."

"You have to stay objective, Hunter. Getting rid of him helps her to stop throwing good money after bad. Not to mention she gains a story for her show and garners a lot of public sympathy." She paused and stared him in the eyes. "I'm starting to be concerned about your seeming inability to look at all the angles. This could hinder your career in the long run."

"What are you suggesting? Ella is harming those few people in her life to rid herself of a financial burden and to improve her podcast ratings? I can tell you with the utmost certainty that she didn't knife her brother."

"She could have hired somebody. People have been killed for less, and from what you've told me, she doesn't have much of an attachment to people. In some circles, this would be called a psychopath. Again, you have to keep your mind open to all possibilities, Hunter."

"Josie Wheatly's killer was definitely a male, going by the assault and the video taken at the hospital."

"Exactly. Two different perpetrators." Greta sighed. "We can debate these cases until our faces are blue, but until you get some solid evidence one way or the other, all we're doing is blowing smoke. What are your next steps with the Wheatly murder?"

"I'm expecting a forensics report with an analysis of her laptop and phone today. Hopefully there'll be a lead or two. I'd also like to reinterview her fiancé and parents. Leavitt's early return to Canada and the fact he omitted to tell me about Josie's letter breaking up with him have me curious."

"Does Leavitt have any connection to Danny Tate and Paul O'Brien, or Ella Tate, for that matter?"

"None that I'm aware."

She didn't say anything, but her expression spoke volumes. She'd never bought in to his theory that Ella was at the centre of all the assaults. She'd become skeptical of all his working theories ever since they'd gone out for a drink. He regretted that slip in judgment more with every passing day. He hadn't missed her veiled threat to his career and knew she could hold him up with one bad report.

"Well, make sure Boots is okay with your plan, since you're reporting to him."

"If there's nothing more, I'll get back at it." He waited for her to nod and stood. "I'll check in with him."

"Keep me updated. I'll be in meetings the rest of the day."

"Any news on Julie Quade?"

"She expects to be done the course by Friday and back in the office Monday. I'll count on you to bring your partner up to speed."

"I'll try to touch base with her on the weekend."

"She'll need to come in running. Good to have another set of eyes on the murder cases. A woman's perspective." She picked up her laptop and stood. "I'm off to the first meeting. I likely won't be back in my office until late this afternoon."

He shrugged off her not-so-subtle undermining of his work, because reacting would only bring her simmering aggression into the open. At least leaving her anger unspoken let him keep working without her overt interference. He returned to his desk and watched her lock her office door and disappear around the corner before he picked up the phone and called his contact in Forensics, only to be told the Wheatly report had been logged into the system an hour ago. He found the file and cursed himself for not checking before he placed the call. The meeting with Greta had him off-balance.

"Shit," he said when he finished reading the details of Josie's online dating. It made sense she hadn't used her real name on Tinder. She was a teacher and engaged to be married. Her reputation needed protecting. What didn't make sense, however, was her decision to use the name Ella T. as her alias. Maybe she found it amusing to steal the name of the woman who'd occupied the apartment before her. Hunter focused his eyes on O'Brien's empty chair. The decision to use the name of the previous tenant in her apartment could very well be what got Josie Wheatly killed.

CHAPTER 28

Tony was waiting for Ella when she started up the stairs to her apartment. Dressed in a black track-suit and silver sneakers, he had Luvy tucked under one arm and a glass of red wine in his free hand. She'd have liked to be alone, but the smell of cooking meat was wafting through his open door, making her weak at the knees.

"I'm hoping you have time for a glass of wine and some beef bourguignon."

"No Sander?"

"Still in Phoenix." Tony's eyes shifted and stared at something over her left shoulder. A blush suffused upward from his neck, making her curious. "I could use some company," he added.

"Let me go wash up, and I'll be back." Her bottled spaghetti sauce would keep for another day.

Tony had set the table with crystal stemware and fine china that sparkled in the candlelight. He'd already poured them each a brimming glass of wine and was serving up plates of food that smelled like the best thing she'd eaten in months. "Sit your pretty fanny down," he said, pointing to a chair.

"Do you eat like this every night?" she asked, sliding into place. He'd put a linen napkin beside her plate that she ignored.

"Dining should be a dance of the senses." He set a plate of beef and mushrooms in front of her that looked like an elegant stew and smelled of red wine, garlic, and thyme. She closed her eyes and inhaled. He returned from the kitchen with a plate of crusty rolls and sat across from her. "Should I say grace, or would you like to?"

She stared at him and blinked.

He laughed. "Just pulling your leg, girl. Pick up your fork and dig in."

She didn't wait to be asked twice. Tony sipped wine and barely ate anything. He refilled her plate without prompting and refilled his own glass once. She turned down his offer of thirds, pushing her chair back and patting her tummy. "God, that was good. Where have you been all my life?"

"Waiting for you to show up." He gave a quick smile and topped up her wine from a new bottle. "I believe we have business to discuss."

"We do?"

"I know this isn't a good time for you, Ella, but we need to decide on Danny's service."

"Danny wouldn't want a service." She glared across the table at him, the food starting to churn in her stomach. "My brother spent most of his life trying not to be noticed."

"He was a musician, so he was used to being in the limelight."

"He played for himself … and to make enough money for drugs. An audience was simply a means to an end."

"Regardless, your brother has many people who would love the opportunity to come together to mourn and to celebrate him."

"What, his homeless buddies? I doubt they'd show up unless I hand out free booze. I can't afford a service, Tony. Nor am I convinced one is needed. It would be the final humiliation when nobody came. Danny doesn't deserve that."

"Well, would you let me look after the burial arrangements for you?"

"I don't know why you'd want to do this. You didn't know my brother."

"But that doesn't mean I don't have compassion for him. I'm also your assistant."

A wave of pain and shame washed over her, and she closed her eyes. "Okay," she said after a pause. "I'll take out a loan if I need to pay for sandwiches and the hall or wherever. That crack about needing to serve booze to attract his friends was uncalled for." She wasn't convinced the bank would loan her more money, but she'd have to try.

"What about your parents?"

"A nurse at the hospital called them. They said thanks for letting them know, but they have no interest in claiming his body. I suspect my father's behind that decision."

"How very sad. They don't sound like people I'd want to know."

"No, they're not." She looked around the apartment. "Where is Sander, really?"

Tony started to say something but stopped. "Phoenix, of course. The company might have him stay on to work with some new clients."

"I saw him coming out of your apartment the other day. He couldn't have been in Phoenix at the same time."

If their partnership or whatever they'd become to each other was going to work, he had to tell her the truth.

Tony's shoulders dropped. He slumped back in the chair. "Phoenix was a ruse. Sander never went." He pushed aside his glass. "He met his old girlfriend, the one he lived with before me. They were engaged for a couple of years, and turns out she was pregnant when they split."

"He didn't know?"

"Apparently not. The child has drawn him back. A son, about two and a half years old."

"I'm sorry, Tony."

"He has to follow his path. I say that, but I'm selfishly wishing he'd pick me over his kid. I was stalling for time, giving him a chance to come back."

"You'd be superhuman not to feel that way. You and Sander were the real deal, from what I saw. Does his ex know about you?"

"Thank you. I believed the same. I don't think his girlfriend knew or knows now. Sander asked me to stay away from her. He's stopped answering my texts." He paused. "So what were you up to today? Make any progress on the Wheatly murder?"

She studied him for a moment and knew now was not the time to press. "I haven't had a chance to update you. Detective Liam Hunter came by to tell me that Paul O'Brien's death was suspicious. O'Brien was my friend on the force and the cop I was supposed to meet for breakfast. They believe now that he was murdered."

Tony was in the process of taking a drink and spat the wine back into the glass. He wiped the back of his hand across his mouth. "Oh, my God! That's two people close to you, Ella. Someone is totally targeting you. What is this Detective Hunter doing to keep you safe?"

"I don't need his protection. We have Luvy, remember?"

"This is not the time to joke. Your life's in danger, or are you too stubborn to see what's going on?"

Her body went still. Everything she'd been thinking but avoiding crystallized. She made her voice angry. "The police can't protect me if this person is hell-bent on killing me. However, they seem more interested in hurting the ones I'm close to than finishing me off. Perhaps you should rethink our partnership while you still can."

"You don't appear close to many people."

"I'm not." Terror ripped through her. "Finn." She jumped out of her seat. "He's got to be warned."

"Can you call him?"

"My phone's upstairs in my apartment."

"Then don't just stand there. Let's go get it."

She rushed upstairs with Tony and Luvy galloping behind. Her phone was next to the computer. She stood motionless while the phone rang three times on Finn's end before going to voicemail. She tried a second call with the same result. This time she spoke after the beep. "Finn, this is important. Call me when you get my message, no matter what time it is."

She lowered the phone and stared at Tony, panic making her wail. "What if I'm too late?"

"Well, don't just stand there, girl. Get your jacket, and I'll drive us over. We'll make sure he knows what's going on, and until then, don't you dare think the worst."

CHAPTER 29

Finn and Adele lived in a small house in the French quarter of the city called Orleans, about fifteen kilometres east of the Glebe as the crow flies. Tony accessed the Queensway at Bronson to avoid driving through city streets now slick with rain that had started while they were eating supper. He leaned toward the windshield and cursed with every slap of the wipers. "Goddamn weather report called for clear skies and no chance of precipitation until morning. Why can't they ever get it right?" He drove as fast as he dared while Ella sat huddled with Luvy on her lap.

Twenty minutes later, Tony exited the highway by the Jeanne D'Arc off-ramp. They followed the boulevard past shops, restaurants, and businesses to a residential suburb. Finn's house was a bungalow with yellow siding and brown trim set on a large treed lot in the middle of the block.

She groaned as they get closer. "That's their blue Fiat in the driveway, but Finn's truck is gone. Let's hope Adele knows how to reach him."

Tony pulled in behind the Fiat and turned off the engine. "Luvy and I will wait here."

Nobody answered the doorbell, and she didn't detect any sign of movement inside the house. The lights were off except for the outdoor porch light. She leapt back down the steps and slid in next to Tony. "Now what?"

"We wait to see if one of them comes home. I'll pull onto the street across from the house."

"If you're sure it's not too much trouble."

"A stakeout on a chilly, foggy night in October? What could be more deliciously noir?"

It didn't take long for the car to cool down, but Luvy alternated between Tony's lap and hers, keeping them somewhat warm. At one point Tony ran the engine for ten minutes with the heat on high. She dozed off for a bit and wakened to Tony's hand shaking her arm. "Is that your friend, Finn?"

She rubbed away the bleariness from her eyes and then used the back of her hand to clear the fog from the windshield. She craned her neck to see through the darkness. "Oh, thank God. It's him."

Finn's truck had pulled into the driveway, and he was already walking toward the house. Ella leapt out of the car and raced across the street and up the driveway in an attempt to waylay him before he reached the front steps. The rain had changed to a mist that shrouded the houses in a white haze and dampened her face. Finn turned at her approach, and the smile on his face quickly turned to concern. "Ella. What's going on?"

"Something's happened since Danny died. Another friend … you remember Officer O'Brien from Danny's trial?" She panted to catch her breath. "Well, he died last week too. The police first thought it was a heart attack, but turns out someone murdered him as well."

Finn held up a hand to stop her from talking. His

expression was incredulous. "Are you telling me that somebody is killing off people close to you?"

"Well, when you put it that way, the idea sounds out there."

"Kind of, yeah." He turned and climbed the steps. With his back to her, he said, "Adele's in labour. Three weeks early, so I'm still in a bit of shock. I'm home for a quick shower and change before I go straight back to the hospital."

She noticed then that he was dressed in his sweats and runners, and his hair was dark with sweat. Of course he'd be consumed by the baby's birth, but his dismissive tone angered her. "I won't keep you then."

He got the door open and turned. "Thanks for coming all this way to warn me, but I truly doubt anyone is trying to kill me. It's kind of a crazy idea."

"And I hope nobody will come after you, Finn, but there really is somebody out there who killed Danny and now O'Brien. I'm worried for you."

Finn flashed his most disarming grin. "He or she might wish they hadn't if they try anything." He jumped back down the steps and gave her a quick hug. "I'll be careful," he said into her ear.

"All my best to Adele," she replied. "Let me know when the baby arrives."

He moved back and held her at arm's length. "I'm going to be a dad, Ella. An honest-to-God dad. I can hardly believe it's really happening."

He left her and hurried up the steps into the house. She ran across the street and got into the car. Tony's eyes were bright with curiosity. "Well?"

"Yeah, he doesn't buy our concern. His wife Adele's in labour at the hospital, and he's having a shower and heading back over."

Tony studied her. "You're upset."

"He blew off my warning. I mean, I know he's preoccupied with the baby coming, but this … this dismissive side of him is new in our relationship."

"What do you want to do?"

"Would you mind waiting until he leaves the house to make sure there isn't any trouble?"

"I was going to suggest it if you didn't."

They sat huddled inside their jackets, watching the house and not speaking. Finn emerged half an hour later and bounded down the steps and into his truck. He was holding a travel mug and carrying an overnight bag, which Ella guessed had Adele's toiletries and nightgown inside. He didn't even glance their way.

"We could be Jack the bloody Ripper sitting here and he'd be oblivious," she said. The rain had started up again and drummed a steady beat on the roof. "Do you mind following him to the hospital?"

"I'll give it my best James Bond."

Finn drove fast for a rain-soaked night, but he reached the General Hospital and turned into the parking lot without incident. Tony pulled over to the shoulder, and they watched Finn park. He stepped out of the truck and jogged through the mist and rain toward the main entrance. Tony waited until the sliding glass door closed behind him before pulling back onto the road.

"Hopefully, his wife takes her time popping out the kid and he stays put for a while," Tony said, grinning at her. He looked otherworldly with his face half in shadow. "It'll give us a bit of time to figure out our next moves."

She glanced sideways at Tony's profile as he focused on getting them safely home through the rain-slicked streets. Every so often, he reached down and rubbed Luvy's fur and called her his good girl. Ella looked out the side window at the passing houses and blinked back the tears that blurred her vision. Odd how she could harden herself to the grief and nastiness, but one iota of kindness from this man broke down the defenses. As sidekicks went, Tony continued to surprise her.

THE RAIN INTENSIFIED at midnight and eased off close to dawn. At first light, Ella forced herself out from under the covers and boiled the water for a cup of instant coffee. Another breakfast of champions. Luckily, she was still full from Tony's meal the night before.

She hadn't completed compiling her list of possible suspects from her days working the crime beat that Hunter had requested. She'd stowed her hard copy work files under the bed when she'd first moved in, and they'd sat there collecting dust ever since. She pulled out the first box and dragged it over to her computer, opening the electronic file she'd created the day before when she'd done a search through her news stories. She wished that she still had access to her computer files at the office, but at least she'd kept these paper copies.

It took the entire morning to go through the boxes and make notes. Upon completion, three promising names sat at the top of her list, in addition to the two cons she'd earlier confirmed were still behind bars. Colin Waters, convicted of indecent exposure and child luring two years ago. Suspended sentence but made the offenders' list and forced to take rehabilitation classes. Manny Geico, murdered his mother four years ago. Got life when the judge didn't buy his temporary insanity plea and still behind bars. Last but not least, James T. Ramsay, served three years for gang-related crimes, including shooting two opposing gang members in the legs. Released six months ago.

All three had taken offense at her coverage of their trials. All three had threatened to harm her in various creative, horrifying ways. Manny was still in prison, but she followed Hunter's instructions to include the dead and the locked-up. Hunter had the resources to check out Manny's contacts. In her view, Ramsay was the most promising. He was also one scary son of a bitch.

She saved her changes and attached the file in an email to Hunter. After hitting *Send*, she stood and stretched, trying to work the kinks out of her shoulders. It was nearly two thirty. Time for another cup of coffee and a peanut butter sandwich before she tackled the script for her next podcast.

After eating, she sat back at her desk and kept working for a few more hours. She'd finished distilling the latest information on Josie Wheatly's murder, when her cell rang. Besides the calls from Hunter, she hadn't received a phone call in days, maybe weeks. People either texted or emailed. The number was private. "Yes?" she said, half-listening while continuing to read her computer screen. She was about to hang up as the silence stretched. *Another damn telemarketer*. She started to lower the phone.

"Lying bitch."

She was instantly on guard. "Who is this? How did you get my number?"

"You deserve everything you get."

"Who the hell are you?" she asked angrily, but she was speaking into the dial tone. Her heart pounded so hard that she was lightheaded. Could the person who'd left the threatening message below her podcast have tracked her down?

She tossed the phone onto the desk like a hot potato,

jumped up, and crossed to the window. Nobody was standing below watching her apartment. Was the caller the same person who'd tried to break in, or was this somebody new? Were the trolls and weirdos multiplying like rabbits? She sat down at her desk, wiped the beads of sweat from her forehead with the bottom of her sweatshirt, and glanced at her computer screen. Six o'clock. No wonder she was lightheaded. It was time to boil spaghetti and heat up sauce and get some carbs into her. The answer to worry was to keep busy.

She replayed the phone conversation in her mind as she opened the package of pasta. A man's voice. Definitely a man. He'd spoken quietly and deepened his voice so that she couldn't identify him. Suspicion made her pause as she stirred the sauce. Could this be somebody in her orbit? Greg was still hanging around and not all that happy with her. He and Sander seemed to have had a peculiar bromance going when Greg lived here, always getting together while she and Tony were away, keeping in touch after Greg left. Was it strange timing that Sander also moved out right after Greg? She gave her head a shake. Greg was definitely not into men, even if Sander went both ways. Tony had given a very real reason for Sander to leave him. She couldn't let fear make her distrust those few people close to her. At this rate, she was on track to becoming the crazy old woman believing in conspiracy theories and talking to herself outside the liquor store. She inhaled deeply, and her shoulders loosened. It could be one of the five men on the list she'd sent to Hunter. Even incarcerated Manny Geico had access to a computer and a phone in Millhaven Pen.

She served up a heaping plateful and stood in front of the living room window, eating spaghetti while scanning the shadows below. A sudden movement near the cedars made her stretch onto her tiptoes and crane her neck. One of the bushes began shaking before a cat broke through and darted across the road. Ella turned away from the window and laughed at her foolishness. Tony wasn't due home for a while, and the silence from his apartment had unnerved her, making her as jumpy as that cat.

After finishing her meal, she sat at the computer and checked her phone for messages. Finn had sent a text half an hour earlier: *It's a girl! Seven pounds even. Lena Isabelle Nyberg. Can't wait to introduce you.* Ella's finger hovered over Finn's number, but she stopped herself from phoning. This was Adele's moment to shine and to bond with the baby and Finn. She wouldn't interrupt their family time. Instead, she sent Finn a text of congratulations and asked him to call when he could. She said how happy she was for them both and to take care.

She settled in and started working on her podcast script, not satisfied with the wording and flow of the piece, until past midnight. By then, she was happily worn out, both mentally and physically. The thought of Finn and Adele's new baby helped her mood. Tony had come home a few hours earlier, and music had thumped through the floorboards for a bit, but all was silent now and had been for an hour or so. She decided to call it a night too and shut down the computer.

Ten minutes later, she'd crawled under the covers and was dead to the world. She was sound asleep until the ringing of her phone pulled her back. She groaned, rolled onto her side, and checked the clock. Four thirty. She closed her eyes for a second and started to drift. The ringing started again. *Danny!* For one moment between sleep and wakefulness, she forgot that he was gone. She threw back the covers and staggered across the room. Her phone was next to the computer. She snatched it up and pressed it against her ear.

"Yes?"

"Ella? My house is on fire! What the hell is going on? What didn't you tell me?"

Her mind scrambled. *Shit. Shit. Shit.* Sirens were screaming in the background, making it difficult to concentrate "Finn, are you okay? Oh God, I never thought … I'll be there as quick as I can."

"This is insane, Ella. Fucking over-the-top insane."

The line went dead in her hand like an angry slap on the wrist for her sins.

CHAPTER 30

Ella dressed in record time after booking an Uber, clattering down the stairs with her shoes undone while shoving her arm into a sleeve of her jacket. The driver pulled up as she stepped onto the stoop. Even though the rain had stopped, the air was misty and cool. The chill cut through her raincoat and pullover sweater on her sprint to the back seat.

The driver was young, early twenties she guessed, and seemed hopped up on Red Bull. A couple of empty cans lay on the seat next to him, supporting her observation. The streets were virtually empty, and he zipped along, humming to a tune on his headphones. She was happy not to have to make small talk or listen to his music selection and twisted sideways to watch the world whiz by the side window. They were at the Orleans off-ramp in half the time it had taken Tony to cover the same distance.

The black, billowing smoke from Finn's burning house was visible as they turned into his neighbourhood. It thickened as they got closer, and an acrid burning smell permeated the inside of the car. The driver craned to see out the windshield and said, "What the hell?" He slowed as he turned onto Finn's street and yanked out an earbud. He met her stare in the rear view. His eyes shone with excitement. "Somebody's house is completely ablaze. This where you want to go? I can't get any closer. Ugh, the smell."

"This is good. Stop here and I'll get out."

"If you're sure. Want me to wait for you around the corner?"

"No. I'll be here a while."

"You're the boss."

The smoke filled her nose and throat as soon as she stepped outside the car. She coughed, and her eyes watered before her body adjusted somewhat to the foul air. Two fire trucks blocked off access to the block, along with a couple of police cars and an ambulance. She could get no closer. A group of people were gathered on a lawn to her right. She started walking toward them and spotted Finn through the smoke, speaking to a young couple dressed in pajamas with coats thrown overtop. He was making motions toward the crackling orange flames shooting from the roof of his house, and the woman had a hand resting on Finn's shoulder. He turned when Ella called his name.

"Ella." He crossed the space between them and wrapped her in a hug. "Sorry I sounded so unhinged on the phone. Thanks for coming. I shouldn't have gotten you out of bed, but I'm glad you're here."

"I need to be here, Finn. This is unbelievable." She took a step back but stayed close to him. "What happened? Are you okay? Are Adele and Lena still in the hospital?" She noticed then that he was fully dressed in street clothes, including a black overcoat and skullcap.

He nodded. "I stayed at the hospital with Adele and slept in the chair beside her bed. I woke up when Lena started crying for her feeding and decided to come home for a better sleep and to get the last-minute things we'd need to bring Lena home. The back of the house was on fire when I drove up the street. I called 911 right away but it was too late. All the baby furniture and clothes are gone. I managed to move the vehicles, thank goodness. The police told me to wait over here while they talk to the neighbours to see if anybody saw anything."

"I'm so sorry, Finn. You and Adele don't deserve this."

They stood leaning against each other and watched the fire. More neighbours approached Finn, giving hugs and words of support, offering to help in any way they could. He was popular, it seemed, but she wasn't surprised. He liked helping people and had a quiet friendliness about him.

An hour later, the police singled him out and took him back to the squad car for a longer chat while she searched the shadows. Could whoever have started the fire be lurking in the darkness, watching their handiwork? She didn't know the people on this street well enough to pick out who didn't belong. The fire seemed to be contained, the frame of the house still standing with gaping holes in the roof and blackened hollows where the windows and doors once were. The fire hoses kept pouring a steady stream of water on the charred remains. People began slowly disappearing into their houses as the excitement passed.

The sun was peeking over the row of houses facing her, and gradient shades of blue and peach had lightened the night sky when a familiar sedan pulled up on the street behind her. She watched as Liam Hunter stepped out of the driver's side, the dark circles under his eyes showing his exhaustion. Black stubble on his cheeks meant he hadn't taken the time to shave. He spotted her standing off to the side and crooked his finger for her to join him at the squad car where the officers were speaking with Finn. She sauntered over.

Hunter nodded at Finn. She listened to one of the cops tell Hunter what they'd found so far. Not a hell of a lot, as it turned out. "I'd bet my first-born that the fire was deliberately set," Hunter said, "based on other recent events."

"Could you possibly be any more mysterious?" The cop with a bald head and grey goatee winked at Ella as if they were sharing a joke.

"I don't want to put ideas in your head, but make sure to do a careful search," Hunter said to the cop without cracking a smile. Hunter's sharp blue eyes swerved over to focus on Ella. "We need to talk," he said.

"So talk."

"I want to be in on your conversation," Finn said. "Ella tried to warn me to be careful, but my wife was in labour and I didn't pay any attention. I'm sorry. I should have listened, Ella."

"Well, none of us could have predicted this," she said before looking at Hunter. "Does your sergeant buy your theory about me and my friends being targets now?"

"She doesn't know about the fire yet. I'll brief her when I leave here."

"So, let's say for sake of argument that someone is systematically destroying the people close to me. How are you going to protect them?"

Finn added, "Especially since my wife and new baby were supposed to be coming home this morning."

"Full protection won't be easy." Hunter paused. "Finn, is it? I suggest we register your family in the suites downtown under a different name until we get a handle on what's going on. I'll take care of the reservation."

"It's not like I have a choice with my house burned to the ground."

"No." Hunter gave Ella the trying-to-look-inside-her-brain stare. "How many other friends *do* you have?"

"None. Looks like being antisocial is saving lives."

"Surely to God you have more than three people in your life?" Hunter looked from her to Finn and back.

She rested her pointer finger on her chin and pretended to think. Shook her head. "I mean, I have acquaintances but nobody I'd call a friend."

"She's not kidding," Finn said. "Ella doesn't like a lot of people around. She's not one for a party, say."

"I'm right here," she grumbled. "I can speak for myself." She gave Finn a little shove to let him know she wasn't kidding around.

Hunter's mood appeared to be darkening. "I'd still like you to come up with a list of people that you have regular contact with. Include your family members. And Finn, I'll take your contact information."

Ella mused aloud. "You want an addendum to my other list of people possibly trying to kill me."

"Let's hope there are no crossovers."

Finn started rhyming off numbers that Hunter typed into his phone. She watched them and tried to piece together what was happening. Three people had been harmed because they got close to her. Three people she loved. What if something she did was causing all this horror? Finn lifted his eyes and met hers. He put an arm around her shoulders and squeezed. "We'll catch the bastard."

"One way or the other." Inside, she wasn't so certain. This person had an enormous advantage. They were patient, relentless, and thorough, not to mention anonymous. She couldn't even nail down the motive.

Finn said to Hunter, "What are you doing to protect Ella?"

"I'll have to get clearance from my boss, but once I do, Ella and I are going to become joined at the hip." Hunter gave a curt nod and strode toward his car, leaving her and Finn silently watching, fixated on a picture in their heads that wouldn't go away. Finn cleared his throat first. "Well, you could do worse. He's got pretty nice hips."

"You know that bit about me not liking many people? Well, Hunter's on the list, and he's vying for first place." She saw Finn's truck parked partway down the side street and pointed toward it. "Do you have to stick around here, or can you go be with Adele?"

"I'm supposed to wait until the first cop I was talking to gives the okay, but I'll check and take you home."

"No need. I can Uber easily enough."

"I want to take you home. Then I'll go to the gym and shower up before going to get Adele. She'll freak when I tell her that our house is gone."

"Well, if you're going my way…"

"Always." He smiled at her, and all felt right between them again. Nothing like the threat of death and destruction to help old friends reconnect.

CHAPTER 31

Tony was gone when Ella arrived home, likely at the salon. Sander had told her once that Tony was one of the better-known stylists in Ottawa and could work as many hours as he liked. "His clients are the rich and famous, but he's so discreet and knows just what to say to make them laugh. That's why they adore him. Well, that and he gives fabulous cuts and colours."

She spent the day in her apartment, recording the next podcast, happy to focus on something other than Danny and Paul O'Brien and Finn's fire, even if her focus involved true crime. Reporting on Josie Wheatly's life and murder took her mind off the danger that she and everyone around her were in and let her stop thinking about the people she'd lost.

Her podcast update didn't reveal much new, although she introduced Josie's colleague, Mr. Rivington, without giving his real name, and related his observations about Josie's dating life. Rory Leavitt wouldn't be pleased to hear this latest information, although the idea that there'd been more men in Josie's life widened the suspect pool — a plus in his column, all evidence weighed. Ella got up a couple of times to eat peanut butter sandwiches and boil water for coffee. Her jar was getting low, and she started cutting the spoonful of coffee granules in half.

This life of poverty wasn't ever a state she'd courted, yet she wouldn't change a thing if she had it to do all over again. She'd borrowed money to finance Danny's two stints in rehab at a residential setting out of the city for months at a time. The interventions hadn't worked, but that wasn't the point. Danny had known that she loved him above all else — that his life was worth fighting for. She'd gladly spend the rest of her days in poverty if this would bring him back, but she had to settle for knowing she'd done all she could to help him while he was alive.

Tony clumped up the stairs to his apartment as she was ready to go live with her podcast. She lifted her head. The bright light of midday had greyed into late-afternoon shadows, and she reached over to turn on the desk lamp. Time went quickly when she was engrossed in her work. She finished uploading the podcast and added the descriptive text. Then she copied the link and sent out notices on her social media sites. Rather than sit waiting for the comments to dribble in, she lay down on the floor and worked through some yoga poses. One final stretch and she thought about getting up and putting on a pot of water to boil the last of the spaghetti while Tony's music thumped through the floor. A Shania Twain night. Tony's second-favourite go-to. It took her a moment to isolate the knocking on her apartment door.

"Coming!" she yelled and scrambled to her feet.

Tony was standing on the other side waving a bottle of red wine. He was dressed in a grey suit that fit him like melted butter. "Get into your black dress, girl. We have time for a drink, and then we're expected at the Mission for seven. I'll meet you in my apartment in five. Have your coat and things ready to go."

"I was about to make supper."

"I've got appetizers. Get moving." He turned and left before she could argue. She started to call out to him but thought, *What's the point?*

The dress had fallen off its hanger and was lying in a heap on the floor of her closet. She put it on anyway and was surprised when the wrinkles all fell away. What kind of fabric did that? She found the matching shoes and coat and carried them downstairs to Tony's apartment. He'd set out a plate of brie, pâté, seed crackers, and purple grapes and was pouring two brimming glasses of wine.

"What is all this?" she asked before sitting down and tucking into the food. "The wine is lovely. Much better than the plonk I buy," she said between mouthfuls. "Where's Luvy?"

"Sleeping in the bedroom. She's knackered." Tony sat across from her and picked up his glass. "I organized..." he started to say when a loud knocking at the front door of the house interrupted. "One minute. I need to check on who that is."

She set her glass on the table. "Tony, we need to be careful who we let in. I didn't have a chance to tell you about Finn."

Tony's face paled, and he covered his mouth with one hand. She hurried to reassure him. "Finn's house burned down this morning, but nobody was hurt."

His hand dropped to clutch his chest. "Good Lord, girl. You scared the bejesus out of me. I thought another one of your people bit the dust."

The knocking was getting louder at the front door as they descended the stairs. Tony had picked up a baseball bat that he kept beside the boot rack as they left his apartment. "You stay back. We'll let Slugger do the talking."

He clicked open the deadbolt. "We really should have asked Alex for a peephole." He peered through the crack in the door before shoving the door open wide. He rested the bat on his shoulder. "Detective," he said, stepping aside to let Hunter into the hallway along with a whoosh of cold air.

Hunter stopped when he saw her standing behind Tony. His eyes flicked over her dress and back to her face. He frowned. "Good, you're here."

"But on our way out," she said.

"Yes," Tony added. "We're about to leave for the Mission. Care to join us, Detective? Always room for one more."

She poked Tony in the ribs. "Can you be any more obvious?" she said under her breath.

He turned his head. "I could bat my eyes." They shared a quick smile before turning their stares back at Hunter. His eyes were steady on them, and he wasn't smiling.

"It's better if you both stay in for the night. I can't guarantee your safety if you're roaming around the city in the dark."

"It's Danny's memorial service," Tony said. "I thought it might be a chance to scan the crowd. See if any strangers show up."

Hunter thought for a moment. "Your idea might have merit, if you both want to take the risk."

"Of course we do," Ella said. "Anything to stop this person from hurting somebody else."

"Then I'll call in for some reinforcements." Hunter pulled out his phone.

"And we'll go get our coats and will meet you back

here." Tony grabbed Ella's arm and pulled her toward the stairs. "Thanks for backing me up."

"Was that really your plan? To lure the killer to Danny's service?"

"No, but we still get to hold it, and now we have protection. I'd say a win-win."

"Give me a minute."

She ran upstairs to her apartment and switched her purse for a shoulder bag before going into the kitchen. She grabbed a paring knife from the butcher block and tucked it inside the bag. If the bastard dared showed his face, he'd live to regret it. Going to prison would be a small price to pay for putting an end to him.

Danny and Paul O'Brien would do the same for her.

THEY ARRIVED AT THE MISSION, and Tony found a parking spot in the lot next door. She felt overdressed, but he'd assured her she wouldn't look out of place. "You're honouring Danny's memory," he said. "Everyone will appreciate the effort."

They entered through the main doors and were greeted by silence. The hallway was empty of men. The lights were dimmed. She stopped and Tony bumped into her. "What is it, Ella?"

"This is a mistake. Nobody cares about my brother. He spent his life on the outside looking in." She turned to leave, but Tony grabbed onto her arm.

"You're paying for sandwiches, so you may as well take some home."

"Damn, I sure hope you didn't order too many."

"Follow me." He led her down the corridor and stopped outside the door to the mess hall. "In here."

She was muttering curses at him under her breath, but he opened the door, and she stepped in behind him. The heads of nearly eighty men turned in unison to look at them standing in the doorway. She tried to take everything in as they made their way to the reserved seats in the front row. The lighting was low with candles strategically placed on tables at the perimeter of the seating area. Beside the candles were flower arrangements: mums, daisies, and eucalyptus. A vase of pink roses sat on a table next to the urn. *Danny.*

"This is … beautiful," she said.

"You're welcome." His warm hand rested for a moment on her shoulder.

"Is this where you were all day?"

"Not all day."

A man dressed in minister's robes came over to welcome them before taking his place at the podium. "We're gathered to remember our dear friend Danny Tate," he began. "I had many wonderful chats with Danny during his stays at the Mission and grew to love him as a brother. I'm grieving with you at the loss of such a gentle, loving soul. We're blessed to have Danny's sister Ella with us today. Danny often spoke of his love for you, Ella, and I know he'll always live in your heart."

She nodded at the minister and lowered her head to study her hands folded in her lap. He continued by saying that some of Danny's friends would come forward to celebrate his life. A series of men not used to public speaking gave moving statements about what her brother had meant to them. The last and most upset speaker was Cal, the man she'd spoken with in this very room after Danny's assault.

"Danny kept tellin' me that life was going to get better. All we had to do was keep the faith. He'd had some bad knocks in his life, and it wasn't weakness why he took to drugs. Was his soft heart. He loved music and poetry and his sister Ella here. I'm sure gonna miss you, buddy."

The minister ended with a Bible reading and a prayer and then invited everyone to stay for a cup of tea and some sandwiches and baking. Chairs scraped across the floor, and the chatter started as the men stood. They lined up at the refreshment table and then gathered around the room in groups, awkwardly balancing cups and plates. They took turns coming over to speak with her about Danny. Whenever there was a break, she looked around the room, trying to recognize someone from her past or someone who looked out of place. She spotted Hunter at the back of the room and another officer unobtrusively taking photos. She was glad that nobody else appeared to notice.

The minister was the last one to come over to speak with her. He took her hand in both of his. "I'm always here for you if you ever want to talk."

"Thank you. I don't even know your name."

He laughed. "Pastor Mike. It's what everyone calls me."

"Danny was lucky to know you, Pastor Mike."

"I was the fortunate one."

Tony was waiting for her by the exit. He had the urn with Danny's ashes cradled in his arms and handed it to her when she stepped up next to him. "I wasn't sure if you wanted him interred in a mausoleum, but I can look into that if you like."

"You've done enough, Tony. More than enough. I'll look after Danny's ashes from here on. Thank you for everything." For now, all she wanted to do was bring Danny home.

Hunter and the other officer followed them outside. "I'm not sure if the killer showed, but we'll go through all the photos and will work with the pastor to get names to faces. You two driving back to the apartment?"

"We are," Tony said.

"Then I'll be right behind you."

"And if we're lucky, maybe he'll tuck us in," Tony whispered to Ella as they walked away. "Lord knows I wouldn't say no."

CHAPTER 32

Hunter followed her upstairs to her apartment while Tony stopped at his floor to take Luvy for her nightly walk. Hunter made himself busy while she changed in the bedroom. He'd put the kettle on and had instant coffees ready by the time she joined him dressed in sweatpants and a baggy sweater.

"You need some new java. This is the last of it." He pointed to the empty coffee jar on the counter.

"I plan to shop tomorrow. Cupboards are getting low." She accepted the mug. "Would you like milk?"

"Black's fine."

She recalled that he put milk and sugar in his coffee in the restaurant but accepted his answer without question. They both knew that her fridge was all but empty. Her chin jutted out as she strode past him to her desk chair in the living room, his earlier comment about her life choices not forgotten.

He followed and eased onto the couch. "I spoke with my sarge. She agrees that coincidences are piling up, but she can't afford to put a detail on you without a direct threat to your life."

Ella shrugged and sipped from the mug. "I can look after myself."

"I wish I could believe that." He set his mug on the floor, stood, and began pacing. "That one name you gave me is a definite possible. J.T. Ramsay. He's living downtown in a house with a couple of prostitutes. I've convinced my boss to put eyes on him for the next couple of days."

"Why him and not me?" She was curious but not particularly upset by the decision.

"We think he's dealing drugs and pimping, so there are some crimes in progress we can use. He's violating his parole, for starters."

"Sounds like he's picking up right where he left off." A shadow passed over her as she remembered the look in Ramsay's eyes when he stared her down in the courtroom before his sentencing. A premonition shivered up her spine. "He's capable of killing Danny and Paul. He also wouldn't hesitate to start a house fire. He might have followed me to the gym and figured out I'm friends with Finn. I wasn't looking for him then and likely wouldn't have recognized him even if he was standing next to me. He threatened to hurt me after the judge gave him a couple of years for gang shootings. I'd tracked down two of the bystanders and managed to get them to make statements that ultimately convicted Ramsay. The judge kept their names anonymous for their protection, but my name was out there, of course. Nobody died, but one gang member came close."

Hunter stopped walking and stared at her. "I'm going to see about getting a panic button to you that you can press and it'll bring help any time, day or night."

"Thanks, but I don't need one." Ramsay would do her in before any help arrived, but she kept this thought to herself.

"It's what we give women in abusive situations."

She was hardly an abused woman but didn't say that either. "I don't want a panic button. What about Finn and Adele and their new baby? How are you going to keep them safe?"

"They're housed in the hotel suite under my name. Unfortunately, Finn plans to open the gym against my advice. I've asked for a patrol to make regular checks."

"Finn won't back away from a fight."

"I got that sense. Hopefully we'll pick up Ramsay before he tracks down Finn or hurts anybody else."

"You really believe he's behind all this?"

"If I were a betting man, I'd play the odds. There's one more thing."

"About Danny?"

"No, about Josie Wheatly. Forensics on her laptop and phone came back. She was using an alias on the dating apps."

"I could see that she would. She had a teacher's reputation to uphold."

"She was using Ella T."

"My name."

"Pretty much." He watched her face as she reasoned this through.

"If someone still thought I lived in that apartment…"

"You looked alike when your hair was longer. The photo she was using could be mistaken for you, if someone hadn't seen you in a while."

She stood and crossed to the window. "I'd be foolish not to be scared." She spun around. "But I'm more angry than anything."

"We'll catch him. In the meantime, you have to stay vigilant."

He hung around until his coffee was gone. At the doorway, he stopped and gave her face another searching stare. "I wish I'd had a chance to meet your brother. I would have liked him."

"Thanks." She looked down at her hands and waited for the sound of the apartment door clicking shut. She got up from her chair and returned to stand in front of the window with her arms crossed, trying to rub some warmth into them. She thought about Danny and all she'd lost.

A light tap at the door pulled her back from her reverie. Tony and Luvy were standing in the hall when she opened the door. He held a bottle of Drambuie and two small crystal glasses. "Nightcap?"

She opened the door wider, and he followed her inside. "You're going to turn me into an alcoholic," she said, accepting a full glass.

"I prefer to think of this as helping you to get through these dark days. You don't strike me as having an addictive personality."

He was right about that. She could give up vices, possessions, people … most people … and not look back. They took their places. The liquor burned her throat and warmed her chest. For a few moments, her body relaxed.

"So what's next?" Tony asked. Luvy curled into his lap, and he lazily stroked her back while watching Ella.

"I'm going to finish this drink, you're going to return to your apartment, and then I'm going to fall asleep."

"That's not what I meant. Did the good detective who just left have any updates?"

"The police are watching an ex-con named Ramsay. I'll milk my resources to see what he's been up to the last few weeks." She thought of Felix and realized she hadn't checked her messages or podcast site all evening. Suddenly she was eager for Tony to leave so she could catch up. She threw back the last of her drink and set the glass on the desk. "Should we call it a night and regroup tomorrow?" She didn't tell him that she planned to start working on her own. She couldn't chance having him end up dead too because he'd gotten too close to her.

Tony pursed his lips as if to stop himself from saying anything. He also drained his drink before standing. He cradled Luvy in his arms like a baby. "It is that time," he said. "I have a full day in the salon tomorrow, but I'll check in when I get home."

"Perfect." She walked him to the door. "Thanks for today, Tony. Danny would have liked that sendoff."

"I was happy to do it."

"Let me know the cost of the food and flowers. I'll reimburse you."

"The flowers are my gift. There's no rush for the food."

"I can't let you do that."

He left without answering. She wondered where she was going to get the money but was determined now to pay him back in full. She looked at Danny's urn where she'd set it on the wide window ledge and took comfort from the idea of his presence in this room with her. Someday she'd release his ashes in a wooded area in the Gatineau Hills, a place dappled with sun and smelling of moss. A warm, safe place far away from anyone who could hurt him. But not yet. For now, she needed him with her.

She opened an email from Felix that arrived around the time she was driving to the Mission with Tony. The message gave the contact information of the sponsor O'Brien had lined up before he died, with instructions to deal with them directly. There was also an attachment with two photos of a man and Josie Wheatly exiting the hospital, date-stamped the morning of her death. The pictures were stills from a video. The man's face appeared to be deliberately averted from the camera, but she could tell that he was at least a half-foot taller than Josie, who, according to the police report, stood at five foot four. He was wearing a black hoodie and a bulky jacket that hid his size. No distinguishing logos on the clothing. He had hold of Josie's arm, almost as if he was keeping her from collapsing … or escaping. She enlarged the photos. He was wearing gloves, but a gap under the cuff of his jacket sleeve showed a sliver of skin. She zoomed in until the pixels were too large to make anything out, pulled back. He was light-skinned, as far as she could tell.

Ramsay had olive skin, but the photo wasn't clear enough to rule him in or out. He was the right height, certainly. She printed the photos and added them to her paper file before deleting the email and emptying the trash. Next, she opened her text messages. Greg had sent two, both asking to meet up. Part of her was flattered that he felt remorse for leaving so easily. Another part was irritated by his persistence. She sent a reply saying she'd meet for coffee in the morning. It was time to find out what he was up to.

Finally, she brought up her latest podcast. The comments were benign for the most part. No threats or nastiness to ruin her peace. Subscribers were up by sixteen hundred. She shut off the computer. She wasn't lying about being exhausted. She'd get a good night's sleep and would plot out her next moves in the morning. Hopefully, a new day would bring fresh leads while her desire to avenge Danny and O'Brien still burned red-hot. The need to see someone pay was all that was keeping the grief from overwhelming her.

CHAPTER 33

She woke early and lay in bed, watching the shadows of tree branches crisscrossing the ceiling like spindly arms while she planned her day. She'd start in the ByWard Market, where Danny had his regular busking spots. Perhaps not all the vendors had been canvassed. One might remember seeing a man hanging around the day Danny was stabbed, or even a day or two before. After that, she'd check out the apartment where Ramsay was staying. Maybe speak with one of the women living with him, if she could get one alone. At eleven, she'd meet Greg in the Starbucks on Bank.

She beat Tony to the shower and luxuriated in the hot water that didn't cool after five minutes. The radio announcer said it was twelve degrees outside and windy, so she dressed in a warm pullover under her denim jacket. Faded jeans, black ankle books, a grey skullcap, and a blue-and-white-striped scarf completed her look. Her hair was growing fast and already getting shaggy, but it was still at the stage where the messy style could be intentional. She raked fingers through the tangle and convinced herself not to take the scissors to it yet.

Instead of taking her bike, she walked along the canal to the downtown. She stopped a few times to make certain that nobody was following her. The knife within reach in her handbag gave her enough courage to keep going. The red and gold leaves lay in soggy heaps on the path and littered the expansive lawns, branches black against the deep indigo sky that paled to shades of blue as she strode along. Dog walkers and joggers kept her company. Two women stayed a distance behind her most of the route, engrossed in a conversation punctuated by sporadic laughter. She was comforted by the normalcy.

She neared the spot where Danny had been found lying on the path. She'd studied the photos and scanned the area as she drew close to where she'd estimated the stabbing took place. It wasn't hard to find. She crouched and traced a finger where the pavement was still faintly stained in his blood, now brown and faded. Soon the rain would wash the last traces away.

She swivelled around on the balls of her feet and scanned the trees and bushes from the direction she'd come. Danny once described a spot where he liked to sleep when he needed to be alone. She closed her eyes and tried to bring his description into focus. She began walking back along the edge of the grass, pushing branches aside and peering into the cool shadows. A thicket of bushes made her pause. Overhead, feathery branches from conifer trees wove together, reminding her of children holding hands. She parted the bushes and stepped deeper into the shrubbery until she found a flattened spot where Danny could easily have curled up and slept or hidden from a threat. The ground was cool but dry as she sat and pulled the branches back into place. The path was visible, but she was hidden from passersby. If Danny had been here, he'd left no trace. This wasn't a surprise. He was always careful not to leave garbage behind and sometimes walked the shore of the Ottawa River picking up litter. A bird landed on the branch above her, and she watched it for a while, thinking that this was the right place. Danny's presence felt strong here. "I wish you could tell me what happened that night," she said. "I wish you could come back to me." She stayed crouched in place until the bird flew away.

Her phone rang as she stepped on to the path. She checked call display before answering. "Have you found something?" she asked before Hunter had a chance to speak.

"Where are you?"

"I'm fine. Thanks for asking." She looked both ways, relieved to see the path empty, and resumed walking toward the downtown.

"I'm sitting outside your apartment and finally realized you weren't inside."

"Haven't you got anything better to do?"

"What's better than trying to keep you alive?"

"And I appreciate that, Hunter, but I don't want to be babysat."

"Tell me where you are."

She hesitated. Between Tony and Hunter, their attentiveness was claustrophobic. She liked working … being alone. How much of a handicap would it be to have a cop trailing along behind her? She took too long answering, and he seemed to interpret her silence as a refusal to reveal her location. His voice softened. "I can't protect you if you won't meet me halfway, Ella. Tell me what will work for you."

She cleared her throat. "We could meet for lunch if you like."

"Say where and when."

"Daisy's café at twelve thirty."

"I'll be there. Until then, stay out of trouble." He clicked off.

Out of the corner of her eye, somebody was jogging close behind her. She stepped nearer to the metal railing separating the path from the canal and turned to watch him pass. He smiled as he drew abreast, and she relaxed. Was this how it was going to be from now on? Watching over her shoulder? Frightened when somebody got close? She scowled at the thought, and the jogger's smile disappeared. He quickened his pace and soon rounded the corner and was out of sight.

The path led past the National Arts Centre and the outdoor patio. The chairs were stacked, and she wondered if the café was closed for the season or would open later in the day. She kept walking and climbed the stone steps, emerging at street level across from the Château Laurier, the castle-like hotel to the east of the Parliament Buildings. People were strolling by on the cobblestone sidewalk, and several waited at the bus stop as she continued on her way to the Sussex-Rideau Street intersection.

She crossed Rideau Street with the flow of pedestrians and walked past limestone buildings converted into shops and cafés on her way into the ByWard Market. There were more people gathered here, many heading toward the outdoor stalls that sold produce from across the Ottawa Valley: maple syrup, freshly cut flowers, fruit and vegetables. Pumpkins took up a corner spot, lined up in bright orange rows. Farther on, a line of shops sold cheeses and fish, baking and meat. Shoppers lingered over the displays and pointed at the food they'd like to purchase as the vendors whipped apples, beans, and cauliflower into shopping bags. She stopped for a moment and soaked in the activity and earthy smells that mingled with the scent of coffee and baking. This was where Danny felt most at home. The place where he'd found comfort.

The vendors that she approached were wary at first but warmed up once they realized she was Danny's sister. They all knew him. One man selling homemade fudge told her that Danny's music was the background to his day. The tourists would linger longer when Danny was playing nearby. Nobody remembered a stranger, that is until she reached the stall where Danny got his free apples. Ella had met Hannah, the owner, many times when she'd come to hear Danny play. She was serving a customer when Ella arrived. The young man with her behind the counter asked if he could help her pick out some fruit. Ella rightly guessed that he was Hannah's fourteen-year-old son.

"I want to ask if you knew my brother Danny. He used to play guitar and sing over there." She pointed to the spot while watching his eyes dart to Danny's corner and back at her.

Hannah put her arm around the boy. "I'm so sorry for your loss. We thought the world of Danny. He was the sweetest man and always came early to help me set up in the morning. He was teaching my boy Gavin here how to play the guitar."

Gavin nodded. "He was a good guy."

Ella was learning so much about her brother and all the people in his orbit. His life had been joyous in so many ways. "Did you see him last Tuesday or the week leading up to that day?"

"I already spoke to the police. It was raining and cold, and Danny took the day off. I'm sorry, but I didn't see anybody hanging around."

"There was a man scoping out the street the day before," Gavin said.

"We talked about that," Hannah said quickly. "You decided it was your imagination playing tricks."

"He was dressed in black and had his hood up over a ball cap. I know what I saw, Mom. You didn't want me getting involved, but it bugs me not to say anything."

Ella tried to keep her voice calm. "Can you describe him further, Gavin? Maybe how old he looked? His skin colour?"

He stared at his mom as if for permission. She nodded, and he kept talking. "He was a white guy. Older than my brother but younger than Mom."

The woman added, "His brother's eighteen."

Ella smiled her thanks and looked back at Gavin. "Did he have a beard or moustache that you saw?"

"I didn't see his face clearly, so he might have had a 'stache or a beard. Not sure."

"What made you notice him?"

"He walked the length of the street and then came back and stopped in the spot where Danny always played, but it was Monday, so Danny wasn't there. The guy seemed to be looking around for something on the ground, and he checked over his shoulder a few times, you know, like he was making sure nobody was watching him."

"Then what did he do?"

"He went around the corner, and I didn't see him again." Gavin thought for a second. "He didn't look like he was living on the street. His clothes were too new. My buddy owns the same leather jacket he was wearing over his hoodie, and it's not cheap. He had on Doc Martens."

His mother shook her head. "Expensive boots that Gavin's been after me to buy him for Christmas."

"Do you think you could find pictures of what this guy was wearing online and send them to me if I give you my email?"

Gavin nodded. "Okay."

"He has the Doc Martens bookmarked." His mom gave him an affectionate poke in the side.

SHE FOUND the address where Ramsay was living. The house was pebble stucco, two storeys with a tilted front porch, wedged between a Chinese food takeout and a five-storey apartment building. Ella scanned the cars lining both sides of the street. A couple was sitting in the front seat of a black Town Car a few doors down. They had to be the undercover surveillance team.

Ella walked with purpose and stopped in front of the Chinese takeout. She stepped closer to the building and pretended to be studying the menu taped to the plate glass window. The front door of Ramsay's building opened, and she turned her head slightly to see a woman in a short jean skirt and high-heeled boots starting toward her. Ella backed onto the sidewalk, nearly colliding with the woman as she strode past.

"Sorry," Ella said.

"No problem."

"Say, can you tell me what it's like living on this street? I was looking at a vacant apartment in the building next door to the house where you came out. Is it really noisy?" Ella started walking in the same direction as the woman, and they fell into step. Her perfume was strong to the point of overwhelming.

"I've never found the noise a problem." She dug around in her purse and pulled out a pack of cigarettes and a lighter as they rounded the corner. "Smoke?"

"Sure." Ella accepted one and dipped her head toward

the flame as the woman lit their cigarettes. Her dark eyes squinted as she exhaled and assessed Ella.

"You looking for somewhere cheap? We have a spare room for rent. My name's Fawn, by the way."

"Nice to meet you, Fawn. I'm Jen. How many live with you now?"

"Two. Sue Ann and James. We get along fine."

"Won't James mind living with three women?"

Fawn choked on a laugh. "He'd live with more if he could." She leaned in closer. "He did some time for doing something stupid … nothing too bad … so we're helping him get back on his feet. He's working hard to turn over a new leaf. He's a stand-up guy."

"That's okay then." Ella knew Fawn would say anything to reel her in. "How about I take your phone number, and I'll text you when I figure things out?"

"Well, don't wait too long. I'll try to hold off the other girls looking at the room for a couple of days. I think you'd fit in real well."

"I'd appreciate that, Fawn."

GREG WAS SITTING at a table near the window, watching for her to arrive. He motioned that he had a coffee for her through the glass. She entered and slid into the seat across from him.

"You're looking great, Elle. Thanks for seeing me."

"I was surprised you wanted to get together. Nothing has changed since you moved out."

"I know. I'm really, really sorry about Danny. You tried so hard to get his life back on track."

"He didn't deserve to die that way."

"No, he didn't."

Ella bit her bottom lip to stop it from trembling.

Greg locked eyes. "I've missed you."

"I'd be lying if I said I haven't missed you too." She looked away and sipped her coffee, buying time. She set down the cup. "The thing is, Greg, you want a life that I don't, or that I don't want right now. You shouldn't wait around for me."

"I wish it were that easy."

"Just give it time. You'll find the right person, and I'll be a distant memory." She leaned closer. "I need to ask you something, and I want you to be honest."

"Always."

"Did you try to get into my apartment a couple of nights ago? Work the front door lock?"

"I wouldn't do that." He hesitated. "Not sober anyway."

"Were you drinking that night?"

"Maybe. Probably. I have no memory of trying to break into your place. I'm pretty sure I'd remember that, even if I was drunk."

She sat back in the chair and picked up the coffee cup. "Pretty sure doesn't instil confidence." She remembered other times when he'd blacked out while on a bender.

"I'd never hurt you, Ella. Not intentionally, anyway."

"Shit, Greg. What are you telling me?"

"Nothing. I've been to a couple of AA meetings. I'm cleaning up my act. Do you think we could go out on a date sometime? Not this week, but sometime?"

"What about Lucy? Aren't you living with her?"

"It's temporary. We're not taking up where we left off, if that's what you're thinking."

She watched his hands and thought about how she'd always admired their strength. Loved their gentleness. "Let me sleep on it." She paused. "I'm not sure if you're at risk, since we aren't dating anymore, but it seems someone has it in for anyone close to me."

"What the hell are you talking about?"

"Danny was stabbed, my cop friend Paul O'Brien was killed in a parking garage, and Finn's house was burned to the ground."

Greg's face paled. "Shit, Elle. This is serious."

"I know. The cops have a suspect under surveillance, but you need to be careful too. No getting drunk and not having your wits about you."

He nodded. "I'll be careful. Are you safe?"

"Getting there." She picked up her cup and stood. "Thanks for the coffee. I have a meeting with the cop on Danny's case. I'll be in touch." She would not give in to the regret she was feeling as she looked at him.

He flopped back in his seat and shook his head. "The craziness you get into. Take care of yourself too, Ella. I'll be waiting for your call."

CHAPTER 34

Liam greeted Daisy and chose a seat facing the entrance so he could watch for Ella. He was too wired to read the paper that Daisy dropped onto the table, not entirely convinced that Ella was going to show. He'd received still photos on his phone of her outside Ramsay's house from the surveillance team twenty minutes earlier. He'd wanted to throttle her.

The front door opened, and he relaxed his shoulders at the sight of her standing in the foyer, hands in her pockets, blonde hair sticking out every which way, surveying the room until her unusual green eyes lighted on him. She started shuffling toward him. He worked to keep his face neutral. He hadn't known her long, but it was long enough to understand that she wouldn't react well to anger.

"Have you ordered?" she asked as she sat down and wriggled out of her jacket.

"Not yet." He signalled to Daisy. She took their sandwich orders and filled their coffee mugs before leaving. He waited. "How was your morning?"

"Not very insightful." She sighed and slumped back in the chair. "I did learn that whoever was tracking Danny the day before he died wasn't another homeless guy, because he was wearing expensive clothes. A leather jacket and Doc Martens. The son of one of the vendors remembered him."

"Anything else?

"No, that was it so not much to go on, really."

"Every little bit." He kept his voice level. "I got word that you were outside Ramsay's house."

She looked away. "I wanted to check him out. I wasn't planning to confront him." She reached into her pocket for her phone. "I met one of his roommates with the unlikely name of Fawn coming out of his building. She offered to rent me a room after I told her I was looking at an apartment next door. I took her phone number with a promise to call and told her my name was Jen." She pushed her cell across the table with Fawn's number on the screen. "Every little bit, right?"

Liam took out his phone and added Fawn's contact info. "It might be best if you steer clear of James T. Ramsay from here on in."

He stared at her until she nodded. He wasn't convinced she'd follow through, but he didn't plan to let her have the opportunity to roam around the city on her own.

Their food arrived, and they suspended conversation while they ate. He tried not to stare. She wolfed down her meal as if she was half starved. As far as he could tell, she was thin for a woman of her height under all the baggy clothes. Her cheekbones were pronounced and her wrists slender, if these were tells. He remembered her underfurnished apartment and empty fridge. Her battered bike.

"Feel like a piece of pie?" he asked. "I could use one with another coffee if you're up for dessert."

"No, I'm good."

He spotted Daisy at the counter and motioned her

over. "Two pieces of apple pie … with ice cream?" He waited for Ella to nod. "And coffee refills."

"I thought I said no to the pie," she said after Daisy left.

"Call it my treat. I'm never sure when I'll get my next meal, so may as well stock up."

"I know the feeling." She smiled for the first time since she sat down. "So what are our next steps?"

"After we finish the pie, I'm driving you home, and I'm hoping you'll stay in for the rest of the day. I have a meeting downtown and then will be back and can escort you anywhere you need to go."

"You're putting me on house arrest?"

"Hardly, but I think we need to be careful for the next while. Will you work with me on this?"

"Do I have a choice?"

"You always have a choice."

"Well, I have some editing to do on my podcast, so I'll stay put for the rest of the day. After that…" She shrugged and grinned. "We'll just have to see."

HE WAITED until Ella was safely inside. It was midafternoon and windy, a late fall day with a whisper of snow in the air. The kids would be getting their costumes ready for Hallowe'en and carving pumpkins. He'd have to make time to drive over to see his nephews before they went out trick-or-treating. They'd been sending him text messages all week with reminders.

He parked in his reserved spot in the station's underground parking garage and hurried to the staff meeting room on the second floor. The Major Crimes team was already assembled, and he tried to slip in unnoticed. Greta gave him the evil eye as he stepped over legs and feet to take the last empty seat against the wall. She was standing at the head of the table and broke off talking so that everyone turned and looked at him. He met her stare.

"As I was saying," she said without taking her eyes off him, "we have three murders. It's been suggested with the same killer, but we have no evidence to link the cases. The audit on Ella Tate's finances is in." She held up a paper. "She owes sixty-four thousand dollars on bank loans that she took out to pay for the deceased Danny Tate's residential drug rehab visits. Her brother was back on drugs after two stints in the place and was likely to cost her a third visit. He was bleeding her past dry. She was laid off from the newspaper only three months ago, so it's a safe guess that she was at the end of her rope."

Hunter looked around at the attentive faces. He wondered at Greta's motivation in steering the investigation in this direction. She'd been opposed to his theory linking all three murders from the start. She'd never wavered in doubting Ella Tate's innocence. "If I might interject," he said, waiting for Greta's curt nod. "Danny Tate had been off drugs for three weeks when he died. Another stint in drug rehab wasn't in the plans."

Greta's mouth tightened. "Ella didn't know he was off drugs, though, did she, Detective Hunter?"

"No."

"So she wouldn't have known that another costly rehab stint wasn't necessary. Not to mention three weeks sober is far from cured."

"There's no evidence linking Ella to his stabbing."

"Does she have an alibi?"

"Nothing rock-solid."

"She was friends with O'Brien. He helped her out over the years, even in her move with Danny to Ottawa. If he knew she'd stabbed her brother, she had reason and means to do him in as well in order to keep him from talking."

The room was silent as the other detectives took in the exchange. Hunter wasn't going to gain ground by challenging her any further. Her leaps in logic were idiotic, but she was in charge, and he'd have to work around her. He leaned back in his chair and lowered his eyes.

"I guess you have some serious investigating to do then," she said. "Boots, what can you share about O'Brien's case? Any developments?"

Boots stood. "The video cameras in the garage captured someone dressed in black with the hood of their sweatshirt pulled up exiting from the stairwell on the fourth level moments before O'Brien arrived through the same door. The image isn't good enough to ID anybody or even tell if it's a man or a woman. They left the same way four minutes and twenty seconds later. We're quite certain this was O'Brien's killer. I've uploaded the file, and you can access it on our shared drive. Jingles and I are going back to the bar where O'Brien spent the evening to re-interview the staff to see if anyone remembers hoodie person being there that night."

"And anything on the Wheatly murder?"

"She was a serial dater and had broken off with her army boyfriend. He was back in Canada five days before her murder. We're working with Hunter on this one."

"That's something then. Does anybody else have something new to add to the conversation? No? Well, then get on with it. I'm expecting you to make some progress today."

Boots followed Hunter to his desk. "You're a brave man contradicting our fearsome leader." Boots glanced toward her office. "Notice she didn't ask you for an update. Something going on between the two of you?"

"I'm not her favourite person at the moment."

"No kidding. Anything you want to talk about?"

"Nothing comes to mind." Hunter turned to his computer screen. "I'll have a look at that video in the parking garage."

"The bugger was good at avoiding the cameras. Almost skirted the angle."

Hunter found the file. It was difficult watching O'Brien during his last minutes. Boots had uploaded an edited version that showed O'Brien exiting down the same staircase early in the evening. The time stamp moved three hours. The person in the dark clothes and hoodie arrived ten minutes before O'Brien and left four minutes after he must have reached his car out of sight of the camera. Both times, they were fleeting images on the camera, shot at an overhead angle that revealed little. Hunter backed up the footage and froze on the hooded figure. His heart sank. This person didn't appear to be a match with the hooded man who'd walked Josie Wheatly out of the hospital. He enlarged the photo as much as he could without distortion and printed a copy. He pulled out his murder book for Josie Wheatly and compared the stills. Nothing conclusive, but not the same person, as far as he could tell. "Damn it," he said under his breath.

"Something not working out for you?"

He turned and grinned. "I thought you weren't due back until Monday."

"The course wrapped up early, and I figured you could use me. Hearing you cuss out those two photos makes me think I came back none too soon."

"You're right. How was the course, Quade?"

"Good. Informative. I believe I aced the final exam, if I may be so immodest."

"I have no doubt. You'll be moving up the ladder soon."

She took a seat next to him. "That I doubt. I'm forty, female, and how do you white folks put it? Not white." She grinned. "I'm not even convinced I want to move into management."

"We sure could use you." He looked toward Greta's closed door without thinking.

Quade followed the track of his eyes. "She been up to anything I should know about?"

"Let's say I ignored your wise counsel and went for a drink alone with her."

Quade's eyes widened. "You idiot. God, Hunter. How bad was it?"

"She asked me to be her set of eyes and ears, reporting on my fellow detectives. I told her that was not going to happen." He didn't mention the flirting that led up to her request or his awkward retreat from her suggestion they go back to her place. She hadn't taken his refusal well.

They both flinched at the sound of Greta's door opening. "We'll talk later," Quade said. "I'll get started going through the case file." She wrote down the file number from Hunter and moved over to her desk. Greta didn't emerge from her office, but the open door signalled caution.

Hunter made some entries into his computer file and waited for Quade to finish going through the material. When she finally leaned back in her chair and looked across the desk at him, he motioned toward the main door. "Want to grab a coffee at the Happy Goat before I head out?"

"You read my mind. I need a pick-me-up before I retrieve the girls from their dad's and the homework battles commence."

They left the station and walked up Elgin to the coffee shop. They got their drinks and found a table. Hunter did a visual sweep of the room and relaxed. No cops that he recognized. "Initial thoughts on the case?" he asked.

"Danny Tate didn't have it easy in life. It'll be a miracle if we track down his killer."

"I believe the same killer might have attacked O'Brien."

"I could barely believe it when I heard he died. It's so, so sad. But I thought it was a heart attack."

"We thought so initially, but Brigette Green concluded that he was hit on the head and a drug was administered through a syringe in his neck that stopped his heart. She's still working on the tox screen."

"Good God. Who's lead?"

"Boots and Jingles."

"Should have been us. Are you working the Danny Tate murder?"

"Greta shifted it over to Boots, along with the Wheatly case. He still has me doing the legwork, though, for both. Says the politics are nonsense, and he plans to give me the credit if I solve the Tate murder. Doesn't matter to me, really."

Quade shook her head in disgust. "Someone's got to rein in that woman."

He decided not to pursue her opening. Venting about Greta Warner might feel satisfying for the moment but wouldn't last or do any good. "The reason I was cursing when you came up behind me was that the surveillance photos of the probable killers for Josie Wheatly and O'Brien don't appear to match, although even that's inconclusive. You can't ID anyone from them."

"You thought the same killer who murdered Danny and maybe O'Brien also killed Josie Wheatly?"

"I was going on that premise, but I'm willing to revise. I'm still thinking O'Brien and Danny Tate were killed by the same person, and I believe there's a link between Josie Wheatly's attack and murder and the other murders. I just don't know what. It seems that Ella Tate is a common denominator, but I have no idea how or why. Greta thinks Ella had a hand in both deaths, but I'd be blown away if she did."

Quade sipped her coffee while she thought. "Could two men or a man and a woman be working together?"

"Maybe. Everything's worth considering at this point."

She rested her elbows on the table. "So what do you want to do about our sarge? She's obviously not giving you the important cases or any credit."

He shrugged. "It's more her narrow-minded focus on a single suspect without evidence. She seems to think that Ella Tate killed her own brother to get rid of the responsibility of caring for him. Ella owes sixty grand plus for his stints in rehab. She's also lost her job on the paper and lives in a bit of a hovel."

"Wait, Ella Tate, *The Capitol* reporter?" Quade hit her forehead with the palm of her hand. "Of course. I should have made the connection right away. She and Greta have a history."

"Really?"

"Oh, sweet Jesus, yeah. Ella investigated Greta and wrote a blistering piece on her racial profiling and skirting the rules, oh, about two years ago before you arrived. Greta was fit to be tied. She's not a woman who takes criticism lying down." Quade shook her head. "This is going to get ugly."

It was Hunter's turn to shake his head. "I couldn't figure out the hate on she has for Ella. I'm glad you're back, Quade."

"How's Ella doing with all that's happened?"

"Amazingly well, but she's challenging to deal with. She's running a parallel Wheatly investigation and posting updates on her podcast. She's biking around the city on her own, making me extremely nervous. She even went to check out James T. Ramsay."

"The main suspect under surveillance?"

"You really did read the file thoroughly." He sometimes forgot she had freakish total recall. "Ella met one of Ramsay's roommates named Fawn and pretended to be looking at renting next door. Fawn offered to rent a room in their house. Ella gave me Fawn's phone number and promised me that she wasn't going to follow up. She was smart enough to give Fawn the fake name Jen. Her years on the crime beat paying off."

"Ramsay would recognize Ella if she showed up on his doorstep." Quade thought for a moment. "What if I follow up instead? I could say Jen passed along Fawn's phone number, since I'm also looking to rent. I can wear one of those down-on-my-luck, torn bodice costumes. Play the poor Black woman card."

"Let's sit on that idea for a bit."

"Okay. Well, I'm leaving to do kid duty. I'll be in the office tomorrow."

"I'm grabbing some supper and heading back to Ella's house to do some surveillance on my own time. I still believe she's the key to all this ... or at least two-thirds."

"I'll free up the next few evenings, and we can work it together." She stood and gave him a quick hug. "Remind me never to leave you on your own for a month ever again."

"You'll get no argument from me, partner."

CHAPTER 35

Ella hit *upload* and sat back in her chair. The podcast was short, but she'd put a lot of her heart and soul into it. This was her tribute to Danny and a plea for information about his attack. She'd even included a private email that she'd created for this express purpose.

Exhausted, she glanced at the time. Ten o'clock. She'd forgotten to eat, and the light-headed feeling was back. She'd heard Tony come home some time ago, but he hadn't blasted any music or made his usual noise. All was quiet, and she guessed he'd gone to bed early.

She checked the fridge. Eggs and cheese and half a loaf of bread. She pulled the lot out and got busy making fried egg sandwiches and ate while she checked her messages. She skimmed the first of three from Sherry Carpenter, asking her to call, no matter the time. Ella sighed and deleted the first message. The second and third were progressively more forceful. She paused before deleting the last but decided to make the break with Sherry once and for all over the phone.

Sherry picked up on the first ring. "Ella. Thanks for

calling me back. I found something. Josie Wheatly was using a fake name on a dating site that she appears to have been using exclusively. You'll never guess whose name."

"Whose?"

"Yours. Well, a variant. Ella T. She was living in your old apartment and probably thought it was funny."

"Hunter — the detective on the case — already told me. Whoever raped her might have thought they were dating me."

"Exactly, if you also consider how much the two of you look alike on a superficial level. She went on a date with someone who either believed she was you, maybe even after he raped her. He might have found out who she really was in the news reports afterwards."

"Or she told him during the date, and he got mad at being lied to."

"I don't buy that theory. People lie about their real identities on these sites all the time."

Ella forced herself to breathe deeply to calm her racing heart. "So how do we track down her date from that night?"

"I've got a friend on the inside."

"The inside of what, exactly?"

"I don't like to talk about him over the phone, but safe to say, we'll have a name by tomorrow."

"A name that we'll take to the police."

Sherry laughed. "Are you crazy? Not before I get this person on the record."

"By broadsiding him and hoping he doesn't kill you too?"

"I thought we could do this together. You could confront him and my friend will film his reaction. Then I'll question the guy on tape. It'll be pure media gold."

"Sherry … I'm not sure this is a good idea."

"Come on, Tate. Where's that hardnosed reporter everybody envies?"

"This isn't about my career. This is my life we're putting on the chopping block." But Ella couldn't deny that the idea of seeing Josie's blind date was tempting. She felt inklings of the old excitement from tracking down a lead, cornering this guy and getting his reaction on film. "Let's touch base after you have a name, which I doubt will be real."

"But it'll be a way to make contact. My web guru will sift through the roadblocks, that is, unless this blind date is a computer genius. Not bloody likely, though." She hung up after saying, "I'll call you tomorrow ... partner."

Ella stood up and crossed to the window. Hunter's car that had been parked across the street two doors down for most of the evening was gone. She knew he was working on his own time and making an effort to protect her. It wouldn't be enough if somebody was really out to get her, though. She turned and began pacing the length of the living room.

Could the same person have killed Josie, Danny, and O'Brien? Was the unease she felt around Rory Leavitt misplaced? Going with the same killer theory, Leavitt had no reason to kill Danny or O'Brien. He didn't even know them, as far as she was aware. He had no reason to come after the people in her life. Yet Leavitt had lied about when he returned to Canada and lied to his commanding officer about why he needed to come back early. He had to be upset to rush home after getting Josie's letter breaking off their engagement. She couldn't rule him out. Not yet.

Tony and Luvy put in an appearance the next morning as Ella finished dressing. Tony had timed their visit perfectly after her shower. He'd have heard the pipes clanking and the water running. He brought a carafe of brewed coffee and a plate of croissants hot out of the oven.

"I've got a busy weekend. Two weddings, so I won't be in the salon."

"You go to their houses?"

"All the bridesmaids and mothers and flower girls gather at the bride's home. It's easier for me to go to them."

"I couldn't imagine."

"Getting married or having your hair done?"

"Spending all that money and energy on one day."

"Happily for me, you're an anomaly. Anyhoo, I won't be around to help with our investigation."

"That might be for the best."

"Now why would you say that?"

"People who spend time with me are ending up dead."

"You sound like you've developed a complex, girl. Kind of egocentric, really."

Ella glared and reached for a second croissant. "Since when did you become my shrink?"

Tony smiled and fed a piece of pastry to Luvy. "Any leads from your podcast about Danny?"

"I haven't checked." She turned around in her chair and opened the site. Three thousand and twenty-four likes. Ninety-one comments. Her project was gaining an audience. She scanned the comments. None gave any new information, until she scrolled to the bottom. Tony was standing over her shoulder and read it at the same time she did.

"*Danny got what he deserved*," Tony read out loud. "*You're next*? Holy fuck, Ella! Have you gotten any others like this?"

She shut down the screen. "A couple, but it's trolls. They see an opening and get nasty." No point mentioning the phone call and getting him more worked up.

"You should report these to your detective. I'm not kidding."

"You're overreacting."

"And what if I'm not?"

Hunter had asked a similar question. What was she willing to leave to chance? "Okay, I'll do something about it, and to be clear, he's not *my* detective."

"Good. I came up to tell you that I'll be back late tonight and tomorrow night. I'm not only the wedding party hair stylist, but I'm also a guest at both wedding dinners."

"What about Luvy? Won't she need a walk?"

"Would you be able to take her out later? She's good for eight hours, but it's a strain on her tiny kidneys."

"Of course, but I'll need a key."

"You should have one anyhow. I'll bring up a duplicate on my way out."

After he'd dropped off the key and left for work, she checked the email account she'd set up for tips on Danny. There were a couple of repeat emails telling her that her package was held up at the post office. Click the link for more information. Too bad she hadn't ordered anything. Someone else had sent a link to a clairvoyant. She emptied the mailbox and closed her computer screen.

Her phone rang. She glanced at call display. It was her licence bureau contact. "Hey, Brooke. Thanks for getting back to me."

"No problem. I've been home sick so just got your message. How can I help you?"

"I need a plate traced. It concerns a case I'm working on." Finding out the name of the cop who was the other half of Felix didn't seem important now, but she may as well follow through.

"I thought you left the paper?"

"I'm doing a true crime podcast. I'm sorry if this came out of nowhere."

"Give me the plate and a couple of days to slide this one in with other requests."

"Perfect."

Ella recited the number, signed off, and walked over to the window. No sign of Hunter's car. Hopefully, he was actually working on the two lists of names she'd sent him. The cloud cover was low and rain looked imminent. She returned and found a local radio station on her computer. A storm watch with severe lightning was predicted to start in an hour and go on all day. Not a nice day for a wedding — or taking Luvy for a walk.

She started pacing again. She was restless to get moving, to take action and not sit around waiting for something else terrible to happen. There was an hour before the storm was due to hit. She'd get Luvy and take her around the block. Get her little legs working.

Luvy was happy to see her and even happier when Ella clicked the lead onto her collar. For a miniature dachshund, she was surprisingly strong once they started down the stairs. Ella was laughing by the time she got the front door open and Luvy yanked her onto the top step. "Hold on, Luvy. We've got an hour." She bent over to untangle her leash, lifted her head, and stared. Detective Hunter and a fit-looking woman were getting out of his car. Luvy tugged, and they raced down the steps, meeting Hunter and the woman on the sidewalk.

"Are you stalking me, Detective Hunter?" she asked. "And bringing recruits?"

"This is my partner, Detective Julie Quade. We were hoping to have a chat."

She nodded at Quade. They'd crossed paths when she worked on the paper. "Nice to see you again, Detective Quade. I'm taking Luvy around the block. You're welcome to walk with me."

Hunter and Quade exchanged looks. "I'll come with you. Detective Quade has some emails to catch up on."

"As you like."

Luvy trotted along for short stretches but became distracted by any bush or plant near the sidewalk. "Do dogs really pee this much, or does she have a problem?" Ella asked. She was only half-joking.

"She's marking her territory. My last dog did the same thing."

"What kind of dog?"

"Beagle."

"Did it pass away?"

"No. My ex took him when she moved out."

"Oh, sorry." *And Tony will be really sorry to hear that you prefer women.*

"No need to be. They'd come as a package and left the same way." He shoved his hands in his pockets. "I listened to your podcast on Danny. Anyone send new info?"

"No." She thought of Tony's lecture and sighed. "I had a nasty message. It was the third one for this round of podcasts."

"Nasty how?"

"Threatening. This last one told me Danny got what he deserved and I'm next."

"I'll want to see them. We might be able to trace the sender."

"I deleted the first two, but you can see yesterday's."

"Quade has some questions to ask you about the list of

possible suspects so she can have a look at the message. They might not have anything to do with the murders, but we need to be thorough. She's spending the day tracking those people down."

"What will you be doing?"

"I'm completing some background research on Ramsay. I've got a call with his parole officer in about an hour. My sergeant wants me to bring him in for questioning."

"Do you?"

"Not my decision." His mouth settled into a grim line. "But I'd prefer to continue surveillance and not tip him off."

Luvy had found an ice cream sandwich wrapper, and Ella squatted to wrestle it out of her mouth. She couldn't help laughing as Luvy released her hold and licked her hand instead. Ella glanced up. Hunter had the trace of a smile on his face.

"You have a way with animals," he said.

A stab at dry humour. She straightened. "Time to head back. Luvy looks like she could use a nap."

"That's not what I'm seeing, but okay."

Quade escorted Ella upstairs while Hunter took the car back to the station. Ella wasn't happy to be spending the rest of the morning dredging up her past but couldn't see any way around it. Instead of dropping Luvy off, she brought her upstairs, liking the idea of having her nearby.

CHAPTER 36

A squad car picked up Quade just before lunch. As she put on her raincoat, she grumbled about having to go out in the storm that had built in intensity since midmorning. The rain lashed against the windows, the glass rattling in its panes with every gust. After she was gone, Ella remained at her desk with Luvy sleeping at her feet. The dog was unfazed by the rolling thunder and sudden flashes of lightning.

An hour later, Ella went into the kitchen and made a peanut butter sandwich that she took back to her desk. Her cell phone rang, but she ignored it and took a bite of sandwich. The phone shut off and immediately started up again. She groaned, checked call display, and picked up.

"We've found the blind date and are meeting at the pub at Lansdowne Park in twenty minutes. We'll be in front of your house in ten to pick you up."

"What's his name?"

"He identified himself as John Smith."

"He's playing you, Sherry. He probably won't even be there."

"Oh, he'll be there. We tracked down where he works, and he doesn't want us showing up at his office."

"All right. I'll be downstairs waiting." She might as well play along and see where this led.

She put on her green raincoat and left Luvy sleeping on the couch. It wasn't long before a black SUV pulled up to the curb. Sherry was sitting in the front passenger seat and waved at her through the window. Ella ran through the pouring rain and got into the back seat. Sherry half-turned to face her.

"Mark, meet Ella Tate. Ella, Mark."

Mark raised a hand, and their eyes connected in the rear-view mirror. He was wearing a Yankees ball cap and looked to be in his twenties.

"Mark's going to film our encounter and be our backup if this guy gets nasty. Nice raincoat, by the way. A ballsy colour choice."

Mark looked more like a computer nerd than a street fighter. Ella bit back a couple of retorts and said, "So what's the plan?"

"Mark and I will meet him first, and I'll signal you to join us when it's time. Mark will have the video running on his phone."

"Brilliant." Ella stared out the window and tried not to think about all the ways this could go sideways.

The drive took mere minutes, and Mark lucked out with a parking spot across from Lansdowne on Bank Street. They exited the car and dodged traffic and puddles on their way across the busy road. They entered the restaurant slightly out of breath, shaking water off their coats. It was a large, noisy room, half-filled with late lunchers lingering over their beer. A girl dressed in a tight-fitting black pantsuit greeted them. Sherry positioned herself in front of Mark. "We're meeting a guy named

John Smith. He was supposed to leave his name with you."

The girl checked her reservation book. "Yes, he's here." She picked up three menus. "Follow me."

They exchanged looks, their doubt turning to relief. Ella held back and watched Sherry and Mark slide into a booth facing her. She couldn't see the man waiting for them on the other side. She tried to stay out of the way near the bar while keeping an eye out for Sherry's signal. She shook her head at the bartender who asked what she'd like to drink. By the time Sherry waved her over, she was starting to feel that she should place an order or give up the space. She crossed the room, stood at the head of the table, and looked at the man who'd gone on the blind date with Josie Wheatly the night she died. She studied his face but had no idea who he was. Sherry motioned for her to sit next to him, but Ella remained standing.

"No, it's okay," Sherry said. "He didn't actually date Josie. His name really is John Smith, by the way. I checked his ID."

"What do you mean?" Ella tried to imagine this man as a killer. He was movie-star handsome, with wavy black hair and attractive dark eyes. He looked up at Ella without any sign of recognition.

"I was telling your friends here that a guy contacted me through Tinder and asked me to help set up a reunion surprise with this woman named Ella T. He said they were friends from years ago, and he wanted me to arrange the date, and he'd be in the pub instead of me. He told me that she was a teacher and he'd donate one hundred dollars to a kids' charity if I helped him out. He planned to film the reunion and would send me a copy. It would be the surprise of her life because he'd been living in England for the past ten years."

"And did he send you the tape?"

"No, but I honestly believed the guy. His story seemed sincere, and he followed through on giving the money to the Children's Hospital. He forwarded a copy of the receipt in my name."

"You know that she was raped that night, right?"

"I didn't know until your friend here told me before you came over. I'm still trying to process how he … well, it's simply devastating to know I set her up with him."

"How could you not have known? It's been the top story in all the news sites."

"I knew that a woman was raped and died by suicide afterwards, but the name I heard was Josie something. I had no idea they were the same person." He hung his head. "I feel like a major idiot. I can't believe I got sucked into his con."

"Can you describe this man?"

"We, uh, didn't actually meet in person. We corresponded by email and once by phone."

Mark had been fiddling with John's cell phone and slid it across the table. "I've forwarded myself the messages," he said, "and will see what I can find out about the sender."

"You need to go to the police with this information," Ella said.

John nodded. "I'll call them as soon as I leave here. I'd have made a report earlier if I'd known."

Sherry slid out of the booth and stood next to her. "We've got all we're going to get here. Now Mark and I need to track down this other guy. I'll be back in touch when we've cracked his identity."

Ella held out little hope but stayed silent. Sherry didn't much care what she thought anyway.

Ella had Mark drop her off at Finn's gym. She was too restless to go home. An intensive workout would tire her out and would be a chance to catch up with Finn. Maisie greeted her on her way in.

"Finn will be by later to close up."

"So he's doing okay?"

Maisie nodded. "He's tired with the new baby and getting the insurance claim in and lining up contractors for estimates to fix his house. So far the consensus is to tear down what's left and start over."

"Yeah, it was pretty much a charred shell. What will he do in the meantime?"

"He plans to sell the lot and buy a new home closer to work, or at least that's what he was thinking yesterday. He changes his mind every other minute." Her eyes met Ella's and slid away. She seemed to be choosing her words with care. "Finn hasn't been himself. He's become … unreliable."

"Well, he has a new baby, and his house burned down, so that would give anyone reason to become scattered. Could that be what's going on?"

"I guess."

"I'm going to change now and get to my workout." She'd had enough of the veiled innuendos. If some drama was going on between Maisie and Finn, she didn't want to hear about it. This gym was her sanctuary, and the less she engaged in their relationship the better. Maisie might be finding out the hard way that Finn's kindness was nothing more than that, even if she'd become attracted to him.

She managed an hour on the bike, followed by twenty minutes on the elliptical. She saved the weights for last. A few people came in, worked out, and left by the time she finished her cooldown. She was alone except for Maisie, who was in the office, speaking loudly on the phone with the door slightly ajar. No sign of Finn.

She thought about showering at home, but her clothes and hair were soaked with sweat. The idea of walking outside into the chilly night air wasn't inviting, nor was the thought of the length of time it would take to heat up the hot water tank back in her apartment. Decision made. She'd shower here and catch an Uber home.

She stood in the hot stream of water, rinsing conditioner out of her hair when the lights flickered … once, twice. The wind had picked up when she arrived almost two hours earlier, and this building was in an older part of town. The power lines were always a concern. She held her breath, and the lights flickered one last time before snapping on. She didn't need a second warning. She quickly rinsed off the last of the soap and conditioner and turned off the water. The towel was hanging on a hook right outside the shower, and she wrapped herself in it before walking to her locker to get dressed.

The locker room was strangely silent. Usually, music played through the speakers in the ceiling, but Maisie had turned the sound system off for some reason. Ella dressed quickly and was bent over pulling on her boots when the lights flickered a final time and went out for good. Only the red exit light glowed above the door to the gym, but the rest of the room was in total darkness. Caution stopped her from calling out to Maisie. She felt around for her workout clothes and running shoes and stuffed everything into the locker. Her purse was on the bench next to her, and she slung the strap across her chest and started toward the door, hands outstretched to keep from smacking into anything.

The row of windows near the ceiling on either side of

the gym cast gloomy light into the room, but it was sufficient for her to make out shapes. She skirted around the boxing ring and walked on silent feet toward the exit sign over the main doors. Where the hell was Maisie?

She slowed her steps as she approached the office. The door was now completely shut. She tried the handle. *Locked.* "Maisie," she called out. "Are you okay? Maisie?" She leaned an ear against the wood. If somebody was inside, they stayed silent.

She started to turn at the same time as a rush of movement came toward her through the dark. Her hands rose to block a blow as her body tensed. The rush of motion stopped.

"Ella? I thought you'd left already." Maisie was out of breath. "What are you still doing here?"

"I took a shower. Where were you just now?" Ella lowered her hands and inhaled deeply to still her racing heart. Maisie was standing inches away from her face.

"Trying to find the fuse box, with no luck."

"I think it's a power outage." *And not a murderer waiting to surprise us in the dark.*

"I'm glad you're still here. This place is spooky with no lights on. Do you have all your stuff?"

"I do."

"Then let's go outside and I'll lock up. Looks like Finn isn't going to make it." Her voice was wistful.

The nearby buildings and streetlamps were in darkness. Ella stepped in a puddle and swore. She pulled out her phone and opened the Uber app. "Do you have a way to get home, Maisie?"

"I'm taking the bus. Are you okay waiting here alone for your ride?"

"If you're okay walking alone to the bus stop."

Maisie grinned. "I'm small, but I'm mighty. I'll be fine. See ya later."

Ella watched her cut through the parking lot toward the street. Maisie stopped and waved before rounding the corner. Ella checked her app. The Uber driver was only two blocks away. She followed in Maisie's footsteps to wait at the corner, shivering inside her jacket, eager to get out of the wind and away from the darkness that had her very much on edge.

CHAPTER 37

Liam climbed into the back of the white surveillance van and ducked his head as he slid into a vacant seat. Officer Pete Jenkins handed him a set of headphones. "Been a while since our last stakeout," Jenkins said. He glanced at Liam's face. "You look worried, buddy."

"It's never easy having your partner confront a potential killer alone." Liam had fought Quade's insistence on checking out the spare room in Ramsay's building. He wasn't surprised when Greta took Quade's side over his own. He'd managed to get Quade to wear a wire, an idea she'd initially turned down.

The van started moving. Quade was sitting up front with the driver. As agreed, they pulled over as soon as they reached a side street in the ByWard Market, and Quade got out to walk the final distance. She pounded on the side of the van as it pulled away. They took the next street north, and Liam felt the van stop and turn at the corner. Street parking in the Market was notoriously difficult to find, but they'd cordoned off a spot a few houses down from Ramsay's place. Their driver parked in the middle of the street and got out to move the orange cones before angling into the spot. A few seconds later, he slid the back door open and climbed in beside Liam.

Quade was speaking into her mic. "I'm at the corner and approaching the house. Fawn sent me a text a few seconds ago telling me that the front door is unlocked and to walk right in."

Liam didn't like the sound of this, but Quade wouldn't turn back now, even if he voiced concern. She'd pinned a camera to her handbag in the shape of a plastic daisy, and it captured images of the sidewalk as she walked. She'd vetoed an earpiece because Ramsay might notice one too easily.

"She fits in anyhow," Jenkins said, perhaps sensing Liam's unease. "Her Afro is epic."

The driver nodded. "You'd never take her for a cop."

"Here I go," she said, and the camera scanned a hallway with a linoleum floor and a crooked red lampshade hanging from the ceiling halfway down. Quade was moving her handbag so that they got a good view of the layout.

"I'm betting on rats in the basement," Jenkins said.

The house was long and narrow, kitchen and bathroom at the end of the hall and living room to the right. A woman called for Quade to come through to the kitchen. The camera swept across the faces of three people sitting at the table, Ramsay and two women, one of whom had to be Fawn. A smoky haze from cigarettes and weed hung in the air.

Ramsay: "Take some weight off and have a seat."

Quade: "Don't mind if I do." *The sound of a chair scraping.* "Which one is Fawn?"

Women's voices introduced themselves and bottles clinked.

Ramsay: "Hope you like Labatt Blue."

Quade: "I do. Thanks."

The mic picked up the sound of her drinking. Chatter and laughter. The camera remained focused over Ramsay's right shoulder.

Quade: "Fawn, any chance of seeing that room?"

Ramsay: "What, don't you like our company? Lots of time to see the room. Have another beer."

Quade: "Well, if you insist." *The camera angle changed as Quade adjusted her purse. The volume increased.*

Ramsay: "So, Fawn tells me your friend passed along her phone number. You new to the city or what?"

Liam liked this turn of conversation. Quade could spin out the story they'd agreed on without being obvious. He relaxed slightly and leaned in to hear her reply.

Quade: "Yeah, I moved here from down east. I'm looking for a bartending job and have one potential lined up. I'll be able to walk to work if I take the room."

Ramsay: "No family in the city?"

Quade: "No." She paused. "My brother's living in Kingston, and it'll be easier to visit him."

Ramsay: "Won't he want to visit you here?"

Quade: "He's, uh, in Millhaven Pen. *Embarrassed laugh.* Ten years to go, but hopefully he'll make early parole."

Ramsay: "What's he in for?"

Quade: "Armed robbery. Just about killed our mother. I mean that figuratively and not literally." *Laughed again, likely realizing she'd spoken over his head.*

"Is she nuts?" Jenkins asked. "He's gotta know she's educated and not struggling to find work in the hospitality industry."

Ramsay: "Yeah, I get it. Say, ever do any dancing?"

Quade: "Like in a bar?"

Ramsay: "Yeah. Strip, you know. You can make a shitload of money if you get in the right place. You've got a smoking bod."

Quade: "I did a bit in Halifax. I'm up for anything, really."

Fawn and the other girl started talking loudly and overrode their conversation. Liam wondered how Quade was going to get back to talking about prison. He shouldn't have doubted her.

Quade: "I hope me mentioning my brother won't eliminate me from getting the room."

Ramsay: "Nah. Truth is I'm out on parole myself."

Quade: "Is that a fact? What for?"

Ramsay: "Nothing too bad. Press misreported and turned the public against me. The judge said she hadn't read the papers, but I'm sure she did. Anyhow, I'm out, so what does that tell you?"

Quade: "Those reporters. Always embellishing. My brother went through the same shit. There was one reporter who slandered him like she had a personal axe to grind."

Hunter and Jenkins exchanged glances. Had she shown her hand too early?

Ramsay: "Tell me about it. There's this one bitch." *Bottle top popped.* "She lost her job but started up this true crime podcast."

Quade: "Oh, yeah? Did she talk about your case?"

Ramsay: "Not yet. I'm getting her rattled, though."

Jenkins looked at Liam. "Is that an admission?"

"Sounds close."

Quade: "How are you doing that? My brother would love to know."

Ramsay: "Let's say I've got her looking over her shoulder, scared of her fuckin' shadow."

Someone turned on the radio, and music drowned out their voices. The camera jumped when Quade picked up her bag. She was walking out of the kitchen. They listened to her heels click on the linoleum. Ramsay's back bobbed up and down in the camera lens. Quade was following him up the stairs. The two women hadn't budged from their seats in the kitchen.

"Well, this can't be wise," Jenkins said.

Liam focused on the screen. They'd gone over the danger if she was alone with him. Quade reached the upstairs landing but was staying behind Ramsay. She slowed as he walked to the far end of the hallway. He was motioning her to have a look in the last bedroom. She moved up next to him.

Ramsay: "There's a double bed. Comes with the room. We could try it out if you want." *Suggestive chuckle.* "Break it in."

Quade: "Tempting as that might be, sugar, I have that interview to get to, so maybe next time?"

Ramsay: "Sure thing. Say, I can get you work that brings in a lot more than a bartender. All you gotta do is say the word."

Quade: "What are you offering exactly?"

Ramsay: *His low laugh rumbled through the mic.* "Talk to Fawn about that. Let's say we have an arrangement."

More activity and rustling, and the camera angle started back down the stairs. Liam relaxed into the seat. He'd come close to going in after her. A few minutes later, Quade extricated herself from the house and started strolling away from them toward Sussex.

"Mission accomplished," she said into the mic. "We have enough to bring him in for questioning. Looks like we'll be spending the rest of the morning working up a warrant to pick the weasel up, although what I'd like to do is go home and have a long, hot shower to get the grime off."

CHAPTER 38

Ella checked call display and didn't recognize the number. She hesitated but clicked to accept.

"Ella? It's your mother."

"Mom?"

"I've been wanting to talk to you about Danny. I'm in town for the night. Is there a chance we could meet for coffee?"

"Why are you in Ottawa? Did Marianne have her baby?"

"A boy. The day I arrived."

"That's good." She wanted to tell her mother that they had nothing more to say to each other. The years of silence had put too much space between them, but she couldn't bring herself to cut the last tie to her family with Danny's death so raw. "Where?" she asked.

"I'm staying at the Sandman Hotel near the airport, but I can cab to wherever you say."

"I'll come to you in an hour or so. I'll call when I arrive. This is the number?"

"Yes. Thank you, Ella, but I'll be waiting in the restaurant downstairs."

Ella's phone rang again as soon as she hung up. She groaned but accepted the call.

"Ella, it's Detective Hunter. I wanted to let you know that we've brought James Ramsay in for questioning. We'll be charging him with a number of offences, including parole violations and soliciting for prostitution. We're gathering evidence to charge him for the three murders as well."

"I'm … surprised. This happened awfully fast. Did new evidence surface?"

"Detective Quade got him on tape saying that he's been working on payback. He said he had you scared of your own shadow."

She wanted to believe they caught the right person, but skepticism tempered hope. "That doesn't sound like an admission he killed anybody."

"No, but we'll be working on getting him to confess when we question him."

"Let me know when that happens."

"You'll be the first. I'll be at the station for the rest of the day if you need to reach me. I wanted you to know about Ramsay to ease your mind about where the case is heading. Take care of yourself, Ella."

She sat for a moment, the phone pressed against her ear, barely registering the buzz of the dial tone. Was Ramsay Josie Wheatly's blind date? He was violent enough to rape and kill her. He would have used John Smith to set up the date because he'd thought Josie was her, and she would have recognized him from his trial. Had he done to Josie what he'd fantasized about doing to her while he was in prison? If so, Josie's mistake had been using her name as an alias on the dating site. Such a terrible price to pay for an innocent fib.

She lowered the phone and opened up the Uber app.

Thank God it wasn't rush hour, and their rates to the airport hotel would be lower. Her depleted finances could hardly withstand any more hits.

When she arrived at the Sandman Hotel restaurant, her mother was waiting at a booth for two next to a window. She was holding a cup of tea and staring out at the empty sidewalk as Ella took the seat across from her. Once again, Ella was struck by how small and frail her mother seemed. Her smile was tentative, and her hands trembled as she set down the cup.

"Ella."

"What are you doing back in Ottawa, Mom?"

"I have something to tell you. I also needed to see you after Danny…" Her voice faltered.

"He never woke up. I was with him at the end."

"That's a blessing, at least. I would have come back if I'd known his condition had worsened." She wrapped her hands around her cup and paused as the server approached. "What would you like, Ella?"

"Tea would be great."

After the server brought Ella's order, her mother said, "I've left your father."

Ella went still. "You what?"

"I left your father. It's taken me a long time to make the arrangements. I met a woman at the church who works with abused women. She's been helping me."

"Where will you go?"

"You have to promise not to tell if he comes to you."

"I doubt that he will, but of course I'll never tell him anything."

"Winnipeg. I have a friend who moved there, and she owns a house and is happy for my company."

"Why, Mom? I thought you and Dad were together on … things. Was he hurting you?"

"No, no, nothing physical." Her mother sighed. "I'm sixty-four years old, Ella. I've stopped feeling like I have any worth. It took my friend at the church to validate my unhappiness and help me to find a way out."

"You haven't told Dad you're not coming home?"

"Lord no. He's joined one of those far right, anti-everything groups. He's angry all the time, and I fear what will happen when he learns I'm gone for good. I mailed him a letter yesterday."

"I'm surprised but not surprised Dad joined a group like that."

"Him and Gordon both. They even went to meetings. Gordon never got over being sent to prison. They fed off each other's conviction that they'd been hard done by. You know how they were. Always in each other's pockets. Since Gordon's been so sick, your father's been insufferable."

"You came for the birth as an excuse to throw Dad off your trail."

"Yes. I took a chance visiting Danny. If your father ever found out, he'd have made the trip to Peterborough to bring me home. I half-expected him to show up the entire time I was there." She stared out the window. "I'm watching for him all the time."

"I had no idea how bad it was for you. I always believed you and Dad were on the same page about things."

"Well, people can change. For what it's worth, I came to believe you and Danny about that sexual abuse. I wish I'd been stronger and spoken up, even if it wouldn't have made any difference after the trial. I know it's a lot to ask, but I hope someday you can forgive me. I misspoke in the hospital earlier about forgiving you and Danny. It's me who's in need of forgiveness for being so weak. What I said came out wrong."

"It's okay, Mom." Ella didn't want to hurt her, but she couldn't leave this unsaid. "It would have mattered to me and to Danny if you'd spoken up."

Her mother nodded but kept her eyes downcast. "I should have said the truth and left a long time ago. I was a coward."

Ella reached out and covered her mom's hand with her own. "We can start over. I'd like to try if you want to."

Her mom turned her hand over and grasped onto Ella's. "I'd like that. I just wish I'd seen Danny before…" Her voice cracked, and Ella knew she'd reached the breaking point. She squeezed her mother's hand before pulling hers back. She sipped from her mug.

"How's the new baby? Is that Marianne's third or fourth? I can't remember."

Her mother's face lightened. "Fourth. He's a real sweetheart. They named him Billy."

"And how are my other cousins, Sally and Lance?"

"Sally and her husband split up over five years ago She's living in Calgary and working in a grocery store, believe it or not. She's got custody of their daughter. Now Lance and his wife Teena split a year ago. Lance moved back in with Ruth and Gordon, and their kids went to live with Teena. Lance lost his teaching job around the same time and has been looking for work. He's had interviews all over the place but no offer yet. Of the three kids, only Marianne managed to make a good marriage."

"Goodness. I always thought my cousins had ended up much better off than me, but maybe not. Remember how they thought Danny made up the abuse because he was jealous of Lance's hockey prowess while I was supposed to be in on the lie to spite Sally and Marianne?"

"That seemed ridiculous even from the get-go. I always felt sorry for your cousins. Gordon expected them to excel at everything. Lord knows they each tried to meet his standards for a long time. Do you still see your friend, Finn? He was usually around somewhere, and it felt like I lost three children when you all moved away."

Her mother kept surprising. "Finn owns a gym and got married. They just had a baby girl. I see him now and then." This seemed like the moment to ask, "How's Aunt Ruth? Has she ever doubted that Gordon was telling the truth?"

"She's too much invested in their marriage to question him. She's bought into a lot of his right-wing nonsense, including that women should be in the kitchen and keeping their opinions to themselves unless their ideas concern housework or child-rearing."

"That's craziness."

"It's tragic is what it is."

They finished their tea and left the restaurant together. Ella hugged her mom goodbye in the lobby. "When will I see you again?"

"When it's safe. I'll contact you through my church friend. I'll be following your podcast. I'm proud of you, Ella." Her mom held her a moment longer before moving back to hold her at arm's length. "I'm glad Danny had you with him. It brings me some solace knowing that you were there for him." She let go of Ella's shoulders, nodded, and turned away. She waved when she stepped inside the elevator.

Ella watched until the doors closed before walking outside to find her Uber. The day had flipped on its head, and she needed time and space to regain her equilibrium and to process what had led her mother to this place — to absorb that her mother was back in her life and her parents were no longer together.

CHAPTER 39

They let Ramsay stew in the interview room for an hour. On the way to question him, Liam and Jenkins met Quade in the hallway.

"We'll go in first and get him to commit to some answers. Then you come in and surprise him. We'll see how he responds," Liam said to Quade.

"Let's hope we get him on tape contradicting himself."

Ramsay didn't say anything as they took the seats across from him. Liam introduced himself and Jenkins and told Ramsay that everything they said was being recorded. Ramsay shook his head. "This is all bullshit, man."

"We'd like to confirm that you've waived the right to have a lawyer present." Liam waited.

"I don't want none of them scum-sucking leeches."

"So noted."

Liam settled back in the chair. "We understand you're living with two prostitutes, which violates your parole conditions."

"They're my friends, nothing more. They charge me rent."

"Are you working as their pimp?"

"Absolutely not."

"Where are you working?"

"I'm looking for a job in construction. I've got my name in a couple of places. There's not a lot of choice when you have a record, as you well know."

"Ella Tate. You threatened her when you were convicted. Have you made contact?"

"Not sure who you mean."

"She was a reporter with the *Ottawa Capitol* and covered your trial. You sent her a letter from prison outlining what you'd like to do to her."

"We weren't allowed to send letters like that."

"Someone smuggled it out for you."

Ramsay's smile widened. "I'd like to see the proof. Somebody else must have written it and signed my name."

"Are you still angry with her?"

"No way. I had a lot of counselling. They worked me through … my issues. Are you arresting me for something, or is this a fishing expedition?"

"You wrote in the letter that you'd like to choke her until she passed out and then rape her."

"Wasn't me, man. Must have been another con using my name."

"Now why would they go to all that trouble?"

"I had a few cellmates who were psycho."

Liam heard the door open behind him. Jenkins stood, and Quade took his seat. She set her phone on the table. Ramsay's eyes widened for the briefest of moments before his expression hardened. Quade pressed a button on her phone, and her conversation with Ramsay in his kitchen and the hallway filled the room. They focused on each other in grim silence while the tape played out. Ramsay slumped in the chair and crossed his arms across his chest. He stared at the table.

Liam studied his face. Hollowed cheeks and pale blue eyes that were constantly moving. Thinning blonde hair gelled back from his forehead. He had a husky build, tall and broad across the shoulders. He could be either of the men on tape from the hospital or the parking garage. Lines deeply etched around his eyes and mouth gave him a cruel appearance. Ramsay raised his head and glared at him.

"All right, I might have lied about being in contact with the bitch. She has this podcast, and I sent comments. Phoned her once anonymously. Maybe you could take that as threatening. I just wanted to scare her a bit, but I wasn't going to actually do anything."

"Did you ever go to her apartment?"

"Never. I don't know where she lives, for starters."

"What about her brother? Did you ever interact with him?"

"Didn't know she had one, so no. If this is all you got, you can't hold me."

Quade leaned forward. "You offered me escort work in exchange for the room. That's solicitation. You said that you, and I quote, have an arrangement with the girls."

"I told you to speak with Fawn. I offered you sweet fuck-all." He glared at her with enough venom to make Liam's skin crawl. His gaze shifted to Liam. "I'll take that lawyer now. I ain't saying another word until I get one of those scumbags on this side of the table."

GRETA CALLED him and Quade into her office when they broke for supper. They took seats in her meeting area in front of a bank of windows.

"He's not going to admit to the killings," Quade said

with finality. Liam silently agreed, but Greta jumped in before he could back up his partner.

"We have him on tape practically admitting to harming her. He lied when we asked him about making contact with her since he got parole, and we have that on tape too. I say we squeeze him."

"I don't see how," said Quade.

"We have him breaking parole. That could be used as a wedge." Greta's tone implied that they should have thought of this themselves.

Liam had long tired of her inept leadership, if one could call it that, but he kept his voice neutral. "Not wanting to admit to killing three people might override that bargaining chip. He's too smart to incriminate himself for murder."

"I agree with Hunter." Quade spoke quietly but firmly. "I think we have to let him walk and keep the tail on him. Maybe we jumped the gun bringing him in. I'll take responsibility for that."

Greta stood and began pacing. "I hate the idea of letting a possible killer back on the streets. You two have to think outside the box and get him to slip up during the next interview."

"What if he only posted threats on her podcast and made a call to her cell, as he claimed?" Liam asked. "The real killer could still be out there. Ella Tate could be in danger. We should put a detail on her house."

"I can't justify the expense." Greta whirled around to face him. "Don't dismiss the idea of Ramsay's guilt. You still need to prove to me that he isn't behind the three murders. He's a violent man and he had axes to grind with Ella and O'Brien. It was O'Brien who arrested and interviewed him in the first place. I'm finally convinced the three deaths are linked, and you want to quit on your theory now, Hunter? Is there some personal animosity with me that's hindering your objectivity?"

Liam marvelled at her quick shift in logic, her ability to project her own hostility onto him. It wasn't the first time he'd witnessed her gaslight someone who'd challenged her. "I'm open to all theories. I haven't made up my mind about Ramsay except to consider that he might be telling the truth about his interactions with Ella. She already told us about the threatening messages left on her podcast page." *But not the phone call.*

Greta calmed a notch. "Then pursue his guilt while we have him at the station and leave no stone unturned. If you fail, we'll have to put a team on him and hope he does something in plain view."

Quade looked at Liam and pointed toward the door. "We'll get on it then."

Liam nodded and followed his partner out of Greta's office. It wasn't as if they had any other choice but to follow her instructions as long as she was in charge.

CHAPTER 40

Luvy was ready for another walk when Ella got home at eight thirty. She decided to take him outside before sitting down at her computer. Once she began working on the next podcast, hours would go by and she'd forget all about the dog. Her ability to tune out everything around her didn't bode well for having children.

She checked Tony's apartment in case he was home, but he was still at the wedding party. She'd settle Luvy in her little bed on the floor in Tony's room after the walk. The air had chilled considerably since sunset but the cloud cover had blown over. She found herself scanning the shadows as they made their way to the corner and turned onto Fourth Avenue. Luvy was doing her dog thing, sniffing and peeing on every bush. She trotted along between foliage but never for long before another bush tempted. Ella finally realized that if she moved onto the road, this put distance between Luvy and people's lawns and greenery, and she hiked along at a better clip.

At the next corner, Ella heard footsteps pounding on the pavement, gaining on her with every second. She spun around, ready to face whoever was coming at her. Luvy stood at attention and growled. Two women joggers drew abreast, and one waved as she sped past. Ella waved back before bending to pick up Luvy. "We need to get home," she said into the dog's ear. Ramsay was being held for questioning, but the fear she'd been living with the past week was still with her. She felt exposed on the deserted streets.

Luvy weighed less than ten pounds. She snuggled against Ella and licked her chin as she walked. Ella carried Luvy the entire block and as a reward let her down to pee on bushes the last few houses before their own. "You almost make me want to get a dog," she said. Almost, but not quite. Dogs took work, and she didn't want anything or anyone dependent on her for their survival.

Her phone rang as she was unlocking the front door. Finn's gym popped up on call display. "Hey, buddy," she said, expecting Finn at the other end. She was surprised to hear Maisie's voice instead.

"Ella, thank God I reached you." The phone seemed to slip from Maisie's hand as her voice faded away. A moment later, she was back on. "Sorry about that. Finn asked me to call you. He wonders if you have time to come by the gym."

"What, now?"

"Yeah, it's got something to do with the fire and insurance on his house. Anyhow, he needs to speak with you and have you sign something."

"I'm sure it can wait until tomorrow."

"He … he needs to get the paperwork in tomorrow."

Ella stood at the top of the steps and looked out over the yard. She wanted to hole up in her apartment and spend the night working. She sighed. This would only put her out an hour. "All right. I'll grab an Uber and should be there within half an hour. Tell Finn to get the beer chilling."

"Great, I'll tell him. The side door will be unlocked."

"Maisie..." Ella was surprised they'd closed up before ten o'clock. She'd wait and ask why when she got there. She looked down. "Let's get you settled, Luvy. Then I've got another place to be."

THE DRIVER LEFT her at the corner in front of Finn's gym. Ella stood on the sidewalk and surveyed the building. The lights were on, but the neon red closed sign was lit up in the front window. It was nine thirty, and a half hour before the regular closing time. Finn's truck was not in the parking lot. Perhaps he'd walked from whatever hotel he and Adele were staying in downtown. The distance would take less than half an hour on foot.

Something felt off about Maisie's call. If Hunter hadn't contacted her to say that they had Ramsay at the station, she'd be more on edge. She told herself to relax. It was understandable that she was hypersensitive, with everything that had happened. Even so, as she neared the side door she pulled out her phone and held it in her hand.

The door opened easily, and she stepped into the gym. Only a bank of lights near the office was on. From where she stood, she could see that the office door was slightly ajar. She crossed the gym and knocked lightly before pushing the door open. It took a few seconds for her brain to catch up with the surreal scene before her.

Maisie sat tied to the chair, her hands behind her back, duct tape covering her mouth. Her terrified eyes darted between Ella and the man leaning against the desk. Ella turned her head to look at him. He seemed vaguely familiar, and she ran the cons who'd threatened her through her memory. This wasn't Ramsay, but could he be an accomplice? He was dressed in hunting camouflage pants and jacket and a black ball cap. His eyes were deep brown and hard as flint. The beginnings of a beard made him look like someone who spent time in the bush and lived off the land. The knife he was holding reinforced the image. His voice froze her in place.

"Ella Tate. You don't know how glad I am to finally hunt you down."

Could it be? She stared at his face, searching for features of the boy she'd known. He was sixteen the last time they'd been together in the same room. "What are you doing here, Lance?" She tried without success to keep the tremble out of her voice.

"Evening scores."

"You don't have to do this."

"But I do. You and Danny lied and ruined my father's life. Made him out to be a pedophile faggot. He's dying."

"His dying has nothing to do with what he did to Danny."

"He did nothing to Danny. The story you and your brother concocted made him suffer like you wouldn't believe." Lance's voice rose to a shout. "Stress causes cancer. Everyone knows that. Your lies. Made. Dad. Sick."

He sounded so earnest in his craziness. Ella tried to signal Maisie with her eyes that she'd get them out of this. She wished that she could convince herself too. She kept her voice low, steady. "Nobody else needs to die. You and I can leave Maisie and go wherever you want." Her phone picked that second to ring, startling all three of them. She'd forgotten she held it in her hand.

"Who is it?" Lance asked, straightening from the desk.

She glanced down. *Tony.* Lance would never let her

answer. "It's the cop who's been working on Danny's case. He said he was going to check in with me around now."

"Answer it then. Tell him you're fine, and don't say anything else or, well, you know what will happen."

Ella nodded and held the phone to her ear. Lance moved closer so that he could hear both sides of the conversation. "Hello Detective Hunter. No, I'm fine."

Tony had started to say something but was instantly silent.

She glanced at Lance as she added, "Yeah, sorry you came by and I was gone. I'm out with friends. It's going to be … another late night."

Tony said, "Okay. I'll check in again. You take care."

"I will. Thanks."

She began to slide the phone into her pocket, but Lance held out his hand. "I'll have that," he said. He took the phone from her and put it into his own pocket. "We're going for a drive."

Ella stepped backward, but Lance grabbed her arm and wrenched it behind her back. He set down his knife and pulled a plastic packing tie from his pocket that he used to secure her wrists together. He shoved her toward the door, and she went willingly so that he'd forget about Maisie and leave her alone. Her plan was naïve, as it turned out.

"Stop there," Lance yelled. He picked up the knife and leapt behind the desk. "Sorry you had to be part of this. Consider yourself in the wrong place at the wrong time." He rammed the knife into Maisie's stomach and withdrew it in one vicious movement. Maisie's eyes bugged out of her head, and a muffled screech broke through the tape. Her entire body stiffened. Blood gushed from the wound, and her head dropped forward.

Ella's knees buckled, and she cried out. Lance waved

the bloody knife in her direction, and she stopped herself from lunging forward. He grabbed a white towel from a stack in a basket next to the desk and wiped long streaks of blood onto the cotton with the knife blade. He took a last look at Maisie before jumping over to Ella and pushing her into the gym. "Get moving."

Somehow, she stayed on her feet. The horror of what had just happened numbed her brain so that she didn't register crossing the gym and leaving the building through the side door. She stopped and sucked in the cold night air in gulping mouthfuls. Her body was shaking uncontrollably. She felt Lance's fingers dig into her flesh where he grabbed her arm. He frogmarched her across the parking lot and onto the sidewalk. She saw a couple walking toward them, but Lance's grip tightened and he whispered into her ear, "Don't even think about it." He hustled her across the street to a black 4 x 4 truck, opened the door of the cab, and shoved her into the passenger seat without saying another word.

CHAPTER 41

Tony set down his phone and ran into the bedroom to find his laptop. He accessed the page of apps and opened up the tracker linked to Ella's phone. She hadn't known he'd added it, and he never would have told her if he hadn't needed to use it. Sneaky was wise in hindsight.

A map filled the screen with Ella's location pinned at Finn's gym. Without hesitating, he called 911 and said that a crime was in progress. He read the address of the gym from his laptop. He said that the assault concerned an investigation being run by Detective Liam Hunter. As soon as he hung up, he grabbed his jacket and ran down the stairs and raced to his car. He should arrive at the gym within ten minutes if he managed to hit green lights.

He wheeled into the parking lot as Hunter was getting out of his car. A fire truck and police car were already on scene. The wail of a far-off ambulance siren could be heard approaching. Hunter spotted him and waited while he jumped out of his car. They fell into step.

"Was it you who called this in?" Hunter buttoned up

his leather jacket as he walked. "Luckily, I was still at the station."

"I called Ella, and she said the secret code that we'd agreed on if she was ever in trouble. She was also pretending to be speaking to you. I tracked her here with the app I put on her phone."

Hunter turned his head and stared at him. "I'll get you to fill me in more fully after I find out what's going on." He started running toward the side door with Tony a few steps behind him. An officer met them as they stepped inside. Hunter flashed his ID. Her eyes went from Hunter to Tony, but she seemed to assume they were together and didn't ask for Tony's ID. She spoke directly to Hunter.

"The woman's critical. Stabbed in the stomach while tied to the office chair. Paramedics are working on her, and the ambulance should be here any second."

"Oh my God." Tony covered his mouth with his hand. *Ella!*

Hunter turned. "Stay here. Better yet, wait outside. I'll come find you."

Tony stepped back and watched as the front doors opened and two paramedics hurried in with a gurney. The cop moved to block his view. "Outside, sir," she said, and Tony had no choice but to walk ahead of her outdoors.

He hurried around the building to the front entrance, figuring that Ella would be taken out through the main doors. The ambulance was waiting on the street, red and blue lights pulsing through the darkness. He positioned himself out of the way but in line to see when they wheeled her out. If he hadn't left the wedding party when he did — he couldn't bring himself to go any further with this line of thought. He kicked himself for leaving her alone. She'd become more withdrawn the last few days, and he'd known she was shutting him out. He shivered as a sharp blast of wind cut across the open space. The cold, dreary weather only added to this awful night.

Within minutes, the doors slammed open and a paramedic burst outside, pulling the gurney. The other paramedic was holding a bottle of something hooked up to her arm. Tony leaned in and jumped back, relieved for a split second before the horror returned. He had no idea who this woman was, but it wasn't Ella. Still she was somebody's daughter, sister, wife. Somebody fighting for her life. His eyes met Hunter's as he followed the paramedics outside. Hunter stopped next to him.

"It's not Ella. Can you track her phone with that app?"

"I can try." He pulled out his cell. His fingers were cold, and he fumbled with the keys, cursing as he tried to bring up Ella's phone location. The red dot was on the move.

Hunter peered over his shoulder. "They're heading west on the Queensway. Let's get my car."

They ran around the building and hopped into Hunter's front seat while Tony kept his gaze on the phone. "They're making good time, wherever they're heading."

Hunter sped out of the parking lot and onto Catherine Street. He circled the block to get to the westbound on-ramp. "Do you have any idea who's behind this?" he asked, stealing a sideways glance. His eyes reminded Tony of a feral cat's glinting in the light from the dashboard.

"If I did, you'd be the first to know. Ella thought it was a con from one of the trials she'd covered when she worked at the paper."

"We were going with that theory and thought we'd got the right guy. Unless he has an accomplice, we were dead wrong."

"Are you calling this in?"

"And tell them what? We have no idea who she's with or what he's driving, if it even is a he, although I'd be surprised to find a woman behind this. All we have is your tracking app, and that's worrisome. This person could decide to pitch her phone out the window if they realize she has one. I'm frankly surprised they haven't found it yet."

"He must have it. I called and he was there when she answered. So our plan?"

"Track them until the phone tells us they've stopped. Then we play it by ear."

"Shee … it. What could possibly go wrong?"

"The only thing in our favour is that whoever took her has no idea we're on their trail."

Tony didn't say what he was thinking. What was the point? The killer, for there was no doubt that's what they were, had a several-kilometre head start and wasn't slowing down. Assuming it was a man, he'd stabbed the woman who'd been taken out on the stretcher and wouldn't hesitate to kill Ella. There was a small chance they'd reach him in time, let alone save Ella from someone who would go to these crazed lengths to destroy her life. All Tony could do was hope. "Who was that woman they took out on the stretcher?"

"They found ID in her bag. Maisie Kruger. She works at the gym."

"Is she going to make it?"

"I'm not sure." Hunter looked over at him. "What I do know is that she'd have had no chance if you hadn't called it in."

"Ella and this girl Maisie don't deserve any of this."

"You think a lot of Ella."

"She dresses like a bag woman, eats like a stray cat, and has the personality of a cranky old man, but yeah, she's grown on me." Tony checked his phone again. "They've slowed down. Maybe they're looking for a turnoff."

"Show me."

Tony held the phone close to Hunter's face, and he took quick glances at the screen.

"That's the exit toward Carp. Lots of farmland and places to dispose of a body."

Tony shuddered. "Can this heap go any faster?"

"I was leaving the station parking garage when I got the call, so this is my own car. I'm going as fast as I dare without a flashing light on the roof."

"You have your gun, at least?"

"No."

"Then how are we going to stop this person?"

Hunter's face was grim in the dashboard light. "I've got a baseball bat in the trunk."

"Better than nothing, I guess."

"Listen, when we get there, I want you to stay in the car. Out of harm's way."

"Probably not happening, but okay."

"I mean it, Tony. No point you getting hurt too." He looked over. "Nice suit, by the way. Last time I saw you at Danny's service, you were wearing a suit."

"Pure coincidence, I assure you." He didn't like the underlying implication. Hunter had him pegged as a dandy who needed protection. Stereotypes. He'd spent his life giving his finger to the pigeonhole. "Are you on a team?"

"A team?"

"Baseball. Why else do you carry a bat?"

Hunter nodded. "I play on a fastball team."

"Position?"

"Centre field."

"Well, at least you know how to swing the bat. That offers a modicum of comfort."

CHAPTER 42

The tie dug into her wrists, and Lance had neglected to buckle her seatbelt, but these were the least of Ella's worries. She was in the truck with an unhinged monster with no easy way to escape. She looked at his profile out of the corner of her eye. His complete concentration was centred on the road, with occasional glances at the GPS set up on the dash. Ottawa and the surrounding countryside were foreign territory to him by the looks of it. She realized that she had no idea where he'd travelled the last ten years. She tried to remember what her mother had said about him. He lived in Edmonton now with his parents, and his marriage had broken up. She'd taken the kids. He'd lost his teaching job. Any one of these topics could set him off, but she had to risk it in getting him to talk.

"My mother says you have kids?"

Her question startled him. He looked over at her and back at the road. "A boy and a girl. Rick is five and Becka's four."

"And Marianne just had a baby. Have you seen her?"

"Not this trip."

He was silent for the next few minutes. She tried again.

"I don't understand why you're doing this, Lance. We're family."

"You weren't concerned with being family when you smeared my dad." He turned his head. His stare was cold and unflinching. "I promised my father I'd handle things before he died. This is all that will bring him peace. It's all that's going to make him proud of me."

"Killing off your cousins?"

"An eye for an eye. The Bible says so. Dad would have come himself and finished this if he could. It's all he talked about the last couple of years."

"You killed Danny and Paul O'Brien. You were trying to hurt me." She wanted him to admit what he'd done.

"I needed you to feel the pain I suffered when they sent my dad to prison. Three years of our lives, gone, including the trial. Nothing was the same afterwards. Dad was angry and talked about finding you and making your life the same hell you'd made ours. I'm just doing his will now that he can't. God's will." He glanced at her. "I found out where you lived and staked out your house for a day. I was planning to just kill you that night I broke in and would have except for that damn dog. As it turns out, the mutt did me a favour. Made me see that making you suffer some more was much more satisfying."

"You burned Finn's house down."

"I was hoping he'd be in it. Such a self-righteous jerk. You know he had the nerve to tell me off before he followed you to Ottawa? He was the easiest one to find, since he named the gym after himself. He always had a big, swelled head."

She hadn't known, but Finn standing up to her bully family sounded like something he'd do. "Josie Wheatly had nothing to do with this."

"Josie who?"

"The woman who used my name to go on blind dates."

"Oh, her." He paused. Smiled. "She was all right as dates go."

"You had John Smith set up the meeting because you thought she was me."

"What a joke. I knew right off when I saw her that it wasn't you. She eventually fessed up and told me how she came to be in your old apartment. She thought using your name was a big laugh. I took her out for supper anyway and dropped her off at her apartment. We even made out for a bit in my truck. If I'd had more time—"

"Making out. Is that what you call it?"

"I thought I'd found you. Luckily, she knew where you'd moved, so the date wasn't a total loss. That woman across the hall…"

"Clare."

"Yeah, Clare told her where you'd gone. I pretended we were old friends and I'd been trying to surprise you by setting up the date. Josie even wrote down your address for me."

Traffic was light on the highway tonight, and he was keeping slightly over the speed limit. He'd left Ottawa proper and stayed right at the split toward the adjacent city of Kanata. He moved into the middle lane and drove another fifteen minutes until they'd outdistanced the suburbs. The landscape became rural, with spaced houses on large lots and a string of trees lining the road. Ella felt the truck slow as Lance pulled into the right lane. A few minutes later, he eased onto the off-ramp. The lights flickered past as he slowed at the stop sign and turned right. A large working quarry was somewhere close by, but he passed it, and she breathed easier. She didn't want to die in a pile of rubble. The town of Carp was twenty minutes farther on this long stretch of road lined by farmland and woods. It was darker out here away from the houses and the streetlights. She knew that time was running out.

"You must be in a lot of pain, Lance. I know this isn't who you are. The boy I remember is kind and shy. Loving."

"Yeah, right. Nice try. The boy you knew was a wimp."

The truck was going slowly now. Lance was leaning into the windshield, scanning the road ahead. "It's different in the daytime," he said.

"Good to know." She tried to wriggle her hands so that the cord didn't bite into her wrists. Her fingers were going numb and tingled as she flexed them to keep the blood circulating. She wouldn't be able to grasp a weapon, even if she was in a position to use one. She told herself not to give in yet. Lance had to get her out of the truck, and an opportunity to get away might happen. She'd be ready.

"Do you believe in anything outside yourself, cousin?" she asked. It wasn't an idle question; she was honestly curious to know.

"You really want to talk about the meaning of life?" He barked a laugh. "You always were something else. Hard to believe I once looked up to you. Yeah, I believe in a man taking care of his family and doing whatever it takes to keep this country free and strong. I believe in retribution and standing up to liars and evil-doers, and that includes you and your homo brother."

"Danny was a good man. I loved him."

"He was a sinful liar who deserves to burn in hell."

She knew then that there'd be no reasoning with him. She could appeal to the past and his sense of compassion until the cows came home, and he wouldn't budge from his dangerous worldview, from his need to prove himself by killing her and everyone involved in his father's shame. Her mother had said that her dad and Gordon got involved in white supremacy. She'd neglected to mention Lance. She could pity him for having Gordon as a father, but Lance had made his own choices.

He slowed even more. A car passed them going over the speed limit, horn blaring to let them know they'd made the driver slow down for no good reason. Lance raised his middle finger and cursed. He looked at her. "If you weren't with me, I'd chase the fucker down."

"Don't hesitate on my account."

"Shut the fuck up."

"Do you eat with that mouth?" She couldn't help herself. How much more dead could he make her anyway? She'd be joining Danny and O'Brien, and this thought gave a certain courage. It couldn't hurt to keep Lance off balance. Maybe her salvation was in his rising rage.

Lance slammed the steering wheel with the palm of his hand. Ella pushed herself against the side window. A dull red suffused upward from his jacket collar. "Shit, now look what you've made me do. We've missed the turnoff."

He drove a mile farther up the road before he found a driveway to make the turn, cursing under his breath all the way. He calmed down as they got closer to the spot where the car had passed them. He eased his truck onto the shoulder, stopped, and checked the GPS. He started inching forward until a road appeared on Ella's right.

"Ah, here we are." He grinned at her before making a sharp turn onto the road. The track was unpaved, bumpy, and closed in by scrubby bushes and balsam and cedar trees. The truck jostled and shook its way down the single lane into an even darker stretch of land. The lights of a house shone some distance away through the woods on their left, but it was too far away to be of any help.

Some half a kilometre farther on, they broke through

the trees lining the track into a clearing. Before them was a manmade lake, oval with steep sides leading into deep black water, moonlight sparkling on its surface. On the far-off bluff to the right sat a row of houses. Nobody would be able to see Lance dispose of her from that distance. Nor would anybody think to look for her body in this remote location. Lance had done his homework well.

He stopped the truck next to bushes that offered some protection on the remote chance someone was looking their way. He shoved the keys into his pocket. "End of the road." He tilted his head and smiled at her. "Ready for a moonlit dip? You always did like to swim, if I recall."

She planted her feet and waited for him to round the hood of the truck to open her door. He'd put the knife on the floor behind his seat, and he opened the back door and reached for it before circling the truck to her side. Her chances were slipping away fast. He swung her door open, grabbed her by the arm, and dragged her onto the ground. She stumbled and fell to her knees. He lost his grip for a second, and she pushed herself up and backed away from him.

"Fight all you want, bitch." He held up the knife and grinned like crazy Jack Nicholson in *The Shining*. "The outcome is never in doubt."

God. He was enjoying this. His smugness turned her fear into anger. "So why did your wife leave you, Lance? Why did she take your kids if you're such a good, God-fearing father?" She took a step backward.

"Shut up. Leave my family out of this." He waved the knife over his head.

"Isn't that what this is about? Our families? What did you do, Lance? Why doesn't your wife want anything more to do with you? Why did you lose your teaching job?"

Another step backward into the darkness. They were now two metres apart.

"None of your business."

"Do your kids know what kind of a father you are? Can't hold a job. Can't keep your wife happy. I'll bet she can't stand it when you touch her."

He was waving the knife in front of him now, shredding the air with brutal cuts. Screaming at her to shut up. Ella turned and started running. Her wrists were still tied behind her back. No way to break her fall if she stumbled, but she had to chance it. She could hear him behind her and deked to the left into a thicket. She tripped, and the full length of her body landed flat on the hard-packed ground, the right side of her face smashing against the side of a tree trunk.

This is it then, she thought as his laughter cut through her pain. She rolled onto her side and pulled her knees into her chest as his boot connected with her ribs. She gritted her teeth and held in the scream. He was a dark shape wavering above her as she fought to keep from passing out.

CHAPTER 43

T*his is going to get ugly*, thought Liam as he glanced over at Ella's friend in the designer navy suit with the long, pewter-coloured hair. Tony was bent over his cell phone and looked like the least likely backup a cop could ever want. He should have called Quade from the gym, but that would have eaten up valuable minutes that he didn't have if Ella was to have any chance at all. In his gut he knew that whoever stabbed Maisie had a bigger ending planned for Ella. She was the final prize in his crazed killing spree.

"They're turning around," Tony said, looking up. "We're gaining on them, but for some reason they've changed directions."

"There's the off ramp. Keep an eye on how far back they come. Maybe they missed the turnoff and are looking for it."

"They've slowed, so perhaps that's it."

Liam had pushed his car way over the speed limit for the last ten kilometres and luckily hadn't been pulled over. He took the exit at a higher speed than was comfortable, but the traffic had dropped away, and he made the right-hand turn onto the Carp Road without coming to a full stop at the stop sign.

"They've turned onto a side road." Tony enlarged the map on his phone. "I know where they're heading. There's a manmade lake at the end of it. The spot is quite isolated, although a new subdivision is being built nearby."

"You know this area?"

"I grew up in Stittsville. If you'd turned left instead of right at the stop sign, Stittsville is a few minutes up the road. We drank at this lake all through high school, so yeah, I know it well. They've taken the back road in. It's not paved and goes through some bush and woods."

"Is this the quickest route?"

"I'd say so."

Liam gunned it. The road was straight, and there was no traffic. His car had an eight-cylinder engine that responded to his foot on the accelerator like a bat fleeing hell.

"Just ahead on the left." Tony pointed toward a stretch of woods on the far side of the road.

"Good." He slowed and pulled over to the shoulder. "I want to have the baseball bat ready to go."

"Pop the trunk, and I'll jump out and get it."

"There are a couple in the equipment bag. Pick any one."

The car came to a full stop. Tony leapt out his side and returned a few seconds later while Liam drummed his fingers on the steering wheel and craned his neck to see into the woods across the road. Tony set the metal bat on the floor within Liam's reach and slammed his car door. "All set."

Liam wheeled back onto the road and immediately turned left onto the dirt track. The opening through the brush was straight, with a curve that swooped to the right a few minutes in. No streetlamps, only the light of the moon to illuminate their way. He held on to the steering wheel with both hands and struggled to keep control as the wheels bounced and jostled and branches whipped across the windshield.

"Turn off your headlights and park before the bend if you want to surprise him," Tony said. He was hunched forward, peering into the shadows.

Was this the best plan, or should he drive full bore and use the element of surprise? Liam was torn, but the fact this person had stabbed Maisie and still had the knife made him err on the side of caution. He shut off the lights and eased the car over as far as he could onto a scrubby bit of grass. "Stay here," he said and got out. He wasn't surprised to hear Tony's door creak open. He'd have done the same in his position.

"We should split up," Tony said. "The lake is more of a quarry than an actual lake and is straight ahead. Just at the end of this wide path before the quarry is a flat, open space where the kids hang out. It's a long drop to the water."

"I'll go on ahead. Don't do anything to get yourself hurt."

He began jogging, the bat resting on his shoulder. The night had turned cold, but the wind was still and the sky clear. The moon was coming on to full, fortuitous as the landscape had a golden glow. He rounded the corner, and a wide-open space appeared ahead of him. He could see several feet ahead and spotted a black truck near some bushes. The road ended at a cliff that plunged into a small but deep-looking lake, moonlight sparkling across its surface. He scanned the expanse, searching for Ella and her abductor, but couldn't locate them. He moved stealthily forward, swivelling his head from side to side, peering into the dark corners, trying to find them. His stomach churned with anxiety. Was he too late?

He reached the truck and felt the hood. Still warm to the touch. He skirted around it and kept running to the cliff's edge. The water was black and as flat as glass, no sign of Ella. He squinted and searched for any ripples in the water. A noise behind him made him spin around, but he was too far away to see anything beyond the truck. He ducked and ran back the way he'd come, peering around the truck toward the woods. He scanned the perimeter. At the right edge of the tree line, he made out a dark form hunched over, their back toward him, pulling someone out of the bushes. Whoever was being dragged was putting up a hell of a fight, writhing and digging into the dirt with their heels. The person pulling them punched and kicked as they dragged their victim forward. A woman's scream pierced the silence, and Liam leapt forward. His footsteps pounded on the packed earth, and the man swivelled his head and saw him before he'd covered half the distance. He hoisted Ella into a standing position with one arm and stuck the long blade of a hunting knife under her chin. Liam stopped and stared into her terrified eyes. Blood smeared one side of her face, and her eye was swelling closed.

The man dug his hand into Ella's arm and jerked her sideways. "I don't know who you are, but don't even think about coming any closer."

Liam dropped the bat against his leg and held up his hands, palms facing outward. He tried to keep his voice low and calming. "Let's talk about this. Let her go, and you can leave without any trouble."

"Not going to happen."

Liam cursed himself. He'd been stupid to plough in here, thinking he could solve things with a baseball bat.

The expression on Ella's face tore at his heart, reminding him of a trapped animal awaiting its fate. The guy who held her wasn't overly big, but he was strong and working off adrenaline and rage. With her hands tied behind her, she was helpless to fight him. Liam took a step forward. "Why don't you put down the knife and we can talk things over? Figure out what you need to resolve things."

"What I need is for this lying bitch to join her brother. Toss that bat into the lake."

He hesitated, but the man tightened his grip on the knife and forced Ella's neck up with the tip. Liam wanted to take a running lunge at the man and would have if the distance hadn't been so great. He'd never reach them in time to stop the guy from slicing her ear to ear. He picked up the bat and walked over to the cliff edge. It hit the water with a splash and bobbed in place. Liam pivoted to face them. The man had relaxed the hand holding the knife, but he kept a firm grip around Ella's shoulders. "Sit down next to my truck," he yelled.

Liam walked toward the truck and lowered himself to the ground. The man started marching Ella closer to the cliff edge, keeping a wide berth. Liam waited until the man's back was turned and got onto his feet in a crouch. He braced himself to lunge forward and attack. Ella was trying to pull back from the brink of land, digging in her feet and writhing like a hooked fish.

Out of the corner of his eye Liam saw a flash of movement. He'd forgotten about Tony, never considering him a viable part of the solution. He turned his head and squinted toward the tree line as Tony broke free of the woods. He was keeping to the shadows and scooting toward Ella and the man whose identity Liam still didn't know. Ella was standing now with her back to the cliff's edge, the man looming in front of her. He was yelling at her and had the knife raised, preparing to stab her in the stomach.

"No!" Liam yelled and started running. There was no time to reach her. He stumbled as an object whizzed past his head. On his knees, he heard a thunk and lifted his face toward the cliff's edge in time to see the knife slipping from the man's hand as he fell forward onto the ground, clutching onto his stomach. Ella broke free and started running clumsily toward him, her hands behind her back. The man tried to stand and staggered like a drunk after her. Another missile landed squarely in his face and flung him backward so that he landed full out on his back. Liam grabbed on to Ella as she barrelled into him. Her entire body was vibrating like a tuning fork. "I've got you," he said. "I've got you."

She let him hold her for a moment before twisting out of his grasp, bending over at the waist, panting and trying to catch her breath. Liam put a hand on her back to steady her. After a couple of shuddering breaths, she straightened. "I'm okay. I'm okay. Where's Tony?"

They both turned to look at Tony running toward the man, who was now lying motionless on the ground. He held a third baseball raised over his head, but he didn't throw it. Liam wouldn't have believed Tony's aim if he hadn't been here as witness. He grabbed Ella's arm and pulled her toward him. "Are you really okay?" He tilted her head and looked for blood. Her cheek was bruised and swollen. Scratches seeped blood, but he couldn't see any deep wounds on her neck.

She shook his hand away. "Maisie … he stabbed Maisie at Finn's gym."

"We've got her. Tony called 911. If you're sure you're all right, I've got to check on that guy. Do you have any idea who he is?"

"Lance Jamieson. My cousin from Edmonton."

Liam paused but didn't ask her yet. There'd be time to sort out the who and the why. He ran ahead of her toward Tony, who was standing over the man named Lance. Tony glanced at Liam and looked past him. "Looks like you needed me after all."

Tony stepped around him and grabbed Ella, pulling her into a hug. "And here I thought you'd only been humouring me about the secret words." He let her go and spun her around. "We have to untie your hands, girl."

"That can't happen soon enough. Thanks, both of you." Ella kept her gaze on Tony. "I have no idea how, but you saved me."

"Just your valued assistant doing what I can."

"I'm going to triple your pay."

"Ha. Good one."

Liam squatted down and checked the man's pulse. Still breathing but unconscious. He looked up. "Where'd you learn to throw a baseball like that, buddy?"

"I pitch on a men's fastball team. I'm the starter."

"I can see why. You never mentioned that when we were talking baseball."

Tony smiled at him. "And you never asked."

He'd assumed Tony wasn't athletic, and he'd been wrong. He'd been wrong about a lot when it came to this case. Liam stood, pulled out his phone, and hit 911. He breathed in the frosty night air and let relief wash over him as he waited for someone to pick up. He'd need to remember this gift of a moment as the glimmer of light at the end of a horrendous case that would have him questioning all the missteps and keep him from restful sleep for many nights to come.

CHAPTER 44

Ella slept in Tony's spare room after they returned from the hospital where her wounds had been inspected and tended to. He convinced her that nobody should be alone after what she'd been through. When she woke midmorning, she had to admit that having him and Luvy nearby had helped her to relax enough to sleep. Her body ached, and her face hurt like hell. She took one of the painkillers on the bedside table and waited for the throbbing in her cheek to subside. Her eye was nearly swollen shut, but the doctor had assured her there was no permanent damage. The smell of decent coffee and bacon finally got her out of bed. She'd brought a change of clothes and got dressed while listening to Tony singing as he cooked.

He poured her a cup as soon as she entered the kitchen and waved her over to the table. "It feels like a bacon and eggs kind of morning," he said a few moments later when he joined her with full plates. "Comfort food."

"You are a man of many talents, my friend." She took quick glances at him as she ate. He'd dressed in a blue denim shirt with sleeves rolled up, and his hair was tied in a tight ponytail. The way he concentrated on his food reminded her of Danny. The same sweet expression on his face.

"So what's shaking for the day?" he asked, looking at her and catching her one-eyed gaze before she had a chance to look away.

"I told Liam Hunter I'd call him when I got up. He's going to come get me so I can make a statement. I've also gotten a call from my old editor at the paper. He asked me to come in for a meeting at three."

"Are you feeling well enough for all of that?

"I'm okay. What are your plans for the day?"

"I'm heading to the salon for one. A full afternoon of colouring and cutting. Making women versions of their best selves."

"Not a goal I aspire to."

"You already are your best self."

"Debatable, but thanks. My face has been pummelled but good. It'll be a while before I run for another beauty contest."

"I don't know. I kind of like the fierceness of it."

She studied him as he lowered his head to eat. "Any word from Sander?"

"He's not coming back. He sent a text yesterday morning."

"I'm really sorry, Tony. You deserve to be happy."

"And who says I'm not?" He looked up at her and grinned.

She finished eating and returned to her apartment. Hunter showed up half an hour later to pick her up. He looked tired and closed off. She didn't bother making small talk, and they drove to the station in silence. Quade was the one tasked with taking her statement. Ella recounted Maisie's call that lured her to the gym and all the events after that, including her conversations with Lance.

"He said he went on a blind date with Josie Wheatly, but he didn't rape or kill her."

"Interesting. Why would he lie about that and confess to the other murders?"

"Exactly my thought."

"I'll let Hunter know. He's in charge of questioning Lance when his concussion wears off. Your friend has a wicked arm, by the way. He's becoming a legend around the water cooler."

"Tony is a man of surprising talents. Is there any word on Maisie's condition?"

"They operated on her and she's critical. Her parents are with her."

Ella tried phoning Finn when she left the station, but he wasn't picking up. She called for an Uber but was still late for her meeting with François Canard at *The Capitol*. It was strange being back, signing in with security when she used to show her pass and walk right past. François met her at the front desk.

"Thanks for texting to let me know you were held up. You look like you've been through a war. Are you in pain?"

Ella touched the gauze on her cheek. "It felt like a war. The pain is manageable."

They passed through the open offices to his closed one. She searched for Sherry and spotted her talking with another reporter she recognized from the sports beat. Ella accepted a coffee as she sat down in one of the leather chairs next to Canard's desk.

"That was a horrendous tragedy you went through. We got word that girl Maisie is in intensive care but stable."

"She's in good shape physically, which will help her recovery."

"How do you know the assailant?"

Ella had an idea where this was heading, and she didn't have the energy to play games. "You want an interview with me."

"More than that. I'd like to hire you back on the crime beat. Your podcast has attracted a large following, and we can build on that. An interview telling your side of this story would be a start."

A few months ago, she would have jumped at his offer. A steady income and her old beat back. Yet she'd grown to like not having to answer to anybody. If that meant living in poverty, she was willing to make the sacrifice. Not caring about money made her bold. "I'll make you a counteroffer. I'll do freelance articles for pay to complement my podcasts. Instead of giving an interview about my case, I'll write the article and you can publish it. You can haggle over the fee with my agent, Tony, but I'll want to be well compensated or I'm not interested."

He tapped a pen on his leg while he studied her face. "Not what I was considering, but I like the idea. I'll have to run it past the board but don't see a major issue. We'd want the story this week if it all comes together."

"How about I write it in instalments? Build up the suspense and attract readers."

"Sounds great. Give me a detailed proposal, and we'll go from there."

"One more thing. You need someone on the crime beat, if I'm reading your offer correctly."

"I do."

"Sherry Carpenter. We work well together, and she's ready for the challenge. I know she's inexperienced, but she's hungry and could be a decent crime reporter with some guidance and mentoring."

"Sherry? She covers City Hall."

"She did some good digging on the Wheatly murder. I'd enjoy keeping the connection."

"Then I'll definitely consider her for the post."

They stood and shook hands. Ella smiled as she left his office. Not needing the job had given her the bargaining edge to turn the tables her way. Who knew that not giving a crap was the road to success?

At least something in her life appeared to be working out.

CHAPTER 45

Liam made a Herculean effort not to look at his partner. He could tell by the rigid set of her shoulders that she wasn't buying Greta's decision. He jumped in to lay out his reasoning without expecting Greta to budge, but he owed common sense one more shot.

"Lance admitted to stabbing Danny and to waylaying O'Brien in the parking garage. If he killed Josie Wheatly, I believe he would have said. He went so far as to tell us that he met her on the blind date but that he left her very much alive. We have to look at the other people in Josie's life."

Greta sat stone-faced, her stare going between him and Quade and back again. "Of course Lance Jamieson killed Josie Wheatly. He admitted to going out with her that night, and he's confessed to killing two other people in Ella Tate's sphere. Ergo, he killed Josie when he found out she'd lied about her identity. Plus, she could identify him."

"Then why not admit to killing her too?" Quade's voice had a confrontational edge that their sergeant was not going to ignore. She continued digging the hole anyway. "I agree with Hunter. We need to look at other suspects."

Greta's eyes narrowed. "You might have passed that sergeant's course, Detective Quade, but let's remember who's in charge here. Lance isn't admitting to killing Josie Wheatly because he raped her. He doesn't mind being labelled a killer, but he sure as hell doesn't want his wife, kids, and future cellmates to know he's a rapist. Ask any psychologist and they'll tell you the same thing. I want you to lay murder charges for all three deaths and for the attempted murder of Maisie Kruger and the abduction and assault of Ella Tate. We're going to put his sorry ass away for life. I've got media relations preparing the news release now. I'll be making the announcement at a press conference at four o'clock and expect the two of you to be there."

"We will be." Liam spoke for both of them before Quade could respond and harm her career. Greta would write up a negative report to go on her file given any more provocation.

"Good." Greta glared at each of them in turn before spinning around to work on her computer, her passive-aggressive way of telling them they were dismissed.

Quade's mouth dropped open. Before she could say anything, Liam waved a hand in front of her face and signalled for her to leave with him. They weren't going to gain any ground by arguing with Greta. He led Quade outside the main office into the hall. She slammed her fist into the palm of her other hand. "What I'd like to do to that woman. She's so obtuse and bull-headed."

"We need to work around her. I'll get the paperwork done to lay the charges, and we can meet afterward to go through the Wheatly case again. Might be wise to do it offsite."

"Geezuz, Hunter. We shouldn't have to work like this."

"I know, but we do as long as she's our boss." It was the

closest he'd come to badmouthing a colleague, particularly their sergeant. "I'll let you know when I'm ready to go for a coffee."

"And I'll attempt to keep my big mouth shut." She grinned. "Thanks for having my back."

Ella locked herself into her apartment and got to work writing her next podcast. She recounted the events of the day before, including Maisie's stabbing and her own abduction. She steered away from her conversations with Lance, as she'd promised Hunter. The script made writing a story proposal for Canard a piece of cake, and she sent off the draft to him late afternoon. She planned to post her podcast to align with the first instalment. She checked her phone. She'd left two messages, but still no word from Finn.

Tony knocked on her door at quarter to seven. He flopped onto the couch, Luvy on his lap. "You'll never guess who came into my shop today."

"Meghan Markle."

"No, but I have cut her hair on occasion."

"You're kidding me."

"Why would I kid? Anyhoo, the woman who came into my shop today was … Mrs. Leavitt. Maureen."

"Rory's mother?"

"The very same. I happened to give her my business card in the funeral home parking lot and said I'd love to give her a cut and colour. Her hair looks fabulous now, by the way. The salt 'n pepa is now a soft blonde."

"Did she happen to say anything about Josie or her son?"

"She didn't bring them up until I noticed bruising on

her neck and arms and asked what had happened. Tears rolled down her cheeks for a good five minutes while I fussed and made her tea. It doesn't take a genius to know that her son is beating her, Ella, and we have to do something about it."

"Good God." Ella leapt up from her chair and began pacing. "The bastard killed Josie, I'm sure of it. He's the only one with a reason, perverted as it is, to have wanted to hurt her. He must have seen her making out with Lance in his truck and gone off the deep end. His mother has to know, and he's threatening her."

"A few leaping conclusions, but I agree with you. I almost had her talking, but Rory came into the shop early to drive her home. He sat in the waiting area, and she clammed up. That is one scared woman."

"Do you think she wants saving? Will she talk if we can get her alone?" Ella thought of her own mother and how long it took for her to work up the courage to leave her father.

"I don't know. He seems to be keeping her controlled."

Ella stopped pacing. "You have to tell Hunter. If something happens to her because we kept quiet or botched rescuing her, we'll never live with ourselves."

Tony took a moment before nodding. "I was hoping for another romp to Almonte, but you're right. Call up the delicious detective while I go freshen up."

"Looking your best for Sander's potential replacement?" she asked, deadpan.

"If only. I love a good Irish banger. Hold the mash."

She groaned. "You're making it awfully hard for me to look Hunter in the eye."

She put a call in, and Hunter said he'd drop by on his way home. She was surprised that he was still at work but perhaps shouldn't have been. He'd be questioning Lance and charging him. While she waited, she checked the day's news and watched a replay of the media scrum with Hunter, Quade, and their boss, who did all the talking. Ella squinted at the screen. Staff Sergeant Greta Warner. She announced that they'd charged Lance with Josie's murder.

Ella slumped back and thought about what this could mean. From what Hunter had told her about his sergeant, she wouldn't pursue charges without evidence. Had they found something to link Lance to Josie's rape and death? Would Hunter still be open to helping them go after Rory Leavitt if the police had already decided Lance killed her? She was still debating the wisdom of talking with Hunter when Tony led him into her apartment. The two men took seats on the couch while she served cups of instant coffee. She sat down in her desk chair, facing them.

"Maisie's holding her own," Hunter said without being asked. "She's been moved out of intensive care and into a private room. Lance goes before the judge tomorrow to see if he'll make bail, but experience tells me he won't qualify."

"About that," Ella said. "I see you charged him with Josie Wheatly's murder." She stopped talking and watched Hunter. If he believed Lance guilty of Josie's rape and murder, then they were done.

Hunter grimaced. "Let's say Quade and I aren't convinced that charge will stick, but we weren't the ones putting out the press release."

Ella studied his face until she assured herself that he wasn't gaslighting her. "Tony has something to tell you."

Tony turned sideways to face Hunter. "Long story short, I cut Rory Leavitt's mother Maureen's hair today. She's covered in bruises and scared as a jackrabbit crossing a six-lane highway. Before she could tell me what was going on, though, Rory entered and sat where he could watch her. Elle and I believe he killed Josie, and his mother knows about it. This puts her in danger."

Hunter rubbed a hand across his chin and slowly nodded. "Quade and I looked at the timeline and evidence, and he's our top contender. The problem is our staff sergeant believes we have Josie's killer locked up and told us to stand down. We can't officially investigate without her approval."

"Then what are we to do?" Ella couldn't hide her frustration. "We can't let Leavitt get away with this, and we can't leave his mother alone with a murderer, even if he's her son."

"Do you think Maureen Leavitt would be open to talking about Josie's murder?" Hunter asked Tony. "Can you see her turning in her own son?"

"Hard to say for certain, but she was distraught. I thought she was about to spill her guts, but Rory showed up and she shut down."

Ella leaned forward. "She's friends with Josie's mother, Cheryl. In fact, they live on the same street in Almonte. That could be a way to make contact and isolate her from Rory."

Hunter thought it over. "It's not without risk but worth a shot. We need to give her a chance to tell us what she knows in a safe space."

Ella slapped her thighs and smiled for the first time since he sat down. "Rory Leavitt might think he's gotten away with murder, but we're going to show him that he's sorely mistaken."

CHAPTER 46

Maureen Leavitt sat in her recliner and thought about how to get out of the house without Rory seeing her. A copy of the Ann Cleeves mystery *Thin Air* rested on her lap. She wished that she could disappear into the title. Rory had been working out in the basement for over an hour, and if she'd been brave enough to make it out the door, the moment had passed. He'd be upstairs soon for a shower and would hear her leave. Where could she go that was safe anyway?

He hadn't specifically told her that she was being held hostage. Not in so many words. His relentless presence had said all that needed saying. That and the moments of unprovoked violence that had left her afraid of saying or doing the wrong thing. If only she hadn't found his bloody clothes hidden in a duffle bag under his bed. If only he hadn't caught her stuffing the clothes back inside. She thought he'd be working out for a good hour when she entered his bedroom, but he had this sixth sense when it came to danger. He'd somehow stolen up behind her without her hearing.

"What the hell are you doing in my things?" His voice

was as cold as a winter's day. So cold that terror flooded her veins and froze her in place. Since that horrible day, she'd managed to keep the fear below the surface, but it was always with her, waiting for him to make his next move.

"I'm sorry. I'm sorry. I was looking for your dirty clothes." She set the duffle bag on the floor and took a step toward him. Made her voice motherly, knowing he'd seen her holding his tee splotched with dried blood. "How did you get that blood on your shirt, dear? We should have soaked it right away, or it'll never come out."

His eyes studied her, and she flinched at the hardness in his gaze. "An accident overseas when I was on patrol. I didn't have a chance to wash out the stains."

Did he think she was stupid? She forced a smile. "Would you like me to give it a try now?"

"No, I wouldn't. I'll deal with my own clothes."

"As you wish."

She tried to walk past him, but he grabbed her by the arm. His fingers dug into her flesh so hard, she let out a yelp. "What is it, dear?" she asked when she caught her breath.

"I don't need to tell you that I don't want you sharing my business."

"Of course not. I would never do that."

He'd given her another one of his dead-eyed stares before flinging away her arm. She'd made it into the hallway when he slammed her against the wall and grabbed her by the neck. He pinned her for less than a minute without saying anything, his breath hot on her cheek, his eyes rabid.

Later, in her bedroom, getting into her dressing gown, she'd seen the marks on her arms and neck. Puffy, purple bruising tinged with red and yellow. He could kill her as easily as … as he'd killed Josie, she could see this now. The clothes in his duffle bag were the ones he'd worn to Ottawa in the hopes of changing her mind about breaking off their engagement. He'd left so hopeful that even now, knowing what he'd done, Maureen wanted to weep with compassion. He wasn't an evil man. She blamed the change on the trauma working in a war-torn country and the steroids that he kept insisting were safe, approved substances. His aggression rose with every workout and every shot of body-building drug. If only Norm were here to speak reason to their son.

Rory appeared in the doorway without her hearing him come up the stairs. He'd taken to surprising her as a way to keep her off guard. She found herself constantly on edge. Even her sleep was restless, broken by frequent awakenings with hours spent lying awake, listening for him in the darkness. Her clothes had started hanging loosely as she lost weight. Pretending everything was normal was taking a mental and physical toll.

"All done?" she asked.

"I'm having my shower. I'll join you for tea in a couple minutes."

"I'll put the kettle on."

She waited for him to go upstairs and into the bathroom before she got up and went into the kitchen. A phone rang as she stood at the counter filling the kettle. She spun around. He'd left his jacket on the back of the chair. She set down the kettle and kept an eye on the doorway as she felt inside his pockets. The ringing phone was hers. Rory had confiscated it the day she'd found the bloody clothes. Cheryl Wheatly's name appeared on call display. She took another glance at the doorway and hit *receive*.

"Maureen, at last. I've been calling and getting your voicemail."

"Sorry about that, Cheryl."

"Never mind. Would you be free to come for tea today, say two o'clock?"

Maureen glanced at the wall clock. Rory liked to do his kick-boxing workout in the backyard between two and three. Her eyes travelled to the window. The sun was out, so chances were that he'd stick to his routine. "I might be a bit late."

"No worries. We'll have a chance to catch up whenever you get here."

"Okay." Her voice rose barely above a whisper. She ended the call, tucked her phone back inside the same pocket of Rory's jacket, and then resumed making the tea.

Rory entered the kitchen fifteen minutes later dressed in his martial arts clothes. Relief flooded Maureen's chest. "Can I make you something to eat?" she asked.

"I'll have one of my power shakes, so no thanks. You should eat, though."

She wasn't fooled by his solicitous tone. Waffling between anger and concern was a tactic to keep her off balance. The son she'd raised and loved had morphed into a manipulative stranger.

At quarter to two, she set her book on the coffee table and yawned. She looked over at Rory stretched out on the couch. "I'm going upstairs to have a nap. Are you doing your next workout in the backyard?" By asking the question, had she tipped her hand?

Rory looked up from the book he was reading. "It's one of the last warmer days, so I'll take advantage. Have a good rest."

His eyes burned into her as she walked across the living room. She climbed the stairs and lay on the bed fully dressed, waiting for him to go out the back door. Her mind buzzed with anxious thoughts, mostly centred around Rory sneaking up on her and raging like a mad bull. Should she risk leaving the house for twenty minutes? She could visit with Cheryl for the length of a quick cup of tea and be safely home before Rory finished his workout. The idea of a normal conversation with a friend overrode all the reasons she shouldn't go. *This might be your last time.* The thought came unbidden, confirming what she hadn't been able to face. Rory was not going to leave her on her own and risk her telling people what she knew.

Her son was not going to leave her alive when he finally decided the time was right to move on. His entire life had become a battlefield, and he believed himself justified in eliminating every threat, killing anyone who'd betrayed him or who stood in his way.

That was just the way it was.

CHAPTER 47

"She's not coming." Cheryl Wheatly stepped back from the window and turned to face Liam. He was standing behind her, next to Tony.

"It looks that way." He knew this visit had been a long shot.

Ella was pacing in the hallway and stopped on her way past them. "We need to go to her. Knock on the door like we're there for a visit. Just checking in to see how she's doing."

Cheryl caught Liam's eye. "I can bring some baking. Rory won't question that. Maureen and I used to get together for coffee all the time before Josie died."

He tried to reason past the uneasy feeling. Maureen had said she'd come for a visit around two, and it was now quarter to three. Forty-five minutes was a lot late. "Try calling her again."

Cheryl stood near the others when she placed the call. They could hear the ringing and nobody picking up at the other end. The call went to voice mail. She lowered the phone. "Now what?"

Liam wished Quade were here to help with the

weight of the decision and to be his backup. He couldn't put any one of the three people in this room in harm's way. He'd only brought Tony along because he had a relationship with Maureen and would be the best one to get her talking. Ella had insisted on coming to witness whatever took place. He couldn't blame her. She'd been the one chasing down Josie's killer from the outset of the case. They shared the same need to see things through to completion. He let his eyes rest on her. She looked beaten up and in pain, but her one-eyed gaze was determined.

"I'm going to knock on their door," he said. "I'll say that I've come to update them on the charges against Lance."

"I should go with you then," Cheryl said. "You'd be updating me as well, since Josie's my daughter."

"I'll tell them that I've just come from your place." He wouldn't be taking any of them with him, no matter how many scenarios they came up with. He looked at Cheryl. "Do you know if he has a gun in the house?"

Her eyes widened behind the lenses of her glasses. "He keeps his guns in a safe. Maureen showed it to me once. It's upstairs in the middle bedroom she converted into a den."

"If you were here officially, wouldn't you need to contact the local police?" Ella asked.

"Almonte doesn't have its own force. I'd have to call the OPP or an Ottawa detachment in one of the nearby towns."

"I could be your backup," Tony said. "Rory might not remember me from the salon."

Ella reached over and touched his long silver ponytail. "I'd say that's a big no."

Liam agreed. "I'm going over there now alone. If you don't hear from me within half an hour, call 911." He gave a business card with Quade's number to Ella. "And call my partner next."

"Have *you* got a gun?" she asked.

"I do, but I'm hoping not to use it."

The street was typical of any small-town community. Houses on both sides with front verandas, large treed lots, now covered in autumn leaves, and gardens filled with dahlias and chrysanthemums bitten by frost. Wood smoke wafted past as he strode toward the Leavitt house at the end of the road. This seemed like such an unlikely neighbourhood for a murderer to be hiding out in, but idyllic settings could hide horrible secrets. He waved at some kids playing on a tire swing tied to a tree branch in their front yard and kept going.

The Leavitt house was set back farther than its neighbours, and he had to walk up the sidewalk past mature oak trees to get a better view. A well maintained two-storey. Seventies vintage. Looked like three bedrooms upstairs and living room to the left of the front door. He made a quick survey of the windows. No sign of movement. No gun pointing at him from the upstairs bedroom. He couldn't forget that Rory Leavitt was a soldier trained in the art of killing the enemy. He'd be hypersensitive to danger and prepared for attack.

Hunter slowed his pace and attempted a normal, easy stride. He loosened his jacket and opened the side holster of his gun so that he could pull it out easily. He surveyed the windows as he reached the steps to the front door. Nobody answered the doorbell. He tried the handle, but the door was locked. He waited a few moments before pressing the buzzer again. The chimes echoed throughout the house. He pounded hard on the thick wooden door with the side of his fist. *Crickets.*

He stepped back and spotted a metal gate to the right

of the house. He crossed the short distance and kept his hand ready to reach his gun. With his other hand, he lifted the latch and entered the yard. A stone walkway led around the side of the house to a back deck. The lot was deep, conifer trees lining the fence and flowerbeds stretching its length. Hunter climbed the steps to the sliding doors. He pulled the handle, and the door eased open. He hesitated before stepping across the threshold into the dining room. He stopped, held his breath, and listened.

A grandfather clock chimed the hour somewhere deeper in the house. He debated calling out but held back. The hairs on the nape of his neck stood on end, and the uneasy feeling returned more sharply. The room smelled of pine cleaning product, and he took a closer look around. Nothing was out of place, and the surfaces were spotless. He stepped around the oak table and looked in the kitchen. Again, nothing out of place and the smell of a chemical air freshener overriding any food odours.

He should back out of the house now or call out to let them know of his presence. This would be the prudent way to go and might keep him his job if all went south. He figured he could make a two-minute sweep of the house, which appeared to be empty, and retreat the way he'd entered without anyone being the wiser. He'd be able to report back to Cheryl that her friend had likely forgotten about the afternoon tea and had gone somewhere with Rory. They'd try meeting with her again tomorrow. Maybe he'd bring Quade next time.

The living room was where he'd pictured it, at the front of the house to his right. The furniture was well-worn and comfortable-looking, a maple rocker positioned to look out the window. He was relieved not to see Rory snoozing on the couch. The stairs to the second floor were at the start of the hallway. He hesitated. Twenty seconds. That's all it would take for him to bound up the steps, look in each room, and make it back down to assure himself that nothing was amiss. Still, he'd be taking a chance.

He started back toward the kitchen and stopped. He could have sworn he heard a noise upstairs. Moving to the bottom of the steps, he decided it was time to identify himself. "Maureen," he called. "It's Detective Hunter from Ottawa. Your door was open, and I want to make sure you're okay. Can I come up?" He kept his eyes focused on the head of the stairs, his hand on the handle of his gun. This time he was certain he heard someone up there. He began climbing, never taking his eyes off the landing.

The first two bedrooms were empty. The first was where Rory slept. His shaving gear was on the bedside table, and his boots were on the floor next to his bed. The door at the end of the hall was open. Hunter identified himself again and cringed as the floorboards creaked on his way to the last bedroom. He angled himself not to be in the direct line of fire and steeled himself for whatever was on the other side of the door.

The blind was fully down, casting the room in partial darkness. He didn't see anybody on his first scan of the space, but he heard movement out of his sightline and took two steps inside so that his view of the floor on the other side of the bed widened. He paused for a moment to take in the scene before him. Maureen Leavitt lay propped against the wall with her arms wrapped around the bloody body of her son. She was watching him, her face in shadow so that he couldn't assess the expression in her eyes.

"Are you hurt?" Hunter moved carefully toward her, his eyes on the shotgun resting on her thigh. Rory's chest was blown open, and blood pooled around him, staining the carpet bright red. Maureen rocked him like a baby, her own shirt and arms soaked in blood. She was humming softly, brushing his hair back from his forehead over and over. Liam couldn't tell if she'd been shot too and stepped as close as he could without disturbing the bloody scene. "Maureen? Are you hurt?" he asked again softly. He crouched down a metre away from her.

Her gaze sharpened on his face. Her voice was surprisingly strong. "I had no choice. He refused to get help."

"You shot him, Maureen?"

"Only because I love him, the son he was. Not this person who came back from the war zone."

"I'm going to call an ambulance. Are you okay with me moving the gun out of harm's way?"

She glanced down, seeming startled to see it there. "Yes, take it away. I'm done."

He took a photo before using a pillowcase to lift the gun and set it on the other side of the room. He reached the 911 agent and asked for backup before calling Ella. He returned to crouch next to Maureen. He could see now that she wasn't hurt. The blood was all Rory's.

"I asked myself what Norm would do." She continued as if there'd been no break in their conversation. "He always said it was a kindness to shoot an animal in pain that couldn't recover. Rory never would get over killing Josie or the so-called enemy in the Middle East. I know him. I know my son."

"Rory isn't suffering anymore."

She nodded. "No, I suppose he isn't. He's left that burden for the rest of us." She brushed Rory's hair back and kissed his forehead. She raised her eyes and looked at Liam. "I did what any mother in my situation would do. There was no choice, really, and I'm ready to accept the consequences for what I've done."

CHAPTER 48

Liam stopped by Ella's apartment on his way home. Three weeks had passed since Rory's death, and Ella had taken off, left the city, and Hunter had no certainty she'd be returning. He was surprised at how much he missed her slightly cantankerous, intelligent, and always challenging presence. Paul O'Brien had left her in his charge, and he found the idea had grown on him.

Tony answered the front door. Today his hair was ebony and cut short. Liam almost didn't recognize him. Tony sighed. "No word from her. I'd be worried if this wasn't Ella."

"Let me know when she returns. You can reach me on my cell." He turned and started walking toward his car parked on the street.

"I heard Maureen Leavitt made bail." Tony's voice carried from the top porch stair.

Liam stopped and took a step toward the house. "Charges were reduced to manslaughter. She's living with Cheryl Wheatly. I'm hoping she won't have to serve any time, given the circumstances."

"Now that would be a decent outcome. Lance,

however, is another matter. I'd like to see him rot in prison."

"He likely will. How're you doing, Tony?" He should have asked earlier, but Ella's absence had him preoccupied.

"Settling into the boredom. With Ella gone, life has gotten incredibly mundane."

"I know what you mean, but better for her to take some time to put all that happened behind her."

"That appears to be what she's attempting."

The door opened behind Tony. A man carrying a baby stepped outside. "I believe you know our new tenants," Tony said.

"I do. Hi, Finn. You getting settled?"

Finn patted Tony on the shoulder as he descended the steps. "Getting there. This sure beats the hotel. The contractor gives the rebuild a year, so we'll see how that goes."

"Where's Adele?" Tony asked, looking toward the closed door.

"Unpacking." Finn glanced back. His smile disappeared. "Lena and I are going to visit Maisie at the hospital. She'll be home end of the week. Any word on Ella?"

"She's being devilishly incognito." Tony stepped to one side to let Finn pass. "Has she ever done this before, Finn? Gone off and left without telling anybody where she's going?"

"The only thing predictable about Ella is that she's unpredictable. With Danny no longer here, she's lost her tether. We'll hear from her one day when she's ready for some company again."

Liam continued on to his car, all the while thinking about Ella and wondering what it would take to make her stay.

The boat rocked in the swell from the bay, her nose butting gently against the pier. Ella opened her eyes and breathed in the salt air that smelled of halibut and seaweed through the open stairwell hatch. Harry was already up. She could hear him fussing around in the galley, making coffee and toast. He planned to take her through the Digby Gut and south along the shoreline to Whale Cove, where the humpbacks fed.

She shivered under the comforter. "Snow's coming by the end of the week," Harry had said the evening before as they settled with glasses of wine on the deck to watch the sunset. "I'll be docking the boat and moving back home by Friday."

He'd watched her face for a sign of her decision, but she'd kept her gaze averted, watching the play of light sparkling on the water, listening to the gulls circling overhead. Harry's home was Atlanta, Georgia. He'd been coming to Nova Scotia since he was a boy and bought this sailboat because he loved the sea. They'd met on the dock a month before, when he'd offered to take her for a ride around the Annapolis Basin, and she'd been drawn to his gentle demeanour. That and his easy acceptance of her without the need to probe about her past. "There's room for you, if you want to come with me."

"So you've said."

He'd smiled at her, but his eyes lost their brilliance as he turned his face to look out at the horizon. He hadn't raised the subject again.

She slipped out from under the covers and grabbed one of his shirts from the pullout drawer under the bed. She found her jeans where she'd tossed them on the floor the night before and got dressed quickly as the floor rocked under her feet.

Harry had filled a mug for her and laid out toast and jam on the tiny table. He wrapped her in his arms and kissed her before she slid into the seat, cupping the steaming mug with both hands. He was a bear of a man with shaggy brown hair, a full beard, and kind hazel eyes.

"I love it here with you," she said. She turned her gaze on him. "You know that."

"But it's time you returned to your other life." He was leaning against the sink, keeping his distance in the small space.

"I have to tie up some things. An old friend who died left me some property and his car. I need to figure out what to do with all that."

"I'll be back next summer. Open invitation."

"You could be in a relationship next summer."

"We could be in a relationship now."

She was the first to break their stare. "Maybe next summer." It was more hope than she'd meant to offer, and she instantly regretted the words, no matter that the urge to go with him now was strong.

Thinking about returning home brought back the sadness. She hadn't forgotten about Danny and Paul O'Brien, but their deaths had been manageable while she was on the open water with Harry or down below in his bed. She hadn't told him about her past, and being with someone who didn't know her had been freeing. Freeing but not sustainable.

"Let's go see those whales one last time," she said, standing and folding herself in his arms. "And hold on to this moment."

Because time waits for nobody and has no guarantees.

Harry kissed the top of her head and held her a few moments longer before she slipped out of his embrace.

Yesterday, she'd broken her promise to herself not to check messages, and ever since, she had felt the pull of her old life. Canard wanted another story, and comments on her podcast asked when she'd next be posting. Her followers had grown exponentially, now forty thousand plus. Sherry Carpenter had sent an email announcing her promotion to the crime beat and asking Ella to call her. Tony had given numerous hilarious updates. She reread his message telling her that Finn and Adele had moved into the ground-floor apartment, wondering how that would work out, missing Finn and Tony both. Tony also gave a Maisie update — she was recovering nicely and would be back working in the gym in the new year. There was a voicemail from her contact in the licence bureau identifying the owner of the SUV driven by the woman who claimed to be working with O'Brien and calling herself Felix. Ella didn't recognize the name but liked the idea of keeping her as an ally in Victims' Services and saving this last link to O'Brien. Even Clare Daniels had sent a message through Facebook, telling her that Josie's apartment had been rented to a civil servant who liked to throw noisy parties, so she was thinking about moving. The only person she hadn't heard from was Liam Hunter, but then why would he stay in touch?

Her apartment and job were waiting for her. Tony and Finn hadn't gone anywhere. All she had to do was rent a car and drive home — or she could change her mind and go with Harry to Atlanta and spend the winter.

Harry turned on the radio before filling the galley sink with soapy water to do the dishes. Ella went in search of a warmer pullover and joined him a minute later, picking up the tea towel.

"Did you hear that?" Harry asked, turning to look at her.

"Hear what?"

"A university student's gone missing in Ottawa. She was walking home from a party and hasn't been seen since Saturday night."

"How awful."

"Isn't that the type of story you research for your podcast?"

"Maybe." Her heart quickened. She picked up a plate and began drying. Clear blue sky beamed through the open hatch. "Looks like the mist has burned off in time for our outing. I'll finish up here if you want to get ready to shove off."

"Good enough."

He dried his hands and climbed up on deck. She could hear him clumping around, getting ready to set sail. She laid down the tea towel and went in search of her phone, itching to find out more about the girl's disappearance. The story was headline news in all the media outlets. Sherry replied right away to her text asking for an update.

Ella left a message for Tony on his phone. Then she dialled the nearest car dealership and booked a rental car for the morning. If she was on the road early and drove all night, she'd be in Ottawa for breakfast the following day. She tucked the phone into her pocket and started climbing the ladder to join Harry on deck. She'd tell him after they returned to dock in the evening that she'd be leaving at first light.

ACKNOWLEDGMENTS

Many generous people helped to bring *Blind Date* to publication, and I owe each a deep debt of gratitude. Thank you to my thoughtful, dedicated beta readers: Darlene Cole, Derek Nighbor, Carol Gage, Mary Jane Maffini, and Susan Rothery. Each of your contributions strengthened and improved the story immensely. Thank you as well to my editor, Allister Thompson, book cover designer Laura Boyle, and graphic designer Hunter Martin. You've all been wonderful to work with on this project. Also a shout out to Patrick Fleury and Kim Hadley for working your tech and website magic.

The crime fiction community is supportive and tight-knit, and I've been blessed with many mentors and friendships over the course of my career. Judy Penz-Sheluk patiently guided me through the publishing process for this one, and I'm immensely grateful for all the time, effort and patience she put into bringing *Blind Date* to print. Thanks also to Mike Martin for leading the way.

I'd also like to thank you, my readers, for all your support. I hope that my books have brought entertainment and pleasure along with a few shivers and doses of trepidation —I'm writing about murder after all!

Finally, last but not least, thank you to my husband Ted Weagle, who continues to encourage me to keep writing for the love of writing, and to my daughters Lisa and Julia, of whom I could not be prouder.

ABOUT THE AUTHOR

Brenda Chapman is a crime writer who has published over twenty books, including the lauded Stonechild and Rouleau series, the Anna Sweet mysteries for adult literacy, and the Jennifer Bannon mysteries for middle grade readers. A former teacher and senior communications advisor in the federal government, she makes her home in Ottawa.

CPSIA information can be obtained
at www.ICGtesting.com
Printed in the USA
LVHW012004230622
721997LV00001B/80